Countdown to Independence

A Revolution of Ideas in England and
Her American Colonies: 1760–1776

Countdown
to
Independence

A Revolution of Ideas in England and
Her American Colonies: 1760–1776

Natalie S. Bober

Atheneum Books for Young Readers
New York   London   Toronto   Sydney   Singapore

Atheneum Books for Young Readers
An imprint of Simon & Schuster Children's Publishing Division
1230 Avenue of the Americas
New York, New York 10020

Jacket photograph of teapot used with the permission of the Colonial Williamsburg Foundation
Jacket photograph of fife and drum by David Bohl, used with the permission of the Concord Museum
(Concord, Massachusetts), "Where Concord's History Begins," www.concordmuseum.org and the Lexington
Historical Society (Lexington, Massachusetts), "Flashpoint of the Revolution," www.lexingtonhistory.org

Book design by Angela Carlino

The text of this book is set in Janson Text.

Printed in the United States of America

2   4   6   8   10   9   7   5   3

Library of Congress Cataloging-in-Publication Data
Bober, Natalie S.
Countdown to independence: a revolution of ideas in England and her American colonies: 1760–1776/ by
Natalie S. Bober.—1st ed.
p.   cm.
Includes bibliographical references (p.   ) and index.
Summary: Examines the people and events both in the American colonies and in Great Britain between 1760
and 1776 that led to the American revolution.
ISBN 0-689-81329-5 (lib. bdg.)
1. United States—History—Revolution, 1775-1783—Causes Juvenile literature. 2. United States—Politics and
government—To 1775 Juvenile literature. 3. Great Britain—Politics and government—1760-1789 Juvenile
literature 4. Revolutionaries—United States—History—18th century Juvenile literature. 5. Revolutionaries—
Great Britain—History—18th century Juvenile literature. [1. United States—History—Revolution,
1775-1783—Causes. 2. United States—Politics and government—To 1775.
3. Great Britain—Politics and government—1760-1789.] I. Title.
E210.B57   2000   973.3'11—dc21   99-27086

For Evan
who tells his wonderful stories
with a paintbrush

Author's Note

King George III of England was a tyrant whose wicked plans to do away with the British constitution, which guaranteed liberty to millions of people, were foiled by the courage and resistance of a small group of colonial rebels. He was a corrupt monarch who, in attempting to restore the divine right of monarchy, instead lost the most precious jewel in the crown of the British Empire.

Or *was* he? I had to find out.

My grandmother, who was a constant presence in my life as I was growing up, had grown up in England during the reign of Queen Victoria, granddaughter of King George III.

Over tea and freshly baked cookies every afternoon at four, she told me wonderful stories of England, and kindled in me a love of a country I had never seen, as well as a desire to learn all I could about it. All through school, as I studied English and American history, I wondered why the American colonies had separated from England. How had the American Revolution come about? What was England like in the eighteenth century? Was George III truly a tyrant? Who were his ministers in Parliament? In the New York City schools that I attended, George Grenville, Charles Townshend, and Lord North were portrayed as villains who had lost the American colonies. How could they have done this? Were they really villains?

On numerous trips to England later in my life and in conversations with teachers of history there, it became apparent to me that the loss of the colonies was hardly mentioned. Why not?

Then, as I researched and wrote biographies of Thomas Jefferson and Abigail Adams, two Americans intimately connected with the colonial period, my curiosity was piqued even more. Two of my granddaughters, both of whom love history, began to ask similar questions. Finally I decided that the best way for me to find the answers would be to write the story of what had actually happened.

I have always felt that writing is exploration. Indeed, I write to learn. For me, my drafts become a lens, helping me to see my subject from a new perspective. I would apply that philosophy now and study the period from 1760 to 1776—on *both* sides of the Atlantic Ocean. Perhaps I might discover a story worth telling.

The biographer is a portrait painter who sets her subject against the canvas of history. In fact, biography has been described as the human heart of history. Now I would attempt to portray history through the eyes of the people who made it happen. I would ask the question: What forces were at work that swept these people into a conflict that ultimately precipitated a shocking revolution and severed the ties between Britain and her American colonies?

Four years of research and writing, in both England and America, have resulted in this book. Along the way I needed much help, and I owe a debt of gratitude to many people.

English historian Peter Griffin and American historian Mark Peterson set me on my way with an inspiring week-long debate at Harvard University entitled, "In Defense of the Crown; In Defiance of the Crown." Both men continued to offer encouragement and advice.

Distinguished American historian Bernard Bailyn graciously gave of his time and depth of understanding, and made fine suggestions. He brought the relationship between Samuel Adams and Thomas Hutchinson into sharper focus for me.

Leonard Robinson of Sussex, England, located and sent materials in use in English schools.

Members of the staff at Colonial Williamsburg were extraordinarily helpful. I thank particularly Mary Wiseman, Anne Willis, Nancy Wilton, Barbara Luck, Connie Graft, Liz Ackert, Cindy Gunther, Diana West, Marianne Martin, and the staff at the John D. Rockefeller Library for their part in it. Jack Flinton brought the character of John "the Tory" Randolph to life for me. Brenda La Claire, Director of Education at the DeWitt Wallace Gallery, has become a treasured friend. She, along with Bill Cole and dear friends Fran and

Arthur Post, and my niece and nephew Lisa Ehrich and Dr. Robert Bernstein and their daughters, Allison, Emily, and Jill, made an extended stay in Colonial Williamsburg both pleasant and rewarding.

The librarians at the British Library in London, the American Antiquarian Society, the New York Public Library, and the Boston Public Library were most gracious and helpful. As always, the staff at the White Plains Library never failed to locate a book for me, no matter how difficult.

I owe a tremendous debt of gratitude to Dr. Allen Terdiman, who did extensive preliminary research for me on two trips to England. He tracked down material at the Institute of Historical Research, London University, and the British Library, then spent countless hours reading, analyzing, and discussing with me concepts as well as key figures who played a role in the unfolding drama. His help was invaluable.

I am deeply indebted to both Jeremy Black, distinguished professor of eighteenth-century English history at the University of Exeter, England, and Joseph Ellis, Ford Foundation Chair in History at Mount Holyoke College. Professor Black, author of *Pitt the Elder* and *An Illustrated History of Eighteenth Century Britain*, shared insights with me during an enlightening, if chilly, week at Oxford University. His final reading of the manuscript verified details of the English story and clarified for me numerous questions I had regarding some of the players on the stage in London.

Professor Ellis, author of *Passionate Sage: The Character and Legacy of John Adams* and *American Sphinx: The Character of Thomas Jefferson*, and winner of the 1997 National Book Award for Nonfiction, read the manuscript carefully and wrote a candid evaluation of the whole.

Marcia Marshall, my friend and editor these many years, continues to offer encouragement and support as well as an astute editorial eye. She somehow managed to organize the many aspects of a very complicated book. It was she who envisioned its format as a countdown to independence. Her colleague, Caitlin Van Dusen, helped immeasurably with picture research, tracking down hard to find British sources for me, and read the manuscript with meticulous attention to detail. They asked the kind of questions every scholar needs to hear and every writer cherishes.

To dear friends Wallace Green and Renée Karas for their close reading of the manuscript, and their perceptive questions and thoughtful suggestions; and Sylvia Bernstein, who became for me a lee port in a storm, my deep appreciation.

My granddaughters, Melanie Lukens-Bober and Joelle Bober Polivy, both of whom share my love of history and my passion for writing, read the manuscript aloud to each other during a snowy week in the tiny town of Rensselaerville, New York, then honestly and lovingly articulated its strong and weak points and helped me to see it through their eyes. Their ability to express the philosophy behind their suggestions, and even to supply some necessary changes, was extraordinary. It is they who keep me writing.

Joelle spent her summer of 1998 actually working with me. She meticulously created the cast of characters and the chronology, helped with reference notes and bibliography, searched out pertinent material about eighteenth-century London, discovered the announcement of the death of King George II in the *Boston Gazette* of January 1761 at the New York Public Library and suggested a design for the jacket. She even took over her father's role of unraveling the mysteries of the computer for me. To both girls, my gratitude and my love.

As always, my son Stephen read the manuscript with the critical eye of a talented writer, a teacher of young adults, and a lover of American history. He constantly fuels the fire of my interest in, and enthusiasm for, the eighteenth century. His unique contribution made this a better book.

My husband has for many years borne the burden of living with a wife who was living in the eighteenth century—not an easy task! But he has done so with grace, willingly undertaking any twentieth century task that would allow me the freedom to write. His careful reading of the manuscript at every stage along the way, and his probing questions have been invaluable. Accompanying me on numerous research trips throughout England and "the colonies," all the while taking his extraordinary photographs, doubled the joy. His patience, his understanding, and his love make it all possible.

In fact, it strikes me that, over the years, my research and writing have served as a bond that has brought our family even closer together. It is an unexpected corollary—a joy that has helped me keep a legacy alive.

—N. S. B.

Table of Contents

Chronology

Fifteen Years to Independence

15 [1760]

October 25–George III becomes king of Great Britain.

14 [1761]

February 24–James Otis speaks out against the writs of assistance.

October 5–William Pitt resigns from Parliament.

13 [1762]

May 26–John Stuart, third earl of Bute, becomes prime minister.

12 [1763]

February 20–The Treaty of Paris ends the Seven Years' War.

April 1–Bute resigns as chief minster.

–George Grenville becomes first lord of the Treasury and leader of the House of Commons.

May–Pontiac's Rebellion begins.

October 7–The Proclamation of 1763 is issued.

11 [1764]

March–George Grenville's Sugar Act is passed.

10 [1765]

March–The Stamp Act is passed.

–The Quartering Act is passed.

May 29–Patrick Henry's Virginia Resolves are passed in the House of Burgesses.

July 13–Charles Watson-Wentworth, marquess of Rockingham, becomes head of Treasury.

August–Stamp Act riots occur in Boston.

October–The Stamp Act Congress meets in New York.

9 [1766]

January 14–William Pitt defends colonists in Parliament.

February 13–Benjamin Franklin testifies before the House of Commons.

March 18–The Stamp Act is repealed, but Rockingham's Declaratory Act is linked with it.

July 30–William Pitt becomes Earl of Chatham.

August–The Duke of Grafton becomes first lord of the Treasury.

8 [1767]

Monthly from December 1767 to February 1768–John Dickinson's *Letters from a Farmer in Pennsylvania* are published.

May–The Townshend Acts are passed.

7 [1768]

February–The Massachusetts circular letter is distributed to other colonial legislatures.

March–The nonimportation agreement begins.

June–The *Liberty* Riot occurs in Boston.

September–The Massachusetts Convention assembles.

September 30–British troops arrive in Boston.

6 [1769]

May–Virginia adopts the nonimportation agreement.

5 [1770]

January 22–Lord North becomes prime minister.

March 5–The Townshend Acts are partially repealed.
        –The Boston Massacre occurs.

August–The nonimportation agreements break down.

4 [1772]

June 9–The *Gaspée* is burned.

December–Committees of Correspondence are established in Massachusetts by Samuel Adams.

3 [1773]

March–A Committee of Correspondence is established in Virginia by Thomas Jefferson and Patrick Henry.

May 10–Lord North's Tea Act is passed.

December 16–The Boston Tea Party takes place.

2 [1774]

January 29–Benjamin Franklin appears before the Privy Council.

March-June–The Coercive Acts are passed.

September 5–The First Continental Congress assembles.

October–The Continental Association is adopted.

1 [1775]

February–Lord North offers Conciliatory Propositions.

April 19–The battles of Lexington and Concord take place.

May–The Second Continental Congress meets.

June–George Washington becomes commander in chief.

July-March 1776–The siege of Boston takes place.

Independence
[1776]

January 10–*Common Sense,* by Thomas Paine, is published.

May–The Virginia Convention votes in favor of independence.

June–Richard Henry Lee of Virginia moves that "these United Colonies are, and of right ought to be, free and independent States."

June–Thomas Jefferson writes the Declaration of Independence.

July 2–Congress votes for independence.

July 4–Congress adopts the Declaration of Independence.

Main Characters in the Colonies

John Adams, brilliant young lawyer with a strong sense of duty to his country; believed in the rule of law; author of numerous legal arguments and historical tracts; perhaps the most intellectually profound of the Founding Fathers

Samuel Adams, known as a behind-the-scenes molder of action; worked tirelessly for independence by letter writing and organizing political meetings

Sir Francis Bernard, royal governor of Massachusetts, 1760–1769

John Singleton Copley, artist, moderator of the Boston Tea Party

John Dickinson, wealthy lawyer from Philadelphia, one of the leading American patriots, author of *Letters from a Farmer in Pennsylvania*

Daniel Dulany, pamphlet writer, lawyer of Maryland

General Thomas Gage, commander of the British army in America

Jeremiah Gridley, a leading lawyer of Massachusetts, sometimes referred to as "the Father of the Boston Bar"

Patrick Henry, member of the Virginia House of Burgesses; known for his "audacity, his tempestuous eloquence, his fighting spirit"

Thomas Hutchinson, lieutenant governor, probate judge, chief justice, president of the Governor's Council, and later, royal governor of Massachusetts

Thomas Jefferson, member of the Virginia House of Burgesses; brilliant thinker and writer who believed strongly in the freedom of the human mind and in the worth and dignity of the common man; known for the "felicity of his pen;" author of the Declaration of Independence

George Mason, member of the Virginia House of Burgesses

Reverend Jonathan Mayhew, influential pastor of the West Congregational Church in Boston

Ebenezer McIntosh, Boston cobbler; leader of the Boston mob, called "First Captain-General of the Liberty Tree"

Andrew Oliver, brother-in-law of Thomas Hutchinson, stamp distributor in Massachusetts, and later, lieutenant governor

James Otis, fiery and eloquent lawyer of Massachusetts; spoke against the writs of assistance

Thomas Paine, impoverished Englishman who, just a year after he arrived in Philadelphia, wrote the radical pamphlet *Common Sense,* a bold and passionate plea for the separation of the colonies from England

Thomas Preston, Private White's commander; known as "a sober, honest man, and a good officer"; was "Captain of the Day" on the night of the Boston Massacre, and was accused of murder

Josiah Quincy, young lawyer who, with John Adams, defended the British soldiers after the Boston Massacre. He later sailed to England to try to explain the American point of view to Lord North

John Randolph, clerk of the Virginia House of Burgesses, attorney general of Virginia; brother to Peyton Randolph and cousin to Thomas Jefferson; Loyalist

Peyton Randolph, attorney general of Virginia, Speaker of the Virginia House of Burgesses, chairman of Virginia's Committee of Correspondence, and president of the Continental Congress until his sudden death on October 22, 1775, revered for his ability to create harmony within the Congress

Paul Revere, express rider, silversmith, and one of the "chiefs" among Boston's radicals

Joseph Royle, conservative editor of the *Virginia Gazette*

Oxenbridge Thacher, lawyer of Massachusetts

Dr. Joseph Warren, revered and much loved physician; one of the leaders of the patriots

Hugh White, private, British soldier of the Twenty-ninth Regiment, on duty in Boston on the night of the Boston Massacre

George Wythe, one of the leading lawyers of Virginia, member of the Virginia House of Burgesses, and law teacher to Thomas Jefferson

Main Characters in England

Colonel Isaac Barré, member of Parliament, friend to the colonies

Edmund Burke, brilliant young Irish lawyer, Rockingham's private secretary, member of Parliament, and friend to the colonists

General Henry Seymour Conway, unofficial secretary of state for American colonies

Edward, Prince, Duke of York, brother to King George III

Augustus Henry Fitzroy, third duke of Grafton, prime minister 1768–1770

Benjamin Franklin, author, scientist, philosopher, statesman; agent for some of the colonies and unofficial voice of America in England

George William Frederick, King George III of Great Britain and Ireland, Duke of Brunswick and Luxembourg, Archtreasurer and Elector of the Holy Roman Empire

George Grenville, chancellor of the Exchequer (or first lord of the Treasury), and prime minister 1765–1767; launched an aggressive program of taxing the colonists, and initiated the Stamp Act.

Samuel Johnson, great Tory writer and lexicographer, author of the pioneering *Dictionary of the English Language*

John Locke, political philosopher, writer, teacher, and hero to Englishmen on both sides of the Atlantic. Believed in the natural rights of man.

For Locke, property was the source of life and liberty.

Frederick Lord North, second earl of Guilford, head of the Treasury; prime minister 1770–1782. Pleasant and easygoing, he was trusted by the king and was always dutiful.

Thomas Pelham Holles, first duke of Newcastle, known as "First Whig" prime minister, 1760–1762

William Pitt, secretary of State, prime minister 1766–1768; later, earl of Chatham; known as "the Great Commoner"; friend to the colonies

John Stuart, third earl of Bute, tutor to the young George; later known as Groom of the Stole, prime minister, 1760-1762

Charles Townshend, member of Parliament; chancellor of the Exchequer, 1767. A flashy young politician, known as "Champagne Charley," he was brilliant but unscrupulous. He introduced the Townshend Acts to further tax the colonies.

Charles Watson-Wentworth, second marquess of Rockingham, leader of a small group of Whigs in Parliament; prime minister, 1765–1766

John Wilkes, a member of Parliament, radical newspaper editor and writer. Arrested for his attack on Lord Bute's government in his paper, *The North Briton*, number 45. Became symbol of the fight for constitutional liberties.

William, Prince, Duke of Gloucester, brother to King George III

"As to the history of the Revolution, my ideas may be peculiar, perhaps singular. What do We Mean by the Revolution? The War? That was no part of the Revolution. It was only an Effect and Consequence of it. The Revolution was in the Minds of the People, and this was effected, from 1760 to 1775, in the course of fifteen Years before a drop of blood was drawn at Lexington."

John Adams to Thomas Jefferson, August 24, 1815

Introduction

A special kind of Englishman

At the time our story opens, near the end of the year 1760, the magic words, "The rights of Englishmen," had been casting their spell over a group of thirteen British colonies strung out along the eastern coast of North America for well over a hundred years. During that time, Great Britain (comprised of England, Ireland, Scotland, and Wales), three thousand miles across the Atlantic Ocean, had allowed her "children" to grow in their own way, with very little interference from the mother country. Though the colonies had been founded under the authority of the king of England, with the vast ocean separating them they had been able to achieve a considerable degree of independence.

At that time, the name of Great Britain was held in higher esteem by the nations of the world than ever before. Although not perfect, her unique form of government—a monarch and two houses of Parliament*—the House of Commons and the House of Lords, representing the common people and the aristocracy, and responsible for the government of the country—was looked on with envy by neighboring European nations. This three-legged stool of monarchy, aristocracy, and commons seemed the best defense against corrupting tyranny. Until 1760, her North American colonies had been the least significant part of the British Empire.

*Parliament can be loosely translated to mean "discussion."

xxi

This period of what is often called "salutary neglect" of the American colonies contributed to the growth of self-reliance and the love of freedom among them. As Britain permitted the tradition of local liberty to take firm root in America, the colonists, governed by popularly elected representative assemblies with the power to impose taxes and propose changes in the law, began to think of themselves as being beyond the mother country's control.[1]

Indeed, an American named Benjamin Franklin predicted in 1760 that "the foundations of the future grandeur and stability of the British Empire lie in America, and though, like other foundations, they are low and little seen, they are nevertheless broad and strong enough to support the greatest political structure human wisdom ever yet erected."[2]

In England, Parliament was growing increasingly powerful. King George I, a distant cousin of Queen Anne (who had died leaving no living children), had been brought in from a German state—the Electorate of Hanover—to rule the British Empire in 1714. He understood little English, and less about British government. Therefore he, and his son George II, who succeeded him, rarely attended meetings of the cabinet, a small group of ministers from the House of Commons who were appointed as royal advisers. Over the years, the influence of the king gradually diminished. Parliament, on the other hand, grew stronger, and its most influential ministers, these members of the cabinet, grew strongest of all. Thus, the principal decision makers responsible for the government of the country were a relatively small number of ministers accountable to Parliament.[3]

Among the Americans, however, major decisions were made at almost every point by large bodies of colonists assembled in local or provincial meetings and responsive to a far broader base of the public.

Most of the earliest settlers of North America had come from the southern part of England. They put down their deepest roots in the northeast and called it New England. They had crossed the ocean seeking religious freedom, free land, and economic opportunity. They found abundant land, divided it into holdings for all who were ready to clear it of trees and till it with their own hands. They trusted themselves and one another, and had a common, strongly held purpose.

Faced with long, hard winters, thin, stony soil, forests that came down to the sea, and, occasionally, Native Americans raiding their lonely farmsteads, they quickly developed strength, self-confidence, individualism, and a spirit of independence. Rugged pioneering conditions changed their patterns of living and, therefore, their habits of thought. Every acre was won from nature by the ax and the plow, and guarded by the sword and the gun. These settlers overcame the hardships because of their special character. It was they who held the key to the future of North America.

Most New Englanders lived along the coast, with its fine harbors and inlets. Their capital was Boston, a merchant city on the sea. The forests on the water's edge of the Atlantic made shipbuilding easy for them.[4] In fact, the town drew its life from the sea.

Virginia, the largest of the thirteen colonies, was the jewel of British America. While it had no major cities like those of New England and the middle colonies, its population was larger than that of any other province. Many of its inhabitants lived in comfort and grace on huge plantations run by slave labor, whose carefully tended lawns swept down to the river, where vessels tied up to deliver English goods ordered by the plantation owner, and to take on loads of tobacco grown on the plantation. Land was rich and abundant, and was there virtually for the taking. Virginia was the anchor of the South, as Boston was of the North. Its lifestyle most nearly imitated that of the English country gentleman.

North Carolina differed substantially from its neighbor Virginia. While it had some great plantations worked by slaves, it was primarily a colony of small farms operated by fiercely independent farmers.

South Carolina combined plantation life with the bustling port city of Charleston, then known as Charles Town. Its economic base was its rice crop. Maryland, also, had a number of large, slave-holding plantations in addition to a thriving seaport in its capital, Baltimore.[5]

In the middle colonies, New York boasted prosperous urban merchants and manors along the Hudson River founded by the early Dutch settlers. New Jersey mingled numerous religious and ethnic groups; Pennsylvania was dominated by Quakers.

Though most of the colonists came from England and were proud of their English descent, there were two large exceptions: the Scotch-Irish and the Germans who settled in the backcountry from Pennsylvania southward; and a half million African slaves who were scattered throughout the colonies, with the greatest numbers on the tobacco and rice plantations of the South. The Africans were the great exception to everything that can be said about colonial Americans. They did much of the work but enjoyed few of the privileges and benefits of colonial life.

Over the years the colonists began to change. They had a strong sense of their roots (a great majority spoke of England as "home" even though they had never been there), but they also had a dawning sense of themselves as a special kind of Englishman. Within each colony they took pride in their common heritage. In Massachusetts they were gradually developing the notion that as Puritans (dissenters from the Church of England), successful merchants, and loyal subjects of England, they were better than just Englishmen. By the early 1700s they were beginning to think of themselves as the way Englishmen *ought* to be. The colonists developed a group identity and became, in a sense, "citizens" of their particular colony, each with a destiny of its own.

As colonists, they held certain values in common. They shared a sense of opportunity and the freedom to take advantage of it. And they shared a common commitment to the future. They accepted the doctrine that the colonies existed for the benefit of the mother country and were proud to claim membership in the world's most powerful empire. They were proud, too, of Great Britain's tradition of political liberty and civil rights guaranteed by the British constitution.[6]

But the British constitution was not a written document. It was the constituted (meaning "existing") system of government, defined by the law laid down over centuries and centuries of custom. The colonists' colonial "constitutions," however, were written documents describing specific powers.

Gradually, ideas began to take hold in the colonies that would precipitate a shocking revolution against Great Britain. What was happening on both sides of the Atlantic Ocean?

A revolution has been described as a change in human society so large that no one quite understands it. For fifteen years between 1760 and 1775, before a drop of blood was shed at Lexington and Concord, ideas were the weapons with which Americans and Englishmen waged a revolution. Words of protest did not become deeds of resistance until both sides came to realize that only force could decide the issues that divided the empire.[7] This is the story of those years.

Chapter I

"George, be a King!"

London: 1760–1761

At half past seven on the morning of Saturday, October 25, 1760, the young Prince of Wales, George William Frederick, set out for his morning ride, accompanied by some of his servants. He had been staying at Kew Palace, a small royal residence on the river Thames just outside of London. The prince loved this palace, with its beautiful gardens that his father had filled with exotic plants and trees.

Now, at eight o'clock, as he crossed the newly built Kew Bridge, he was overtaken by a messenger on horseback. The messenger handed him a note from the king's valet informing him that his grandfather, King George II, had

OPPOSITE: A formal portrait of the young King George III in his coronation robes, painted just after he ascended the throne in 1760, at the age of twenty-two. *By Allan Ramsay, 1761.*

had an "accident" at Kensington Palace in London. The twenty-two-year-old prince immediately turned his horse around and headed back to Kew.

Suddenly, the impact of what the note implied hit him: He might at any moment become king of the British Empire! Ten years ago, when he was only twelve, his father had died, and he had become next in line to the throne.

Back at Kew Palace, he hastily wrote a note to his dear friend, tutor, and adviser, the earl of Bute, who was living nearby, telling him what he had just learned, and concluding, "I . . . shall wait till I hear from you to know what further must be done." [1]

He had just dispatched this note to Bute when a letter arrived from his aunt, the king's daughter, to say that King George II was dead. The new king ordered his coach and set out at once to consult Bute.

George William Frederick was now King George III of Great Britain and Ireland, Duke of Brunswick and Luxembourg, Archtreasurer and Elector of the Holy Roman Empire. He had been born in London two months prematurely, on June 4, 1738, the second child and first son of his parents, Frederick Lewis and Augusta, Prince and Princess of Wales. The infant was baptized immediately, as there was little hope that he would live.

His grandfather, King George II, son of George I, was the second of his line to wear the crown of Great Britain. His ancestors were, at the beginning of the eighteenth century, the rulers of Hanover, an area in the north of Germany, that was part of a jumble of states known as the Holy Roman Empire. George I and George II had both been born in this German state of Hanover. They knew little English, preferred Hanover to England, and enjoyed being kings of England mainly for the money that it brought them. Having been raised in Germany, they had had to adapt themselves to the British system of government. George III was the first of his line to have been trained from childhood in the history and political traditions of England.

When his father, Prince Frederick Lewis, died on March 20, 1751, the twelve-year-old George had suddenly found himself heir to an empire. Frederick had been an affectionate and devoted father, concerned for his children's welfare. Two years before his death, at age forty-two, Frederick had written a letter to his son, with instructions that it be read to George from time to time if Frederick should die before he became king. The letter said, in part, "I shall have no regret never to have worn the crown, if you do but fill it worthily."

His one concrete recommendation in his letter to his son was that George live with economy and endeavor to reduce the national debt and the rate of interest. He concluded: "When mankind will once be persuaded that you are just, humane, generous, and brave, you will be beloved by your people and respected by foreign powers."[2] George III would take his father's suggestions to heart.

With his father's death, the adults around George recognized that his future conduct and the welfare of the nation would depend on the influences he absorbed during his adolescence. They became so concerned about the heir apparent that they forgot about the growing boy. As a result, George lived in an adult world, constantly

Edward Augustus, Duke of York, with his older brother, the future King George III, at the time of the death of their father, when George was about twelve. The two boys were good friends. *By Richard Wilson, circa 1751 (detail).*

watched over and never alone. He was a silent and shy youth, with no friends of his own age except for his younger brother Prince Edward, Duke of York, to whom he was deeply attached.

His mother, Augusta, Princess of Wales, was named regent and guardian of her son George. Edward, though, had always been her favorite, and she openly praised and petted him. On the other hand, if George were to offer an opinion, she knocked him down immediately with, "Do hold your tongue, George. Don't talk like a fool!"

She constantly kept after him to watch his table manners: "George, sit up straight! Take your elbows off the table! Don't gobble your food! George, be a King!" [3] She never let him forget who he was. Although she loved him, she seemed not to recognize her son's good sense, innate integrity, kind heart, and genuine manliness of spirit. Her criticism tended to increase his shyness.

George was of average intelligence and greater than average intellectual curiosity, but he had no experience of the world, and he was intensely lonely. His intellectual curiosity had first been roused by his father, who was a lover of art and science, and who had a passion for landscape gardening, which he practiced at Kew.

Soon George's schoolroom became a battleground between contending sets of politicians, with the favor of the future king as the prize of victory.

Then, in 1755, when George was seventeen, John Stuart, third earl of Bute, took charge of his education. He became George's tutor and his friend. Directly and indirectly, he had a greater influence over the course of George's life than any other person.

Bute, as he was called, was twenty-five years older than the prince— old enough to take the place of his father. He was an extremely handsome Scotsman and a man of culture and learning, an intellectual with a remarkable interest in science, eager to apply his knowledge to the business of politics. But he lacked an understanding of human nature. He strove to teach a boy how to become a king by seeking the answers in books. He was unable to guide the young George in how to deal with people.

When George began his studies with the earl of Bute, he had no knowledge whatsoever of life beyond the school-room and the royal court except what he had read in books or what his previous tutors had told him. He did have some knowledge of French and German, he knew Latin and the elements of Greek, had a wide but not detailed knowledge of history, and had studied science and mathematics. He was beginning to de-velop what would become a life-long in-terest in astronomy. He had learned to draw and had studied military fortifica-tion. He had also acquired the social skills of dancing, fencing, riding, and music. (He played the harpsichord and the flute.) And he was beginning to de-velop an interest in art and architecture.

John Stuart, Earl of Bute, was tutor and friend to the young King George. *By Sir Joshua Reynolds, date unknown.*

He had been taught the doctrines of Christianity according to the creed of the Church of England, and he had learned and understood the British system of government. Although he had not learned to read fluently until he was eleven, he had developed a passion for books and had begun to collect them. Bute opened his mind and encouraged his curiosity in art, literature, science, and politics. His tutor fanned the spark that grew into a flame, immeasurably enriching his student's life.

What had not been provided for were his emotional needs.

Bute was the first person after George's father's death to treat him with kindness and affection. He broke through his young charge's shell of loneliness. Here was a man in whom George could confide, and who would show him the way his father would have wanted him to go. George put all his trust in Bute. He called him "my dearest friend," and wrote to him: "I am young and inexperienc'd and want advice. I trust in your friendship which . . . assists me in all difficulties." He hoped that Bute would help him to perform his duty "to restore my much loved country to her ancient state of liberty . . . free from her present load of debts and again famous for being the residence of true piety and virtue."

Bute taught George that it was the first duty of a king to lead a moral life and to refrain from indulgence in sensual pleasures. Bute himself set the young prince a fine example. He was happily married, with a growing family that was held together by strong ties of family feeling, and he was pious and upright in his personal life. It was a lesson Prince George learned well.

But the earl of Bute was not content just to be the prince's friend and adviser. His real ambition was to be the tutor who became prime minister.* He won the confidence of his pupil and encouraged him to learn. But he allowed his own vanity and jealousy to obscure the true interests of the young man destined to be king. Under Bute's direction the prince became a tool to further Bute's own ambition.

Although he was not a member of Parliament, Bute soon became one of the most important politicians in Great Britain. He was given the title "Groom of the Stole," which meant "first place in the prince's household." Even so, he coveted the post of prime minister, a post then held by Thomas Pelham Holles, Duke of Newcastle, and he expected to have it when George became king.

In 1756, just a year after Bute had assumed the role of tutor to Prince George, William Pitt, one of the most dynamic members of the House of

---

*The office of prime minister—the man who was at the same time the representative of the king in the House of Commons, and of the House of Commons to the king—helped to establish a stable and civilized system of government in Great Britain. It made it possible for monarchy and popular representation to go hand in hand.

Commons, became one of the two secretaries of state. Pitt was to direct the British effort in the war that had recently begun in North America and spread to Europe. The duke of Newcastle would control the finances and attempt to convince members of Parliament to support government policy. Newcastle was considered head of the Whig party, which strove to limit the power of the king over Parliament.

Ever since William Pitt had entered the House of Commons in 1736, when he was just twenty-eight years old, he had always stood above party politics, a maverick loner among the Whigs. Yet it was he who was best able to maintain a harmonious atmosphere within the House of Commons, where he provided a sense of vision, a steady nerve, and an iron will.

Now, with an incomparable grasp of world strategy and complete confidence in himself, Pitt began to organize the conduct of the great conflict then being waged.

This war, known in Europe as the Seven Years' War, fought from 1756 to 1763, pitted Britain and Prussia against France and Austria. During it, under Pitt's leadership, much of the French overseas empire would be destroyed. In 1759 Pitt had ordered an all-out attack on the French colony of Canada. It was a brilliant success for the skillful young generals he put in command. When the English general James Wolfe captured the city of Quebec, the capital of Canada, the collapse of the French Empire in North America was assured. It

William Pitt, known as "The Great Commoner," was a strategic genius who provided a sense of vision, a steady nerve, and an iron will in the House of Commons. *Painted by William Hoare in 1745.*

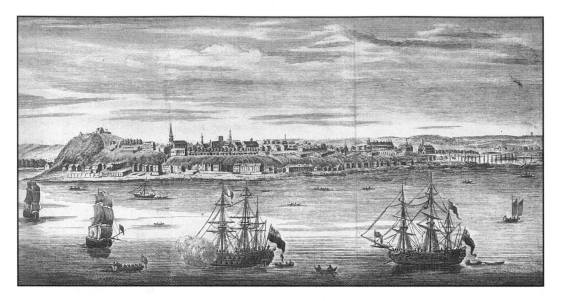

A view of the city of Quebec, the capital of New France (Canada), as seen from the shore of the St. Lawrence River. British warships are in the foreground. *Engraving by Captain Harvey Smith, one of British General Wolfe's officers.*

was a glorious victory and a pivotal moment in both the war and the history of North America. Church bells rang in celebration all across England.

William Pitt's strategic genius, his political courage, and his faith in his own leadership, which was sometimes difficult to distinguish from arrogance (he was certain that he, and only he, could save the country), gave others the basis on which to fight and win the war. No British war minister had ever achieved such success. He became known as "The Great Commoner."

Tall, pale, and thin-faced, with a long, threatening hawk nose and bright piercing eyes, and always in formal dress and wig, his ankles swollen from gout, a painful and often crippling disease, Pitt made a theatrical appearance. He was eloquent, fiery, bold, and original, often composing "on his feet." His oratory was spellbinding. [4]

"At a whisper his voice could be heard in the farthest corners, often swelling like a great organ to its fullest register, so the volume filled the House." There was absolute silence when Pitt stood up to speak. [5]

He was devoted to his wife and clearly delighted by his five children. He called them "the sum of all delight." He was a private and intense man who hated being separated from his family. Outside his family, he was considered cold in his relations with other people. In spite of this, he had the gift to create in all who listened to him the sense that he was the voice of destiny, that he would lead Britain to greatness. The people trusted and loved him. His honesty took men by surprise. By late 1760 he appeared indispensable. [6]

Pitt's administration was particularly important for Britain's American empire three thousand miles across the Atlantic Ocean. Pitt had close ties with British merchants who traded overseas and who had long encouraged support of the thirteen colonies that comprised British America. He strongly urged Parliament to protect their colonial trade. Four decades of colonial growth had greatly increased the sale of British products in America.

King George II died on a Saturday, so most of the ministers were in the country for the weekend. Pitt was the only cabinet member in London, and he, too, was about to depart for the country. His coach was standing ready at the door of his house in St. James Square, his grooms dressed in the striking blue-and-silver uniform familiar to all, when he received a summons to come at once to Kensington Palace. There he learned of the king's death. After sending messengers to all the Privy Councilors, Pitt drove to the palace at Kew. The Privy Council was a formal body of nobles who served as the king's private advisers. They were appointed as a high honor and were made up of the great officers of state, including the archbishop of Canterbury.

When Pitt arrived at the palace, he was greeted first by Bute, whom the king had quickly named to Privy Council membership so that he could attend this elite gathering. It was only after an hour that Pitt was able to see the new king. Newcastle, the prime minister, also saw Bute first, then the king. Both men were complimented by the king and reassured that their services would be valued in the new reign. But both were left with no doubt that Bute would be the power behind the throne.

"My Lord Bute is your very good friend; he will tell you my thoughts at large," the new king told both men. He reassured them that they would retain their positions. Then he confided to both men his concern of "how unequal he was to the load now come upon his youth, but he doubted not he would have the assistance of all honest men."[7]

At six o'clock that evening the Privy Council met to sign the proclamation of the king's formal accession to the throne and to hear his address. Bute was prepared. He had written the speech, and it was in his pocket. But it would provoke the first clash of the new reign.

As William Pitt listened to the king read the final sentence, he was enraged. Bute had written: "As I mount the throne in the midst of a bloody war, I shall endeavor to prosecute it in the manner most likely to bring an honourable and lasting peace."

As soon as the king concluded his speech, Pitt cornered Bute. Pitt saw the reference to the war as derogatory to himself, he told him, and the reference to peacemaking as implying abandonment of Britain's ally Prussia. After an angry discussion between the two men that lasted two hours, and a sulky reconsideration by the king that lasted even longer, the king's speech was formally published the next day as having announced: "As I mount the throne in the midst of *an expensive, but just and necessary* war, I shall endeavor to prosecute it in the manner most likely to bring an honourable and lasting peace *in concert with our allies.*"

This would make the king's speech a justification of Pitt's war policy. Pitt triumphed, and the change was made.[8]

On October 26, the day following his accession, George III was proclaimed "George the Third, by the Grace of God King of Great Britain, France, and Ireland, Defender of the Faith, and so forth."* An old and tired

*The British claim to the throne of France, which dated back to Edward III and had long since been abandoned, still appeared in the royal title. George's German connection was not mentioned.

king had been succeeded by a young and fresh one who fervently hoped "that my subjects will in time come to esteem me worthy of the crown I wear." [9]

The new king made a good impression in public. He had grace and dignity, and none of the surliness of his grandfather. It was said about him that "so much unaffected good nature appears in all he does or says that it cannot but endear him to all." [10] He seemed "the most amiable young man in the world." [11]

King George III was the first unmarried monarch to ascend the throne in a hundred years. Now he needed a wife.

He had recently been smitten by the very young and beautiful Lady Sarah Lennox, the great-great-granddaughter of Charles II by his favorite mistress. George wrote to Bute that his "passion" increased every time he saw Sarah. "She is everything I can form lovely," he told him.

But Bute—and George's mother—advised against her. He should not marry anyone from the English aristocracy. As he was also a prince of Hanover, he must select a bride who would be acceptable in the German states as well as England. George reluctantly agreed.

He began, secretly, to make inquiries about suitable princesses. The qualities he considered important were a pleasant disposition, a good understanding, and the ability to bear children. Beauty was not a factor. Nor did he want a wife with intellectual interests. Above all, he did not want a wife who might meddle in politics.

Princess Charlotte of Mecklenburg-Strelitz was chosen in June. When she accepted the request for her hand, the king indicated his desire for the marriage to take place as soon as possible so that she might be crowned with him in September. He wrote to Bute, explaining: "How disagreeable would it not be for a young person to appear, almost at her first arrival, in Westminster Abbey, and go through all that ceremony. . . . Indeed, she ought to be above a month here before that day that she may have a little recovered that bashfulness which is beautiful in a young lady on her first appearance." [12]

Someone was sent to take her measurements so her wedding clothes could be made in England.

But there were delays. On July 12 Princess Charlotte's mother died, and on July 20 the king caught chicken pox. But a tress of the princess's hair—"of a very fine dark colour and very soft"—was sent to him, and it gave him great pleasure.[13]

From the beginning of their marriage, in order to shield Queen Charlotte from outside influences, the king instilled in his young bride a fear of becoming involved in the corrupt political world. He was so successful that she would later say she had a horror of "medling in Politics." She took English lessons and learned to speak the language fluently. She tried hard to please her husband.

When she was finally able to sail from Germany to England, Charlotte spent part of her time on the voyage learning to play "God Save the King" on the harpsichord. She was at sea for ten days, arriving at Harwich on September 7. The next morning she continued her journey to London.

When Charlotte arrived at St. James's Palace at three in the afternoon, the king's brother Edward, now the duke of York, was waiting to hand her out of the coach and lead her to the king. They met in the garden.

As the princess prepared to curtsy, the king raised her up, embraced her, and took her into the palace to meet his mother and the rest of the royal family. After dining with the family, she was dressed in her bridal clothes, then took her place in the bridal procession to the Chapel Royal, just across the road from the palace. The duke of Gloucester escorted her. When she began to tremble as she walked, he said to her (in French, for she spoke no English), "Courage, Princess, courage."

George and Charlotte were married that evening, September 8, 1761, at nine o'clock by the archbishop of Canterbury. Afterward, they moved on to the drawing room, where the guests had assembled, and while supper was being prepared, Charlotte played the harpsichord and sang. They retired at three in the morning. Charlotte was seventeen years old.

Two weeks later, on Tuesday, September 22, 1761, King George III and Queen Charlotte were crowned in Westminster Abbey. Despite all the splendid pomp and pageantry of the day, there was a certain simplicity in the ceremony in keeping with the style of the king. The king and queen went from St. James's Palace to Westminster Hall on their way to the abbey in sedan chairs, much like ordinary citizens going to the theater. But the king, wearing crimson velvet robes, walked from the hall to the abbey under a canopy of cloth of gold. Charlotte walked under a canopy with silver bells at its corners.

St. Edward's Crown, worn by George III at his coronation. The crown weighs almost five pounds and is used only for the crowning ceremony. Its great diamond fell out on the king's return trip to Westminster Hall, but was quickly found and restored.

King George and Queen Charlotte were crowned at 3:30 P.M. A coronation banquet followed. At ten o'clock the king and queen returned to St. James's Palace as unobtrusively as they had come. The only mishap for the king occurred when the great diamond in his crown fell out of its setting on their return to Westminster Hall. It was immediately found and restored. It had been a perfectly planned ceremony of symbolic significance for the entire British Empire. The king never forgot it, and he observed the oath he took—to rule according to law, to exercise justice with mercy, and to maintain the Church of England—to the end of his reign.

A young man named John Hancock lingered on his only trip to London from the American colonies, in order to witness the coronation.

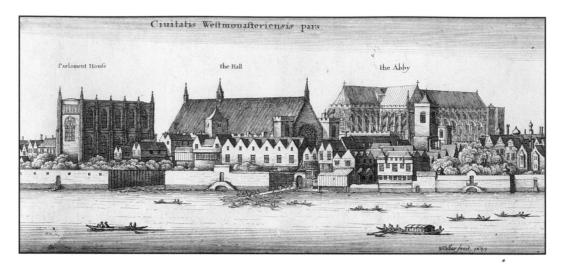

The buildings at Westminster as they appeared in the seventeenth century. St. Stephen's Chapel, on the left, had become Parliament House, where the House of Commons met. The huge roof of Westminster Hall can be seen in the middle. Westminster Abbey is on the right. *By Wenceslas Hollar.*

And another colonial, Benjamin Franklin of Philadelphia, who had been agent* for Pennsylvania in London since 1757, managed to get back to London from Belgium and Holland in time for the coronation. Affection for the young "Patriot King" was as fervent in the American colonies as it was in England.

"The very best in the world, and the most amiable," Ben Franklin characterized the king to an English friend. When his friend mused that the colonists would one day want their independence, Franklin disagreed. The colonists would never unite against their mother country. It was "not merely improbable, it [was] impossible," he argued, unless they are made to feel "the most grievous tyranny and oppression."[14]

---

*Agents were distinguished men elected by the colonial legislatures and sent to England to plead the cause of the Americans before the court, the Privy Council, and occasionally, Parliament. They were not regarded as representatives of the colonists in the British Parliament because they had no official standing or power. They had no right to speak in the House of Commons or the House of Lords, or to make binding decisions for their governments.

Chapter II

"brought to a collision"

Massachusetts Bay Colony: February 1761

His Majesty has declared himself, by his Speech to his Parliament to be a Man of Piety, and Candor in Religion, a friend of Liberty, and Property in Government, and a Patron of Merit. . . . These are sentiments worthy of a King—a Patriot King.

—*From the diary of John Adams, February 9, 1761*

On December 27, 1760, two months after King George II died, the news of his death reached Boston from London. Customs officers immediately prepared to petition the superior court of Massachusetts for a renewal of writs of assistance.

"Writs of assistance" was a common legal term for general search warrants that were granted to customs officers by the colonial courts. In the colonies, the writs gave customs men the authority—without a specific search warrant—to break into and search ships, shops, homes, and warehouses where they suspected that smuggled goods might be concealed. It also empowered them to arrest those merchants who were responsible. The warrants had been legal in England since 1662 and in America since 1696, but they automatically expired six months after the death of a reigning monarch. The death of the king on October 25, 1760, made their renewal mandatory.

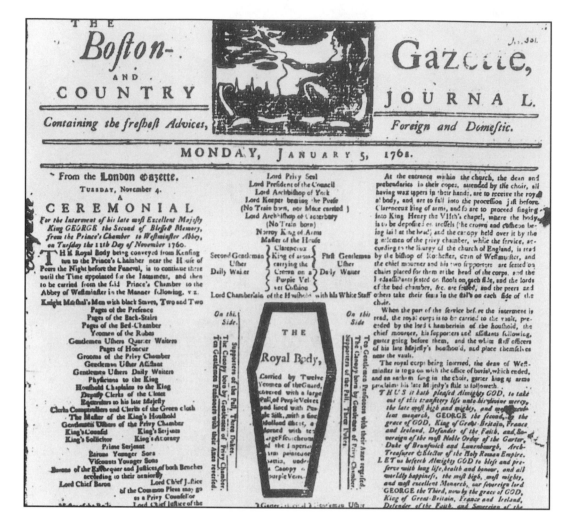

The death on October 25, 1760, and burial of King George II were announced in the *London Gazette* on Tuesday, November 4, 1760. It took two months for the news to travel across the Atlantic Ocean. The notice was reproduced in the *Boston Gazette* and *Country Journal* on Monday, January 5, 1761.

These writs had not been used in the colonies for more than half a century. It was the golden age of smuggling. So many complicated regulations existed to limit trade with other countries that there was no way they could be enforced effectively, and for many years customs collectors had just ignored foreign cargoes coming into port. Consequently, no duties had been paid on the goods.

Little guilt was attached to smuggling because the colonists looked on it as a means of survival, a highly profitable, although illegal, enterprise. In fact, smugglers were regarded as respected members of the community who helped their neighbors get needed goods at fair prices. In addition to the high duties imposed on British goods, there was also a requirement that many items be bought only from England at high prices in order to keep English merchants in control.

Things changed during the conflict known in Britain as the Seven Years' War and in America as the French and Indian War. Before the war the smuggling of foreign products into the colonies had been so common in New England that it had caused little stir, but with the beginning of the war in 1754, smuggling was suddenly considered to be an unpatriotic act, especially because it often involved trade with the enemy, France. The French troops in North America were being supplied with food and other provisions by merchants in the colonies, even though these troops were fighting against Britain.

William Pitt, otherwise the colonists' champion in Parliament, attacked this as an "illegal and most pernicious Trade,"[1] carried on by America with the French enemy, and early in 1760 he ordered colonial governors to enforce the laws governing trade. British customs officers, armed with writs of assistance, began to break into warehouses and ships to seize illegal cargoes in Boston on a large scale. In a moment, the most lucrative trade New England possessed was about to be ended. Sixty-three Boston merchants objected, calling the writs unconstitutional, and petitioned the court to "be heard by themselves and counsel upon the Subject of writs of assistance."

When the doors of the Boston Town House opened on the cold, clear morning of Tuesday, February 24, 1761, John Adams was in the forefront of those who pressed for places in the great council chamber, with its nine tall windows, deep fireplace, and glistening chandelier. Adams was an obscure young lawyer from the little town of Braintree, Massachusetts. Convinced that the case that was to be tried in superior court that day would be a historic one, he had come prepared with paper, pen, and a pot of ink. He would record it in order to study it later, at his leisure, the only written account history would have of the trial. At issue were "writs of assistance."

Adams found a seat in the chamber, along with officers of the government,

The Old State House, also known as the Boston Town House, as it appeared in the 1760s is the middle building in this view of Boston. Built in Boston in 1713, it is one of the oldest public buildings still standing in the United States. It was the center of British authority, where the governor and other royally appointed officials met. But it was also the meeting place of the Massachusetts Assembly, freely elected by the people. As such, it became the scene of many confrontations between the colonists and the British.

Boston attorneys, concerned merchants, and many others interested in hearing the arguments who were jammed into every available space. He was impressed by the majesty of the scene: the judges in their immense white wigs and robes of scarlet English cloth, with the full-length portraits of the Stuart kings, Charles II and James II, framed in gold, looking down on them. Newly appointed Superior Court Chief Justice Thomas Hutchinson presided.

The attorney representing the British government was Jeremiah Gridley, the distinguished lawyer with whom John Adams had recently studied law and who had sponsored him to become a member of the bar. "His words seem to pierce and search," John Adams wrote of the sixty-year-old Gridley in his diary. "He is a great Reasoner. . . . [His] Grandeur consists in his great Learning . . . and his majestic Manner." He was sometimes referred to as the "Father of the Boston bar."[2]

James Otis Jr. and Oxenbridge Thacher, two of the most eminent young lawyers in the colony, who had also been trained by Gridley, represented the Massachusetts merchants.

In order to lead the battle against the writs, Otis had given up his royal appointment as advocate general in the Massachusetts court system, a post that required him to argue cases on behalf of the provincial government. As such, he had been the official legal adviser of the government. Thacher was described by John Adams as one whose "amiable manners and pure principles united to a very easy and musical eloquence [that] made him very popular."

John Adams knew of the tensions that existed between Chief Justice Hutchinson and Otis. Hutchinson had a reputation for integrity, industry, judiciousness, and devotion to public service, and as Adams himself described, "99 in an 100 of [his Countrymen] really thought him the greatest and best Man in America."[3]

Earlier, an appointment as chief justice had been promised to James Otis Sr., a distinguished lawyer, by the royal governor at the time, William Shirley. But when Chief Justice Stephen Sewall died soon after scheduling a hearing on writs of assistance for February 1761, the new governor, Sir Francis Bernard, decided to fill the vacancy by offering the chief justice post to Hutchinson instead, even though he was already lieutenant governor of the colony *and* probate judge.

Governor Bernard was anxious to please the British government and to receive a share of the fees collected from the confiscation of smuggled goods. He needed a chief justice who would enforce the trade laws. Thomas Hutchinson was his man. It was a decision he would come to regret.

When this portrait of John Adams was painted two years after his marriage to Abigail, John Adams was a struggling young attorney who had confided, "I want to do something that will surprize the world." His soft, chubby, bland face reveals little of the character that would later develop. *Pastel by Benjamin Blyth, 1766.*

James Otis Jr. never forgave Hutchinson and took every opportunity to attack the man he thought had cheated his father.

It was against this background that the trial began.

Jeremiah Gridley opened the argument for the writs. He was, as always, informed and learned. He pointed out that such writs had been authorized by Parliament since the reign of Charles II. They were needed to assist in the proper enforcement of the law. He embellished his presentation with rhetoric and logic.

"If it is the law in England, it is the law here, extended to this country by act of Parliament," he said. He went on to cite precedents for the writs, then bowed to the judges and sat down.

The fiery James Otis, whose stirring speech against writs of assistance would have lasting repercussions, was a hero to John Adams. *By Joseph Blackburn, 1755*

Mr. Thacher, in his reply to Mr. Gridley, soberly appealed to reason. His argument rested on the law itself. Writs of assistance were only temporary warrants—special warrants that must be renewed for each search, Mr. Thacher countered. He was moderate and restrained, informed and thorough, and he brought a sense of respectability to the cause. Yet it appeared to John Adams that the weight of precedent and authority was on the side of Gridley and the crown.

By the time James Otis rose to speak, the stage was set for him. The crowd that filled the council chamber had had its fill of formal reasoning. Those opposed to the writs were tired—and uneasy at the array of facts that Gridley had been able to set before the justices. They feared that they were about to lose what they considered a cherished constitutional right in a dispute over points of law.

Otis, at thirty-five, was a giant of a man, with a short neck, a plump, round face, and bold eagle eyes. John Adams described him as "extremely quick and elastic, his apprehensions as quick as his temper. He springs and twitches his muscles about in thinking." Perhaps he was beginning to show signs of the mental instability that would eventually disable him.

Now, with his characteristic flare and fire, his magic power over men's minds and sensibilities, Otis immediately drew everyone's attention. His opening sentence brought the issue out of the maze of legal terms and precedents and into the light of common understanding: "This writ," he declared, "is against the fundamental principles of laws." It did not matter that Parliament had authorized the writs. "A man who is quiet and orderly is as secure in his house as a prince in his castle," Otis told the court. The right of property to an Englishman, native or colonial, was the primary and essential right on which all others rested. Only for flagrant crimes or "cases of great public necessity" might that privilege of privacy be invaded, or through special search warrants "issued on good and sufficient grounds for suspicion."

If general warrants were approved by the court, every petty customs official would be free to enter and search anybody's house at will. It was more important to follow the known principles of the law than any one precedent, Otis contended.

Otis's speech carried his listeners back to Runnymede, where in June 1215, King John had issued the great charter of English liberties known as Magna Carta.* He stressed the natural rights of man as later expressed by John Locke, a great British political philosopher, teacher, and hero to Englishmen on both

*Magna Carta established for the first time a constitutional principle of immense significance: that the power of the king should be limited by a written grant. It is a landmark in the transition from an oral to a written society.

sides of the Atlantic. For Locke, property was not merely a possession to be hoarded and admired. Property was the source of life and liberty. A man could be sure he was free *only* if he knew that his person and his property were his own. Property and liberty, therefore, were one and inseparable.* [4]

The writs were illegal, Otis concluded, for "an act against the constitution is void." [5]

As Otis spoke, John Adams thought that what was being acted out here under cover of a trial was the opening scene in a drama whose consequences, when he considered them, chilled the blood in his veins. For the first time since the initial settlement of Englishmen on the continent of North America, "the views of the English government towards the colonies and the views of the colonies towards the English government [were] directly in opposition to each other." By the imprudence of the British ministry they had been deliberately "brought to a collision." Britain, John Adams felt certain, would never give up its claim to having complete authority over the colonies, and the colonies, in turn, "would never submit, at least without an entire devastation of the country and a general destruction of their lives."

By the time Otis concluded, after three hours of eloquence, the sun had gone down and candles had been brought in to illuminate the chamber. The audience was emotionally exhausted. And Jeremiah Gridley was filled with pride for both his pupils. "I raised up two young eagles," he said later of Otis and Thacher. "They pecked out both my eyes." [6]

John Adams was among many who were deeply stirred. "Every man . . . appeared to me to go away, as I did, ready to take arms against the writs of assistance," he noted later in his diary.

Chief Justice Hutchinson, aware of the anti-British sentiment that pervaded the room, and fearful of how the vote might go, persuaded the court to postpone a decision. He knew that general search warrants were valid in

*James Otis Jr. here struck the first blow in America for what has recently been called the right to privacy. General search warrants were ultimately made illegal by the Fourth Amendment to the U.S. Constitution.

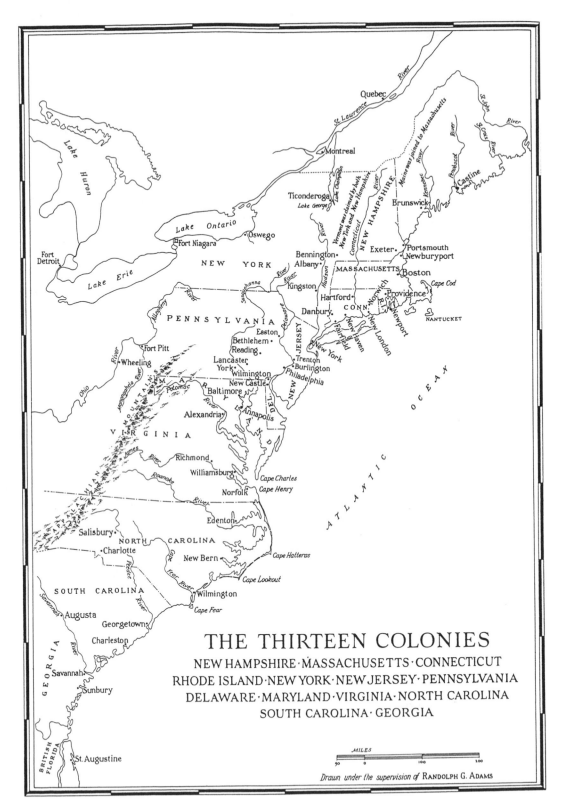

Map of the thirteen colonies at the end of the French and Indian War, 1763.

English law, and that their use in the colonies was specified by law. But it was to the higher law of "natural equity," the moral basis of the law, the *principles* of law, that Otis had directed his plea. Hutchinson decided he would buy time: They must write to England for instructions.[7]

Six months later, the attorney general in London ruled that the writs of assistance were legal. James Otis had lost the case. But the issue of writs of assistance spread to all the colonies and, over the next five years, was dragged through every superior court in America.

James Otis's stirring speech would have lasting repercussions.

Chapter III

Salutary neglect

London: 1761–1764

13

As he ascended the throne of Great Britain, George III vowed to himself that he would be as different from his grandfather as possible. George II had kept a mistress. George III remained faithful and devoted to his wife all his life. He was a genuinely religious man, as opposed to his grandfather, and took his role as head of the Church of England seriously. George II had cared more for Hanover than for Great Britain. George III, with his own hand, inserted in his first speech to Parliament, "Born and educated in this country, I glory in the name of Britain."[1]

He would be King of *all* his people. He considered political party distinctions a disturbing element in national life. He would put an end to them. During the reign of George II, members of the Whig Party had held all the important offices and other lucrative jobs in the administration. Since neither

George I nor George II spoke much English, generally they had been content to allow the Whig leaders to govern as they liked. They were ready to accept the large sums of money their positions as king afforded them.[2]

Now, the new young king decided, if the prestige of the monarchy were to be restored, the power of the Whigs must be broken. He believed that political parties disrupted the nation's harmony.

There were two opposing parties in Parliament: Whig and Tory. They were made up of groups, each wanting power, but held together by ties of friendship, intermarriage, and patronage, rather than by clear policies. *Whig* was a slang term for Scottish bandits and was given to those who believed Parliament ought to be as important as the king. Their aim was to limit the king's power. *Tory* was slang for Irish bandits and was the nickname of those who believed the king ought to have more power than the constitution then allowed. Whigs were the larger group.

George felt that his grandfather and great-grandfather had given too much power to the Whig politicians. They had been "kings in chains." He would gain back for the monarchy those powers it had lost during their reigns. He would make the prime minister a mere instrument of the royal will and reduce the cabinet to a group of the "King's servants" in fact as well as in name. He would welcome many of the old Tories back to court and give them titles and honors. He would appoint men whom he liked and trusted, rather than powerful party leaders, and would choose his advisers from the best men of *any* party. He would deal with "those proud Dukes," as he called them. "The sword is drawn; vigour and violence are the only means of ending this audacious faction," he told Bute.[3]

This attempt at "personal rule," he knew, was not unconstitutional, and no one would argue against it. What George didn't know was how to accomplish it.

He immediately appointed Bute to his cabinet and decided that he would consult him on everything and would follow his advice. Bute would remain tutor to his pupil even though his pupil was now king of England.

George III was well grounded in the British system of government and politics. He believed it represented the height of human political wisdom. Now he saw it threatened by factions within Parliament, but his responsibility for making it work and preserving it intact terrified him. Young, inexperienced, and naive, he found himself hemmed in between William Pitt and the earl of Bute, both of whom craved power.

The best hope of political stability at the outset of the new reign lay in an alliance between Bute and Pitt. But such an alliance demanded compromise on both sides, and this neither man was willing to do. Pitt made it clear to Bute right from the start that he would accept no changes, and that he must continue to be able to act as an independent minister or not at all. This attitude was unacceptable to the king.

Until this time, William Pitt had dominated the cabinet in the conduct of the war. He chose commanders and planned operations, exercising an authority over the armed forces far greater than any other politician had in the past. He felt strongly that two aims should drive English policy: supremacy at sea and the capture of French trading posts abroad. To him, trade meant wealth and power. His ministry was one of the most successful of the eighteenth century, laying the foundation for an empire that circled the globe and brought Britain great wealth.[4]

But George III had been brought up to believe that his grandfather, the former king, had been almost a prisoner of the corrupt politicians of his cabinet who were interested only in the spoils of office—and were indifferent to the needs of their country. He sincerely believed that Pitt's measures were leading the country to ruin. He saw Pitt as a traitor and called him "the blackest of hearts." Newcastle, the prime minister, fared no better in his mind.

William Pitt had been a staunch friend of Britain's American colonies. He felt it was politically wrong to attempt to force the colonies to contribute to the expense of the war against France and its Canadian colonies that was then in progress. In fact, he went so far as to promise them reimbursement for war expenditures, so as to encourage their enthusiastic participation in the war effort to conquer French Canada. As a result, the Seven Years' War became the most expensive war Britain had ever waged.

By now the war was going well for England, and peace negotiations between Britain and France began in the spring of 1761. Britain had defeated France in Canada, India, the West Indies, and part of West Africa. But Pitt knew that Spain would not stand aside and watch this onward march of British power. He was certain that Spain would secretly form an alliance with France to help defeat Britain in the future. Therefore he proposed attacking Spain before she was ready to go to war. "Loss of time is loss of opportunity," he warned.[5]

But George III didn't heed his warning. He had been immersed in the plans for his marriage and coronation, and he didn't want a war to spoil the festivities.

Members of the cabinet, though they considered Pitt's plan brilliant, were fearful that their nation was on the brink of bankruptcy because of the cost of Pitt's war policies. They voted against him.

Bute sided with his king and pressed for peace as quickly as possible. On October 5, 1761, less than one month after George had been crowned king of Great Britain, Pitt resigned, telling the king that it would only create problems if he remained in office. But, he assured the king, he would not oppose the royal measures, nor attend the House of Commons except to defend his own policy.

Soon Pitt was proved right. Spain did enter into a military compact with France. "This fresh enemy makes my heart bleed for my poor country," King George wrote to Bute in November.[6]

Throughout the winter of 1761–1762, negotiations between Britain and France and Spain continued. Pitt kept the promise he had made to the king on his resignation. He only attended one meeting of the House of Commons, on November 13, 1761, in order to defend his position in person. But his gout had flared up again and he was in such agonizing pain that he had to be carried into the House of Commons, his legs wrapped in flannel and his hands in thick gloves. During his speech, which lasted for three and a half hours, he was allowed the indulgence of sitting from time to time. It was a magnificent, but tragic, scene.

Pitt's popularity and the esteem in which he was held was evident when he arrived at St. Stephen's Church, where Parliament met. As he stepped out of his carriage, the joy of the gathered crowd was overwhelming.[7] City merchants, particularly, adored him. The years of war had stimulated Britain's industrial and agricultural production to new levels. A vision of increased wealth and glory had been dangled before their eyes. More importantly, the professional classes and the new industrialists—men who were making their fortunes in steel, cotton, coal mining, and porcelain—believed that England was destined for great wealth if her opportunities were not ruined by the incompetence of her king and his ministers.

When William Pitt resigned on October 5, 1761, George III named Bute his chief minister in charge of war and foreign policy. Bute immediately took command. He ignored Pitt's recommendation that such crushing terms must be imposed on both France and Spain that they would never again be able to menace the British Empire. England, Pitt said, had an unusual opportunity to destroy for all time the fighting power of her "eternal" enemy, France, if she dealt firmly with both countries.

But Bute and the king, in their eagerness to present the people of England with a victorious peace, did not take full advantage of their strong position at the negotiating table. Great Britain did win control of much of India from France, and gained Florida from Spain. But instead of claiming all the French possessions in North America, as Pitt had insisted they should, they accepted the French demand that they choose either Canada or Guadeloupe and Martinique. Guadeloupe and Martinique were two of the French West Indian islands that had been captured by the British during the war. They were rich in sugar and would therefore contribute to a self-sufficient British Empire. But to Bute, the long-term security of British North America counted for far more than quick profits from sugar, and he chose Canada. British possession of Canada, Bute thought, would put an end to the long series of wars waged by the French and the English for control of North America,[8] and put Britain in control of the lands belonging to the American Indian tribes, who had long been a threat to the western frontiers of the colonies when they fought for the French.

Benjamin Franklin, in London at the time, agreed. He published a pamphlet anonymously (which guaranteed that it would attract attention) in which he described America as the western frontier of the entire British Empire. Canada must remain British, he counseled, in order to secure all of North America. In fact, he predicted that "America might one day number a hundred million people." He ended by dismissing the possibility that the colonists would ever unite against Great Britain:

> If [the colonists] could not agree to unite for their defense against the French and Indians who are harassing their settlements, burning their buildings, and murdering their people, can it reasonably be supposed there is any danger of their uniting against their own nation, which protects and encourages them, and [in] which they have so many connections and ties of blood, interest and affection? . . . I venture to say that an union amongst them for such a purpose is not merely improbable; it is impossible . . . without the most grievous tyranny and oppression.[9]

In December 1762 the House of Commons voted in support of the king and the peace. The nation was tired of war. The Treaty of Paris was signed on February 20, 1763. It had taken nearly three years to negotiate.

The peace of 1763 was the first important achievement of George III's personal rule in foreign affairs. In fact, when the preliminaries of the treaty were approved by Parliament, the Princess Dowager exclaimed, "Now my son is King of England!"

In his American colonies there was rejoicing from New England to the Carolinas. Bonfires were lit, church bells tolled, and guns were fired in celebration. There were festive banquets and colorful parades.

Yet there were many in England who feared that they would one day be obliged to fight France again. William Pitt predicted that the peace would last, at best, ten years. He was certain that it contained the seeds of a future war.

There were even some who speculated that once the threat of France was removed from North America and the colonists no longer needed Great Britain's protection, they would "strike off their chains." In fact, it was true that when the French flag was lowered throughout the North American continent and Canada became British, the strong bond of protection against the common enemy, France, which had bound the colonies to the mother country was snapped.

When the new Parliament opened in April of 1763, George III expected Bute to continue as his chief minister, but Bute had lost heart. He had no powerful friends in Parliament, and he found the stress of politics almost unbearable. The Whigs had made him one of the most hated men in England for ousting William Pitt. He was jeered at in theaters and stoned in public by London mobs. In fact, Londoners, who adored Pitt, burned tartan bonnets and other Scottish emblems in bonfires as a symbol of their hatred of this Scottish minister. Bute was thoroughly alarmed. Concerned for his life, he informed the king that he wished to resign from office. The king, who never lacked courage himself, was stunned.

George III then asked Pitt to come back. When he, too, refused unless the king met all his demands, the king, at Bute's suggestion, named George Grenville, Pitt's brother-in-law, chancellor of the Exchequer (sometimes referred to as first lord of the Treasury) and leader of the House of Commons. The chancellor of the Exchequer controlled finances, and therefore wielded great power. Despite the fact that George personally disliked Grenville, he hoped that the new minister would be willing to conduct affairs under the guidance of Bute. Indeed, Bute dictated all the key appointments to the ministry, even making certain that his own brother, James Stuart Mackenzie,

Countdown to Independence

would continue as minister for Scotland. But it turned out that Grenville was not a man who would tolerate "dictation from behind the curtain." [10]

A member of a wealthy Buckinghamshire family and married to William Pitt's sister, Grenville was an able parliamentarian and an efficient businessman. He had wide experience in various branches of government, especially those concerned with trade and finance.

But Grenville was stiff, opinionated, and dour. He had none of the tact, judgment, or persuasion essential for governing. Despite the extraordinary efficiency of his ministry, from the moment he became first minister on April 1, 1763, he began to sow the seeds of a revolution.

When Grenville came into office, Britain was at the peak of her power in the world. With her victory at the conclusion of the Seven Years' War, she had not only defeated France and Spain, but had won a dominant position in Europe's trade with Africa and Asia, and had taken firm control of much of India. She was now, undoubtedly, the financial heart of the world, and her navy rode triumphant on the seas. It was a golden age.

But if Britain was victorious, she was also exhausted. The struggle with France had lasted over fifty years. It had been a costly battle—at sea and in Europe, Asia, and North America. Now Britain possessed, along with one of the largest empires in the world, the largest debt—one hundred and forty million pounds, half of which had been incurred defending the American colonies from French and Indian attacks. Great Britain was close to bankruptcy.

Alarmed for his country's financial stability, George Grenville determined to correct the situation. In fact, he regarded himself as the *only* man who *could* save England. He was a man who would dare anything he believed right, and he believed himself always right.

For nearly a century British thinking about colonial relationships had been dominated by the principles of what is called mercantilism. Mercantilism shaped and justified English exploitation of her empire. According to this doctrine, British colonies existed for the benefit of the mother country. They were considered possessions, rather than independent territories. Their defense and

32

much of their administration were paid for out of British taxes. Therefore, Parliament felt it had a right to control the trade of the colonies to ensure that Britain, and only Britain, gained the maximum benefit from them. The colonies must add to the mother country's wealth and self-sufficiency, while remaining economically dependent on her. Most of the other colonial nations, including France and Spain, also enforced the principles of mercantilism.

George Grenville, chancellor of the Exchequer, initiated the Stamp Act, a bold and fateful policy to deal with "the American problem." His Stamp Act would enrage the colonists and set in motion a series of events that would precipitate a violent response. *By Sir Joshua Reynolds, 1764–1767.*

Under this system colonists were expected to produce raw materials for the use of the mother country. The colonists would also support British manufacturing by buying only British products, transported only in British or colonial ships, thus ensuring Britain's naval supremacy. Never were the colonists to manufacture products themselves. They would keep gold and silver money within the empire by growing products such as sugar, tobacco, cotton, and rice, which would otherwise have to be bought from foreigners, but they could not send these commodities to any countries outside the British Empire. They could be exported to countries in Europe only *after* they had first been shipped to England. These rules persisted despite the fact that the profit to the colonists would be far greater if they could ship these products directly to the European market.

The colonists were expected to contribute to the general welfare of the entire empire, just as they would have if they had remained inhabitants of England. But for more than half a century colonial merchants and ship captains had been successfully bypassing these rules by routinely resorting to smuggling. Customs duties were evaded or ignored. In fact, Grenville learned, it was estimated that approximately seven hundred thousand pounds worth of merchandise was being smuggled into the American colonies annually without any duty being collected. He was horrified.

Until now, Parliament had employed the policy of salutary neglect, adopted earlier by Sir Robert Walpole, the great prime minister under Kings George I and George II. Walpole believed in the principle of "letting sleeping dogs lie," and applied this to the American colonies. If the colonists were left to run their own affairs, with little interference from England, Walpole counseled, they would produce more wealth and commerce and give their mother country less trouble. As the colonists prospered, they would bring added prosperity to England. Walpole was not going to be drawn into schemes to tax the colonists.

Grenville resolved that he would put a stop to the smuggling. He would see to it that the Navigation Acts were strictly enforced. These laws, also known as the British Acts of Trade, translated the theory of mercantilism into laws that governed commerce. They had regulated British shipping and colonial trade since they were originally passed in 1651.

Grenville's plan was simple. He would follow the established doctrine of mercantilism, but with an added sense of urgency. He would extend the usefulness of the colonies as a captive market for British manufacturers by adding more commodities to the list of those that must first pass Britain, more than had been on it during the entire period since the original passage of the Navigation Acts.

With the young king's approval (George III had finally realized that however much he disliked Grenville, the minister had been his own choice, and therefore he must give him his full political confidence), Grenville launched Parliament on an aggressive program of imperial reform. No Britons had gained more from the defeat of France than the colonists in North America, and Grenville resolved that they would pay for it. He would change the way those colonies were run. He initiated a bold and fateful policy to deal with "the American problem."

The British ministry recognized that their North American colonists had made a significant contribution in men and supplies to the British victory during the Seven Years' War. But when they tallied the cost of victory in blood and money, they realized that most of it had come from Britain. Surely, Britain could expect something in return?

American resources were not being fully tapped, they felt, and an excessive burden was being placed on the subjects in England. Expecting the colonists to shoulder part of the expenditure seemed reasonable.

Then an unexpected problem appeared. Word arrived in London that the Indians in North America who had been allies of France were fearful of what they perceived as the land-hungry British, and they had formed an alliance. In May 1763, led by Pontiac, Chief of the Ottawa Indians, they had risen up against the British and the colonists in the Ohio River Valley and the Great Lakes region. This uprising, which came to be known as Pontiac's Rebellion (although from the Indian point of view it was a war, not a rebellion), had caught the British off guard and succeeded in wiping out a number of British army posts.

The ease with which the Indians had accomplished this was proof to the British statesmen that the mother country must protect her colonies. The Indians, they were certain, were the allies of France and Spain. By their strategic position on the exposed frontiers of the British

In 1763 Chief Pontiac of Ottawa led a rebellion against the colonists and the British in the Ohio Valley.

colonies, these Native Americans posed a major threat to the colonists' security. The British recognized that until they outnumbered the hostile French and Indian population, there would be a constant danger that the French would try to repossess the land in a future war. The upper Ohio River Valley was an important area that the westward-pushing settlers hoped eventually to populate. The promise of lush lands and lucrative fur trading made this very appealing.

Unfortunately, the colonists had rejected a plan put forth by Benjamin Franklin in 1754, called the Albany Plan of Union, which called for the colonies to band together for defense against the Indians. Representatives of seven colonies had met in Albany to discuss this. It was the first time the colonies had ever conferred on the possibility of unified action. But, marked by vast social and economic differences, separated by long distances, and extremely jealous of one another, they had not been able to come to any agreement.

Benjamin Franklin created this rattlesnake cartoon to urge the colonies to unite during the French and Indian War. A rough picture of a snake separated into eight pieces marked with the initials of New England, New York, New Jersey, Pennsylvania, Maryland, Virginia, North Carolina, and South Carolina, it appears to be the first American cartoon. The colonists would revive it a decade later.

Disappointed, Franklin had published in his *Pennsylvania Gazette* a cartoon destined to become one of the most famous of the period. It showed the separate colonies as parts of a disjointed rattlesnake and bore the slogan, "Join, or Die."

Now the government of Great Britain issued the Proclamation of 1763, which forbade further settlement by the colonists beyond the Allegheny Mountains and west of the Ohio River.* By cordoning off the entire area of the Great Lakes and the Ohio basin as an Indian reserve, they hoped to satisfy the Indians and to encourage the flow of new colonial settlements into French-populated Canada, Nova Scotia, and the Spanish Floridas for both commercial and strategic purposes. Alarming reports were already coming out of France by September of 1763 that the French navy was being rebuilt in preparation for another war. An attack might be made on Newfoundland in 1764.

By confining Americans to the seaboard, the British hoped to ensure that the colonists would remain dependent on trade with England. What the British didn't comprehend was the vastness of the country. They had no sense of the geography of the land. But colonists who had fought with the British beyond the Allegheny Mountains had seen for themselves how fertile the land was. In fact some, including Benjamin Franklin, had been speculating in land there for years. They felt entirely capable of handling any Indian assaults themselves.

The hastily drawn Proclamation, designed only to meet a temporary emergency, would become the foundation of a permanent British policy toward the American West.

In order to enforce the Proclamation of 1763, the British needed an army in America to police the frontier and protect the colonists. Accordingly, ten thousand British soldiers were immediately sent to the colonies to perform this task. Part of the considerable cost of this protection, the British decided, must be borne by the American colonists. Therefore, Grenville determined to tax the colonists directly and use the tax money to maintain the army. But the British failed to make clear to the colonists why the army had been sent.

On March 9, 1764, George Grenville presented his proposals for raising

*This included the whole of the present states of Ohio, Indiana, Illinois, Michigan, Wisconsin, Kentucky, and Tennessee, as well as parts of Minnesota, New York, Pennsylvania, Maryland, West Virginia, North and South Carolina, Georgia, Alabama, and Mississippi; and the Canadian territories of Ontario and Quebec.

money from the American colonies as a series of resolutions to an attentive House of Commons. Madeira wine would bear a duty for the first time. New duties would be imposed on coffee, pimientos, foreign indigo dye, and foreign sugar. Certain commodities from the colonies, such as lumber and iron, would be added to the list of products that could be exported to countries in Europe only *after* they had first been shipped to England. The list included products not produced in the British Isles, but essential to the wealth and power of Great Britain. Foreign rum was to be prohibited. Foreign textiles were to be taxed.

Perhaps the most important proposal concerned the duty on foreign molasses. The making of rum was an enormous and profitable business in America. The colonists illegally imported molasses from the sugar plantations of the French Caribbean and distilled it into high-quality rum. The rum was sold at a large profit. The colony of Rhode Island declared that distilling rum from smuggled molasses "was the main hinge upon which the trade of the colony turns."

Now Grenville offered to reduce the duty on molasses from six pence to three pence a gallon. But the penalty for violating the law and evading the tax would be increased substantially. Further, since Grenville recognized that colonial juries would not convict local smugglers, new vice-admiralty courts were created for prosecuting them. Under the newly expanded authority of these admiralty courts, all those accused of smuggling or otherwise violating commercial regulations could be sent to Halifax, Nova Scotia, where the courts were located, and be tried by a judge. This would effectively do away with trial by a jury of the colonists' peers. A single judge in faraway Halifax would hand down the verdict—and he would receive a five-percent commission on all fines collected.

The only resolution that did not call for immediate action by Parliament was the fifteenth, the most ominous measure of all. It provided that "towards further defraying the said Expences, it may be proper to charge certain Stamp Duties in the said Colonies and Plantations." This would establish the right of Parliament to lay an internal tax upon the American colonies.

The Stamp Act would require placing a stamp that certified payment of a tax on all legal and commercial documents, including birth certificates, marriage licenses, death certificates, wills, diplomas, pamphlets, freight bills, and even newspapers and playing cards. All official documents would have to be stamped with an ink stamp similar to a postal cancellation.

Test impressions of the hated stamps issued by the British government for use in the American colonies.

Printed revenue stamps could be purchased at a stamp office. Documents without stamps would be considered illegal. The Stamp Act would reach into the pockets of every citizen throughout the country. It affected every court of law, every ship, every school.

It was not scheduled to go into effect until November 1765. Grenville indicated that, in the meantime, notice of the stamp tax should be sent to the colonies, with the idea that if the colonists could agree to tax themselves and raise an adequate sum, he would accept the money raised in place of the stamp tax revenues. But Grenville never stated how much was "adequate." Nor did he send specific instructions to the governors of the colonies. The stamp tax was not even mentioned in Grenville's correspondence with the king.[11]

Grenville apparently had no real intention of allowing the colonies to make up the revenues the stamp tax would provide. Postponing it for a year was simply a political maneuver. He had already made up his mind to levy the tax.[12]

With the exception of the Stamp Act proposal, Grenville's resolutions were drawn into a bill and enacted into law, the Plantation Act of 1764, sometimes called the Sugar Act because the part that was to draw the most attention was the three-pence tax on molasses, a by-product of sugar manufacture.

Only one member of Parliament voted against it, and he had been born in Boston, Massachusetts.

Although the new law appeared to be simply a revision in trade regulations, its main purpose was stated in its preamble: It was "just and necessary, that a revenue be raised, in your Majesty's said dominions in America." Because the Stamp Act was not scheduled to go into effect until the end of 1765, the Sugar Act became the first law ever passed by Parliament for raising revenue in the colonies for use by the British government. Until now, no law had ever been passed in England to raise money within the colonies. The colonists had always taxed themselves directly through their own legislatures.

In London, feeling ran strong that Parliament was the supreme legislature of the nation, with unlimited power and the authority to levy taxes. Parliament, therefore, had the right to legislate for all British subjects, including Americans, though they were not represented. Unless they had that power to tax the American colonies, Parliament had no power at all over them. Most members of Parliament were in no mood to let Americans say how they should be governed.

On the other hand, there were some in England who felt—with the colonists—that Americans should not be taxed unless or until they were allowed to send representatives to Parliament. Although Americans were British subjects, they were represented in their own colonial assemblies, not in Parliament. There was a strong feeling that colonial assemblies could tax Americans, but Parliament could not. On this issue, as on most issues of constitutional law, there was a good legal case on both sides.

Chapter IV

"the privileges of Englishmen"

Boston: 1764

When news of George Grenville's Sugar Act and the impending stamp tax reached Boston by ship in April 1764, James Otis, Oxenbridge Thacher, and their friend Samuel Adams, who was a cousin of the Braintree attorney John Adams, were among the first to read the new law. Immediately the three men recognized that hidden in a brief clause in Grenville's preamble to the Sugar Act was a justification for the British government to raise revenues within the colonies. This, they knew, was a challenge to the doctrine "no taxation without representation," which had been one of England's political maxims since the Middle Ages. Five hundred years before, Edward I had said: "What touches all should be approved by all." The colonists were not represented in Parliament. Therefore, the right to tax had been given solely to the Massachusetts legislature by its charter of 1691. Samuel Adams feared, correctly, that the tax, concealed as a duty on trade, would not be noticed by many who read it.

Samuel Adams considered the charter of Massachusetts a "Sacred Ark" against all encroachments by the British government. But it is doubtful whether George Grenville, or any of the first lords who dealt with the colonies, knew or even cared what was in the Massachusetts Bay Charter.

Adams and his followers regarded the Massachusetts legislature, also known as the General Court, as a local parliament. It consisted of the House of Representatives, or Assembly, which was the lower house, and a Governor's Council, appointed by the king, which comprised the upper house. These corresponded to the House of Commons and the House of Lords in the English Parliament. Most of the colonies were headed by a royal governor, appointed by the king, who had the power to set aside any decisions made by the assembly. The relationship of a governor to the people of a colony was similar to that of the king to the British people.

Sam Adams and his friends insisted that the Massachusetts legislature be given equal dignity with the British Parliament. They promoted this idea in a newspaper they had founded in 1748, called the *Independent Advertiser*. Adams' contributions to this newspaper, based largely on the writings of John Locke, popularized Locke's political thought in New England.

The most important local political organizations within the New England colonies were the town meetings. These were assemblies of the voters in each town. Men who had shared in the founding of a settlement gathered in annual town meetings to elect local officials. They distributed town lands, levied taxes, and took action on such other matters as schools, roads, and bridges. At these town meetings each individual was free to offer his opinion, and differences were often hotly argued.

Perhaps most importantly, town meetings appointed small committees that were sent as representatives to the legislature of their colony. In theory, the actions of these representatives were limited: They were instructed by the town meeting as to a course of conduct. In practice, though, these representatives often acted on their own judgment.[1]

The town of Boston had a very effective town meeting.

When a committee of the town of Boston was appointed to prepare four newly elected members of the Massachusetts Assembly on how to deal with the new British taxes, the task of drafting the instructions was given to Samuel Adams. He submitted them at the town meeting of May 24, 1764, at Faneuil Hall, and soon after, they were published in the Boston press. From there, they spread to the other colonies.

In a delicate but firm hand, Adams, worried that these unexpected tax laws might lead to "more extensive Taxations," had written: "For if our Trade may be taxed why not our Lands? Why not the Produce of our lands, & every thing we possess or make use of? This [would cancel] our Charter Right to govern and tax ourselves. . . . If Taxes are laid upon us in any shape without our having a legal Representation where they are laid, are we not reduced from the Character of free Subjects to the miserable State of Tributary Slaves?"

The danger, Adams warned, was not limited to the merchants of Boston. A tax on molasses could easily extend to the farmers' crops. Parliament was overstepping its authority. His document also hinted that if the burdens of taxation were not removed, no British goods would be imported into any of the colonies. Samuel Adams ended his instructions with the suggestion that all the North American colonies unite in dealing with this important undermining of local rule.[2]

This was the first *public* denial of the right of the British Parliament to tax the colonies. Further, as a result of these instructions, the assembly sent a circular letter to the other colonies, urging them to ask their agents in England to unite in a strong protest against the Sugar Act and the proposed Stamp Act.

By no means was Sam Adams opposed to *all* taxes. He was opposed only to those imposed on the colonies by the British government. He himself was the tax collector for the town of Boston, and when he experienced difficulty collecting taxes from the colonists, he inserted a notice in a Boston newspaper, threatening "steps of law being taken" if delinquents did not pay.[3] Yet the people knew that his bark was worse than his bite. Sam Adams was everything a good tax collector should *not* be: a kind-hearted, easy-going man who listened sympathetically to hard-luck stories and never pressed his debtors once he was convinced it would be a hardship for them to pay.

New England was appropriately named, for it was the most English part of British America. It was precisely because New Englanders were so British that they became the first of the colonies to rebel. "We claim nothing but liberty and the privileges of Englishmen," they would say.

Massachusetts Bay was considered the leader among the thirteen colonies. As Massachusetts led the colonies, so Boston led Massachusetts. And it was Samuel Adams who was coming to be recognized as the leader of the town of Boston.

Though not quite forty-two years old, Adams looked older. His hair had turned gray prematurely, and he had a palsy that made his hands, and sometimes his voice, shake. But in spite of his appearance, he was remarkably healthy.

He was of medium height, muscular, and well built, with clear, steel gray eyes, heavy eyebrows, and a prominent nose. His gaze, which could be quite stern, was more often genial and pleasant. His face reflected his cheerful spirit. But it also mirrored his iron will.

Adams had a high speaking voice that often squeaked, and he was not considered an effective public speaker, but he was a behind-the-scenes molder of action. He won the minds of his fellow men by his earnestness, his genuinely democratic instincts, and his unselfish dedication to preserving their liberty.

As a child, Samuel Adams had attended the Boston Latin School, then entered Harvard College at the age of fourteen. His father paid his tuition in molasses and flour. Adams went on to earn a master of arts degree in 1743, when he was twenty-one. His master's thesis, written in Latin, was based on the thinking of John Locke and addressed the question: Is it lawful to resist the government if the welfare of the republic cannot otherwise be preserved? In his paper, Adams reasoned clearly in favor of the legality of an illegal action.

None of the dignitaries who heard his commencement address seemed to recognize that the young man who was speaking was asserting the right of resistance by the people to oppressors. His political radicalism was considered to be in the best Harvard tradition. Had members of the Massachusetts Patriot Party been in attendance, there is little doubt that they would have agreed that in Sam Adams they had a promising recruit.

Adams' father, Deacon Samuel Adams, was a prosperous brewer who owned a small malt house. As a merchant and the owner of one of the wharves on Purchase Street, Deacon Adams was considered one of the most substantial citizens of Boston's South End. He was a pillar of the Congregational Church and a leader of the community. Sam's mother was a woman of strict religious principles, and she instilled in her son the orthodoxy of the old Puritanism. Both parents expected their son to enter the ministry.

Samuel Adams, a great patriot who was a master at the use of propaganda, worked quietly behind the scenes for American independence. He came to be known as the Father of the American Revolution. Governor Francis Bernard called Sam Adams "the most dangerous man in Massachusetts." In 1775 Josiah Quincy wrote of him from England, "The character of your Mr. Samuel Adams runs very high here. I find many who consider him the first politician in the world." *By John Singleton Copley, 1770–1772.*

But young Adams found himself drawn to politics. He had no appetite for business and, as a young man, was suspicious of people of privilege and wealth. He tried several business ventures but was not very successful. Money always managed to slip through his fingers. His seedy clothes reflected his financial failure.

He was a loner who shied away from intimate friendships, yet he came to life in political circles. Even though he decided that he would make politics his lifework, he did not hold public office until he was thirty-one, although less gifted men were going to the General Court in their twenties. Politically, Samuel preferred to pull the strings and set the stage, then let someone else take the limelight.

In eighteenth-century Massachusetts, a large tavern acquaintance was essential for a politician. Sam spent much time in the taverns. Although he was fond of a pot of ale and a good fire, he drank only moderately, cultivating the company of laboring people with radical political opinions.

Sam was also an active member of the Caucus Club,* which his father had founded with some friends "to lay plans for introducing certain persons into places of trust and power." [4] The members met in an upstairs attic. Sam felt at home among the shipyard workers, artisans, mechanics, masons, and politicians who crowded in there. But he was equally at home with the intellectuals with whom he met on some evenings to discuss the classics, as well as the poetry of John Milton. His friends Paul Revere and Dr. Joseph Warren were members of both groups also.

Little by little, Sam came to be regarded as a spokesman for the common people of Boston. At the same time, his social position gave him influence among middle-class citizens. His second cousin John Adams said of him: "He was more cool, genteel, and agreeable than common; concealed and restrained in his passions." [5]

At Harvard College Sam had read deeply in Roman history and literature. He was thoroughly familiar with Plutarch, Cicero, and the other Roman historians. Because of this, even his political writings, designed to rouse the common people of New England, are filled with classical allusions. He was appealing to an audience that, like himself, knew the literature of Rome far better than it did the literature of England. [6]

Samuel had also learned to use the power of the press for his own purposes,

*A caucus was a way of deciding in advance on a policy or strategy, and who the leaders would be.

often speaking out against men whose opinions differed from his own. Among those men were Francis Bernard, who had become the royal governor of the Massachusetts Bay Colony in 1760, and Lieutenant Governor and Chief Justice Thomas Hutchinson. Hutchinson considered Sam and the other members of the Caucus Club the "rabble" of Boston.

Now Samuel went so far as to warn the British government in the newspapers that New Englanders would forcibly resist the Sugar Act. The doctrine of passive obedience had no followers in America, he cautioned the British. The Sugar Act was a violation of their right to no taxation without representation in Parliament.

Even Thomas Hutchinson, a loyal servant of King George III, saw the folly of this tax. "It cannot be good policy to tax the Americans," Hutchinson said. "It will prove prejudicial to the national interests. You will lose more than you will gain. Britain reaps the profit of all their trade." Hutchinson regarded the British Empire as a great commercial entity in which all could find opportunity for profit.[7]

Although not all the colonists took Samuel Adams's radical stand, most objected to the tax. They simply wanted to save their businesses from ruin. Massachusetts merchants knew they could not obey the act and remain in business. Reducing the tax on molasses from six pence to three pence was not enough to overcome the loss of profit from smuggling, which was now no longer practical, for the risk of seizure was so great.

"We are all link'd in a Chain of Dependence on each other," a New York merchant commented. The Sugar Act would be harmful to the prosperity of Great Britain *and* the northern colonies. It was a departure from the fundamental principles of the empire.[8]

Benjamin Franklin was sure that the British would not be foolish enough to take actions that would damage themselves as well as the colonists. "You cannot hurt us without hurting yourselves," he wrote from Philadelphia to an English friend. "All our profits center on you, and the more you take from us, the less we can lay out on you."[9]

Governor Bernard, too, foresaw trouble. He wrote to England that the publication of orders for the strict execution of the Sugar Act had caused great alarm in New England. He strongly opposed it.

A reform of colonial administration was needed, and he was sure he was the one to direct that reform. He would be happy, he wrote to everyone who might be interested, to sail to England at a moment's notice to advise the Ministry on how to reorganize the colonies.

Bernard felt that the charter of Massachusetts, and of the other charter colonies, were only temporary trusts and could be revoked by Parliament at any time. He recognized that the colonial constitutions varied as widely as did the different times and conditions of their founding. Colonial governors were the chief civil officers, but some were appointed by the king, as in Virginia and Massachusetts; others were nominated by a proprietor and approved by the king, such as William Penn in Pennsylvania; and a few were elected by representatives of the community. The rights and privileges of the people within those colonies varied as much as their governments. Bernard deemed this unfair.

Colonial governments, he felt, should be reorganized and made to have one and the same form of government. They should all resemble England as closely as possible. Furthermore, he saw no reason why the colonists should not send representatives to Parliament.

Bernard recognized that the time was ripe for this in both England and America. Many influential colonists were beginning to feel that the structure of colonial governments should be altered, with the likely addition of colonial representation in Parliament, and even, some thought, the establishment of an American nobility. This reform of colonial organization, Bernard suggested, should be brought about by an act of Parliament.

In the spring of 1764, Bernard convened the Massachusetts Assembly in Concord in order to avoid an epidemic of smallpox that was raging in Boston. While there, he began to put his ideas concerning colonial government on paper. With characteristic orderliness he listed them as ninety-seven propositions, which he called *Principles of Law and Polity, Applied to the Government of the*

British Colonies in America. His plan was clear, simple, and concise. In it he stressed the need for a "balanced" government, based on the British theory of monarchy, aristocracy, and commons, which he thought should be established in all the colonies. The concluding proposition in his plan was prophetic: "This is therefore the proper and critical time to reform the *American* governments upon a general, constitutional, firm, and durable plan; and if it is not done now, it will probably every day grow more difficult, till at last it becomes impracticable." [10] His superiors in London ignored it. Instead, Parliament sent him two revenue acts to enforce, acts that Bernard had urged the ministry not to pass.

A few months later, James Otis expressed his apprehensions in a pamphlet entitled *Rights of the British Colonies Asserted and Proved*. Otis was passionately attached to the British Empire, which, he said, "was best calculated for general happiness of any that has yet risen to view in the World." Yet in his pamphlet he asserted that Parliament, without American representatives, although supreme in its authority, had no right to tax Americans.

By the law of nature, Otis said, every British subject was entitled to "all the natural, essential, inherent, and inseparable rights of our fellow subjects in Great Britain." The colonists must be granted representation in Parliament. [11] The Massachusetts Assembly voted their approval of this statement and sent it to Dennys Debert, their agent in London.

Sam Adams disagreed. While he proclaimed that God had decreed New Englanders were "upon equal footing" in point of liberty and privilege with the inhabitants of Great Britain, to him it was "utterly impracticable" that the colonies be represented in Parliament. They were separated by three thousand miles of ocean. Further, Sam recognized that if American representatives were admitted to Parliament, they would be too few in number to carry any weight against the "King's Friends."

The colonial assemblies must be the sole taxing power in America. If they were recognized as such, Adams contended, Great Britain and her colonies would "long flourish in one undivided Empire." [12]

Sam Adams and James Otis were taking opposite stands.

By October of that year the Massachusetts Assembly had drawn up a petition to the king that so firmly denied the authority of Parliament to tax them that the governor's council feared it would give offense in England and do more harm than good. Therefore, under the leadership of Lieutenant Governor Hutchinson, the council met with a committee of the representatives and pleaded so successfully that the assembly withdrew their strong words in favor of tamer ones supplied by Hutchinson. The new document was submitted not simply to the king, but to the House of Commons as well, which was a significant recognition of Parliament's authority.

Omitting entirely the question of "rights," and even the word, it asked instead for the continuation of the "privilege" that the colonies had hitherto enjoyed of levying their own internal taxes. The argument, aimed at the proposed Stamp Act, was such a model of restraint and loyalty that Governor Bernard himself endorsed it.

Rhode Island's governor voiced stronger sentiments. He called the stamp tax "a manifest violation of [the colonists'] just and long enjoyed rights." The Assembly of New York declared flatly that the Sugar Act violated colonial rights.[13]

Late in 1764, the House of Burgesses of Virginia, Great Britain's largest colony in North America, formally petitioned the king and both houses of Parliament concerning the proposed stamp tax. In their statement to the king, they quietly denied the right of Parliament to tax the colonies, explaining that the charter of Virginia granted the right to Virginians to tax themselves, and they had been doing just that for more than a hundred years. Taxation required their consent, and their consent could only be given if they were represented in Parliament.[14]

But Parliament refused to consider *any* colonial petitions.

Soon, a furious gale of resistance blew up all along the Atlantic coast.

Chapter V

"the approaching storm"

London: February 1765

On Wednesday, February 6, 1765, members of the House of Commons arrived at St. Stephen's Church, where Parliament met. The debate on the Stamp Act was scheduled to begin, and little controversy was anticipated.

In England the first of four volumes entitled *Commentaries on the Laws of England* had just been published. It comprised a series of lectures that had been delivered at Oxford University by Sir William Blackstone, a professor of English law there, and has been called the most important legal treatise ever written in the English language. It achieved broad circulation in Great Britain and soon found its way across the ocean to America. It quickly became the dominant law book in both England and America.

Blackstone wrote that "there is and must be in all forms of government a supreme, irresistible, sovereign, and uncontrollable authority." In England, he

St. Stephen's Chapel assumed the name Parliament House in 1547 when it became the permanent home of the House of Commons. At that time the altar was replaced by the Speaker's chair. The House met there until the building was destroyed by fire nearly three hundred years later. Because worshippers had sat facing each other, the members of Parliament also sat facing one another. Today, the modern House of Commons is arranged in the same way.

stated, this authority is vested in Parliament. According to Blackstone, Parliament included the king, the House of Lords, and the Commons.

"The power and jurisdiction of [P]arliament . . . is so transcendent and absolute, that it cannot be confined . . . within any bounds," he wrote. "It can do every thing that is not naturally impossible. . . . So long as the English constitution lasts . . . the power of Parliament is absolute and without control . . . [and] no authority upon earth can undo [its actions]," he asserted.

Blackstone's writings quickly became the foundation of the English claim against the colonists. It seemed logical to Englishmen that "a power to tax is a necessary part of every supreme legislative authority." Therefore, if Parliament did not have that power over America, they had none, and America would become "a kingdom of itself." [1]

Those in England who read Blackstone believed strongly that the Stamp Act must become law. In fact, most Englishmen were certain that the stamp tax was insignificant enough that it would meet with no opposition in the colonies.

"They must be the veriest beggars in the world," remarked one, "if such inconsiderable duties appear to be intolerable burthens in their eyes."

Now when George Grenville rose in Parliament to deliver a typically lengthy speech in which he urged passage of the Stamp Act, he invoked Blackstone's theory, pointing out that if Parliament could not tax, then neither could it legislate in other ways. Colonial charters, he argued, could *not* grant any exemption from parliamentary authority. He declared that he "hop'd in God's name . . . none would dare dispute their Sovereignty" over the colonies.

Grenville said that although the colonists believed that the prosperity of all of Britain was dependent upon the colonists themselves achieving prosperity, the financial burden in England of the recently ended war was immense and frightening. He refused to believe that the colonists could not afford to pay the stamp tax, and indeed, the colonists were as, if not more, wealthy than the people of Britain. Stamp duties, he insisted, were an ideal form of taxation for the American colonies: They would be cheap to collect and easy to enforce.

General Henry Conway, a member of the Commons who served as unofficial secretary of state for the American colonies, viewed the Stamp Act as a mistake. He urged Parliament to acknowledge the petitions that had arrived from the colonial assemblies opposing the bill. His plea was "elegantly refuted."

Colonel Isaac Barré, an Irish member of Parliament who had lost an eye when he fought with General Wolfe at Quebec during the Seven Years' War, had many friends in America. Now he rose and countered Grenville by questioning his fellow ministers: "Who of you reasoning upon this subject feels warmly from the heart for the Americans as they would for themselves or as you would for the people of your own native country?"

The climax of the debate came when the towering, one-eyed Barré responded angrily to remarks in favor of the bill by Charles Townshend, another member of the Commons. Townshend had concluded his talk: "And now will these Americans, children planted by our care, nourished up by our indulgence until they are grown to a degree of strength and opulence, and protected by our arms, will they grudge to contribute their mite to relieve us from the heavy weight of that burden which we lie under?"

Barré, "with [his] Eye darting Fire, and an outstretched Arm," jumped to his feet and countered:

> They planted by your care? No! Your oppressions planted 'em in America. They fled from your tyranny to a then uncultivated and inhospitable country where they exposed themselves to almost all the hardships to which human nature is liable. . . . And yet, actuated by principles of true English liberty, they met all these hardships with pleasure, compared with those they suffered in their own country, from the hands of those who should have been their friends.
>
> They nourished by your indulgence? They grew by your neglect of 'em. As soon as you began to care about 'em, that care was exercised in sending persons to rule over 'em . . . men whose behavior on many occasions has caused the blood of those sons of liberty* to recoil within them. . . .
>
> They protected by your arms? They have nobly taken up arms in your defence. . . . The [American] people I believe are as truly loyal as any subjects the king has, but a people jealous of their liberties and who will vindicate them if ever they should be violated; but the subject is too delicate and I will say no more.[2]

---

*The phrase "sons of liberty" would resound throughout America and come to symbolize colonial rights in the face of British oppression.

Here Barré broke off abruptly. The entire House sat stunned and silent. Nonetheless, despite Barré's eloquence, the Stamp Act passed the House of Commons by a vote of two hundred and forty-five to forty-nine, and was soon approved by the House of Lords. George III, obstinately determined to be king of *all* his people, for what he considered their own good, and to draw even the colonies three thousand miles across the ocean into his power, gave his assent on March 22, thereby making the Stamp Act a "statute of the realm." It would go into effect November 1.[3]

The battle over the stamp tax had been transformed into a test of Parliament's authority. The main issue was no longer raising a revenue. Rather, it was putting the Americans in their place. Few men in Parliament fully grasped the extent of the emotional affront to the colonists that this would be. British leaders were blinded by the logical aspects of their situation. No one predicted the approaching storm.

Sir Isaac Barré, an Irish-born member of Parliament, was a staunch defender of the colonists. He had lost an eye fighting the French at Quebec. In a historic speech in Parliament he christened American patriots "sons of liberty." *By Gilbert Stuart, 1785.*

Chapter VI

"Liberty, Property, and no Stamps!"

The American Colonies: 1765

Early in May 1765 word reached the American colonies of the passage of the Stamp Act. By then, Americans were so "sower'd and embitter'd" toward the British government that "even the most constitutional tax would have been thought a hardship."[1]

Resentment was further inflamed by the Quartering Act of 1765. This required that colonies provide housing and food for the British troops that had been sent to protect them from the Indians west of the Allegheny Mountains. This took place even though the mere idea of a standing army carried with it the worst connotations of oppression.

It wasn't surprising that a showdown occurred in New York, which was the headquarters of General Thomas Gage, commander of the British Army in America. New York refused to provide for the soldiers. The New York Assembly believed that the mother country was planning "to fix upon us a large number of troops under pretense of our Defence but rather designed as a rod and check over us . . . to keep [us] in proper subjection."[2]

Now the colonists attempted to bring pressure on England by reducing colonial imports of British goods. New York merchants were the first to boycott English imports. Philadelphia and Boston followed soon after. John Hancock, who owned a large fleet of ships in Boston, wrote to his agent in London: "In case the Stamp Act is not repealed, my orders are that you will not . . . ship me one article."[3] Letters to the editors of many newspapers urged the virtues of homespun fabrics. A society was formed in New York to encourage local manufacturing. In fact, homespun woolen garments became fashionable, and volunteer firemen announced in the newspapers that they would increase the American supply of wool by not eating lamb chops. Wool-bearing sheep must be allowed to mature.

Great Britain and her colonies were on a collision course.

The first real act of defiance against Parliament came on May 29, 1765, from Patrick Henry, a newly elected member of the Virginia House of Burgesses, the oldest representative assembly in America. Henry was already known by the other members for his "audacity, his tempestuous eloquence, his fighting spirit."

Henry had dominated the scene in Williamsburg, the capital of Virginia, from the first moment of his arrival there. He was poor, and a failure as a merchant, but he came from a good family and was far more intelligent and cultured than he appeared. In spite of his coarse and worn clothes, whenever he pleaded a case his eloquence on the rights of man caught the admiration of the assembly. He quickly became "Mr. Henry" to all of Williamsburg, an indication of respect and honor.

Patrick Henry was in Williamsburg to take his seat at the spring session of the assembly. As he frequently did when he was in the capital, he stayed with his young friend Thomas Jefferson. Jefferson was studying law at the College of William and Mary, and although still too young (he was twenty-two) to enter the House of Burgesses, he often stood at the door of the assembly room to listen to the debates going on inside. As in many of the colonies, sentiment against the Stamp Act was high in Virginia, but no one knew quite what to do. There was no thought of formal resistance.

Now Patrick Henry sat, day after day, waiting for one of the older members to reopen the subject. Only three days of the session remained.

Then, on Thursday morning, May 29, Henry's twenty-ninth birthday, he and Jefferson walked to the capitol, on Duke of Gloucester Street. They were a study in contrasts as they made their way together. Jefferson was dressed in the height of fashion, wearing a coat of elegant red fabric, its large cuffs trimmed with braid and buttons, a tight-fitting waistcoat, and breeches that stopped at the knee. The buckles on his shoes had been polished until they shone. Henry was wearing plain hunting clothes. He carried an old copy of an English law book, borrowed from Jefferson, under his arm. Jefferson had noticed his friend hastily scribbling on the flyleaf of the book earlier that morning.

Patrick Henry was a member of the Virginia House of Burgesses and his "audacity, [and] eloquence" caught the admiration of the whole assembly. *By Thomas Sully.*

When they reached the capitol, Henry proceeded to his seat in the House of Burgesses, and Jefferson took his place at the door to the Assembly Room. The other burgesses, all members of the wealthy planter aristocracy, were dressed in the best London had to offer, pointing up even more the shabbiness of Henry's clothes. But Henry seemed unconcerned about the impression his appearance made. Shortly after the meeting was called to order, with an unfailing instinct for choosing the right psychological moment, Patrick Henry rose slowly from his seat and began to speak haltingly in a flat, quiet voice. Only his eyes revealed his passion. There was tension in the air.

Slowly, he began to read what he had scribbled on the flyleaf of his friend's book:

1. Resolved, That the first . . . settlers of this His Majesty's Colony . . . of Virginia brought with them . . . all the liberties, privileges, franchises, and immunities held . . . by the people of Great Britain.

2. Resolved, That by two royal charters . . . the colonists aforesaid are entitled to all the liberties, privileges, and immunities of . . . citizens and natural born subjects as if they had been born in . . . England.

3. Resolved, That taxation of the people by themselves, or by persons chosen by themselves to represent them . . . is the distinguishing characteristic of British freedom, without which the ancient constitution cannot exist.

4. Resolved, That . . . [the] people of this most ancient and loyal Colony have without interruption enjoyed the . . . right of being governed by such laws, respecting their internal policy and taxation, as are derived from their own consent. . . .

5. Resolved, therefore, That the General Assembly of this Colony have the only and sole exclusive right and power to lay taxes and impositions upon the inhabitants of this Colony. Every attempt to vest such power in any . . . persons . . . other than the General Assembly . . . would destroy British as well as American freedom.

6. Resolved, That . . . the inhabitants of this Colony, are not bound to yield obedience to any law or ordinance whatever, designed to impose any taxation whatsoever upon them, other than the laws or ordinances of the General Assembly aforesaid.

7. Resolved, That any persons who shall by writing or speaking assert that any . . . persons have any right or power to impose . . . any taxation on the people shall be deemed an enemy to His Majesty's Colony.[4]

When Patrick Henry finished reading the resolutions, he began to speak in his usual faltering way. But as he spoke he seemed to gain confidence. Gradually, he straightened his shoulders and stood erect, his voice picked up, and soon his words rang through the room. People were hearing for the first time words that they had thought but had been too afraid even to whisper to themselves. Sir Edward Coke's comments on the Magna Carta were suddenly being transformed from dead law into living truths.

Thomas Jefferson stood spellbound as he heard his friend thunder, "Caesar had his Brutus, Charles the First his Cromwell, and [pausing] George the Third . . ."*

"Treason!" cried the Speaker of the House.

"Treason! Treason!" echoed from every part of the room.

But with his amazing presence of mind, and not hesitating for an instant, Patrick Henry calmly concluded—"may profit by their example. Sir, if *this* be treason, make the most of it." [5]

The burgesses were dumbfounded.

There was much confusion and wild shouting. The first five resolutions were passed by a narrow majority. The sixth and seventh were defeated. The sixth resolution clearly implied the colonists' right to resist taxation by Parliament. And the seventh, had it been passed, would have suppressed freedom of speech in the name of American liberty.

The fifth resolve, the strongest of all, was passed by just one vote after a "most bloody" debate. Here, for the first time, was the rhetoric of revolution

---

*Brutus was one of the principal assassins of Julius Caesar, the great general, orator, and ruler of ancient Rome. Oliver Cromwell was a powerful champion of Parliament against the despotism of King Charles I. Cromwell ultimately oversaw the trial and execution of Charles for treason against Parliament.

against the king of England. Here was the legal battle cry: Taxation without representation is tyranny. But many were not ready to renounce their loyalty to England.

Distressed by the passage of this resolution, portly Peyton Randolph, attorney general of the colony, came puffing out of the door saying, "By God, I would have given five hundred guineas for a single vote."

Now Patrick Henry, not used to the politics of legislation and always impatient with detail, assumed his job was done. He put on his buckskin breeches, mounted his horse, and rode home.

But the fight was not yet over. A conservative group of burgesses persuaded the governor to allow the House to sit for another day. The group included Peyton Randolph; his brother John Randolph, clerk of the House of Burgesses; and George Wythe, the first professor of law in the colonies. With Henry gone, they managed to have the fifth resolution erased from the record.

These men were opposed to Patrick Henry's resolves *not* because they were in favor of the stamp duties, but because they considered it treasonous to resist the laws of England. They believed that the law, even a disagreeable law, could not be overturned without a judicial procedure. They understood, too, that Patrick Henry and his supporters were using the resolves as a challenge to established authority.

With his speech Patrick Henry became a spokesman for the common people, a champion of colonial liberty in what was rapidly becoming a struggle against the old order. Henry had been a member of the House of Burgesses for less than a month, yet he had scored a triumph over men who had dominated the Virginia Assembly for years.[6]

Suddenly, Virginia was divided into two parties: the Patriots, or Whigs; and Loyalists—those who remained loyal to England—also called Tories. Henry's words gave the signal for a general outcry across the country. In a sense, this was the beginning of the revolutionary movement in the American colonies.

Ironically, it was a Loyalist whose actions, or rather inactions, caused Patrick Henry's Resolves to be spread throughout the colonies. Joseph Royle, the conservative editor of the *Virginia Gazette*, agreed with some of the older members of the House of Burgesses that Henry's speech was treasonous. Therefore he reported nothing at all about the resolves in his newspaper. Patrick Henry's friends and supporters, however, distributed copies of all seven resolves throughout the colony. People who read them automatically assumed that they had all been officially adopted by the House. Soon the Virginia Resolves were published in newspapers up and down the seaboard. Every newspaper printed them as though the fifth, sixth, and seventh resolves had been adopted. Soon other colonies passed similar resolutions. When Mr. Royle complained that other newspapers were printing false news, the *Maryland Gazette* replied: "If Mr. Royle had been pleased to publish those Resolves, the Authenticity of his Intelligence would have been undisputed, and he would not have had any reason of complaint on that score."[7]

Virginia was on the road to separation from the mother country, pointing the way to freedom. The colony had ruled out parliamentary interference in American internal affairs and recognized a connection only with the king. Parliament's supremacy, Virginia contended, did not extend across the Atlantic Ocean to include the colonies. The colonists claimed the right to have to consent to Parliament's legislation.

The colonists now had the framework of an ideology—an intellectual basis from which to conduct their struggle against British rule: Americans and Britons were *equal* within a unified British Empire.

The British were caught unprepared.

To Americans, to be taxed by Parliament was far more than a way to gain revenue. Taxation trespassed on rights of property and of sovereignty.

George Grenville, on the other hand, believed strongly that the power of taxation lay solely with Parliament: "If Great Britain, under any conditions, gives up her right of taxation she gives up her right of sovereignty, which is inseparable from it, in all ages and in all countries," he warned.[8]

Soon the colonies began to realize that they must act in concert with one another against the Stamp Act. "What a Blessing to us has the Stamp Act . . . prov'd," exclaimed Sam Adams. "When the Colonys saw the Common Danger they at the same time saw their mutual Dependence."[9]

Accordingly, James Otis proposed in the Massachusetts Assembly that an intercolonial congress be summoned. All the colonies must come together, he advised, in order to consult on the problems facing them. His plan was adopted, and the Stamp Act Congress was scheduled to meet in New York in October 1765. The twenty-seven men who were chosen to attend were among the most distinguished and respected citizens in the colonies. For the first time in one hundred and fifty years, the colonies would unite for the common good in spite of all past predictions by both the British and the Americans that this would never happen. This was a cause the colonists considered worth fighting for. American unity was being forged in the fire of opposition.

Governor Bernard, who a few months earlier had genuinely believed that the colonists would submit to the Stamp Act without actual opposition, now reassessed the situation and predicted that the publishing of the Virginia Resolves would prove an alarm bell to the people. And, indeed, an alarm bell rang loudly and persistently throughout the colonies, but nowhere more so than in Boston in August.

Until then, the battle between the mother country and her children had been one of words only. The colonists had resolved, they had petitioned, they had defined their rights. They had reached for their pens to justify their resistance to British authority. Now spontaneous and violent action against those whose job it was to collect stamp duties became the preferred method of voicing their displeasure—and distrust.

The post of stamp distributor, one for each colony, was bestowed as an honor. It was expected to provide income, power, and prestige for the chosen colonists. Benjamin Franklin had proposed a friend as tax collector in Pennsylvania. Richard Henry Lee applied for the position in Virginia. Andrew Oliver, brother-in-law of Thomas Hutchinson and a wealthy merchant, was named stamp distributor in Massachusetts. But these men would not be allowed to assume their positions.

In Boston, a group of artisans and shopkeepers who called themselves the Loyall Nine would see to that. The group met in a room on the second floor of a distillery. Sam Adams, though not a member of the Loyall Nine, maintained a close connection with them. Members looked to him for leadership.

Eventually the Loyall Nine became the steering committee for a larger secret group called "the Sons of Liberty," who enthusiastically adopted their name from Isaac Barré's reference to American patriots as "sons of liberty" in his passionate speech in Parliament in defense of the colonists. Most of these Sons of Liberty also belonged to the Caucus Club that Sam Adams's father had founded.

Although it cannot be proved, it is highly likely that the group maintained close contact with James Otis and Samuel Adams, as well as with Paul Revere, a young man who was rapidly becoming one of the best silversmiths in the colonies, and Revere's friend, Dr. Joseph Warren.

Members of the Sons of Liberty exchanged cryptic signs and passwords and wore a special insignia that may have been made by Paul Revere: a silver medal with a Liberty Tree and the words, "Sons of Liberty," engraved on its face.

Governor Bernard called the group "Sam Adams's Mohawks," since Sam proved particularly adept at harnessing mob activity for the patriot cause. It was the Loyall Nine who would incite the mobs that were to terrorize Boston. Adams justified forcible resistance *if* it were in defense of the people's liberties, *and* every other method of securing those liberties had been tried.

One member of the Loyall Nine, Benjamin Edes, a printer of the *Boston Gazette*, published a continuous stream of articles in his newspaper to stir up feeling against the Stamp Act. The Loyall Nine had also enlisted the aid of a twenty-eight-year-old Boston shoemaker named Ebenezer McIntosh, who could control two thousand followers with the precision of a general. McIntosh was a colorful figure, given to wearing a blue-and-gold uniform, strutting about with a cane, and using a horn to bark out orders.[10]

On August 14, 1765, Bostonians awoke to find that a large crowd of men had gathered in Hanover Square. Here, from a huge elm tree that had been planted some one hundred and twenty years before and was soon to be known as the Liberty Tree, they had hung an effigy of Andrew Oliver. Pinned to one arm of the effigy was a paper bearing the words:

What greater joy did New England see
Than a stampman hanging on a tree.

Hanging alongside the effigy of Oliver was another of a huge boot with a "green-vile sole" and a devil peering out of it. The boot and its sole were puns on the names of the hated figures of Lord Bute and George Grenville.

Bostonians gathered at the Liberty Tree to stare at an effigy of Andrew Oliver and a boot with a devil's head sticking out, meant to satirize Lord Bute.

When the effigies were first discovered, Lieutenant Governor Thomas Hutchinson ordered the sheriff to take them down. But when the sheriff arrived and saw the crowd of thousands, he refused. The dummies remained hanging.

Throughout the day, a group of men enacted a vivid dramatization of what the Stamp Act would mean. Standing under the Liberty Tree, they stopped every passerby, requiring each one to participate in a mock ceremony of buying a stamp. In this way they demonstrated just how burdensome and annoying the new tax would be. Carts with goods and foodstuffs rumbled back and forth from the town all day. No one who passed could fail to learn the lesson: The Stamp Act would make a difference in everyone's life.

Toward evening, a funeral procession was formed, and Andrew Oliver's effigy was carried up to Tower Hill and placed on a huge bonfire. Then the procession moved to the state house, where Governor Bernard and his council sat in the council chamber. As the crowd marched, they chanted, "Liberty, Property, and no Stamps!" With the coming of darkness, they converged on a building under construction on Oliver's Wharf, believed to be his intended stamp office. They pulled the building down.

Still not content, the crowd moved on to Oliver's house, where they smashed windows (which were made of glass imported from England and were expensive to replace), tore down fencing, and then forced their way through the front door searching for Oliver himself. They might have carried out their declared intention of throwing him out of his smashed windows along with his broken furniture, wainscoting, glass, and silver, had not Thomas Hutchinson arrived on the scene with the sheriff. The rioters met them with shouted insults and a volley of broken bricks, then went on their way.

The next day, a delegation presented itself at Oliver's house to warn him that if he did not resign his post as stamp distributor immediately, "his house would be destroyed and his life in continual danger." [11]

Andrew Oliver complied.

The Sons of Liberty had achieved their goal. But they were not finished.

Now the crowd focused its wrath on Thomas Hutchinson.

Samuel Adams, like James Otis, had a personal grudge against Thomas Hutchinson. This was his chance for revenge. Years before, Deacon Adams, Sam's father, had been a director of the Land Bank and had invested most of his fortune in it.

The Land Bank had been established as an attempt to alleviate the economic depression of 1740. It was a plan to issue paper money backed only by the value of land in order to help debt-ridden farmers and artisans. But Hutchinson, whose greatest strength lay in his thorough understanding of financial matters, felt that the colony's currency would be more stable if it were based on silver than on land. Therefore, in 1741, by means of appeals to Parliament, Hutchinson had dissolved the Land Bank.

Andrew Oliver, brother-in-law of Thomas Hutchinson and a wealthy merchant, was named stamp distributor in Massachusetts. He was so hated by the patriots that when he died, in March, 1774, both his brother Peter and Thomas Hutchinson feared attending his funeral because of the "rude and brutal behavior of the rabble." *By John Singleton Copley, circa 1758.*

When the Land Bank closed, Deacon Adams lost his money. Sam Adams blamed Thomas Hutchinson for his father's plight. Then, nine years later, Hutchinson had encouraged parliamentary legislation to outlaw paper money. The immediate effect of making their paper money worthless was to bring upon Hutchinson the wrath of colonial radicals. When his house caught fire shortly thereafter, the citizens stood by crying, "Let it burn!" [12]

Hutchinson, wealthy and aristocratic, represented everything Sam Adams opposed. To Adams it became a question of whether the common people or the wealthy gentry would control the political life of Massachusetts.

Hutchinson was a member of one of the oldest families in Massachusetts. He was envied by many for his wealth and was widely disliked for simultaneously holding several offices. Privately, Hutchinson disapproved of the Stamp Act. In fact, when it was first proposed, he had urged that it be abandoned. He believed that parliamentary taxation of the colonies violated the rights of the people. "You must not deprive the colonists of their right to make laws for themselves," he said privately. But his loyalty to the king and to Parliament prevented him from revealing his views publicly in Boston. Thus, the people of Massachusetts, knowing nothing of his private views, feared that he was prepared to sacrifice their rights.

Thomas Hutchinson as a young man. He had a reputation for integrity, industry, judiciousness, and devotion to public service, but he was a loyal servant of King George III. He was governor of Massachusetts from 1769 until 1774. He would become Samuel Adams's archenemy. *Oil portrait by Edward Truman, 1741.*

Although Hutchinson had played no part in the passage of the Stamp Act, when it was passed by the House of Commons it became his duty as the chief justice of Massachusetts Bay to enforce it. While he believed in both the Massachusetts Charter and the natural rights of the people, he also believed in the supremacy of Parliament. Parliament might have been wrong to tax the colonies, but that was no reason for the colonies to commit the further wrong of resisting, he argued. It was his opinion that submission to Parliament, and request for a change in the law rather than defiance of it, were the most effective means of persuasion.

It was this attitude that gave

Hutchinson his reputation in Massachusetts as an enemy of the people's rights. And they had not forgotten that in 1761 Chief Justice Hutchinson had refused to rule against the writs of assistance.

Now Sam Adams and James Otis, who both hated Thomas Hutchinson for "cheating" their fathers, spread the rumor that it was Hutchinson who had planned the Stamp Act and sent it to England. The people were ready to believe them.

As further provocation, Jonathan Mayhew, the influential pastor of the West Congregational Church in Boston, suddenly became a leading player in the controversy. On August 25, despite a long-standing prohibition against religious leaders directly participating in politics, Mayhew preached a sermon that lent his dignity and the sanction of his office to the battle for the repeal of the Stamp Act. He urged his listeners to take action in the cause of liberty.[13]

Reverend Mayhew had already warned his friends in England that the Stamp Act could only be enforced "at the point of the sword, by a large army," in effect, by "Great Britain's waging war with her American colonies."

"No people are under a *religious obligation* to be slaves if they are able to set themselves at liberty," he had written.[14]

On the next night, August 26, a crowd formed, led by Ebenezer McIntosh, and, drinking rum and ominously shouting, "Liberty and Property," they marched to Hutchinson's elegant mansion. The mob turned vicious.

Hutchinson, a widower, had just sat down to supper with his three sons and two daughters when someone shouted, "The mob is coming!" Intending to stay himself, he begged his children to flee.

His elder daughter, twenty-year-old Sally, came back and declared that she would not leave without him. "I couldn't stand against this," he said, and left quickly with her. The two ran to the nearby house of his sister. When someone came to warn him that the mob was looking for him, his little niece took him by the hand and led him through back paths and dark alleyways to the more remote home of a neighbor, where he remained until 4 A.M.

Hutchinson himself described the devastation a few days later:

> Not contented with tearing off all the wainscot and hangings and split-
> ting the doors to pieces they beat down the partition walls . . . cut down
> the cupola . . . and began to take the slate and boards from the roof. . . .
> The garden fence was laid flat and all my trees &c. broke down to the
> ground. . . . Besides my plate and family pictures, household furniture of
> every kind, my own my children and servants apparel, they carried off
> about £900 sterling in money and emptied the house of everything what-
> soever . . . not leaving a single book or paper in it and have scattered or
> destroyed all the manuscripts and other papers I had been collecting for
> 30 years together besides a great number of public papers in my custody.[15]

Enemies as well as friends shared his horrified reaction. Among his books
and papers, which had been strewn in the mud outside his house, was a manuscript for a history of Massachusetts that he had been writing. Parts of it were
rescued by a neighbor.*

Reverend Mayhew was charged with a major role in inciting the riot.

It is highly unlikely that even Sam Adams or James Otis expected the
mob to go so far. The large amount of rum distributed to them earlier had
undoubtedly egged them on. In fact, Sam Adams condemned the attack on
Hutchinson's home as an act of "a truly *mobbish* Nature." It was, to him, "a
lawless attack upon property."[16] And Otis, whom Hutchinson described as
a "designing, wicked man" who had deliberately planned the attack, begged
his fellow townsmen to stop the riots that were destroying both property
and law.[17]

The next morning, the day on which the superior court session was scheduled to begin, Hutchinson, as was his duty, went to the Town House. He arrived, not in his scarlet robe and wig, but in his rumpled clothes of the night
before. The court rose as he entered, then, seated, listened silently as he addressed them.

---

*Thomas Hutchinson later wrote *History of the Province of Massachusetts Bay*. It marks the beginning of modern historical writing in New England.

Explaining that he was obliged to appear, since without him there would be no quorum, he went on to apologize for his dress: "Indeed, I had no other." He was "destitute of everything . . . but what I have on." His own clothes lay trampled in the street.

Then, with tears in his eyes, he called upon God as witness to his innocence of any hand in the Stamp Act. He swore that he had striven to prevent it. But the Boston patriots immediately circulated a false story that letters had been found in Hutchinson's house the night of the riot that proved he was responsible for the Stamp Act.

The letters were never produced.[18]

Bostonians, particularly, found mobbing an effective weapon. But it was often used wrongly on people who were only suspected of supporting the Stamp Act. Other colonies followed their example. Soon "Liberty Trees" were designated in every town along the eastern coast.

Another type of violence practiced by the mob was tarring and feathering. The victim was stripped naked, put in a cart, and hot tar was poured over his body. Then the contents of feather pillows were dumped on him. The poor creature was then carted through the streets of Boston, often in freezing weather. The hot tar could inflict third-degree burns, causing the victim's skin to peel off in slabs, with the tar still sticking to it.

The planned violence successfully

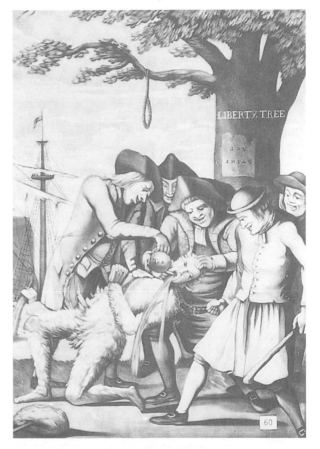

Tarring and feathering was a brutal but common punishment used by the patriots against Loyalists. The victim was stripped and covered in hot pine tar and goose feathers. Here, Bostonians pour tea down the throat of a tarred and feathered customs officer. In the background, men are dumping tea into Boston Harbor.

prevented implementation of the Stamp Act and brought about the resignation of stamp officials. Men from all walks of life—from longshoremen and artisans to wealthy merchants in the North and plantation owners in the South—participated in this form of social protest. Royal governors in the colonies found themselves helpless in the face of this massive display of public sentiment.[19]

The Reverend Jonathan Mayhew, for his part, was shocked and distraught by the riot, and immediately wrote to Thomas Hutchinson: "God is my witness, that from the bottom of my heart I detest these proceedings; that I am sincerely grieved for them; and have a deep sympathy with you and your distressed family." He had not only preached in favor of civil and religious liberty, he told Hutchinson, but "I cautioned my hearers very particularly against the abuses of liberty . . . And, in truth, I had rather lose my hand than be an encourager of such outrages as were committed last night."

In another letter, to a parishioner, a contrite Mayhew acknowledged that he would gladly give "all that I have in the world rather than have preached that sermon." But, he went on to explain, he had preached it deliberately. Boston clergy had recently been "blamed for their silence in the cause of liberty at a time when . . . our common liberties and rights, as British subjects, were in the most imminent danger."

Mayhew would spend the rest of his short life (he died of a stroke in July 1766, at the age of forty-six) apologizing for his sermon and advocating obedience to lawful authority and a conciliation of differences.[20]

In September 1765, Oxenbridge Thacher, who was a member of the Massachusetts Assembly and an ardent patriot, died from an inoculation against smallpox, at the age of forty-five. On September 27, the town elected Sam Adams as his successor to the assembly. Within two weeks of taking his seat, Adams was elected to all the important committees and was recognized as James Otis's chief lieutenant. His age (at forty-three, he was older than many of the other members) afforded him a certain seniority in an era when age merited respect. His flexibility and adaptability made him popular. He was treated with the same respect as James Otis.

Otis's power at that time was so great that at his mere entrance into a town meeting, the members would shout and clap, and when he spoke, he swayed his audience in much the same way as William Pitt did in the British Parliament. But Otis, considered by many until then as a rabble-rouser, had recently changed his view. When news of the Virginia Resolves had reached Boston, the unpredictable Otis had called them treasonable. And while the *Boston Gazette* continued to publish his fiery speeches against taxation, he was overheard to say that "if the government at home [England] don't very soon send forces to keep the peace of this province they will be cutting one another's throats from one End, to the other of it."[21]

By contrast, Samuel Adams was always straightforward and sensible, although he, too, could be impressive. He was persistent, undeviating, and always rational. Within a month of his election to the Massachusetts Assembly, he had begun a life of public service that would last, unbroken, until his death.

Now Sam was asked once again to prepare instructions for the Boston representatives to the Massachusetts Assembly. John Adams, some thirteen years Samuel's junior, was asked to perform the same task for his town, Braintree. The two cousins put their heads together and worked closely, as they would continue to do many times in the coming years.

With these instructions, known as the Massachusetts Resolves of October 29, 1765, Samuel Adams firmly established his importance. The resolves asserted the right of the people of Massachusetts, secured for them by their founding charter, of possessing all the privileges of free-born Britons. They considered representation in Parliament an indispensable condition of taxation, and reaffirmed the right of trial by jury, violated by the establishment of the admiralty courts.

The *Boston Gazette* which had by now become the voice of Massachusetts radicalism, spread the two documents throughout the other towns of Massachusetts, and they became the accepted platform of the Massachusetts Bay

Colony. The Massachusetts Assembly was formally committed to opposing the Stamp Act.

Upon learning of these Massachusetts Resolves, Thomas Hutchinson warned: "They approach very near to independence."[22]

The Boston town meeting at which they were reported thanked General Henry Conway and Colonel Isaac Barré for their bold speeches in Parliament on behalf of the colonists. Then they directed that portraits of the two Englishmen be hung in Faneuil Hall, the building that had been constructed in Boston twenty-three years before specifically to house town meetings.

Faneuil Hall, called "The Cradle of Liberty," was Boston's town meeting-hall where the colonists first dared to speak out publicly against British rule. It was a gift to the town from Peter Faneuil, whose parents had come to America from France, fleeing religious persecution.

Chapter VII

"We may still light candles"

London: 1765

10

Following passage of the Stamp Act, opposition began to arrive in London from the colonial assemblies in the form of letters and petitions for its repeal. South Carolina opposed the stamp duty, declaring it "inconsistent with the inherent rights of every British subject not to be taxed but by his own consent or that of his representatives." Massachusetts and Connecticut sent resolutions affirming the right of Parliament to levy *external* taxes, such as customs duties paid at the port of entry, but disallowing *internal* taxes, such as the Stamp Act. Other colonies, including New York, New Jersey, Rhode Island, and North Carolina also sent protests. Parliament refused even to hear their petitions.

George Grenville ignored the warnings. Instead, he congratulated himself on his plan to preserve the British Empire from financial ruin.

Benjamin Franklin, back in London at the time in his role as agent for the colony of Pennsylvania, was just as blind as Grenville. He, too, failed to foresee the explosion against the act that would take place in America. He wrote to a friend in Philadelphia: "I took every step in my power to prevent the passing of the Stamp Act. But the tide was too strong against us. . . .We might as well have hindered the sun's setting. That we could not do. But since 'tis down, my friend, and it may be long before it rises again, let us make as good a night of it as we can. We may still light candles." [1]

Franklin's main objective at this time was to bring the two parts of the empire together in friendly understanding. In fact, Franklin had made this his crusade more than ten years before. It was at that time that he had found himself unable to resist the call of public duty and for the remainder of his life he would be chiefly engaged in politics and diplomacy.

Benjamin Franklin, the eighth child and youngest son of the ten children born to Josiah Franklin and his second wife, Abiah Folger, was born in Boston on January 6, 1706.* When religious meetings were forbidden in England, Josiah, a pious Congregationalist, had simply taken his first wife, Anne, and their children across the ocean to Massachusetts so they might practice their religion in freedom. Seven children had been born to Josiah and Anne before she died, at the age of thirty-four. Josiah became a maker of soap and candles and provided well for his large family.

Josiah recognized early on that Benjamin was the most promising of all his children, yet in spite of Ben's brilliant mind, his father took him out of school after only two years. Apparently, he realized that Ben was not pious enough to enter the ministry and decided, therefore, that a formal education was not necessary for him. But Ben studied books on his own and eventually became one of the best-informed men of his century.

Taken into the family business at the age of ten, Ben waited on customers and ran errands, but he wasn't happy there. His father, fearful that this

*According to the New Style Calendar, the date became January 17.

son might break loose and go to sea, as an older child had, took him around to the shops of Boston and showed him all the trades from which he might choose. Ben saw joiners, bricklayers, turners, braziers, and cutlers at work. In each place Ben learned something he never forgot, and that he eventually put to use.

Finally, because Ben was fond of books, his father decided on the trade of a printer for his son. He apprenticed Ben to Ben's older brother James, who had learned printing in London and had returned to Boston with types and a press of his own. From that time on, Ben read all the books that came into the shop. He managed to purchase

Benjamin Franklin, American statesman, writer, philosopher, and scientist, had been agent for Pennsylvania in London since 1757. *Painting by Mason Chamberlin, 1762.*

those he loved by eating only biscuits and raisins, and saving his food money for books. He gave himself a classical education, memorizing much of what he read, and taught himself arithmetic.

Above all, he trained himself as a logician, mastering all the stages of the art of reasoning. He learned that he must avoid the use of words like "certainly" and "undoubtedly." He substituted, instead, "It appears to me," or "It is so, if I am not mistaken." He developed a talent for talking people into doing what was for their own improvement and advantage.

At the age of seventeen, he escaped from his brother's printing shop and began the long trek to Philadelphia, arriving in that city with his pockets stuffed with shirts and stockings, but empty of money. He was quite a sight as he strolled along, carrying one roll under each arm and munching on another.

Ben worked hard, lived frugally, and soon became a master printer. He started his own newspaper, the *Pennsylvania Gazette*, and published his highly successful *Poor Richard's Almanac*. He put his great energy, his bold creativeness, and his skill in managing people into the service of his adopted city. In very short order, Philadelphia lacked little that London possessed.

Ben's first project was to found a book club, the forerunner of the modern library. Soon after, he created a volunteer fire company, a paid police force, and a public hospital. He founded the American Philosophical Society and an academy that would develop into the University of Pennsylvania. He developed a street lamp, and he invented a heating stove for sitting rooms (called the Franklin stove), refusing a patent for it on the grounds that he himself had profited so much by the discoveries of others that he was only too glad of an opportunity to repay his debt.

In August of 1753 he was appointed deputy postmaster general for all "His Majesty's Provinces and Dominions on the Continent of North America." It was a post he had coveted. He would share it with William Hunter, postmaster of Williamsburg and publisher of the *Virginia Gazette*.

As a contribution to the cause of freedom of religion, Franklin promoted the building of a meetinghouse expressly for the use of any preacher of any denomination who might have something to say to the people of Philadelphia.

By the time he traveled to England in 1757, his experiments in electricity had made him well known and highly respected among gentlemen scientists of the age.

But now, in London, Franklin was about to make a grave error. George Grenville, in an effort to pacify the Americans, had just directed that only colonists were to be appointed stamp distributors. Grenville believed that Americans would find it easier to pay the tax if it were collected by fellow colonists. Franklin, recognizing that in spite of all the opposition to it the Stamp Act would pass, helped place some of his close friends in the job of stamp distributor. Many wanted the job because it paid a fine salary: three hundred pounds a year. Franklin's enemies in Philadelphia swiftly accused him of having planned the Stamp Act himself in order to profit personally from it. In fact, as he strove to bring the two parts of the empire together, each suspected him of being a supporter of the other.

When Franklin had first read of Patrick Henry's Virginia Resolves in the London press, he had written to a friend: "The rashness of the Assembly in Virginia is amazing." He counseled "a firm loyalty to the crown and faithful adherence to the government" of England. He spoke of the "madness of the populace" and "their blind leaders," who would only bring on greater burdens "by acts of rebellious tendency." In England, Franklin had developed a deep love for the mother country. But his loyalty to America was never in question.[2]

During this period, George Grenville's relations with the king were rapidly deteriorating. Though Grenville was considered the ablest man in the House of Commons and performed the king's business better than any other minister, the king came to dislike him more than any other politician of the time. There was no basic difference of opinion between them. But in any debate Grenville persisted until he got his way in every detail. His favorite occupation was talking.

King George could not bear Grenville's cold self-righteousness and verbosity. The king, with his natural good manners, always let his ministers have their say when they met privately. But of Grenville the king complained, "When [he] has wearied me for two hours, he looks at his watch to see if he may not tire me for an hour more." The king's small revenge was to call his minister "Mr. Greenville." He chose never to remember his correct name.[3]

The king and Grenville, however, thought alike about the taxation of America. In fact, there might have been much to draw them together, for Grenville had a concern for economy that was much like that of the king. But while preaching economy for Britain, Grenville was also careful to provide for his own family, insisting on a large stipend for them. The king could not tolerate his personal greed for money and power.

Unfortunately, too, Grenville had been so busy winding down the war and vying for power with Bute that he had had little time left to concentrate on territories three thousand miles away. He hadn't considered what the American reaction to taxation might be. In spite of his serious desire to benefit the English people, his zeal to erase Britain's debt gave him a narrow perspective, limited to an intense desire to raise money, and his lack of vision in other areas made him the wrong man in the wrong place at the wrong time.[4]

Grenville, who had never been able to win George III's confidence, was jealous of Bute's relationship with the king and was concerned about Bute's influence over him. Whenever any of Grenville's recommendations met with an objection from the king, Grenville immediately blamed Bute. The young king's inexperience and his dependence on Bute aggravated the situation. George was determined to reign *and* to rule. He had been ill intermittently from January to April, and by now, although sufficiently recovered to resume his duties, he was still weak, depressed, and easily fatigued.*

Now George Grenville pushed the king too far. He warned his monarch that if anyone attempted to speak to the king on business without Grenville's prior approval, he would resign as treasury minister.

"Every day I meet with some insult from [Grenville and the other members of his cabinet]," the king cried to Bute. "I have been for a week as it were in a feaver my very sleep is not free from thinking of the men I daily see." He told a friend that he would sooner see the devil in his closet than George Grenville. Soon his patience gave way completely. The king determined to rid himself of this minister.[5]

In their final, frosty meeting Grenville warned the king that the colonies were "the richest jewel in His Majesty's crown." If anyone were to try to change the laws that governed the colonies, that person should be considered "a criminal and a betrayer of his country."[6]

The king hardly needed this warning. To deny the right of Parliament to

---

*In January 1765 the young King George (he was only twenty-six) was stricken with the first major attack of what is now known to have been the rare disease porphyria. Its symptoms in its early stages are much like a cold accompanied by fever, nausea, acute chest and stomach pains, and difficulty breathing. His doctors were bewildered. Today we know that porphyria is caused by a metabolic disorder.

legislate for the entire British Empire was to deny the Bill of Rights. King George had been too well educated in the principles of the British constitution not to know where his duty lay.[7]

On July 10, 1765, King George III called on the thirty-five-year-old Charles Watson-Wentworth, second marquess of Rockingham, one of the wealthiest nobles of England and leader of a small group of young Whigs, to replace Grenville as head of the Treasury. Within a week, Rockingham selected Edmund Burke, a brilliant young Irish lawyer and a newcomer to the Commons, to be his private secretary. Burke and Rockingham would remain close friends and political associates for the remainder of their lives. Burke became Rockingham's intellectual guide, his voice in the Commons, and the

Charles Watson-Wentworth, second marquess of Rockingham, one of the wealthiest nobles of England and leader of a small group of young Whigs, was chosen by George III to replace George Grenville as head of the Treasury. He was well liked, but lacked leadership qualities. *Painting by Joshua Reynolds.*

official pamphleteer of the Rockingham branch of the Whig Party. He would use his substantial literary talents to further the cause of the American colonies.

The new government, known as the Rockingham administration, was a strange cabinet. Rockingham was a shy young man, timid and insecure, well liked but totally lacking in leadership qualities. None of the men who filled the three principal departments of state had ever officially held political office. The next five years would bring with them an unusual period of political instability. For until George Grenville died in 1770, the king's politics were dominated by his determination not to have Grenville in office again. Purely personal issues, not public affairs, spelled the end of Grenville's administration. In fact, Grenville's was the most efficient ministry to govern England during the first twenty years of the king's reign.

Chapter VIII

"a bundle of sticks"

The American Colonies: 1765

At the same time that the Massachusetts Resolves were being read in Boston, twenty-seven representatives from nine of the thirteen colonies were meeting in New York from October 7 to 25 to confer on the Stamp Act. While acknowledging "all due subordination" to Parliament, and assuring the king of "the warmest Sentiments of Duty and Affection," they, too, put forth the doctrine: "No taxation without representation."

Although there was much debate among the delegates, eventually they came to recognize the need for a unified approach, and they soon signed petitions by which the colonies became "a bundle of sticks, which could neither be bent or broken."[1]

Making a distinction between taxation and legislation, the delegates insisted that the right to legislate did not necessarily include the right to tax.

Taxes were a *gift*, they explained, given by the people through their representatives. Therefore, only a representative body could grant them. The delegates to the Stamp Act Congress objected not only to the Stamp Act, but to the Proclamation of 1763 forbidding western expansion, the Sugar Act of 1764, and the creation of the new vice-admiralty court in Halifax.

They went so far as to say that if the colonists could not be taxed without representation in Parliament, and they could not practically be represented in Parliament, then they were beyond the control of Parliament: "The People of these Colonies are not, and from their local Circumstances cannot be, Represented in the House of Commons in Great Britain." Representation in Parliament was no longer the issue. What this meant was that the colonists would not allow themselves to be taxed without representation, and they did not seek to be represented. This was unprecedented.

Perhaps this occurred partly as a result of a pamphlet that had recently been published by Daniel Dulany, entitled *Considerations on the Propriety of imposing Taxes in the British Colonies, for the Purpose of raising a Revenue, by Act of Parliament.* It immediately became a best-seller.

Dulany was an outstanding Maryland lawyer who had been educated in England, and who maintained an interest in political events in England *and* in America. He knew from his reading that in 1764 the House of Commons had debated the question of its right to tax the colonies and had decided in favor of such a right. He knew, also, from pamphlets he had received from his bookseller in London, that a thorough overhaul of colonial affairs was being planned, and that in this reorganization the colonists would be denied their requests for exemption from parliamentary taxation.

Pamphlets were the accepted medium on both sides of the Atlantic for the dissemination of ideas. The careful writer preferred its greater dignity, while the thoughtful reader preferred its greater length. Daniel Dulany was writing in response to those who had already written in defense of the Stamp Act.

Dulany saw in Grenville's program the worst threat that he and other privileged men like himself had ever faced. He discounted the arguments

Parliament was putting forth in favor of the Stamp Act, and decided to refute them publicly. His pamphlet was the first response of a large sector of the American elite.

Dulany recognized that the colonists' arguments in terms of natural rights would carry little weight in the British Parliament. The question, as he saw it, hinged not on natural rights but on constitutional rights. As long as the colonists had the constitution on their side, he reasoned, it would be best for them to base their arguments on it.

As a lawyer, Dulany used tradition and precedent to set the bounds of Parliament's authority. In his pamphlet he explained that the essential difference between internal taxes and trade duties was that internal taxes were levied "*for the single purpose of revenue*" and trade duties "*for the regulation of trade.*"

He continued: "A right to impose an internal tax on the colonies without their consent *for the single purpose of revenue* is denied."

Yet Dulany, like James Otis and Benjamin Franklin, made clear his opinion that although Parliament did not have the right to tax the colonies, still it was the colonists' duty to submit. They must not attempt forcible resistance to British authority.[2]

His pamphlet, designed to influence public opinion, did indeed influence the liberal political leaders both in the colonies and in England, particularly the Great Commoner, William Pitt.

By now, Sam Adams was more certain than ever that colonial representation in Parliament was impractical. He felt strongly that the colonies could not be "fully and equally represented" there. The colonies were too far removed from England and Parliament, and their circumstances so different, that it would not be possible for them to be properly represented: "A representative should be, and continue to be, well acquainted with the internal circumstances of the people whom he represents. . . . Now the Colonies are at so great a distance from the place where the Parliament meets, from which they are separated by a wide ocean, and their circumstances are so often and continually varying . . . that it would not be possible for men, though ever so well acquainted with them at the beginning of a Parliament, to continue to have adequate knowledge of them during the existence of that Parliament."

Sam Adams feared, also, that liberty was quietly disappearing under more and more arbitrary British power. He, unlike Dulany, was beginning to feel that independence from Britain might be the only answer. Until now, he had had only praise for the British constitution. There had been no reason to doubt that the colonists would remain "faithful and loyal Subjects" *if* they were allowed the same governmental powers to which they had long been accustomed.[3] Now he sensed an upsurge in patriotism among the colonists that had not existed before.

By November 1, 1765, when the Stamp Act was scheduled to take effect, no one in America was willing to distribute the stamped paper, which had been safely stowed away in forts and on warships. Boston's stamps were being held

Castle William, the British fortress in Boston Harbor, was situated on an island about three miles out from the town, at the entrance to the Bay. Its armament of over a hundred guns made it the most powerful fort in the British colonies.

at Castle William, the British fortress in Boston Harbor, about three miles out from the town, at the entrance to the bay.

In most colonies there was a pause in business as the people made up their minds which way to nullify the act: by doing nothing that required the use of stamps, or by proceeding in their business without them.

Trade across the Atlantic came to a virtual halt, since no ship could leave an American port for England without properly stamped papers. The courts were closed, and business was at a standstill.

The colonies were in great economic distress. Private debts were exceptionally high, the cost of living had risen, and real estate values had dropped tremendously. There was much unemployment. Many of the most important commercial houses in Boston had failed. Americans up and down the seaboard became convinced that the British government was seeking to destroy colonial prosperity.

Not long afterward, in December, a broadside (a large sheet of paper, printed on one side only) in the town of Boston announced: "The True-born Sons of Liberty are desired to meet under Liberty Tree at XII o'clock, This Day, to hear the public Resignation, under Oath, of Andrew Oliver, Esq., Distributor of Stamps for the Province of the Massachusetts-Bay. A Resignation? Yes."

Andrew Oliver would be forced to repeat his resignation publicly.

On December 17, a cold and blustery winter's day, a humiliated Andrew Oliver, accompanied (ironically, for protection) by Ebenezer McIntosh, walked through the streets of Boston to take an oath beneath the Liberty Tree. Two thousand citizens braved the gusty wind and rain in order to witness the proceedings.

Four days later, John Dickinson wrote a long letter to William Pitt. Dickinson was a wealthy lawyer from Philadelphia who had enthusiastically participated in the Stamp Act Congress and played a pivotal role in drawing up its *Declaration of Rights and Privileges*. In his letter he pleaded with Pitt, as "the Friend and Preserver not only of Great Britain but of these Colonies; as the Friend of Liberty and Justice . . . to form a Plan of Policy that shall establish for Ages the Union of Great Britain and her Colonies."

"My Passion, sir, for the Welfare of Great Britain and of my native Country, is the same," Dickinson told Pitt, "because I think their Interests are the same, and that the Prosperity of the one cannot be infected, without the other's catching the Contagion."[4]

Dickinson had studied law at London's Middle Temple, and in the course of his four-year stay there had witnessed firsthand the workings of the British government. Government officials seemed to him ready to sacrifice public welfare for their own profit. The ministers, he wrote home, were men who would "gratify every desire of Ambition and Power at the expense of truth, reason and their country." Although considered cautious and conservative, Dickinson had begun to believe that there was a conspiracy in England against the British constitution and against the civil liberties that it was supposed to protect.

His attitude toward the British didn't change when he returned to America. He became a member of the Pennsylvania legislature in the early 1760s. The Sugar and Stamp Acts increased his hostility to British authority.[5]

Dickinson also published a pamphlet in which he predicted that the Stamp Act would not affect the wealthy, but would hurt those "who most of all require relief and encouragement." The colonies are being "treated as rich people when we are really poor." Further, he warned, British manufacturers and merchants would suffer along with the colonists, who would spend less money the more they were taxed.

Dickinson went on to remind the British that "the foundations of the power and glory of Great Britain are laid in America." He

Even teapots were used to express American defiance of the Stamp Act.

denied British allegations that the colonists were seeking independence, but threatened that independence could be their goal should the British continue their oppressive measures.[6]

A few months later the ports of Boston were open for business, with no sign of a stamp. The courts reopened, and unstamped newspapers appeared weekly, full of messages encouraging the people to stand firm.

Chapter IX

"saucy Americans"

England: 1765–1766

News continued to arrive in England about the hostile reception that the Stamp Act had received in the colonies. British authorities found it impossible to land the hated stamps in America, and British merchants could not receive payment for goods shipped to the colonies without the proper stamps. British merchants were suffering also, because American merchants from Boston, Massachusetts, to Charleston, South Carolina, had stopped buying English goods. By the end of 1765 it was obvious that the Stamp Act could be carried out only by military force. This, Rockingham was not willing to do.

Now Edmund Burke, Rockingham's secretary, began to gather together a group of British merchants and manufacturers to urge repeal of the Stamp Act. But he was careful to emphasize that repeal would be in the interests of British merchants, not a concession to Americans. Soon Parliament was deluged with petitions testifying that North American trade was the source of England's prosperity, and unless Parliament took action, they all faced financial ruin.[1]

Rockingham was concerned about the violent response in America and was influenced by pressure from the British merchants worried about an American commercial blockade. He was anxious to please the merchants and viewed the Stamp Act as a mistake, but he hesitated taking any action. There were several ministers in his cabinet who were strongly opposed to repeal as a "retreat" before American demands. Was it wise to repeal a tax simply because those who had to pay disliked doing so? the ministers wondered. And Americans objected not only to the tax, but to the principle behind it—to the *right* of the British Parliament to raise taxes on Americans.

Then, on November 10, 1765, Benjamin Franklin, who had shifted his ground to become the leading spokesman for America in England, accepted Rockingham's invitation to dine with him. During dinner, Franklin explained to Rockingham that enforcing the Stamp Act would cause more trouble than it was worth. It would alienate the affections of the Americans and would thereby lessen trade between the two countries. In order to achieve harmony within the empire, he argued, there must be local government in America and representation in Parliament.[2] Still, Rockingham, inexperienced and indecisive, decided to watch and wait.

Unexpectedly, on January 14, 1766, Rockingham got the support he needed. A debate on the Stamp Act had been scheduled in the House of Commons for that day. It was not known whether William Pitt, who had not been seen in the Commons for more than a year, would be able to attend. Since his retirement, he had lived at Bath, helpless with gout. He could not walk without crutches, use a fork at the table, or even write legibly. Pitt had written to a friend that "if I can crawl, or be carried, I will deliver my mind and heart upon the state of America."[3] A few Americans, including Benjamin Franklin and several other colonial agents, listened in the balcony. The air was tense with anticipation.

Well after the session had begun, Pitt—in spite of the intense pain he was suffering and determined to voice his opinion in the growing crisis over America—hobbled into Parliament. He was recognized immediately by the Speaker. He spoke so softly at first that it was difficult to hear him, but he gathered energy as he went along, and soon his voice could be heard in every part of the Commons. He stunned the members by announcing that taxes could be legally imposed only on those whom the imposers represented: "It is my opinion that this kingdom has no right to lay a tax upon the colonies. . . . They are the subjects of this kingdom, equally entitled with yourselves to all the natural rights of mankind and the peculiar privileges of Englishmen." Eloquently, vehemently, he had placed before the Commons the Americans' appeal for no taxation without representation.

Fired by enthusiasm, he continued:

> Equally bound by its laws, and equally participating of the constitution of this free country, the Americans are the sons, not the bastards of England. Taxation is no part of the governing or legislative power. The taxes are a voluntary gift and grant of the Commons alone. . . .
>
> When in this House we give and grant, we give and grant what is our own. But in an American tax . . . we give and grant to Your Majesty the property of Your Majesty's commons of America. It is an absurdity in terms. . . .
>
> The Commons of America, [have the] constitutional right of giving and granting their own money. . . . [But we cannot take] their money out of their pockets without their consent.[4]

An incensed George Grenville, now out of office, retorted:

> I cannot understand the difference between external and internal taxes. They are the same in effect, and differ only in name. That this kingdom has the sovereign, the supreme legislative power over America is granted. It cannot be denied; and taxation is part of that sovereign power. It is one branch of legislation. . . .

> Protection and obedience are reciprocal. Great Britain protects America; America is bound to yield obedience. If not, tell me when the Americans were emancipated?[5]

Pitt shot back: "The gentleman asks, when were the colonies emancipated? But I desire to know, when were they made slaves?

"I rejoice that America has resisted," he continued in one of his most splendid defenses of American liberty. "Three millions of people, so dead to all feelings of liberty as voluntarily to submit to be slaves, would have been fit instruments to make slaves of the rest."[6]

At this point, an incensed member of the Commons jumped up and declared that the Great Commoner ought to be sent to the Tower to be hanged. He was betraying England. He was sacrificing the rights of the mother country "to the pitiful ambition of obtaining an huzza [a cheer] from American rioters." By approving rioting and rebellion in America, the member continued, Pitt had encouraged the colonists in their unruly ways and made more difficult the task of those who upheld the rights of Great Britain over the colonies.

Many in the Commons "immediately joined in the idea and gave such shouts of applause as I never heard," one member reported.[7]

Pitt, startled by the response, attempted to explain: "I am no courtier of America. I stand up for this kingdom. . . . Parliament has a right to . . . restrain America." But they must rule so as "not to contradict the fundamental principles that are common to both."

Then, replying to Grenville, he continued: "If the gentleman does not understand the difference between external and internal taxes, I cannot help it; but there is a plain distinction between taxes levied for the purposes of raising a revenue, and duties imposed for the regulation of trade."

An impassioned Pitt concluded: "The Americans have not acted in all things with prudence and temper; they have been wronged; they have been driven to madness by injustice. Will you punish them for the madness you have occasioned? . . . I will beg leave to tell the House what is really my opinion. It is that the Stamp Act be repealed absolutely, totally, and immediately."[8]

In a moment, in his brilliant and passionate speech, William Pitt had transformed the Stamp Act into a debate on the constitutional rights of Americans rather than the right of Parliament to make laws. Pitt was not advocating American independence. His vision of the British Empire was one in which the American colonies were a strong element. He did not want to see the empire torn apart on an issue of simple finance. The Stamp Act had been founded on a false principle, Pitt argued, and he was urging its immediate repeal.

For the next seven weeks, day after day, Parliament dealt with the American problem as it had never done before. Even King George confided that the fate of the Stamp Act was "undoubtedly the most serious matter that ever came before Parliament."[9]

Now the British newspapers took up the cry: The "saucy Americans" must be taught humility and obedience. They must learn who was master in the household before they felt strong enough to "wrestle with us for Pre-eminence." The "too large and too powerful Colonies" were contrasted with the declining, exhausted, tax-ridden mother country. The growth of the colonies must be stopped. Making America pay what they thought was a fair share was to most Englishmen the goal of British policy. The Stamp Act was valuable because it promised to transfer money across the Atlantic Ocean.

In Parliament, George Grenville had quickly risen to the defense of the measure that he had originally proposed. Now that he was no longer finance minister, he had no responsibility to enforce the Stamp Act, so he had no reason to make concessions. Neither the constitutional dispute with the colonies nor the difficulties of enforcement concerned him.

On the other hand, Rockingham, who had no responsibility for the Stamp Act, saw no reason to enforce an unpopular measure not of his creation. Rockingham did *not* sympathize with the Americans. He and his followers in the House of Commons agreed with the principle behind the Act. They believed that Parliament did have the right to tax the citizens of Boston just as it had to tax the citizens of London. But they had come to the conclusion that it would be unwise to exercise that right in this instance. Rockingham and his followers would have it repealed. With a firmness with which he is rarely credited, Rockingham finally decided to act.

But Rockingham understood the necessity of affirming Parliament's authority. The colonists must not be allowed to think that Parliament had abandoned its right to tax them in the future. Therefore, he recommended that a Declaratory Act, stating that Parliament has the power to pass laws to bind the people of America *in all cases whatsoever*, accompany the repeal of the Stamp Act. He then took the highly unusual step of bringing British merchants and visiting Americans before the House of Commons to testify to the evil consequences of the Stamp Act. Benjamin Franklin was one of those called.

Franklin, whose attitude toward the Stamp Act had by now swung from apathy to one of fierce opposition, had been planning for the last month for the time when he would be allowed to speak out himself. He wrote to his wife in America: "I am excessively hurried, being every hour that I am awake, either abroad to speak with Members of Parliament or taken up with People coming to see me at home concerning our American affairs."[10]

He had recently spoken out defiantly against the British role of parent to the colonists. His ballad, which he called "The Mother Country," expressed this defiance of the "old Mother" at the same time that it expressed the colonists' loyalty:

> We have an old Mother that peevish has grown,
> She snubs us like children that scarce walk alone;
> She forgets we're grown up and have Sense of our own;
>   WHICH NOBODY CAN DENY, DENY, WHICH NOBODY CAN DENY.
>
> If we don't obey Orders, whatever the Case,
> She frowns, and she chides, and she loses all Patience,

And sometimes she hits us a Slap in the Face,
  WHICH NOBODY CAN DENY, ETC.

· · · · · · · · · · · · ·

Know too, ye bad Neighbours, who aim to divide
The Sons from the Mother, that still she's our Pride;
And if ye attack her we're all of her side,
  WHICH NOBODY CAN DENY, ETC.

We'll join in her Lawsuits, to baffle all those,
Who, to get what she has, will be often her Foes:
For we know it must all be our own, when she goes,
  WHICH NOBODY CAN DENY, DENY, WHICH NOBODY CAN DENY.[11]

Now Franklin wrote anonymous letters to the newspapers, and went so far as to publish in the *London Chronicle* letters he had written some years before to the then governor of Massachusetts, William Shirley. The letters contained the fullest statement of the American position that Londoners had ever read.

Franklin was ordered to testify before the House of Commons on February 13, 1766, the final day of the hearings. In a good-humored and carefully rehearsed performance, he gave the marquess of Rockingham exactly what he needed. It has been called Franklin's finest hour of all his years in London.

To some degree, his testimony was prearranged. Consulting with his friends in the Commons, Franklin had helped frame a group of sympathetic questions that would elicit the points he wished to make. The order of questioning, however, was spontaneous, and there were many opposition voices. But he was confident that no point would likely be raised that he was not prepared to answer.

Franklin had always been known as a writer of elegant prose and as a stimulating conversationalist, but never as a public speaker. Now, in the most courteous and restrained manner, but with a wealth of facts at his command and an ability to answer without offending the questioner, this philosopher stood before the members of the House of Commons and put forth his country's position clearly and logically. No one had ever thought so carefully about America, nor could anyone have delivered the arguments as Franklin did. There was not a question for which he did not have a reasoned answer. His comments were simple and fundamental, yet his testimony revealed the depth of feeling against the Stamp Act in America.

Dressed in a plain brown suit, unadorned by any finery, the most distinguished American in England stepped to the bar, a horizontal piece of wood between the rows of opposing benches that blocked passage into the well of the House of Commons, and identified himself simply as "Franklin of Philadelphia." Never again would he consider himself an Englishman. He remained standing for four hours, responding to more than one hundred and seventy-four questions, such as: [12]

> Q. Do Americans pay any considerable taxes among themselves?
> A. Certainly many, and very heavy taxes.

> Q. For what purposes are those taxes laid?
> A. For the support of the civil and military establishments of the country, and to discharge the heavy debt contracted in the last war.

Grenville then asked:

> Q. Do you think it is right that Americans should be protected by this country, and pay no part of the expenses?
> A. That is not the case. The Colonies raised, cloathed, and paid during the war nearly twenty-five thousand men, and spent many millions.

One of Franklin's friends stood to question him.

Q. What was the temper of America towards Great Britain before the year 1763?

A. The best in the world. They submitted willingly to the government of the crown, and paid . . . obedience to acts of Parliament. . . . They were led by a thread. They had not only a respect, but an affection for Great Britain, for its laws, its customs, and manners, and even a fondness for its fashions that greatly increased the commerce . . . to be an Old England-Man . . . gave a kind of rank among us.

Q. And what is their temper now?

A. Oh, very much altered.

Q. Can anything less than a military force carry the Stamp Act into execution?

A. I do not see how a military force can be applied to that purpose.

Q. Why may it not?

A. Suppose a military force sent into America, they will find nobody in arms; what are they then to do? They cannot force a man to take stamps who chuses [sic] to do without them. They will not find a rebellion; they may indeed make one.

When Franklin, in response to a question, turned the tables and called the recent war a *British* war, for the profit of *British* merchants and for the defense of *British* trade, Grenville and his friends were stunned.

Franklin continued to make his questioners appear foolish: The war, Franklin insisted, had been fought chiefly with American men and money. The Americans did not need British help against the Indians. "They defended themselves when they were but a handful and the Indians much more numerous. . . . They are very able to defend themselves."

The conclusion was dramatic in its simplicity, at the same time that it threatened the British economy:

Q. What used to be the pride of the Americans?
A. To indulge in the fashions and manufactures of Great Britain.

Q. What is now their pride?
A. To wear their old clothes over again till they can make new ones.[13]

It was a brilliant performance.

Never did "Truth . . . make so great a progress in so very short a time," Rockingham told a friend.

The bill to repeal the Stamp Act was moved in Parliament on February 22. Once again, there was vigorous debate. When Pitt arrived, on crutches, he was cheered into the chamber by the crowd outside. He spoke for over an hour, telling his listeners that he would be an Englishman first and then an American. Repeal, he said, was in the best interests of England. He reminded them of the miserable state of the country, the distresses of the manufacturers, the unhappy wife, the starving child, the universal bankruptcies. He pleaded for "unconditional repeal." The vote was finally taken at 2 A.M. It carried by a strong majority.[14]

When Pitt appeared outside the chamber shortly after, "gaunt and tired, and hobbling on his crutches," the crowd "pulled off their hats, huzza'd, and many followed [him] home with shouts and benedictions." The bill was quickly carried through the Lords. But it lacked the most important condition of a great compromise. It was not accepted by Grenville and his supporters.[15]

And Rockingham still needed the support of the king.

It was the duty of the king to see to it that laws were obeyed. Therefore, it was almost instinctive for King George to wish to have the Stamp Act enforced. Furthermore, he was alarmed by the temper of the colonists. He saw in their protests a threat to his plans for personal rule, and grew more stubborn than ever. Their defiance, he reasoned, if allowed to go unchecked, would

A British cartoon depicting the burial of the Stamp Act, printed anonymously in 1766. The Stamp Act was not entirely popular in England, and many merchants there were relieved when Parliament repealed it. George Grenville, the author of the Stamp Act (fourth from the left), is seen carrying his failed law in a child's coffin.

fragment the empire and ruin Great Britain. To George III, repeal of the Stamp Act meant surrender to organized rebellion and encouragement of further evil.

Thus, when he was told that the tax was placing a heavy burden on the colonists, and that it was unpopular in America, he suggested amending it to meet any "just grievances" from America. He was told that this was impossible. There was no alternative between enforcement and repeal. The cabinet, Rockingham told the king, would make their American policy an issue of confidence. Unless the Stamp Act was repealed, the Rockingham ministry would resign. Faced with the choice of Rockingham and repeal, or Grenville and enforcement of the Stamp Act, the king chose Rockingham.

The bill to repeal the Stamp Act received the royal assent on March 18. As King George signed it, he pursed his lips and remarked, "It is a fatal compliance." The king, rather than his ministers, seemed to recognize that repeal was a virtual acknowledgment of a victory for the colonists' belief that they could not be taxed without their consent.[16]

There was "great rejoicing in the City of London by all Ranks of People." Ships in the harbor displayed their colors, and bonfires were lit throughout the city. A ship that had been lying in wait in the harbor was dispatched immediately by merchants who traded with America to carry the news across the ocean.[17]

But repeal of the Stamp Act was linked with Rockingham's Declaratory Act, which gave Parliament full authority to make laws binding on the colonies *"in all cases whatsoever."* The last four words were italicized to ensure that the message was understood. The colonists had won no more than a temporary, limited victory.

Chapter X

"glorious tidings"

The American Colonies: 1766

On May 16, 1766, the brigantine *Harrison* dropped anchor in Boston Harbor. She carried news of the repeal of the Stamp Act. The *Boston Gazette* pronounced it the "most joyful, great and glorious news this continent ever before received." But this most important piece of news had taken eight weeks to cross the Atlantic Ocean. For two months after repeal of the hated tax, the colonists had continued to live in doubt of the outcome. Many had been badly frightened at finding themselves in virtual revolt against the mother country.

Now the colonists were filled with a deep sense of relief, and they scheduled a huge celebration for Monday, May 19. On that day church bells began tolling at 1 A.M. In Boston Harbor and off Castle Island ships festooned with flags fired cannons in salute. The Liberty Tree, just leafing out in the early spring, was decorated with ribbons and banners, and musicians strolled the

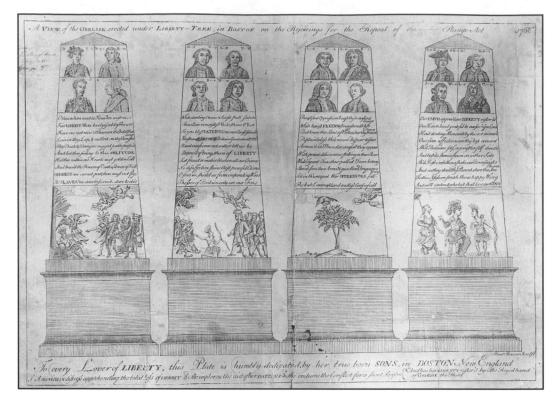

A view of the four sides of the obelisk erected in Boston when news arrived of the repeal of the Stamp Act. The obelisk itself was destroyed by a fire during the celebration. *Engraving by Paul Revere, 1766.*

streets playing. At night, candles burned in the windows, and fireworks blazed over Boston Common, where the servants of John Hancock handed out pewter mugs filled with fine Madeira wine. Those who had homes near the common kept open house, and ladies and gentlemen went from one beautiful house to another, drinking innumerable toasts to liberty. Paul Revere, one of those who had helped organize the celebration on Boston Common, engraved a design for an enormous transparent obelisk of oiled paper. Illuminated from within like a Japanese lantern by two hundred and eighty lamps, and covered with symbols of liberty and defiance, it was inset with portraits of George III, Rockingham, Pitt, and other Englishmen who had supported the colonists.[1]

Unfortunately, the obelisk caught fire, whether from its own lights or from a rocket burst is not known. Paul Revere's copperplate of it, dedicated "To every Lover of Liberty," survived.

Governor Bernard held a congratulatory meeting with his council in the afternoon, then strolled graciously among the people in the evening. The atmosphere was joyous. What the people didn't know, or even suspect, was that this governor, who constantly claimed to be mediating between the colonists and their angry sovereign, was secretly writing to George III and systematically exaggerating the turbulence of the patriots, and at the same time underrating their courage and sincerity.

In January 1766 he had written to London: "The people here talk very high of their power to resist Great Britain; but it is all talk. New York and Boston would both be defenseless to a royal fleet. I hope that New York will have the honour of being subdued first."

Now, with the repeal of the Stamp Act, Bernard set to work even more forcefully. He wrote to England that Massachusetts should be deprived of its assembly. In secret letters to the king he pleaded that taxes should never be repealed or lessened, while in public he falsely assured Bostonians that he had written to the king asking for relief from these very taxes.[2]

"I have spoke to you with Sincerity, Openness, and Earnestness," Bernard claimed, and hoped that the people of Boston would renew their "duty" to the king and to him as the king's representative.

The people, unaware of Bernard's actions, were jubilant. Prosperous merchants even contributed money to pay the bills of Boston's debtors so the debtors might be released from prison.

A poem, written for the occasion, concluded by assuring King George that if he ever found himself menaced by enemies, he could be certain that he might:

> To this Asylum stretch thine happy Wing,
> And we'll contend who best shall love our King.[3]

No doubt George III would have been startled had he read this.

Similar celebrations were held in all the colonies. In Philadelphia, the "glorious tidings" were read to an enthusiastic crowd at the London Coffee House, and the captain of the ship that brought the news was presented with a gold lace hat. A special "extraordinary" supplement to the *Pennsylvania Journal and Weekly Advertiser* was printed bearing the good news in a handsome broadside. But Philadelphians waited for June 4 in order to celebrate the king's birthday and the repeal at the same time. An elegant party was held at the State House, and toasts were drunk to the king, to Parliament, to "the glorious and immortal Mr. Pitt," "America's friends in Great Britain," "the Virginia Assembly," "Daniel Dulany," "the Liberty Press of America," and to "our worthy and faithful agent, Dr. Franklin." Salutes were fired from a barge named the *Franklin*.

Dr. Franklin, in England, determined that his family should truly rejoice, sent his wife and daughter in Boston a lovely present of satin and brocade fabric to replace the clothes of their own spinning that they had worn while the crisis lasted. All good patriots had refused to buy anything that came from England.

In New York, a lead statue of King George III on horseback was erected on Bowling Green, at the lower tip of Manhattan. In all the colonies, a release from fear and tension was evident as the colonists gave vent to their feelings by reaffirming their Englishness and their attachment to their king. There were few who realized how unsympathetic he was to their cause.[4]

John Adams noted in his diary, "The people are as quiet and submissive to government as any people under the sun. . . . The repeal of the Stamp Act has hushed into silence almost every popular clamor, and composed every wave of popular disorder into a smooth and peaceful calm."[5]

Colonists were brought together by a bond of common joy. Within a few weeks, this remarkably diverse group of people, spread out over a vast expanse of territory, were no longer referring to themselves as Virginians or Marylanders or Philadelphians. They stopped talking of "our colony" or "our province." Suddenly, people began speaking of themselves as "Americans." Ideas and actions initiated in one colony were quickly and enthusiastically adopted in another. Few people seemed to pay any attention to the Declaratory Act that accompanied the repeal.[6]

But a Virginia burgess named George Mason, who was a leading citizen and good friend and neighbor of George Washington, was one of those who did recognize the threat inherent in the Declaratory Act. In a letter to the commissioner of London merchants, he ridiculed the English merchants for speaking to the colonists like schoolboys, as if to say: "We have with infinite difficulty and fatigue got you excused this one time; pray be a good boy for the future, do what your papa and mamma bid you, and hasten to return them your most grateful acknowledgments for condescending to let you keep what is your own; and then all your acquaintance will love you, and give you pretty things; . . . Is not this a little ridiculous, when applied to three millions of as loyal and useful subjects as any in the British dominions, who have been only contending for their birth-right, and have now only gained, or rather kept, what could not, with common justice, or even policy, be denied them?"[7] Some members of the Virginia House of Burgesses saw that the matter was a powder keg.

In Boston, Sam Adams was not celebrating. He told his friends that repeal meant very little, that Britain still considered herself supreme over the colonies. He, too, had not missed the significance of the Declaratory Act. He believed that Parliament had repealed the Stamp Act more from fear than from mercy. The colonial boycott of British manufactures and the Stamp Act Congress, Sam said, had forced Britain to give way. American "firmness and resolution" had brought it about. He believed that George Grenville and Parliament had created such ill feeling between Britain and her colonies "as it is to be fear'd will never wholly subside."[8]

But he cleverly suggested that Massachusetts send a letter to England to thank the king.

He would wait quietly, Sam decided, until the political thinking of other patriots caught up to his. He knew that he was far ahead of his associates in his ideas. But he was content to move no faster than their support would take him. "Patience is characteristic of the Patriot," he once advised a fiery young rebel.[9]

John Hancock was a generous young merchant who became the wealthiest man in the colony of Massachusetts. He was considered the financial godfather of the patriots. *By John Singleton Copley, 1770–1772.*

In the same way, Sam patiently watched young men in Boston as they rose to prominence, then enticed them into the Whig (patriot) camp, where he diligently trained them. Sam had the rare ability to recognize that his own strengths were limited, and therefore he recruited others for roles he could not fill.

Among these men was John Hancock, a handsome, generous young merchant who had recently inherited the substantial fortune of his uncle, Thomas Hancock. Thomas Hancock had died in 1764, making the then twenty-seven-year-old John perhaps the wealthiest man in the province of Massachusetts, if not in the entire country.

John Hancock was vain and pathetically eager for praise. Yet he was also sincerely eager to do great and good deeds with the money he had inherited. He had only "moderate" intelligence, and his vanity and pomposity earned him the nickname "the American king." But his liberal sentiments and his reputation for smuggling and flagrant abuse of customs officers endeared him to the people and made him famous. His generous philanthropy ensured his popularity.

Samuel Adams guessed, correctly, that John's hankering for popularity, and his susceptibility to flattery could be used to advantage. He would lend prestige to the patriot cause. From the time Adams first brought him to the Patriot

Club in 1765, John Hancock became the financial godfather of the Whigs. His main fault was that he was sometimes indiscreet: He talked too much. "Such a leaky vessel is this worthy gentleman," John Adams lamented of him.

In May 1766, when elections were held for representatives to the Massachusetts Assembly, Boston returned Samuel Adams and James Otis to office, along with a newly elected

John Hancock entertained lavishly in his mansion, set atop Beacon Hill.

John Hancock. From that time on, Hancock remained in politics alongside Sam Adams.

Hancock had an odd combination of traits for a politician: He was an aristocrat whose rapport was with those beneath him; a lover of luxury who thrived in an age that prided itself on self-denial; and a revolutionary whose greatest hallmark was moderation. From his mansion atop Beacon Hill he would look down on a community that would almost always look up to him.[10]

During the June session of the Massachusetts Assembly, James Otis opened the debates of the assembly to the public, and arranged for a gallery where sessions could be witnessed by all. For the first time in the history of legislative associations, it was made the right of any citizen to see and hear the proceedings.[11]

At this same session, Samuel Adams was made clerk of the House of Representatives, a position that gave him custody of all papers belonging to the House. These Adams published freely in the *Boston Gazette* to keep the people informed of the struggle for freedom being waged by their representatives. For many generations the Massachusetts Assembly had not permitted its addresses to the king or to the Commons to be published before they had been received and made public in the mother country. Sam Adams ignored this. Instead of wasting valuable time waiting for the petitions from Massachusetts Bay to arrive in London, and then for King George and his ministers to ponder them, Adams rushed them through the press and had them in the *Gazette* even before they were stowed aboard ship for England. Such "lack of respect" for the king and his ministry shocked James Otis.

Shortly after Sam Adams took him under his wing, John Hancock began to branch out into new enterprises. By constructing new warehouses and wharves and engaging in trade on a larger scale, he gave employment to so many workers that John Adams estimated that a thousand New England families were dependent upon him for support. It was thought highly unlikely that these laborers would offend their employer by voting against his friend Sam Adams. Soon Adams and Hancock were invulnerable in Boston.[12]

By the time the Stamp Act was repealed, Samuel Adams had become one of the most important figures in Massachusetts politics, second only to James Otis in popularity. People began referring to him as "the great Mr. Adams." Outwardly, he seemed a "plain, simple, decent citizen . . . who lived frugally and took great pride in his poverty." In Revolutionary Boston, he was considered a devout, old-fashioned Puritan who believed that New Englanders' best security against tyranny was the Puritan spirit, and he never overlooked an opportunity to give a religious flavor to his political activities.

He had a fine ear for music, and a fine voice. But some people complained that the singing societies he organized among Boston's mechanics produced more revolutionaries than songbirds.[13]

At the time that Sam Adams began bringing John Hancock to the Whig clubs, Paul Revere was also beginning to stand out as someone worth watching—a man capable of bridging the very real gap between the thinkers and the doers. He thought of himself as an artisan and a gentleman, without the slightest sense of contradiction—a new American attitude toward class. A New England Yankee to his very soul, Paul Revere was, by birth, half English and half French—but always entirely American.

He was a ruddy-faced, plain man with a wide mouth, flaring nose, and quizzical brows arching over his warm, dark eyes.

As a youngster, Revere was educated in Boston's North Writing School, and he became a lifelong learner who loved books. When he was apprenticed to his father, Apollos Rivoire, a gifted French goldsmith, he mastered many skills. He learned to work in gold, silver, and later, in copper and brass. He studied the difficult art of copperplate engraving and did many illustrations for Boston printers. But he was best known for his silver. His blunt, capable hands fashioned some of the most beautiful silver pieces in the colonies. When his father died, Paul was only nineteen, yet he was able to take over the business and become the main supporter of his family.

Paul Revere, who was rapidly becoming one of the finest silversmiths in the colonies, was an important member of an organized network of patriots in Boston. His engraving tools, the burin and needle, are on the table ready for use in engraving the teapot. Revere was also an accomplished horseman, highly regarded for the speed with which he carried secret messages across Massachusetts. *By John Singleton Copley, 1768–1770.*

He faithfully attended church and served his community in many ways. He was known as someone who would get things done. He associated actively with other artisans and mechanics and enjoyed their company, and he joined many organizations. One of these was the North Caucus Club, a branch of the political organization that had been founded by Sam Adams's father.

Paul Revere was also invited to join the Long Room Club, which met above the printing shop where the *Boston Gazette* was published. This secret society was the center of power of the Whig movement in Boston, smaller and more select than the North Caucus. Most of its seventeen members had attended Harvard College and were lawyers, physicians, magistrates, and men of independent means. Paul Revere was the only "mechanic" among them, yet he felt comfortable there.[14]

Now the patriots "went to school" with the great ancient and modern philosophers. They began to read widely all the leading authorities on natural law, constitutional government, and individual rights. They read history and considered its lessons. And in so doing, they became the most learned politicians in history.[15]

Chapter XI

"senseless glory"

London: 1766–1770

King George III was not a politician. He had no desire to be in the limelight, nor was he vain. He disliked emotional scenes and had never learned how to deal with a political crisis. He craved a quiet life, one of order and routine. By 1766 he wished for little more than a settled cabinet of *any* political alliance, provided it did not include George Grenville. As he matured and became more sure of himself during the 1760s, his opinions had become more rigid and obstinate. He firmly believed he had a sacred obligation—to his ancestors and to his children—to defend the empire of Great Britain and its constitution at any cost. Any compromise would be a betrayal of God's trust. To him, his American policy was simple: The colonies must be reduced to absolute obedience, if necessary, by force.[1]

He was angered by the repeal of the Stamp Act. He interpreted it as a weakening of Britain's authority in America. Conciliation, he felt, was an act of unforgivable disloyalty to the crown by his ministers. He began to search for a replacement for Rockingham. Once again, his eye lighted on William Pitt. Suddenly, the man who had been "the blackest of hearts," "a snake in the grass," became his "dear friend." In July, he asked Pitt to form another government. This would be the fifth in the king's six-year reign, an indication of the political chaos in London.

He sent Pitt a direct invitation to come in person, rather than approach him through an intermediary, as he had in the past. Pitt, at his country home, replied immediately: "I shall hasten to London as fast as I possibly can." He would ignore the pain of his gout. The prospect of returning to power now was exhilarating. Pitt departed in a carriage that jostled him over the potholed roads on the long trip to London.

William Pitt had his own agenda. He would humbly serve his king, for he, like the king, believed that it was the existence of factions, or parties, in Parliament that destroyed the "dignity" of the government. He was certain that he could unite those factions behind the monarch. But he wanted something in return. He wanted to run the government as a lord from the House of Lords. His health was steadily deteriorating, and he could no longer bear the long and belligerent debates

William Pitt, when he became the earl of Chatham. After he was elevated to the House of Lords, he lost much of his influence among Londoners. *By Richard Brompton, 1772.*

of the House of Commons. He hoped that the House of Lords would prove less strenuous.[2]

King George agreed, and on July 29, 1766, William Pitt was awarded a title by the king and became the earl of Chatham. In one stroke, William Pitt undermined everything he hoped to achieve. By abandoning the House of Commons, where his strength as the Great Commoner had been built, his power and leadership were diminished. As a commoner, he had been a great statesman, but as the earl of Chatham he was a new peer in the chamber of men who held centuries-old titles. "It argues a senselessness to glory," said the king of Poland, "to forfeit the name of Pitt for any title." Further, the people did not accept his explanation of ill health for this rise in class and status, and their confidence in him was weakened. The *Whitehall Evening Post* summed up the change: "Pitt was adored—but Chatham is quite unknown."[3]

Concerned about his shattered health, Pitt decided not to become first lord of the Treasury. He would direct the cabinet from a less demanding post. He would leave it to the other ministers to carry out his orders.

Accordingly, he chose the young, amiable, thirty-one-year-old duke of Grafton to be prime minister. Charles Townshend would be first lord of the Treasury, also known as chancellor of the Exchequer.

In August, Pitt began to implement some of his policies. His aims were to calm the Americans, form a new European alliance against England's old enemy, France, and bring the East India Company under British control. Satisfied that he had made a good start, he left for Bath for the remainder of the long parliamentary recess.

When Parliament opened in January 1767, Chatham (as William Pitt would now be called) was too ill to attend. Without him the ministry was thrown into confusion. King George strove, in vain, to restore order and discipline to the ranks of the ministers. When, despite intense pain, Chatham was finally able to return to London, the king renewed his promise of support.[4]

King George, who liked plain speech and simple honesty, never felt comfortable with Pitt. He disliked his rhetorical language and exaggerated compliments. When Pitt wrote to the king, "Lord Chatham begs to be permitted to lay himself with all duty and submission at the king's feet, and to pour out a heart overflowing with the most reverential and warm sense of His Majesty's infinite condescension," His Majesty could only think him insincere. Yet he knew that this man was the only one who could hold the ministry together.[5]

Pitt managed to remain in London until early March. Then, his body crippled and wracked with pain, and sinking into a state of melancholy that began to disturb his mind as well, he left for home. He would remain in seclusion for two years. During that time, the duke of Grafton was forced to assume his role. Grafton, who believed strongly in the philosophy of John Locke, and who was devoted to William Pitt, was opposed to taxing the colonists without their consent. But he was politically immature and unwilling to lead, and therefore, ineffective.

As soon as Pitt left London, the "colorful gadfly" Charles Townshend, chancellor of the Exchequer, stepped into the power vacuum created by Pitt's departure, and took command.

Elected to Parliament in 1747, Townshend was considered "the delight and ornament" of the House of Commons. He was brilliant, but unwilling to accommodate himself to others, and he was often unscrupulous.

A flashy young politician, witty and energetic, and with a marvelous talent for mimicry and repartee and a taste for high living, Townshend was known in the London coffeehouses as "Champagne Charley." On May 8, 1767, under the influence of a large amount of champagne, he delivered a speech in the House of Commons that a spectator described as "extravagantly fine. It lasted an hour, with a torrent of wit, ridicule, vanity, lies, and beautiful language."[6] Although later described as "a statesman who has left nothing but errors to account for his fame," Townshend's charm and brilliance in the House of Commons made it impossible to ignore him. It was he who would reawaken discontent in the colonies.[7]

When Townshend taunted George Grenville, who was still angry over the repeal of the Stamp Act, Grenville jumped to his feet and shouted, "You are cowards, you are afraid of the Americans, you dare not tax America!"

"Fear! Cowards! Dare not tax America! *I* dare tax America!" Townshend shot back.

Grenville retorted, "Dare you tax America? I wish to God I could see it!"

"I will! I will!" Townshend declared.[8]

Townshend had been a staunch supporter of the Stamp Act. Now he saw a way to bring the Americans "to heel." With William Pitt, Lord Chatham, incapacitated, there was no one to exercise restraint on him.

Five days later, Charles Townshend introduced into Parliament his plan for "improving the system of government in the colonies." He would "indulge" America in what he considered its foolish distinction between internal and external taxation. He would use their distinction to make taxation acceptable to them. The colonies, he felt, were fair game for taxation by Parliament.

Townshend proposed levying a tax on all imported glass, lead, printer's paper, and paint, which the colonies were required to import from Great Britain, and tea, which was brought to England by the powerful British East India Company and then re-exported in large quantities to the colonies. Next, he boldly declared that the revenue from these taxes, which he anticipated would be about forty thousand pounds per year, would be used to pay the salaries of all royally appointed officials in America. Thus, these officials, the colonial governors and judges, would not have to depend on the colonial governments for their salaries and could act independently of them. This

Charles Townshend succeeded George Grenville as chancellor of the Exchequer. Nicknamed "Champagne Charlie," he was brilliant but often unscrupulous, and was responsible for the hated Townshend Acts which reawakened discontent in the colonies. *By Joshua Reynolds, 1764–1767.*

meant that Townshend, by the use of parliamentary taxation, would take money from the colonists and then use that money to destroy colonial liberties.[9]

Furthermore, Townshend announced, if there were a surplus, the money would pay for troops to protect the colonies. He also proposed the establishment of a new Board of Customs Commissioners to superintend the laws relating to trade. Since Townshend's plan would ease considerably the British tax situation, it found much favor in the House of Commons.[10]

In order to make enforcement of the act more efficient, the writs of assistance, authorizing searches and seizures, which had been so forcefully denounced by James Otis in America six years before, would be formally legalized. Customs commissioners would be assigned to headquarters in Boston, considered the most stubborn focus of resistance to British authority.[11]

Further, since the colony of New York had refused to provide for the British soldiers as required by the Quartering Act of 1765, Townshend now proposed a measure to suspend the New York Assembly until the soldiers' requirements were met.[12]

In the debate that followed, Edmund Burke voiced his fear that the colonists would read in the preamble to the Townshend duties "their own annihilation." Even George Grenville tried to convince Townshend that the colonists would oppose *any* tax, internal or external. Grenville, by now a much wiser man, suggested that Britain require the colonies to pay four hundred thousand pounds for imperial costs, then allow them to raise that money themselves.

King George, too, felt that taxing the colonists was a matter requiring much more careful thought and should not be too hastily decided. But the mood in Parliament at that time was so anti-American that Townshend's measure passed easily and was promptly enacted into law.

During the feeling of well-being that had followed the repeal of the Stamp Act, no serious effort had been made to find out what, if anything, could be done to raise defense funds through colonial assemblies. No royal commission was sent to America to study the situation. Agents of the colonies who were in London at the time were not consulted.

Just one month before, in April, Benjamin Franklin had written to a friend in Scotland, warning that he foresaw trouble. He was concerned that the two countries were moving further and further apart:

> Every act of oppression will sour [the Americans'] tempers, lessen greatly— if not annihilate—the profits of your commerce with them, and hasten their final revolt; for the seeds of liberty are universally found there, and nothing can eradicate them. And yet there remains among that people so much respect, veneration and affection for Britain that, if cultivated prudently, with kind usage and tenderness for their privileges, they might easily be governed for all ages, without force or considerable expense.

Franklin feared that the English were such proud people that they would never allow themselves to think of the colonists as equals: "Every man in England seems to consider himself as a piece of a sovereign over America; seems to jostle himself into the throne with the king, and talks of *our subjects in the colonies.*"[13]

Charles Townshend died suddenly during an influenza epidemic in September 1767, just a few months after the passage of the statute that insured him a dubious immortality. He was forty-one years old. His friend Edmund Burke mourned him as the charm of every private society which he honoured with his presence."[14]

Townshend had been a lesser politician than George Grenville, and his principle accomplishment, the one by which he would be remembered, was to revive colonial fears and animosities. Once again, Great Britain and her colonies were headed toward a collision.

Townshend's death created a new government crisis.

The king's patience was running out. George III was disappointed in Pitt. Instead of the stable government for which he had hoped, he was faced with utter confusion. And as ministry followed ministry, Britain's relations with her colonies were steadily deteriorating.

Now the king offered the post of chancellor of the Exchequer to his friend Frederick Lord North, second earl of Guilford. Lord North was a man he liked. North had been born in London in 1732 and had been elected a member of Parliament at the age of twenty-two. He held a "courtesy" title, not an inherited one, which meant that he sat in the House of Commons, not the House of Lords. He soon became one of the best liked and most respected men in Parliament.

Since the early 1760s, North had been a junior minister with no particular political allegiance. No one was enthusiastic about this appointment by the king, yet no one criticized it. It seemed an obvious choice.

The secret of North's success in the House of Commons and with the king was his immense personal charm. Compared to the brilliant orators in Parliament at the time, North was not considered a great intellect or a commanding speaker. But he was skilled and often amusing in debate. He was sometimes absurd, but always entertaining. He had a droll, sly sense of humor. He never said anything that could not be readily understood, and he never appeared cleverer than the average person. He was acutely sensitive to public opinion.

Men of *all* political opinions enjoyed North's company, and even his bitterest political opponents could not help liking him. But had he been no more than a clever politician, he would not have commanded such universal respect. He was a man one could trust.

A contemporary described him: "He had two large prominent eyes that rolled about to no purpose [for he was extremely nearsighted]. A wide mouth, thick lips, and inflated visage gave him the air of a blind trumpeter."[15] He was a large, clumsy man who walked awkwardly. He bore such a startling resemblance to the king that it was rumored that they must be closely related.

North had been a boyhood friend of King George, and the two had acted together in amateur theatricals. But their boyhood acquaintance was not responsible for North's new favor with the king. Indeed, George III's idea of kingship meant that he would tolerate no insubordination. Though personally very pleasant to North, the king would not allow him, his childhood playmate and now his most congenial minister, to be seated in the royal presence.

Over the course of the next three years, despite Pitt's illness and continued absence from Parliament, King George remained faithful to him. The duke of

Grafton remained acting prime minister. The king continued to hope that Pitt would recuperate sufficiently to allow him to resume his duties.

George III had liked none of his ministers since Bute and was not able to talk to them easily. Dependent on others, he had clung desperately to Bute until he finally came to realize that Bute could not help him. Now he clung to Pitt and to the ineffectual Grafton. The king's attachments were never deep. He was simply unable to adjust to change, or to make a decision.

Very early in 1770, William Pitt officially resigned from Parliament. Once that occurred, Grafton, too, tendered his resignation. The king felt deserted.

Forced now to act for himself, George III invited Lord North to become head of the Treasury *and* prime minister. On January 22, 1770, North accepted the king's offer. He would remain prime minister until March 20, 1782.[16]

When Henry Conway, who had been secretary of state under Rockingham, and the earl of Shelburne (a young supporter whom Pitt had put in charge of the American colonies) resigned as well, Britain's North American colonies were left without any powerful friends in government.

North formed a new cabinet, made up of ministers who believed that the only way to handle the quarrelsome colonists was to coerce them into obedience. He named Lord Hillsborough secretary of state for the new American Department. He would be Great Britain's first official

Frederick Lord North, rumored to be George III's half-brother, became prime minister on January 22, 1770, and remained in office for twelve years. He was a skillful manager and was appreciated for his wit and good humor. He was a staunch and loyal supporter of the king. *From the studio of Nathaniel Dance, 1767–1770.*

colonial secretary. Hillsborough immediately adopted aggressive measures toward the colonies.

Benjamin Franklin, still in London, worried about this appointment. He did not trust Hillsborough, and he disliked Hillsborough's pompous and arrogant attitude. And nowhere were the minister's unbending traits more evident than on questions of American policy. Franklin was especially disturbed by a resolution introduced by Hillsborough and passed in Parliament, that invoked a treason law from the reign of Henry VIII. It called for American "traitors" to be transported to England for "trial," and if convicted, then hanged. High on the list of traitors were the names of James Otis, Samuel Adams, and John Hancock.

Throughout England there was great unrest. The colonies had agreed to ban British imports, and this was wreaking havoc with merchants. Lucrative trade was being cut off, and thousands of men were out of work. There was rioting everywhere. Now merchants in London were urging Parliament to repeal the Townshend duties and to recall Governor Bernard.[17]

Hillsborough, though, refused to consider repeal of the Townshend duties so long as the colonists questioned the *right* of Parliament to impose them. "It is essential to the constitution to preserve the supremacy of Parliament inviolate," he wrote.[18]

King George didn't seem to recognize Hillsborough's lack of judgment and unwillingness to compromise. However, when Hillsborough put before the House of Commons other strict measures for dealing with the colonies, and then submitted his proposals to George III, the king thought them excessive. He felt that altering the Massachusetts Charter, as Hillsborough suggested, should be avoided. The threat to the colony's charter was "of so strong a nature that it rather seems calculated to increase the unhappy feuds that subsist than to assuage them."

But the king continued to denounce Boston for having "a Disposition to throw off their Dependence on Great Britain."[19]

Chapter XII

"further mischiefs"

The American Colonies: 1768–1770

In the early spring of 1768, a messenger rode into Williamsburg, Virginia, carrying a letter from the Massachusetts Assembly to the House of Burgesses. It announced that Massachusetts intended to resist the Townshend duties by all constitutional means, and asked Virginia to do the same. The messenger had already stopped in the middle colonies on his way down the coast. He then continued south to deliver copies of the letter to the Carolinas and Georgia. The letter urged all the colonial legislatures to unite with Massachusetts to inform King George of their collective hostility to the new duties.

A network was beginning to form that would make communication among all the colonies possible.

Peyton Randolph, Speaker of the House of Burgesses, sent word to the speaker of the Massachusetts House that the Virginia representatives "could not but applaud them for their attention to American liberty." He went on to say that Virginia was in full agreement with Massachusetts and would support them.[1]

The colonists were quick to recognize that the Townshend duties were simply new revenue taxes. They had nothing to do with regulation of trade, as England had implied, but everything to do with Parliament's raising revenues without the colonists' consent.

At first, the colonists' response to the Townshend duties differed significantly from their earlier militant response to the Stamp Act. This time, patriot leaders urged moderation and orderly protests, and their reaction was notably restrained.

A series of letters began appearing in leading colonial newspapers, written by "A Farmer in Pennsylvania." The author of these letters was John Dickinson, the lawyer who had drafted the resolves adopted by the Stamp Act Congress in 1765.

In the first of his letters, which was published anonymously in the *Pennsylvania Chronicle* in December of 1767, Dickinson had condemned the Townshend Acts for what they were—arbitrary taxation by Parliament. For Parliament to assert its supreme authority in a matter of taxation was to Dickinson "as much a violation of the liberty of the people of that province, and consequently of all these colonies," as if Parliament had sent an army to compel compliance. Dickinson further attacked the parliamentary act that had suspended the New York Assembly for its refusal

John Dickinson was the author of the famous "Letters from a Farmer in Pennsylvania," which helped to arouse opposition to the Townshend Acts. He was a moderate who spoke out against separation from Britain.

to comply with the Quartering Act. Although Dickinson thought that New York's original behavior had been unwise, he called for statements from other colonial assemblies protesting the suspension of the New York Assembly.

The colonists, wrote Dickinson, were the sole judges of whether a tax was lawful or unlawful. Further, he objected to the use of the Townshend revenues to pay the salaries of royal governors and judges in America. Once the colonial legislatures did not pay their salaries, Dickinson warned, these British officials might sacrifice local welfare in pursuit of selfish ends.

Dickinson's letters met with such acclaim that they were quickly published as a pamphlet entitled *Letters from a Farmer in Pennsylvania, to the Inhabitants of the British Colonies*. The pamphlet appeared first in Philadelphia and then in Boston, New York, and Williamsburg. By 1769 it took its place alongside Daniel Dulany's *Considerations* as one of the most influential publications of its time.

Yet, despite this, the letters were extremely cautious and conservative in tone—as was their author. John Dickinson opposed any idea of independence. He urged his fellow colonists to express their dissatisfaction with Great Britain "sedately." The cause of liberty, he wrote, was "a cause of too much dignity to be sullied by turbulence and tumult." One of the most effective ways to combat the Townshend Acts, he suggested, was in nonimportation. By refusing to import British goods, the colonists would prevent England from reaping any advantage from the duties. There must be a peaceful reconciliation of American and British differences.[2]

In his twelfth and final letter, Dickinson summed up his position: "Let these truths be indelibly impressed on our minds—that we cannot be happy without being free—that we cannot be free without being secure in our property—that we cannot be secure in our property if without our consent others may as by right take it away." Again he cautioned his fellow colonists that by proceeding moderately they would demonstrate to the world that they could "resent injuries without falling into rage."[3]

The letters were read widely, reprinted, and much quoted. They were even translated into French. And they established John Dickinson as one of the leading patriots in America.

While his letters were considered moderate, John Dickinson went on to compose a far more militant song for the patriots to sing. He sent his "Liberty Song" to James Otis with an accompanying note that said: "I enclose for you a song for American freedom." Set to the tune of an old English drinking ballad, it was soon being sung in taverns throughout the land:

> Come join hand in hand, brave Americans all,
> And rouse your bold hearts at fair Liberty's call;
> No tyrannous Acts shall suppress your just Claim,
> Or stain with Dishonor America's Name.
>
> In freedom we're born and in freedom we'll live,
> Our right arms are ready,
> Steady men, steady.
> Not as slaves but as freemen, our lives we will give.

Some eight stanzas followed, including this:

> Then join hand in hand brave Americans all,
> By uniting we stand, by dividing we fall.
> To die we can bear, but to serve we disdain.
> For shame is to freemen more dreadful than pain.[4]

Soon word arrived in the colonies that the British government was angrily demanding that all colonial governments revoke their support of the Massachusetts letter announcing resistance to the Townshend duties or their assemblies would be dissolved. The colonies refused. In Massachusetts, James Otis said, "We are asked to rescind. Let Britain rescind her measures or the colonies are lost to her forever."[5]

Two sides of the Liberty Bowl, made by Paul Revere to honor the 92 members of the Massachusetts House of Representatives who voted not to rescind the Circular Letter. The lower photograph shows the side of the bowl which salutes John Wilkes and his *North Briton No. 45* in which he attacked the king and Lord Bute.

When the legislature voted against rescinding by a vote of ninety-two to seventeen, the jubilant Sons of Liberty commissioned Paul Revere to make a silver punch bowl large enough to hold a gallon of punch. The Rescinders Bowl, also known as the Liberty Bowl, commemorating the "Glorious 92" became a cherished symbol of American freedom.[6]

Governor Bernard responded by dissolving the Massachusetts legislature.

In Virginia, the burgesses, who had pledged to stand by Massachusetts, sent a "humble address" to Parliament in which they declared that they, and not Parliament, had the right to levy taxes on the colony. It was their privilege, they insisted, to petition the crown for a redress of grievances and to join with other colonies in doing so. Parliament must remedy the situation. They further resolved that their resolutions should be circulated to the assemblies of the other colonies.

The Raleigh Tavern was the center of political and social activity in Williamsburg, Virginia. Delegates lodged here during sessions of the House of Burgesses. The tavern contained the post office, meeting rooms, a bar, and game rooms. *Photograph by L. H. Bober.*

They were openly defying the British government.

At the same time, they assured the king that they were "ready at any time to sacrifice our lives and fortunes in defense of Your Majesty's sacred person and government."

The result was inevitable. The newly appointed governor of Virginia, the Right Honorable Norborne Berkeley, Baron de Botetourt, dissolved the House of Burgesses.

The governor might dissolve them, but he could not dampen their spirits. They conferred hurriedly, then "with the greatest order and decorum" went immediately to the home of one of the burgesses. There, they elected Peyton Randolph moderator, and decided to continue to meet as an unofficial body in the Apollo Room of the Raleigh Tavern, where so many of them had only recently danced the minuet.

Early the next morning, a document drafted by George Mason and signed by, among others, George Washington, Patrick Henry, Richard Henry Lee, and Thomas Jefferson was published as the *Virginia Association*. Essentially, the document was a nonimportation, nonconsumption agreement: The colonists would not import or purchase any goods that were taxed by act of Parliament for the purpose of raising revenue in America.

The list of contraband goods was enormous. Designed to stop all trade with the mother country, it included such items as meat, butter, cheese, sugar, oil, fruit, wine, paper, clothing material, and leather. Members of the association agreed to inform their correspondents in England not to send them anything until Parliament had repealed the acts to which they objected. This was the first time a colonial legislature had *officially* engaged in an act of rebellion. There would be a far stricter enforcement of the boycott than had occurred at the time of the Stamp Act.

The women, accustomed at that time to remaining in the background, became ardent supporters also. They dressed in "Virginia cloth," or homespun, instead of the beautiful silks and laces that they had previously imported from England for their ball gowns. Since cloth was England's major industry, the boycott of textiles was the most important weapon the colonists could use against the mother country. Spinning and weaving their own cloth became a patriotic activity. By reducing the American market for English cloth, American women were engaging in economic warfare. Their spinning wheels became their weapons.

Many even gave up drinking tea.

In Massachusetts, women did the same. They wove their own coarse but serviceable cloth at home, and used crude, homemade pins in place of English pins. They, too, began to serve coffee instead of tea, and experimented with brews of local leaves, including sassafras, sage, strawberry, raspberry, and currant. They called these "liberty teas."[7]

And they began to call themselves "Daughters of Liberty."

Colonial women did not vote or hold office, or even attend town meetings. Their lives were centered in the private world of family. They were dependent on fathers and husbands to represent them in the public sphere. But now a subtle change was beginning to take place in colonial America. Men were gradually coming to realize that women were a necessary link in the strategy of rebellion. Since wives were the ones who managed the household, without their support boycotts could not succeed. Women were becoming politically important.[8]

Soon there were threats of violence against the customs commissioners whom Townshend had sent to the colonies. Tension heightened.

In May 1768, six months after the customs commissioners had arrived from England, John Hancock's sloop *Liberty* entered Boston Harbor with a cargo of expensive wine that had been smuggled from Portugal's Madeira Islands. When a customs officer boarded the ship to inspect its cargo, Hancock had the man locked in a cabin while other workers removed all the undeclared wine. Only then was the inspector freed, but with the warning that if he valued his life and his property, he would tell no one what had happened.

A month later, the officer finally found the courage to reveal his experience to the Board of Customs. The commissioners were furious. They issued an order to seize the *Liberty*.

The British man-of-war HMS *Romney*, with fifty guns, had been anchored in Boston Harbor since early May. Now sailors from the *Romney* boarded the *Liberty*, cut her mooring lines, and towed her under the guns of the warship.

The crowd of men on the dock who witnessed this were incensed. They were instantly transformed into a mob. Throwing stones and swinging clubs, they beat the customs officers, dragging one of them through the streets by his hair. Later, spotting an inspector's pleasure boat, "built by himself in a particular and elegant manner," they hauled it from the wharf to the common and set it on fire. Only late that evening, when the voice of one of the Sons of Liberty was heard shouting, "To your Tents, O Israel," did the throng disperse and the rioting end. By then John Hancock's fine Madeira wine had disappeared from the pier.

Governor Bernard arranged for the customs officers to take refuge at Castle William in Boston Harbor. From there they sent reports to London that Boston was ruled by "Rabble," and they renewed their pleas for military forces. Bernard wrote to Hillsborough that he feared the *Liberty* riot was but "a prelude" to still "further mischiefs."[9]

With no one who would testify against any of the rioters, a grand jury made up of radicals who would not indict even if the evidence were provided, and, therefore, with no possibility of a conviction, it is no wonder that Lord Hillsborough would reply to Bernard that Massachusetts was "a Colony in which the exercise of all civil power and authority was suspended by the most daring Acts of force and violence."[10]

By the end of the summer, four thousand British troops were on their way to Boston.

In September 1768, when the arrival of British troops became certain, James Otis, Samuel Adams, and John Hancock held a "small, private meeting" at the home of Dr. Joseph Warren. They were planning a revolt.

The tall, blond, and handsome Dr. Joseph Warren was another of Sam Adams's recruits. A young physician who was rapidly achieving a fine reputation, he was a widower and the father of four small children. Described by

Dr. Joseph Warren, a physician and a staunch patriot, worked tirelessly for independence. He was martyred at the Battle of Bunker Hill, where "he fell gloriously fighting for his country." *Oil by John Singleton Copley, 1774.*

Governor Bernard as one of the "chiefs" among Boston's radicals, Warren had long been a foe of rule by a privileged few. His gift for writing propaganda was an asset to the patriots.

In 1766, when he was only twenty-five, he had written a letter to the *Boston Gazette* accusing Governor Bernard of "wantonly sacrificing the happiness of this Province" to his own passions.

Now in 1768, he publicly charged Governor Bernard with "malice" and described him as a man "totally abandoned to wickedness." Perhaps, Warren speculated aloud, if American grievances could not be solved peacefully, then the sword might be the only alternative. Colonists, he declared, were prepared to sacrifice "lives and fortunes" for the cause of American liberty.[11]

Bernard retaliated by asking the Massachusetts House of Representatives to charge Dr. Warren with libel. The House refused, citing "freedom of the press."[12]

But not all the Massachusetts representatives were ready to bear arms. Instead, even as Governor Bernard refused to reconvene the Massachusetts Assembly and let it be known that the four thousand British troops were about to arrive in Boston, some of the representatives pledged obedience to the king and urged fellow colonists "to prevent . . . all tumults and disorders."[13]

When the warships did arrive in Boston Harbor on September 30, 1768, they moved into siege formation and pointed their guns at the town. Paul Revere, angered at the impudence of the British, described the scene: "[They] anchored round the Town; their cannons loaded, a spring on their cables, as for a regular siege. At noon on Saturday, the fourteenth and twenty-ninth regiments and a detachment from the 59th regiment, and a train of artillery landed on Long Wharf; there Formed and Marched with insolent Parade, Drums beating, Fifes playing, up King Street, Each soldier having received sixteen rounds of Powder and Ball."[14]

As they marched, under the command of Lieutenant Colonel William Dalrymple, the red coats of the soldiers and the yellow jackets of the drummers gleamed in the sunlight. The infantrymen wore black, white-laced, three-cornered hats. Their officers' hats were trimmed with silver. The grenadiers,

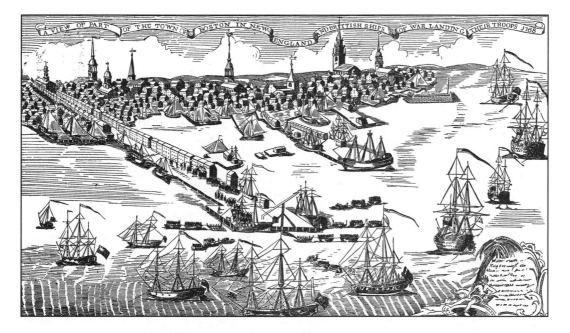

Landing of the British troops at Long Wharf, Boston, on September 30, 1768. Paul Revere watched with mounting anger as the two regiments, with weapons loaded, marched into town. Later, back at his shop, he made an engraving on a sheet of copper of that "insolent Parade," as he called it.

Grenadier of the 29th Foot. Grenadiers, the tallest men in the regiment, seemed even taller in their high, pointed bearskin caps.

the tallest men in the regiment, seemed even taller in their high, pointed bearskin caps. The drummers wore white bearskin caps. All the officers wore crimson sashes over their shoulders and swords on their belts. At Castle William the customs commissioners set off skyrockets and sang choruses of "Yankee Doodle," ridiculing the colonists.*

For the first time, the British army had come to America not to help defend the colonists against the common French and Indian opponents, but to maintain the authority of the mother country against a fractious colony.[15] Governor Bernard described the troops in Boston as a police force "to rescue the Government from the hands of a trained mob and to restore the activity of the Civil power."[16] He hoped that the army would provide peace and security, not bloodshed. Perhaps he didn't recall what Benjamin Franklin had said about soldiers sent to America in his testimony before Parliament almost three years earlier: "They will not find a rebellion; they may indeed make one."[17]

Joseph Warren, Samuel Adams, and other Boston radicals made certain that the soldiers would be as uncomfortable as possible. They would not allow them to be quartered in Boston. They were forced to pitch tents on the Common or sleep on the floor in Faneuil Hall.

*"Yankee Doodle" was originally a British marching tune with words dating back to the Seven Years' War. It was a satiric look at New England's Yankees. "Doodle" meant a foolish fellow, and "macaroni" was slang for a dandy who liked to dress in style. Years later, the Yankees would adopt it to mock the British.

On the next day, Sunday, Governor Bernard arranged to make the Town House, including the room where the House of Representatives usually sat, available for some of the soldiers. The sight and sound of soldiers marching through town on the Sabbath to occupy the seat of government angered the people. Sunday was traditionally a quiet day, with the streets empty except for those walking to church.[18]

Only when General Gage arrived from New York in October and demanded that the town accommodate his men, did the council grudgingly grant the soldiers use of the colony-owned Manufactory House. The British es-

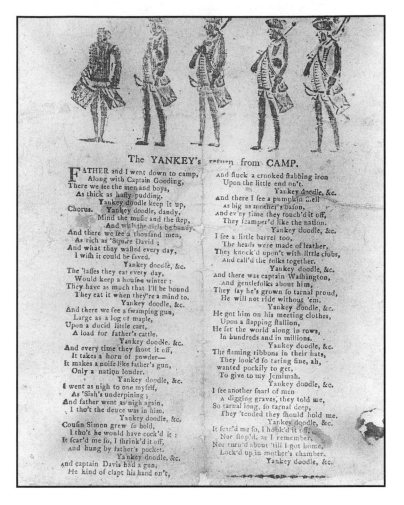

"The Yankees Return from Camp" was a variation on the song originally known as "Yankee Doodle," a mockery by the British troops of the poorly trained colonial militia who had trouble "minding the music and the step." But the defiant Americans adopted the song as their own.

tablished a main guard post opposite the Court House and placed two small cannons there, pointing at the chambers where the assembly was to convene.

By the beginning of the new year, 1769, brawls between the soldiers and citizens became common.

The Massachusetts Assembly, meeting now under its own authority, petitioned Governor Bernard to have the troops withdrawn. He insisted he had no authority to do this. The Assembly, therefore, refused to pay his annual salary.

They then petitioned the king "to remove Sir Francis Bernard forever from the government."[19]

Though this petition probably had no effect in England, Governor Bernard's career in America was coming to a close anyway. The merchants in England, alarmed at the effects of the nonimportation agreements on their businesses, had been agitating for Bernard's removal from office in Massachusetts for some time.

Now Governor Bernard received a letter from Lord Hillsborough in London instructing him to return home to England, ostensibly to help the government with information and advice. But he would never return to the colonies. As a reward for his services, the king would bestow on him the title of Baron. Thomas Hutchinson was named acting governor.

Francis Bernard had no grudge against the colonists, nor had he ever intended to oppress them. He recognized, though, that colonial governments would have to be reformed in order to make them submit to Parliament's authority. He simply didn't have the tact and diplomacy necessary for the task. The people were glad to see him go.[20]

There were thunderstorms over Boston on Monday, the last day of July, and lightning split the masts of two ships in the harbor. In the calm that followed the storm, Governor Bernard was rowed out to the warship *Rippon*, lying at anchor in the harbor, to set sail for England. Here, Bernard was forced to suffer one last humiliation. As he watched from on board ship, the British flag, the Union Jack, was run up the pole at Liberty Tree, banners flew from Hancock's Wharf, church bells rang, and militia cannons boomed. And when the *Rippon* remained becalmed that evening, unable to sail out of Boston Harbor, Bernard could see the great bonfire that had been lit in joyful celebration of his departure. The following Monday's *Boston Gazette* noted that the governor had sailed on the *Rippon*, captain and ship "both worthy of a better cargo."[21]

Shortly after Bernard left, a packet of letters arrived from London. They had been intercepted by colonial agents in England and sent back to Boston. The letters included some from both Governor Bernard and customs commissioners in Boston to the ministry in London. When James Otis learned from this correspondence that he was being accused of treason by the customs commissioners in Boston, he was enraged. To a man who still proclaimed his loyalty to the king, that accusation was intolerable. Both Otis and Samuel Adams felt that the letters, written by Governor Bernard and sent to Lord Hillsborough, were part of a British plot to destroy colonial freedom.

Erratic even at his calmest moments, Otis now resorted to verbal violence. The tension in Boston was taking its toll on him. He attacked the commissioners, particularly John Robinson, in the *Boston Gazette*. He called Robinson a "superlative blockhead," and declared that he had "a natural right . . . to break his head." He was certain that Commissioner Robinson, characterized by others as "gentle and reasonable," was responsible for the slur on his character.[22]

Over the past year, John Adams had been watching James Otis's gradual mental deterioration. Otis had been his hero, and now he saw his friend's foibles become eccentricities, and his eccentricities become madness. Adams was so distressed by what he was witnessing that when Joseph Warren entreated him to harangue a town meeting to stir up partisanship, Adams refused. "That way madness lies," he replied, referring to the madness of James Otis *and* the madness of mob violence.

John Adams was witness to yet another example of Otis's instability when the two attended a meeting on Monday evening, September 4 (the day the *Boston Gazette* article appeared in print). He described Otis's behavior at that meeting as "one continued Scene of bullying, bantering, reproaching and ridiculing" even his friends. "There is no Politeness nor Delicacy, no Learning nor Ingenuity, no Taste or Sense in this Kind of Conversation," Adams continued sadly.[23]

The next day Otis's wildness turned to violence.

On learning that Robinson had purchased a walking stick, the unpredictable Otis immediately purchased "the fellow of it." Then, carrying his new cane, he marched into the British Coffee House, a favorite haunt of the British officers and customs officials, and known as a Tory hangout. Shortly thereafter, Robinson appeared.

"I demand satisfaction of you, Sir," Otis roared.

"What satisfaction would you have?" Robinson asked.

"A gentleman's satisfaction," came the reply. Gentlemen could fight only with their fists. Dueling with swords was against the law.

"I am ready to do it."

But as they moved toward the door, Robinson suddenly reached out to grab Otis's nose. Nose tweaking was considered an insulting, pain-inflicting, yet nonfatal way of expressing contempt. Otis blocked Robinson with his cane. Robinson raised his, and soon they were dueling with their canes. Onlookers quickly took away their sticks, and the two went at each other with their fists.

In the brawl that ensued, the commissioner's friends pinned Otis down, and someone landed a blow on his head that opened a one-and-a-half-inch gash down to the bone in his forehead. When John Gridley, the nephew of lawyer Jeremiah Gridley, passed by the coffeehouse and heard the commotion, he entered and tried to help Otis. In the process he had his arm broken. Still Robinson wasn't finished. Other friends held Otis while Robinson punched him in the face. Finally Otis and Robinson were separated, and Otis went home to have his wounds treated.[24]

Painful as the attack had been for Otis, he was not in physical danger. Two weeks later John Adams found him more subdued and cheerful than he had been.

Otis remained calm for a few months. But by the beginning of the new year his symptoms of madness were becoming more pronounced. John Adams wrote of this man who he considered the single most important influence on himself as a political figure: "Otis is in Confusion yet. He looses [*sic*] himself. He rambles and wanders like a ship without an Helm. I fear he is not in his perfect Mind. . . . I fear, I tremble, I mourn for the Man, and for his Country."[25]

Boston's affections remained with Otis.

Chapter XIII

A study in contrasts

London: 1770

King George was certain that Lord North was the minister for whom he had been searching since the resignation of Lord Bute. North had great skill as a party manager. He could smooth over personal differences between party members, and he kept the king's followers in Parliament contented.

North's moral character, his upright personality, his wit and good humor, and his solid intellectual abilities commanded increasing respect in the Commons. His skill in handling the nation's financial business was second to none.

He himself had only a small estate with which to support a large and growing family, and he was seldom free from financial worry. Yet he was not corrupt. As first lord of the Treasury, he had vast amounts of public money passing through his hands, but even his enemies never accused him of pocketing any of these funds. He won the reputation of being an able and diligent man of business, one who could be trusted, and one who commanded the confidence of both the king and the House of Commons.[1]

Often, bored with the typically long debates that took place in the Commons, North would tilt his large head back on his seat and doze off while the speaker droned on—frequently for hours. On one occasion, when George Grenville embarked on a lengthy speech on finance, North said to a neighbor, "Wake me up when he gets to modern times." When his neighbor eventually nudged him, North listened for a few minutes, then said loudly, "Zounds! You have waked me a hundred years too soon!"

Another time, North closed his eyes while a member of the opposition was speaking. When the speaker complained that the prime minister was asleep, North, in a stage whisper, murmured, "Would to God I were!"[2]

Just over a month after becoming prime minister, on March 5, 1770, North moved in the House of Commons to repeal the Townshend duties—all, that is, except the tax on tea.

"I am clear that there must always be one tax to keep up the right [to tax the colonies], and as such I approve of the Tea Duty," the king wrote to North.[3]

Lord North, ever loyal to the king, would do as his sovereign requested. He would repeal those duties that were hurting English exports—on paper, paint, lead, and glass—and retain the one that did not.

"The properest time to exert our right to taxation is when the right is refused. . . . A total repeal cannot be thought of till America is prostrate at our feet," North explained.

The eloquent Isaac Barré continued to champion the Americans in Parliament. Now he challenged North: "Does any friend to his country really wish to see America thus humbled? In such a situation, she would serve only as a monument of your arrogance and your folly. For my part, the America I wish to see is America increasing and prospering, raising her head in graceful dignity. . . . This is the America that will have spirit to fight your battles, . . . and by her industry will be able to consume your manufactures, support your trade, and pour wealth and splendour into your towns and cities. If we do not change our conduct towards her, America will be torn from our side."[4]

There were those in Parliament who believed that had Pitt still been at the head of the government, his vote and his influence would have carried repeal of *all* the duties. But now, despite Barré's impassioned plea, the tax on tea remained.

North's strength was his total loyalty to the king. But it was also his weakness. He rarely challenged the king's decisions, particularly concerning the American colonies. The king set the policy. North carried it out. He considered himself simply an agent for the king.

The same lethargy evidenced by North's rotund body invaded his mind. He was content to accept the ideas, opinions, and decisions of his king. George III's obstinacy and strongly held opinions were as necessary to Lord North as North's ease and kindness were to his king.[5]

Both Lord North and King George were virtuous husbands and devoted fathers. They spent much time together. Their attitudes were instinctively the same. They scheduled long, private talks four or five times a week. King George enjoyed these talks as he had never enjoyed the time he was required to spend with Pitt, Grenville, or Rockingham. In contrast to those men, North was a blessing—intelligent, affable, amusing, and never forgetful of the difference between sovereign and prime minister.[6]

King George and Lord North were both products of a London composed of royalty, members of Parliament, artists, writers, and scientists.

But the city of London was in actuality a study in contrasts: between wealth and poverty; between splendor and squalor; between continuity and rapid change. A stroll along the Thames could take one past elegant riverside palaces adjacent to pockets of extreme poverty and ugliness. Violence, born of despair and greed, was common among the poor, who lived in desperately overcrowded and filthy dwellings where the stench was often unbearable.

Frequently, when the citizens opposed the king or Parliament, they would band together in vast, unruly mobs and take to the streets in riotous protests. The government was particularly concerned because often these protesters included well-informed, educated citizens.

Londoners' reactions to political events depended very much upon the degree to which their lives were affected by them. City merchants tended to side with the American colonists when they believed that the government was mismanaging national and city interests. Radical Londoners supported the colonists as loyal but ill-treated subjects.[7]

Upper-class Englishmen like King George and Lord North detested what they heard about American mobs, but the colonists had learned these violent acts from the mobs of England herself.

Chapter XIV

"Town born, turn out!"

The American Colonies: 1770

The young Virginia burgess Thomas Jefferson felt vaguely dissatisfied. Word had just arrived from England that, except for the tax on tea, the Townshend duties would be removed. No further taxes would be levied against the Americans for the purpose of raising revenues.

In Jefferson's opinion, nothing had been settled. He considered the tax on tea an affront to the American principle, and the main issue with Parliament no closer to resolution than at the start of the controversy. He considered himself a loyal subject of the king, but he was firm in his belief in colonial rights. He was not alone. Many colonists shared his view.

In January of 1769, Benjamin Franklin had written to a friend, "I am glad to hear that Matters were yet quiet at Boston, but fear they will not continue long so. Some Indiscretion on the part of the warmer People, or of the Soldiery, I am extremely apprehensive may occasion a Tumult; and if Blood is once drawn, there is no foreseeing how far the Mischief may spread."[1] Franklin's premonition took just over a year to become reality.

With the suspension of the Townshend duties, the nonimportation agreement was scheduled to end officially on New Year's Day, 1770. In Boston, cargo had been arriving from London for several months, and patriots and Tories alike there had been secretly buying the goods and selling them. Among these people was Acting Governor Thomas Hutchinson. Hutchinson had stored a great deal of tea in anticipation of being allowed to sell it openly. He had made arrangements to import the tea through letters he had written to London in code.

When the first of January arrived, Hutchinson and his two sons, Thomas Jr., thirty, and Elisha, twenty-five, were eager to begin selling the tea legally and earn a profit. But Sam Adams was anxious to punish those who had been purchasing tea illegally. He therefore insisted that nothing should go on sale before the time it took for a ship to sail to London and back.

The Hutchinsons rejected these new restrictions. They moved their tea to a hiding place.

Faced with this defiance, Samuel Adams arranged a mass meeting at Faneuil Hall. There the patriots voted unanimously to order the merchants to obey the extension. The merchants refused.

Knowing full well that to defy Thomas Hutchinson was to defy the king (Hutchinson was serving as acting governor since Bernard left and, as such, represented the king), the patriots decided to go as a delegation to appeal to Hutchinson. Sam Adams and James Otis led the group. One thousand men and boys followed them to Hutchinson's house in the North End of Boston.

Hutchinson appeared at the window. "It is not you, but your sons we desire to see," he was told.

One of the sons came to stand by his father. Hutchinson asked the crowd to leave. No one moved. He warned them that this was an illegal assembly: "Gentlemen, when I was attacked before [when his house was destroyed four and a half years earlier], I was a private person. I am now the representative of the greatest monarch on earth, whose majesty you affront in thus treating my person."

The delegation dispersed quietly.

Later, some of Hutchinson's fellow Tories persuaded him to give in. The next morning he sent word to Faneuil Hall that his sons would turn over their tea and would also turn over any money they had received from tea already sold. Thomas Hutchinson later called it the bitterest moment of his political life. Even the destruction of his house, he said, had not distressed him as much.[2]

Still, many other merchants were ignoring the nonimportation agreement, and tension between the rebels and the Loyalists continued to grow.

On Thursday, February 22, 1770, a gang of boys set up a wooden board with a large hand painted on it, beneath which was the word IMPORTER. The hand pointed to the house of a merchant who continued to do business with England.

Ebenezer Richardson, who had been an informer for the customs service since 1766 and who lived nearby, tried to take the sign down. The boys pelted him with dirt, sticks, and stones.

Richardson ran home, then came out of his house "in a great rage, doubling his fists," and shouted at some Sons of Liberty who had gathered, "I'll make it too hot for you before tonight."

Richardson continued to shout at the boys, then swore that if they did not leave he would "make a lane" through them.

One of the men picked up a brick and heaved it through a window. As at a signal, the boys surrounded the house completely. Sticks, stones, and eggs began to fly. More windows were broken. In the process, a rock that went through a window struck Richardson's wife, while others whizzed past his two daughters. An enraged Richardson ran upstairs, took his musket, and appeared with it at a window. No one thought he would shoot.

In the street, eleven-year-old Christopher Seider, the son of a poor German immigrant, stood idly watching. As he bent to pick up a stone, Richardson fired. A cluster of small pellets tore into the boy's chest. Eight hours later, in spite of Dr. Warren's best efforts, Christopher died. Another boy, a nineteen-year-old, was also hit in his right hand, damaging two fingers.[3]

On the following Monday, February 26, as John Adams was riding into Boston from Weymouth, his wife's birthplace, on streets still covered with snow from a heavy snowstorm two days before, he saw an extraordinary sight: a "vast Collection of People, near Liberty Tree." When he inquired, he learned it was "the funeral of the Child, lately killed by Richardson." "My eyes never beheld such a funeral," he continued. "The Procession extended further than can be well imagined."

Between four and five hundred schoolboys walking two by two preceded the coffin, which was carried by six boys. Behind them came Christopher's family and friends and two thousand mourners. They marched together in silence, except for the tolling of bells. Thirty chariots and chaises closed the procession, which extended from the Liberty Tree to the Town House—well over half a mile—then up the hill to the Old Granary burial ground, where Christopher was laid to rest.

"This Shewes [sic]," John Adams wrote of it, "that the Ardor of the People is not to be quelled by the Slaughter of one Child and the Wounding of another."

The funeral, the largest ever known in America, had been staged by Sam Adams.

Ebenezer Richardson was tried and found guilty of murder, but he was pardoned by the king. And young Christopher Seider became a martyr for freedom. Attacks on the importers' houses continued in "the dead of night." Some eventually moved away; others slept with a loaded gun by their bedside.[4]

The Christopher Seider murder was but a dramatic prelude to an episode of far greater significance.

In Boston, the soldiers in their bright red uniforms were a daily reminder to the citizens of the power of Great Britain. The clomp of heavy boots on the cobblestones, the beat of the drums, the sound of the fifes, stirred the bitter resentment and even contempt of the citizens. There were incidents almost daily: a soldier cursed by a townsman, or hooted and jeered at; a citizen shoved roughly aside by a soldier; a rock hurled by a daring young apprentice.

John Adams, who had moved from Braintree to Boston with his family, listened regularly to the drilling of the Fourteenth Regiment in Brattle Square, directly in front of his house. The "spirit-stirring Drum, and the Ear-piercing fife" woke them at dawn every day.

"Their very Appearance in Boston was a strong proof to me, that the determination in Great Britain to subjugate Us, was too deep and inveterate ever to be altered by Us: For every thing We could do, was misrepresent[ed], and Nothing We could say was credited," he wrote. "The danger I was in appeared in full View before me."[5]

James Otis complained that "the stench occasioned by the troops in the representatives' chamber might prove infectious," and he therefore recommended that the legislature move to a different location. He also stated that it was "utterly derogatory to the court to administer justice at the points of bayonets and the mouths of cannon."[6]

When some of the soldiers, cold and miserable in their tents on the Common in the middle of a Boston winter, solved the problem by deserting, Lieutenant Colonel Dalrymple offered a reward to any soldier who would identify someone urging him to defect. When a soldier was caught and shot on the Common as a warning to others, Bostonians were horrified. But soon, public lashings of soldiers with a cat-o'-nine-tails became a regular sight.[7]

Sam Adams began writing reports of incidents between soldiers and civilians for publication in some of the other colonies under the title "Journal of the Times."[8]

By now, everyone—the radicals, the Loyalists, and even the military—realized that it had been a mistake to send troops to Boston. General Gage summarized the situation:

> "The People were as Lawless and Licentious after the Troops arrived, as they were before. The Troops could not act by Military Authority, and no Person in Civil Authority would ask their aid. They were there contrary

to the wishes of the Council, Assembly, Magistrates and People, and seemed only offered to abuse and ruin. And the Soldiers were either to suffer ill usage and even assaults upon their Persons till their Lives were in Danger, or by resisting and defending themselves, to run almost a Certainty of suffering by the Law." [9]

Boston was ready to explode.

At noon on Friday, March 2, 1770, William Green was working outdoors with a group of men who were braiding hemp at John Gray's ropewalk (a rope-making factory). Gray frequently hired unskilled workers by the day, and often soldiers who wanted to supplement their meager pay would come there during their off-duty hours. But work in Boston was scarce, and Bostonians resented the competition.

Now, as Patrick Walker of the Twenty-ninth Regiment approached, Green called out to him, "Soldier, do you want work?"

"Yes, I do, faith," said Walker.

"Well," said Green, "then go and clean my shithouse."

"Empty it yourself," Walker retorted.

After a few curses, Walker swore "by the Holy Ghost" that he would have revenge, all the while swinging his fists wildly at the rope makers. In the scuffle, his cutlass dropped from under his coat. Humiliated and disarmed, the soldier fled.

But that was not to be the end of it. Soon Walker returned with reinforcements. He had eight or nine soldiers with him. The rope makers were ready for them with wooden clubs. They beat up the soldiers and threw them off the premises.

The next day, Saturday, another group of soldiers and rope makers tangled. The fighting was fierce. This time a private of the Twenty-ninth Regiment wound up with a fractured skull and a broken arm. The two sides remained quiet on Sunday, March 4, in observance of the Sabbath. But many were predicting trouble.

A maid to Thomas Hutchinson's sister spent Sunday evening with some of the rope-walk brawlers. Afterward, she informed her mistress that there would be a battle Monday evening between the inhabitants and the troops, and that bells would ring. Unfortunately, Hutchinson's sister neglected to tell her brother until it was too late.

The night of March 5 was bitter cold, but clear. Several inches of snow had fallen early in the day, but now the snow had stopped and a thin layer of ice covered King Street. Boston had no street lamps, but a young quarter moon shone in a cloudless sky and reflected on the snow.

The evening began quietly, but small clusters of people could be seen all over Boston: groups of club-carrying townsmen as well as "parties of soldiers . . . as if the one, and the other, had something more than ordinary upon their minds."

At the corner of King Street, Private Hugh White of the Twenty-ninth Regiment kept his solitary post near a sentry box. The captain of the day, Thomas Preston, a forty-year-old Irish officer whom even the radicals called "a sober, honest man, and a good officer," was quietly eating a late dinner at his quarters nearby. Preston was a musician who had frequently performed at Governor Bernard's amateur musicales.

The lone sentry box was just a few feet from the corner of the Customs House, an important building that held all the customs records and all the money that was collected as duties.

Edward Garrick, a young apprentice to a wig maker, came along and began to taunt the sentry. Words were exchanged. Finally, Private White left his post and walked into the street as young Garrick moved toward him.

"Let me see your face," White said.

"I am not ashamed to show my face," the apprentice answered.

Without another word, White swung his musket, striking the side of Garrick's head. Reeling and staggering, the boy cried out in pain.

The ruckus attracted some people. A group of Garrick's young friends began shouting at White and daring him to fight. Knowing that British law forbade the soldiers to fire their weapons without permission of the governor, some of the "townies" were growing more and more aggressive.

"Damned rascally scoundrel lobster! Bloody back!" they shouted as an insulting reference to the soldiers' red uniforms.

More people appeared.

The crowd was increasing and turning into an angry mob. They began pelting Private White with icy snowballs. The frightened soldier retreated to the steps of the Customs House, where he had the advantage of being slightly above the crowd and had a protected rear. He loaded his musket.

As chunks of ice, heavy and sharp-edged, continued to crash around him, he tried to get into the Customs House, but the door was locked.

Now the crowd was shouting, "Kill him, kill him, knock him down. Fire, damn you, fire, you dare not fire."

The town watchman, who had arrived on the scene, tried to reassure White. These are only boys, he told him. They wouldn't hurt him.

Unconvinced, White yelled for help: "Turn out, Main Guard!"

Suddenly, a church bell began to peal. Men began shouting, "Fire!"

During the day, bells might ring for joy or for mourning. But at night, an off-hour church bell meant only one thing: the signal of a fire. Bostonians reacted instinctively. Boston had no fire department, and in this city of wooden houses, the danger of a spreading fire was great. When a church bell sounded the alarm, Bostonians en masse hurried to the site carrying leather bags filled with water and pumps mounted on wheels that they called fire engines.

At the same time that this was happening, broader and more violent confrontations between townspeople and soldiers were taking place throughout the city. There was much noise and confusion. In nearby Dock Square, a crowd of about two hundred had gathered. Wielding heavy clubs and staves of wood, people jammed into the square. Some men broke into the market stalls and broke legs off tables to use as weapons. The shout of "Fire!" was heard repeatedly.

"It is very odd to come to put out a fire with sticks and bludgeons," a man remarked to his companion.

A mysterious stranger, never identified but always described as a "tall large man in a red cloak [like the characteristically stained and shabby one Sam Adams was known to wear on cold nights] and white wig," was heard addressing a crowd gathered around him in Dock Square. Onlookers could not hear what he said, nor did they appear to know who he was. When he finished speaking, there was a cheer and a cry, "To the Main Guard!" [10]

Now, like a magnet, the bells seemed to be drawing men and boys to King Street. Up and down the street they were shouting loudly for additional men to join in an attack on the Main Guard. The cry, "Town born, turn out! Town born, turn out!" was heard.

Captain Preston, having seen what was happening and having heard Private White's cry for help, was deciding what to do. Known for his coolness, he now "walked up and down facing the Guard House for nearly half an hour." The crowd had become so large and angry, and so well armed, that no one could expect the sight of the handful of redcoats Preston had available to frighten it into order. Further, he—and the mob—knew that troops could not be used to quiet civil disturbances.

White's safety was uppermost in his mind. But Preston knew all too well that his superiors might not feel the same way. In England—and in Boston—"soldiers, like slaves, were only with difficulty remembered as human beings." [11]

Now Preston led a group of soldiers, in a column of twos, down and across King Street, their muskets shouldered, empty but with fixed bayonets. As they reached the crowd, they brought their muskets down so the bayonets would prick any of the crowd who pressed too close. Then they continued to the sentry box, halted, and began to load their muskets.

Preston ordered White to fall in. Then he tried to march the group back to the Main Guard. The crowd pressed in closer. There was no way the soldiers could move without using force.

"Damn you, fire!" someone shouted at the motionless Redcoats. "You can't kill us all."

The soldiers, by now, were in a single line, forming a semicircle, with Preston in front. Preston shouted at the crowd to go home. He received more ice balls and curses in reply. Crowd pressure continued to build. The soldiers were trembling, whether from fear or rage cannot be said. Men dared them to fire, called them cowardly rascals, and challenged them to put down their weapons and fight.

A gentleman in the crowd approached Preston: "I hope you don't intend the soldiers shall fire on the inhabitants," he said.

"By no means," Preston answered. He was standing in front of the musket muzzles himself, he pointed out. Further, "My giving the word fire, under those circumstances, would prove me no officer."

Suddenly, someone hurled a club, hitting a soldier. The soldier lost his footing on the ice and fell. Then, as he rose, in rage and in pain, he roared, "Damn you, fire!" and pulled the trigger on his own musket.

Now other soldiers aimed into the mob and fired. Three people were killed instantly, eight more were wounded, two of whom later died. Only one of them had taken part in the actual fracas. He was Crispus Attucks, an exceptionally tall former slave who, brandishing a stick of cordwood about the thickness of a man's wrist, had faced the soldiers and dared them to fight. The rest were bystanders or those who had come at the sound of the bells to learn the cause of the tumult. Three of the dead were just seventeen years old.

Even after the bodies lay in the street, people didn't seem to realize that men had been killed. "I thought," someone said later, "they had been scared and run away, and left their greatcoats behind them."

Since Boston had neither a hospital nor a mortuary, the dead and wounded were taken to various impromptu dressing stations. One boy was carried home to die in his widowed mother's arms.

Within minutes, all that remained as evidence was their crimson blood stark against the white snow, a chilling reminder of the wasted lives.

Sam Adams would call the dead "murdered martyrs to British oppression." He and James Warren quickly spread word of the "Boston Massacre" to the other colonies and arranged to have March 5 set aside as an annual day of mourning, complete with bell tolling, lighted picture displays, and speeches.[12]

This engraving by Paul Revere of the Boston Massacre shows British Captain Preston ordering his soldiers to fire on the defenseless colonists. Hardly a detail is correct.

A few days later, Henry Pelham, talented half brother to the painter John Singleton Copley, prepared a crude but dramatic drawing of the scene on King Street from which Paul Revere made an engraving. Without bothering to ask permission of Pelham, Revere turned out hundreds of hand-colored prints (with a heavy emphasis on vivid reds) that showed Preston, his sword raised, ordering the soldiers to fire on the defenseless citizens. Hardly a detail in the picture is correct. But the engraving helped to fix in the public mind the patriots' version of what had happened.[13]

Chapter XV

"Wilkes and Liberty!"

London: 1757–1774

One of the most charming rascals in Georgian England unwittingly came to the aid of the colonies.

John Wilkes, a member of Parliament, was a wildly extravagant, foul-mouthed but brilliant and witty satirist who hungered for glamour, publicity, and fame. Though tall and muscular, Wilkes had a twisted jaw, a flattened nose, and an incurable squint that made him unusually ugly. "It takes me half an hour to talk away my face," he said of himself. With a quick eye for a weakness in others, his cutting tongue could immediately find expression in a savage phrase.[1]

Soon after his election to Parliament in 1757, Wilkes had become a loyal supporter of William Pitt and championed Pitt's uncompromising stand against France during the Seven Years' War. Pitt called him "the most wicked and agreeable fellow" he had ever met.

Wilkes and the earl of Bute had also been friends and members of the Hell Fire Club, where they and the other members gambled heavily and drank a great deal. When George III had named Bute his prime minister, Bute had put one member of the club, the earl of Sandwich, in charge of the Navy. But he had not given Wilkes, a champion of Pitt, a place in the government. Wilkes was furious.

A radical pamphleteer, newspaper editor, and writer, Wilkes now retaliated by starting his own notorious weekly newspaper, the *North Briton*, on June 5, 1762. In its pages, he consistently attacked the government and all things Scottish, including Lord Bute. It was his hatred of Bute's ideas of government and foreign policy, and Bute's ousting of Pitt in 1762, that had originally led Wilkes to launch the *North Briton* (a sly reference to Scotland, north of England, and so to the Scotsman Bute). When Bute resigned, Wilkes transferred his hostility to George Grenville and his followers, and depicted them as mere tools of Bute.

John Wilkes, a popular hero and martyr, was the idol of a London seething with discontent. His newspaper, *The North Briton, Number 45*, became a powerful symbol for radical reform of government. *By Richard Earlom.*

On April 23, 1763, Wilkes struck directly at the king. Through Pitt, he had obtained a preview of George III's "Speech from the Throne," to be delivered at the opening of Parliament. In it, the king had stated that Frederick II of Prussia was delighted with the Treaty of Paris, the agreement negotiated to end the Seven Years' War. Wilkes claimed that this was not true, and in the *North Briton, Number 45*, issued on that day, he accused the king and Bute (who probably wrote the speech) of having lied, and Bute of having bribed the House of Commons to ratify the peace treaty. And he ferociously denounced the Treaty of Paris. Wilkes even went so far as to hope that the king would not profane St. Paul's Cathedral by attending a thanksgiving service there, and recommended he stay in his own chapel.

King George was so enraged that he had Wilkes arrested for seditious libel in spite of the fact that, as a member of Parliament, Wilkes should have been immune to arrest. Then, while Wilkes was imprisoned in the Tower of London, his house was ransacked and his papers were removed.

Wilkes's arrest came at the time that the new young king had first decided that he must choose his advisers from among men he liked and trusted from *any* party. A widespread dismissal of Whigs from government office by Bute convinced many Britons—and Americans—that King George and Bute had taken over control of the government. It seemed clear to them that constitutional liberties were endangered.

No one doubted that Wilkes was guilty. But he was a member of Parliament, and there were doubts concerning the legality of his arrest. According to well-established privileges of the House of Commons, a member of Parliament could not be arrested except in cases of treason, felony, or actual breach of the peace.

Wilkes fought back furiously from prison, publicizing every action he took and distorting every rash act of the government as an act of calculated tyranny. A legal battle over freedom of the press ensued. Wilkes warned that "the liberty of communicating our sentiments to the public freely and honestly shall not be tamely given up."

Wilkes claimed that he had been wrongfully arrested, then went so far as to sue the secretary of state for damage done to his property during the search.[2] His friends secured a hearing of his case, and he was released from prison pending a trial.

Now he demanded the return of papers that had been taken when his home was searched. When the government refused, he took the ministers to court. The lord chief justice awarded him the case and imposed damages on the government of one thousand pounds. The judge also ruled that a member of Parliament could not be arrested for libel. Wilkes's triumph was acclaimed as a victory for English law and for the liberty of the individual. His standing as a radical hero was ensured. Thousands escorted him home from prison with the cry "Wilkes and liberty!"

George III was furious.

A former friend of Wilkes, turned enemy, now produced a copy of an indecent poem that had been found in Wilkes's papers, called *An Essay on Women*. Wilkes had written it for the amusement of his friends and had printed it on his private press. Appended to it were notes attributing it to a bishop. When it was read aloud to the House with great relish by the earl of Sandwich, the government began a criminal investigation. Wilkes knew he was in trouble. The courts declared the essay an obscene piece of pornography, charged Wilkes with blasphemy, and ordered his arrest.

Wilkes fled to Paris. Hoping for a pardon, he remained there for four years, enjoying the good food, good wine, brilliant conversation, and ardent women. During this time he was supported by some of his friends, including the marquess of Rockingham.[3]

While in Paris, when the French king's mistress, Madame de Pompadour, asked him, "How far does freedom of the Press extend in England?" Wilkes replied, "That, Madame, is what I am trying to find out." [4]

When he failed to return to London, he was expelled from Parliament and declared an outlaw.

Early in 1768, fearful that he would be forgotten if he remained abroad any longer, Wilkes decided to return to England. Not concerned that he had been outlawed in England and found guilty of blasphemy, and knowing full well that he would have to face his punishment, yet jaunty as ever, Wilkes went home. He even sent his footman to the palace with a letter to the king asking for a formal pardon. The king indignantly spurned the message, but he did not order Wilkes's arrest.

A new election to the House of Commons was approaching, and Wilkes decided to run for a seat. To the astonishment of all, he was elected by the radical constituency of Middlesex, a few miles outside London, in spite of the fact that he owned no property there. There were scenes of wild enthusiasm and excitement. Even the king's young son and heir to the throne used Wilkes and his infamous newspaper to upset his father. He climaxed a family quarrel by shouting, "Wilkes and *Number 45* forever!" as he dashed out of the room.

Benjamin Franklin, in England at the time, wrote, "It is really an extraordinary event to see an outlaw and exile, of bad personal character, not worth a farthing . . . immediately carrying [the election] for the principal county." [5]

Wilkes was truly "a showman who could bridge to a wide audience." [6]

On April 20, 1768, once again a member of Parliament, Wilkes surrendered himself to receive his sentence. He was fined one thousand pounds and sentenced to twenty-two months' imprisonment.

In his speech to the court at his sentencing, Wilkes declared his *Number 45* "a paper that the author ought to glory in." King George was horrified. Five days later the king wrote to Lord North that Mr. Wilkes must be expelled from Parliament. How could a man convicted of libel and blasphemy be allowed to sit in the House of Commons? he asked.

Though this was a questionable action for the king to take (it may even have been unconstitutional), Lord North, ever dutiful, complied with the king's wishes and expelled him.[7]

Wilkes was speaking the language of liberty, and he captured the imagination of the public. He became a popular hero and a martyr, the idol of a London already seething with discontent.

The new American embargo on British goods in response to the Townshend Acts was in effect, causing workers to lose their jobs when merchants couldn't sell their goods in the colonies. The beginnings of the Industrial Revolution were crowding laborers into factories with miserable working conditions. Unemployment and lawlessness were on the rise, and poverty was becoming more and more common. Worsening relations with America, with the resulting loss of American demand for British goods, were steadily increasing the unpopularity of the British government. People were worried about the growing power of the king. They saw some of their most fundamental liberties being threatened.

In this setting, Wilkes's image as a folk hero was born. *Wilkes* and *Liberty* became synonymous. And the number *forty-five*, the volume of the newspaper that had angered the king, became a powerful symbol for radical reform of government.

Across the ocean in the colonies, too, Wilkes was seen as a hero. He was fighting against general search warrants, which the colonists had also fought, in the form of writs of assistance. He had defended the sanctity of private property against seizure by the government. His cause was becoming the colonists' cause. Toasts were drunk to him up and down the Atlantic seaboard.

While in jail, Wilkes received a supply of tobacco from Virginia patriots, and the South Carolina Assembly voted to contribute a sum of fifteen hundred pounds to an organization in England that was backing Wilkes. From Boston, the Sons of Liberty wrote letters to him, to which Samuel Adams affixed his signature. Wilkes served his term in relative luxury.[8]

On the opening day of the new Parliament, January 9, 1770, members were astonished to see William Pitt, earl of Chatham, hobble into the House of Lords. He had not attended a session in three years. But he had

This caricature of John Wilkes was drawn by William Hogarth, who was the first British artist to become a social critic. Here he depicts Wilkes with his wig just slightly curled back into the horns of a devil, and his squint exaggerated just enough to turn his grin into the leer of a cynic. Wilkes twirls the cap of liberty on its pole, a laughing man who, according to Hogarth, would exploit the very people he seduced. *Circa 1763.*

recovered sufficiently to resume some of his political activities. Now he had a message for Parliament.

He was concerned about the discontent of the people in America, he told the members. Parliament should be cautious how they invade the liberties of *any* of their fellow subjects. Liberty was a plant that deserved to be cherished. He loved the tree, he told them, and wished well to every branch of it.

And right here in London, he rebuked them, the House of Commons had illegally deprived an elected member of his seat. Pitt was not concerned with Wilkes as a person: "I am neither moved by his private vices nor by his public merits. . . . [But] God forbid, my lords, that there should be a power in this country of measuring the civil rights of a subject by his moral character, or by any other rule but the fixed laws of the land." Once again, Pitt was warning against the abuse of royal power.[9]

While he was speaking, a crowd had assembled outside the House of Lords, "clamouring for Wilkes and Liberty." Another mob attempted to break open the King's Bench prison and rescue Wilkes. Troops were summoned, fighting took place, and a man was killed. The London mob was rioting for more than just Wilkes and liberty. Out of work and starving, they were rioting, as well, for better working and living conditions.

George III never understood this. He never recognized the extreme economic distress of the London poor. His duty, as he saw it, was not to alleviate their distress, but simply to restore law and order.

The king ignored Pitt's message to Parliament. On February 3, 1769, Wilkes was once again expelled from the House of Commons. He immediately announced that he would run again in the next election. On February 16, he was again elected for Middlesex, and the next day expelled again. Then came yet another election and another expulsion. This might have gone on indefinitely, but in April the Ministry promised support to a member of Parliament named Henry Luttrell, and another election was held. Luttrell received only two hundred and ninety-six votes; Wilkes, one thousand one hundred and forty-three. The Commons declared Luttrell a member of Parliament for Middlesex.

Parliament had infringed on the privileges of the freeholders of Middlesex and, by implication, on those of every elector in the country. If the Commons had the right to exclude any member who had given offense, it would effectively put an end to representative government.[10]

When Wilkes was deprived of his seat in Parliament after being duly re-elected by the voters of Middlesex County, colonists in America saw it as a denial of the right of the electors to have a representative of their own choosing seated in Parliament. It focused on principles near to the colonists' own experiences. To Americans as well as Englishmen, Wilkes came to personify Liberty. Colonists saw in Wilkes a champion of their own cause. In fact, many believed that the fate of Wilkes and America must stand, or fall, together. Not only had Wilkes, by his actions and his legal battles, confirmed important liberties, but he had brought Parliament into great disrepute, demonstrating its corruption and prejudice. Worsening relations with America were steadily increasing the unpopularity of the British government both in England and the colonies.

And through it all, the press had been deliberately and carefully exploited. The newspaper-reading public was rapidly expanding, thereby increasing public awareness in the provinces outside of London. Improved communications enabled London newspapers to be reprinted in Liverpool and other English cities within two days. London newspapers were also rushed to ships departing for Boston, New York, Philadelphia, and Charleston, where they were rapidly reprinted in colonial newspapers. Organized public opinion had become a factor in politics.[11]

Wilkes was released from prison on April 18, 1770, and April 18 became an annual day of celebration.[12]

Benjamin Franklin observed that for fifteen miles outside of London "there was scarce a door or window-shutter next the road unmarked with 'Wilkes and Liberty.'"[13]

Soon after, Wilkes was elected to the legislature of the city of London, where the king could not interfere. In 1771 he launched a successful campaign for greater freedom of the press, more open government, and the exercise of greater popular influence over the actions of politicians. He extended the range of civil liberties and liberalized the municipal constitution.

At the next general election, in 1774, Wilkes was triumphantly elected to Parliament once again. A dozen colleagues went with him, members of the new political party, the Wilkites. Their platform was "to redress grievances and secure the popular rights in Great Britain, Ireland, and America."

The storm over abuses of executive power that Wilkes created was one more episode that made American patriot leaders place sinister interpretations on every move made by the British government and its agents in America.* [14]

*Wilkes's name, and that of Isaac Barré, are remembered in the Pennsylvania city of Wilkes-Barre.

Chapter XVI

"My honour . . . my country"

Boston: 1770

John Adams longed to do something that would "surprize the world." From the time he had graduated from Harvard College in 1755 and decided to study law, he had been driving himself relentlessly to become "a lawyer of distinguished Genius, Learning and Virtue."[1]

There were no law schools then, so young men interested in pursuing a career in this field "read" the law, usually studying under the direction of an established attorney. John had been fortunate in that Jeremiah Gridley had been sufficiently impressed with his scholarship to agree to sponsor him as a lawyer. John had read books on many subjects and had already read Coke's *Institutes*, the great law book that records some five hundred years of English law, as well as the new publication, Blackstone's *Analysis of the Laws of England*. John was content with nothing less than perfection in himself.

It hadn't always been that way.

When he was growing up, he had not been interested in books. He much preferred to run barefoot around town with his noisy pack of friends, particularly his closest friend, a minister's son named John Hancock, who was a year younger than he.

In fact, when his father first asked him what he would like to do, his instant response had been, "Be a farmer." But his father had insisted he go to school, and by the time he reached the age of sixteen, the young farm boy had discovered the joy of learning, and recognized his own extraordinary capacity for plain hard work. But he never lost his love of the land.[2]

Now, at the age of thirty-three, he was already known in Boston as a person given to expressing himself bluntly and colorfully. He was considered "likely to make a shining figure at the bar."

"He has a large practice, and I am mistaken if he will not soon be at the head of his profession," a prominent Boston minister said of him.[3]

Five years earlier, John had distinguished himself with his "Braintree Instructions," a legal-style brief denouncing the Stamp Act and defending the town meeting's noncompliance with it. In one remarkable paragraph, he had proclaimed Braintree's "rights and liberties . . . that the world may know . . . that we never can be slaves."[4] And he had been appointed counsel for Boston to plead for the reopening of the courts in defiance of Parliament's law.

He had skillfully defended John Hancock against the charges of smuggling levied against him in connection with his sloop *Liberty*: "An Englishman's property is not subject to confiscation and seizure without trial and prosecution," he had insisted.[5]

In 1768, John had been offered the post of advocate-general in the Court of Admiralty by Governor Francis Bernard. The office, he knew, would mean security for his family for life, as well as immediate success. It would be just the beginning, for behind the governor's patronage lay the power and prestige of Great Britain, and all the places and appointments at a great king's disposal. John described it as "a sure introduction to the most profitable Business in the

Province." He knew it was the first "Step in the Ladder of Royal Favour and promotion."

But he turned it down. He was certain it had implied strings attached. He did not want to place himself "under any restraints or Obligations of Gratitude to the Government for any of their favours." His strict Christian morality, his fierce integrity, would not allow him to compromise. He would not sacrifice "my honour, my conscience, my friends, my country, my God." [6]

While he never doubted that England's policy toward the colonies after the Stamp Act was wrong, he had, on occasion, risen in a crowded room during debates on it to insist that the rights of suspected royal collaborators must not be trampled in the march toward colonial independence. [7]

On the night of the Boston Massacre—March 5, 1770—John Adams was in the South End of Boston, attending a meeting of Solidality, a political club he had recently joined. Shortly after nine o'clock, he and his friends heard an insistent clamor of bells. Fearing the bells signaled a fire, the men broke up their meeting, snatched their hats and cloaks, and dashed out, intending to assist in extinguishing the blaze. But by the time they arrived the conflict was over, and all was quiet.

Thomas Hutchinson had been called to the scene and had gone to the balcony of the Town House, from which he addressed the crowd. He had urged the people to go home, and promised that justice would be done. "The law shall have its course! I will live and die by the law!" he pledged. Captain Preston agreed to surrender, and he was led to jail. [8]

As John hurried home, anxious to get to his pregnant wife, Abigail, to make certain that she and their two small children were all right, he made his way across Brattle Square past a company of soldiers with muskets shouldered and bayonets fixed. As he passed in front of them, in the narrow passage they had left in the street, he kept his head down and tried not to notice them any more than if "they had been marble Statues." [9] He prayed silently that they would ignore him.

When some three hundred men of Boston volunteered for nightly armed watches to ensure that there would be no further bloodshed, John Adams was among them. He took his turn at sentry duty at the Town House, with musket, bayonet, broadsword, and cartridge box.[10]

On the morning following the massacre, John was at work in his office near the Town House when James Forrest, an ardent Loyalist merchant, knocked on the door. With tears streaming from his eyes, Forrest told Mr. Adams he had a "very solemn Message from a very unfortunate Man: Captain Preston wishes for council, and can get none."

Forrest had spoken to Josiah Quincy, who, at twenty-six, was already an outstanding figure among the patriots. Mr. Quincy would accept Preston's case if Mr. Adams would also, but "without it positively he will not."

"Council ought to be the very last thing that an accused Person should want [lack] in a free Country," Adams replied without hesitation. He immediately accepted the case.

"As God almighty is my Judge," said Forrest, "I believe him an innocent Man."

"That must be ascertained by his Tryal," Adams replied in a lawyerlike fashion. "And if he thinks he cannot have a fair Tryal of that Issue without my Assistance, without hesitation he shall have it." The bargain was sealed with a one-guinea fee.[11]

John Adams knew full well the risk involved. His reputation as a patriot could be tarnished, and he himself might become the object of an angry mob. But John Adams was a strange revolutionary. He believed strongly in rule by law. The accused have a right to legal counsel, he felt. If the soldiers killed in self-defense, they deserved to be acquitted. A fair trial would be proof to the British that the colonists believed in preservation of constitutional rights.

When Josiah Quincy Sr. first heard that his youngest son had agreed to defend the British soldiers, his shocked reaction was: "Good God! Is it possible? I will not believe it." His older son, Samuel, had at one time been a Son of Liberty, but had recently been won over to the Tories. Was his young son about to embark on the same path? he worried.

When he asked Josiah Jr. if it were true that he had "become an advocate for those criminals who are charged with the murder of their fellow citizens," Josiah replied that "these criminals, charged with murder, are not yet legally proved guilty, and therefore, however criminal, are entitled by the laws of God and man, to all legal counsel and aid; that my duty as a man obliged me to undertake; that my duty as a lawyer strengthened the obligation."[12]

The trial was scheduled for the fall. The two lawyers prepared their case thoughtfully and carefully. Paul Revere helped supply some of the needed evidence. In their defense of Captain Preston and the eight soldiers who stood accused with him, John Adams did *not* want it to appear that the soldiers had been incited by a calculating mob. He was prepared to agree that the victims *were* part of a mob, "a motley rabble of saucy boys." But he would not permit Josiah Quincy to suggest that they had been manipulated by political puppeteers.[13]

On the other hand, he would not undertake a line of questioning that would be damaging to the town of Boston or the cause of liberty. He would attempt to prove Preston and the soldiers innocent. But he would not track down the citizens who may have been guilty of inciting riot. That was not their job, he stressed to young Quincy.[14]

He insisted that they stick to the law, followed always by his own careful translation of it into plain, understandable terms. In the course of the trial, Josiah Quincy, who had read law under the tutelage of Oxenbridge Thacher, fired the imaginations of the members of the jury with his impassioned rhetoric. John Adams touched their hearts and their minds. And he reawakened their common sense, which had been dormant since the massacre.[15]

Short, plump, and scholarly, he succeeded in court, as he always did, by the force of his conviction and his intellect, rather than by any charm. John Adams won his case. Years later he would call it "one of the best Pieces of Service I ever rendered my Country."[16]

Chapter XVII

"firmness is the characteristick of an Englishman"

England: 1770–1773

Repeal of the Townshend duties, with the exception of the tax on tea, on March 5, 1770, coincidentally the very day on which the Boston Massacre had occurred in Massachusetts, was the major accomplishment of the 1770 session of Parliament. For the next three years, the issue of the American colonies virtually disappeared from Parliament's agenda. It seemed almost as though the ministers felt that if they ignored the "American problem," it would disappear.

Lord North's aim was to give the Americans no fresh grievances, and to keep American affairs out of the House of Commons. He succeeded so well that they were not even mentioned in debates. North (like Walpole years before) was content to let sleeping dogs lie. He himself continued his habit of dozing in his chair in the Commons, much to the annoyance of his colleagues.[1]

During this time, no major crisis erupted. By the beginning of 1771, the nonimportation agreements appeared to be on the verge of final collapse, and trade between England and America was restored—on a greater scale than ever before. In the period from 1771 to 1773, the colonies purchased nine million pounds' worth of goods from the mother country, almost double the amount purchased during the previous three-year period. New Englanders still favored English manufactures. The major exception was tea. Patriots in Massachusetts agreed that it should be blacklisted as long as the duty remained in effect.

The southern colonies, too, remained good customers of the British, and provided them, in turn, with large amounts of tobacco, rice, and indigo. New York and Philadelphia bought almost no tea from England. They imported it from the Dutch.

Parliament was receiving reports from Thomas Hutchinson that the state of affairs in Massachusetts was more favorable than it had been during the past eighteen months. Outwardly, all appeared calm.

Behind the scenes, though, this was far from the case. Contradictory dispatches from the colonies indicated that the colonial boycott was still in effect. And the colonial secretary, Lord Hillsborough, had received worried reports from General Gage about the Boston Massacre. Accordingly, he had directed the general to set Castle William, in Boston Harbor, in a state of defense as a refuge for royal officials, and had ordered British naval forces moved back to the harbor from Halifax, Nova Scotia.

He then made plans to alter the constitution of Massachusetts. He would strengthen the executive branch of government in the Bay Colony. It was Hillsborough's intention to bring Massachusetts under close royal control.[2]

But the "American problem" was not uppermost in King George III's mind. He was far more concerned with creating a stable ministry in Parliament, with John Wilkes and the Middlessex elections, and with the day-to-day business of court functions. He had few, if any, ideas of his own about American policy, other than the wish to maintain British supremacy over the colonies, and he failed to appreciate the crisis that was developing in America.

If America obeyed Great Britain, then Great Britain should be generous to her, he felt. He had been reluctant to use troops to enforce the Stamp Act in 1765 and, four years later, had opposed the extreme measures of his ministers toward Massachusetts.[3]

But George III knew his duty. The Americans must be made to obey, for it was his sacred trust to pass on his empire unchanged and undivided to his heirs. In a confidential letter to his eldest son, intended solely as later instruction for the young boy, the king explained his political conduct. The king's character—his humility, based on a deep religious faith— is evident in it: "I do not pretend to any superior abilitys, but will give place to no one in meaning to preserve the freedom, happiness, and glory of my dominions, and all their inhabitants, and to fulfill the duty to my God and my neighbour in the most extended sense. That I have erred is undoubted, otherwise I should not be human, but I flatter myself all unprejudiced persons will be convinced that whenever I have failed it has been from the head not the heart."[4]

George III's belief in God was the most fundamental fact about him. Over and over in his letters he spoke of "a trust in divine Providence." He began and ended each day with a prayer, and derived much comfort from reading the Bible. He encouraged his children to do the same. As head of the Church of England, George believed that his judgments were fulfilling God's appointed tasks. He was a simple man with a simple code of honor who would not break his word.[5]

But this stubborn disposition—his refusal to consider the opinions of others and his inability to compromise—became a major weakness. He was always certain that he was right. Therefore, he would never waver on the American question. "I know I am doing my duty, and therefore can never wish to retreat, [for] firmness is the characteristick of an Englishman," he insisted.[6]

The foundations of the king's personal happiness were securely rooted in a comfortable marriage. He loved three people deeply: his brother William, Duke of Gloucester; his son Frederick, Duke of York; and the queen. Of these he loved the queen best.

King George didn't fall in love with Charlotte and then marry her. He married her and then fell in love with her. Their marriage was a success because each partner determined from the outset that it should be. Years later, after forty years of marriage, the king would still call her "the Queen of my heart." He was faithful to her all his life.

His love did not include confiding in her or seeking her advice, and Charlotte had no interest in politics. She returned her husband's love full measure. While she was a little in awe of him, she was also, in her own way, a strong personality who took great pride in raising her children. They, in turn, recognized her strength of character and her warm heart, and they adored her. She gave birth to fifteen children. George loved them all, but particularly delighted in his daughters.

Although Charlotte's education had been neglected, she had the ability and the will to learn, as well as a

In the early days of his marriage, King George was considered a handsome young man. To please his wife, for a short while he discarded his wig and allowed his own hair to grow. He was described as "good natured" though "full of dignity." Soon after their marriage, he purchased Buckingham House, across from St. James Park in London, which he would make into "a retreat not a palace."

strong desire to please the king. She shared her husband's love of music, she was adept at needlework, and she became a great collector of furniture and pottery. And she loved to read—in English, French, and German.[7]

Queen Charlotte was a cultured woman, but she was not a beauty. She was

King George III, Queen Charlotte, and their six eldest children. Love, fidelity, and genuine friendship existed between the king and queen, as well as much affection for their children. The queen gave birth with a regularity that could not fail to please her husband, whose approval of large families was well known. He was an extremely loving and indulgent father. *By Johann Zoffany, circa 1770.*

short and extremely thin, with fine, dark hair, a low forehead, a small nose, beautiful eyes, and a large mouth that seemed to dominate her face.

King George was a tall and well-built man who carried himself erect in public. But he, too, was not handsome. He had a high forehead, protruding eyes, a large nose, thick lips, and a dimpled chin. His impaired vision caused him to have a bent and peering look. He spoke with "dignity, delicacy, and ease" in a voice that was described as "particularly full and fine." He shaved his head and wore a small wig that came down to the lobes of his ears. "He had a steady and open expression which commanded respect." Both he and Queen

Charlotte spent as much time as possible with their family. He was frequently seen carrying one or another of his young children about in his arms, or playing on the floor with them.

His servants were devoted to him, and he, in turn, appreciated their loyalty. He would often stroll into the cottages of his farm workers unannounced to talk to them, and he encouraged their children to play cricket and football and to fly kites in Great Park at Windsor Castle.

He admired physical courage and endurance. He himself was physically fit and a superb horseman. Hunting was his favorite recreation.

At his formal receptions it was his custom to speak to all who attended. He had a good memory and developed an aptitude for putting people at ease. He could converse easily on a variety of topics, as he was interested in many things and loved to talk to people about them. This was a great accomplishment for one who had been a shy boy often rebuked by his mother when he attempted to take part in a conversation.

Now, he learned all the gossip of London at his levees. He was never pompous, he loved a joke, and he didn't think it beneath his dignity to speak to the lowest of his subjects. A story is told of his meeting an old woman working alone in a field. When he asked where her companions were, she said they had gone to see the king.

"And why did you not go with them?"

"Because I have five children to provide for and cannot afford to lose a day's work," she replied.

"Then," said the king, slipping her a guinea, "you may tell your companions that the king came to see you."[8]

The colonists in America never saw this side of their monarch.

Chapter XVIII

"a spark of patriotic fire"

The American Colonies: 1772–1773

In March of 1772, the calm that had pervaded the colonies for the two years since the Boston Massacre was suddenly shattered. An armed British schooner named the *Gaspée* sailed into Narragansett Bay off the coast of Rhode Island and began to seize colonial ships entering the port carrying smuggled cargo. Lieutenant William Dudingston was in command.

Narragansett Bay cuts into the southeastern part of Rhode Island, effectively dividing it into two parts. With its many coves and inlets, the bay was an ideal setting for smuggling. Rhode Island merchants had long been taking advantage of this and they had continued to smuggle goods in order to avoid paying any duty, meeting with little interference from the British government. Lieutenant Dudingston would change that. He would teach the colonists a lesson.

Described as "haughty, insolent, and intolerant," Dudingston was determined to stamp out smuggling. As he cruised around Narragansett Bay, he boarded and examined every ship, "ill-treating every Master and Merchant of the Vessels he boarded." When his crew ran short of meat, he stole sheep, hogs, and poultry from the farmers near the bay. He cut down their fruit trees for firewood. He would be happy to see Rhode Island burn, he was overheard to say. Rhode Islanders were furious.

Tension had reached the breaking point when, on June 9, the *Gaspée* hit a sandbar and ran aground while chasing a smuggler. The ship was certain to remain stranded until high tide at midnight. Unable to run, she lay now at the mercy of Rhode Islanders.

The smugglers would make the most of the opportunity.

In Providence, at nightfall, just about the time the shops were closing, a drummer marched down Main Street urging the citizens to gather together to dispose of the *Gaspée*. More than fifty volunteers answered the call.

The men armed themselves with guns, staves, and paving stones. In eight longboats with muffled oars, they silently rowed out to the helpless ship. As they came alongside the *Gaspée*, they demanded the surrender of Dudingston. When he refused, one of the patriots fired, hitting him in the arm and groin.

"I have killed the rascal!" he shouted. But, as it turned out, Dudingston was merely wounded. His wounds were quickly dressed, and he and his entire crew, their hands bound behind their backs, were rowed to shore in small boats. The *Gaspée* was set on fire and burned to its water's edge as Rhode Islanders watched from the shore. The patriots disappeared from the *Gaspée* as quickly and silently as they had appeared.[1]

The dispute between Great Britain and America had reopened.

When an "unconstitutional" court of inquisition was appointed by the British government to investigate the *Gaspée* affair and to hold suspects for trial in England, thereby threatening the most basic of English liberties— every man's right to a trial by a jury of his peers—the patriots rebelled. They displayed singularly short memories under questioning: No one could remember anything about the night of June 9, nor could they recognize any of the rioters. Despite the promise of a five-hundred-pound reward, no one would turn King's evidence. Thus, the commissioners could do nothing, and the British government made no further effort to pursue the matter.[2]

News of the *Gaspée* affair spread rapidly. A ballad sung in many taverns throughout the colonies helped turn men's minds once again to a defense of their liberties:

In seventeen hundred and seventy-two
In Newport Harbor lay a crew,
That played the parts of pirates there,
The sons of freedom could not bear.

That night about half after ten,
Some Narragansett Indiamen,
Being sixty-four, if I remember,
Which made this stout coxcomb surrender;
And what was best of all their tricks,
They in his britch a ball did fix,

And set the men upon the land,
And burnt her up, we understand;
Which thing provokes the king so high,
He said those men shall surely die.

. . . .

But let him try his utmost skill,
I'm apt to think he never will
Find out any of those hearts of gold,
Though he should offer fifty fold.[3]

Americans were beginning to see the Atlantic Ocean as a barrier beyond which even the long arm of Great Britain could not reach.

Then, late in 1772, Bostonians learned that the British government intended to pay the salaries of not only Governor Hutchinson and Lieutenant Governor Andrew Oliver from the revenues collected by the American commissioners of customs, but those of superior court judges and other legal officials—many of them Hutchinson's relatives—as well. These men would no longer be subject to legislative control in Massachusetts. The mother country, Sam Adams warned, was destroying the checks and balances in the Massachusetts Constitution.

In fact, he saw evidence of what he—and many colonists—feared was a conspiracy against liberty. They were becoming more and more certain that there was a deliberate plan afoot to destroy the British constitution with all the rights and privileges it guaranteed, not only in the colonies, but in England as well.

Sam met this crisis by organizing the Boston Committee of Correspondence, which would link all the towns of Massachusetts. "Where there is a spark of patriotic fire, we will rekindle it," Adams vowed. Within three months, more than eighty local committees were formed throughout the Bay Colony.[4]

When the Virginia Assembly, which was by now the southern focus of resistance to Parliament, met in Williamsburg in March of 1773, they, too, were disturbed by the news of how Massachusetts government salaries would be paid. What happened in New England might happen to them. Thomas Jefferson, Patrick Henry, and Richard Henry Lee, realizing that some of the older, more conservative members of the House of Burgesses might not be willing to take action, met one evening in a private room at the Raleigh Tavern. They and a few other "young hot-heads" were convinced that it was urgent to band together with all the colonies and act as a united group.

Concerned about the reported threats to their ancient legal and constitutional rights, the men drew up resolutions to be presented to the House of

Burgesses on the following day. A tense and expectant house convened on the morning of March 12 to hear their proposal: [5]

> Be it Resolved, that a Standing Committee of Correspondence and Inquiry be appointed, to consist of eleven persons . . . whose business it shall be to obtain . . . intelligence of all such acts and resolutions of the British Parliament . . . as may . . . affect British colonies in America, and . . . maintain a correspondence and communication with our sister colonies.[6]

The resolutions carried.

Within a few months, every colony except Pennsylvania had a Committee of Correspondence. Expanding on Sam Adams's circular letter in Massachusetts, Virginia had established an intercolonial information network. By passing along news and information of interest to all the other colonies, these committees would "rekindle" opposition to British policy. The news would move between colonies via post riders who were traveling at the speed of about three miles an hour. Richard Henry Lee's intention "that every Colony on the Continent will adopt these Committees of Correspondence and enquiry" had been realized. The colonies were becoming a unit.

From then on, Thomas Jefferson and Patrick Henry kept track of everything the British did wrong.

It wasn't long before the colonists were given another impetus to unity.

Chapter XIX

"They won't take the tea"

London: 1773

In the midst of the *Gaspée* affair, Lord Hillsborough suddenly resigned as head of the American Department. His successor was the earl of Dartmouth, stepbrother to Lord North, a tactful and moderate man who believed in accommodation rather than confrontation. Benjamin Franklin hoped that the new minister for America would deal more wisely with the colonies than Lord Hillsborough had. Though an intelligent and highly principled gentleman, Dartmouth was also loyal to his stepbrother. Ultimately, Franklin's description of him as a weakling who was "a truly good man, and wishes sincerely a good understanding with the colonies, but does not seem to have the strength equal to his wishes," would prove accurate.[1] While remaining friendly, Dartmouth would be unwilling—or unable—to take the larger step needed to compromise with the Americans.

Lord North's concern at this point was not the colonies—or his brother—but the tangled affairs of the East India Company. The company was on the verge of bankruptcy, and much of its debt was owed to the British government. North had to take action. In fact, the king had warned North, "Any wavering now would be disgraceful to you and destructive to the public, but I know you too well to harbour such a thought." Lord North dared not sleep through this crisis.

Tea weighing seventeen million pounds, valued at about two million pounds in English money, had arrived from India and was moldering away in the company's warehouses. The enormous stock had accumulated largely because of the shutdown of the American market for tea. Now the company petitioned Parliament for a loan and a change in the tea taxes that would allow it to compete with smuggled Dutch tea.*[2]

North knew what he would do. The potential market for English tea in the colonies was huge. He would grant the East India Company a monopoly of the American tea business. He would permit it to export the tea directly to America, duty-free, bypassing the London merchants who normally bought it at auction for later distribution. And the company could ship the tea to dealers of its own selection in the colonies.

Further, the company would receive a rebate of the twelve-pence-per-pound tax that had been collected when the tea was first brought into England. In this way, North reasoned, Americans would be able to purchase tea more cheaply than Englishmen could in England. Instead of costing twenty shillings a pound, it would sell for ten shillings a pound. It would be even cheaper than the tea the Americans were smuggling from Holland duty-free. At the same time, the finances of the East India Company would be put on a sounder basis.[3]

But North would retain the three-pence-per-pound tax on tea in America

---

*One of the main routes for Dutch tea was from Amsterdam to Rhode Island.

left over from the Townshend duties. Certainly the Americans wouldn't object to that.

Lord North didn't understand the Americans.

Despite the urging of opposition leaders in the House of Commons who saw the fallacy in his plan, North wouldn't back down.

"I tell the noble lord now that if he don't take off the duty, they [the colonists] won't take the tea," a member warned Lord North.

North insisted on retaining the tax on tea as a symbol of Parliament's authority to tax America. At long last, he believed, the Townshend duties would provide England the revenues for which they were originally intended.[4] "It is to no purpose making objections. The king means to try the question with America," he retorted.[5]

Lord North's Tea Act was signed into law on May 10, 1773.

An indignant Benjamin Franklin wrote home that Parliament believed "that three pence in a pound of tea, of which one does not drink perhaps ten pounds a year, is sufficient to overcome all the patriotism of an American." Did the ministry not realize that the colonists would see this as yet another attempt at violating their charters? Had they forgotten the colonists' reaction to earlier attempts at taxation? he wondered.

Early in the fall of 1773, the East India Company sent off six hundred thousand pounds (two thousand chests) of duHed tea to commissioners in four American ports: Boston, New York, Philadelphia, and Charleston. Four of the ships carrying the tea were headed for Boston. The smallest of these, a brig named *William*, belonged to the Clarke family, the second largest tea importer in Boston. The largest firm was owned by the Hutchinson brothers, sons of Governor Thomas Hutchinson. The *William* was caught in a December gale and wrecked off Cape Cod, near Provincetown, but its cargo, including Boston's first street lamps, was rescued.[6]

No one was prepared for the reaction when the remaining ships arrived at their respective ports.

Chapter XX

"that baneful weed"

Boston, Massachusetts: 1773

Early in October 1773, the colonists learned of the impending arrival of the East India Company's tea. A protest movement swept along the coast. Suddenly, all the earlier arguments against English tea were revived, and the entire question of taxation without representation in the American colonies was reopened. Many colonists saw in the shipment a devilish plot between the East India Company and Parliament to tempt the colonists into recognizing Parliament's claims by offering them cheap but duties tea. To accept these shipments of tea was to admit the right of Parliament to tax the colonists.[1]

New York was the first to employ organized opposition. A series of inflammatory newspaper articles and broadsides as well as letters to the editor appeared, threatening dire consequences to the consignees (tea commissioners) if they refused to resign their commissions. Harbor pilots would face "the vengeance of a free people, struggling to preserve their liberties" if they dared bring a ship carrying tea up the harbor. Anyone helping to land and store the tea would receive "an unwelcome visit, in which they shall be treated as they deserve." By the end of November the consignees in New York had resigned.

In Philadelphia the scene was much the same. Consignees were reminded of what had happened to stamp commissioners in 1765. Dr. Benjamin Rush, writing under the pseudonym Hamden, declared that the chests of tea contained "a slow poison . . . the seeds of *slavery*."[2] Sons of Liberty met and issued handbills stating "By Uniting We Stand, by Dividing We Fall."[3]

John Dickinson, writing as RUSTICUS, ended his article: "Let the watchmen making their rounds call out, 'past twelve O'Clock, beware of the East India Company.'" The Committee for Tarring and Feathering warned the Delaware River pilots that whoever dared to bring in the tea ship would receive an appropriate reward. By the first of December, all the consignees had resigned their commissions, and the ships carrying the tea to Philadelphia had returned to England.[4]

In Annapolis, Maryland, the ship and its hated cargo were burned.

In Boston the situation was different. On November 28, the British ship *Dartmouth* entered Boston Harbor with its cargo of tea, and on the following day, an announcement appeared in the *Boston Gazette*:

> Friends! Brethren! Countrymen!
> That worst of Plagues the detested tea shipped for this port by the East India Company, is now arrived in the Harbour; the Hour of Destruction or manly Opposition to the Machinations of Tyranny stares you in the Face; every Friend to his Country, to himself and Posterity, is now called upon to meet at Faneuil Hall at NINE O'Clock
>
> THIS DAY
>
> (at which Time the Bells will ring) to make a united and successful Resistance to this last, worst and most destructive Measure of Administration.

Governor Thomas Hutchinson refused to give in to the demands of the patriots that the tea be returned to England. After years of struggle with Sam Adams and other patriots, Hutchinson had reached the end of his patience, particularly since part of the cargo of tea on the *Dartmouth* was consigned to his two sons, Thomas Jr. and Elisha.

Now, in spite of the patriots' pledge that they "would oppose with their lives and fortunes the vending of any tea," Hutchinson was ready for a showdown. He had good reason to think he could win. Two regiments of troops were stationed in Boston, and the Office of Customs Commissioners was there also. Several ships of the British fleet patrolled the harbor. British authority seemed well established.[5]

The governor stubbornly insisted that the chests of tea be unloaded, pending the issue of the necessary clearance forms. He continued to refuse the patriots' demand that the ships (two more ships bearing tea, the *Eleanor* and the *Beaver*, had entered the harbor) return to England with their cargo. In fact, he ordered that the port guns open fire should the master of the *Dartmouth* attempt to leave before the duty had been paid.[6]

Instead of complying with the patriots' demands that they resign, the consignees and the customs commissioners, many of them relatives through marriage and a close-knit group, took refuge at Castle William in Boston Harbor. They knew that they would be safe there from the rough tactics commonly used by the Boston mob.

Since the *Dartmouth* was in Boston Harbor, its captain had to register both his ship and its cargo at the Customs House, and neither could depart thereafter without clearance from the customs collector. Under the trade laws, if the duties were not paid within twenty days, the tea must be landed and confiscated by customs officials. It could not reenter England. With the guns at Castle William commanding the channel, Hutchinson could be certain that no vessel would leave without permission. The decision as to what to do was in his hands.

The patriots were convinced that once the tea was ashore, the commissioners would pay the duty and the tea would find its way into the marketplace. Bostonians had never become as successful at smuggling tea from Holland as had Rhode Islanders. For them to do without English tea meant giving up the habit altogether. For an Englishman, wherever he lived, this was extremely difficult. Thus, only by preventing the landing of the tea could the patriots be certain that no one would purchase it.

The *Dartmouth*, the *Eleanor*, and the *Beaver* were ordered to lie at Griffin's Wharf, where they were kept under guard. *Dartmouth*'s tea would be eligible for seizure on December 17. As that day approached, tension mounted throughout Boston.[7]

The situation affected many citizens of Boston differently.

John Adams's young wife, Abigail, was one of those affected. For several years now she had been serving and drinking

Abigail Adams became her husband, John's, best informant while he was in Philadelphia at the Continental Congress. While many in Congress advocated a conciliatory policy toward Great Britain, Abigail's letters to John reminded him that New England was ready to explode into war. *Pastel by Benjamin Blyth, 1766.*

"liberty teas" in place of the English tea that she used to enjoy. During the spring of 1773, when Abigail accompanied her husband on one of his trips to Plymouth to attend a court session there, she had met Mercy Otis Warren. An elegant lady and the mother of five sons, Mercy was the sister of James Otis and the wife of James Warren, who was a leading Massachusetts radical and brother of John and Abigail's good friend Dr. Joseph Warren. When Abigail first met her, Mercy was rapidly becoming a well-known literary and political figure.

Although Mercy was forty-five and Abigail just twenty-nine when they met, they quickly became good friends. The two women shared fine minds as well as their husbands' interest and involvement in politics. Both were acutely aware of the worsening situation in Massachusetts. They maintained a lively correspondence.[8]

Now, using her pen as an emotional outlet, as she often did, Abigail gave vent to her feelings in a letter to Mercy. Expressing her fears for Boston since the arrival of the tea ships, she wrote to her friend: "The Tea that baneful weed is arrived. Great and I hope Effectual opposition has been made to the landing of it. The flame is kindled and like Lightning it catches from soul to soul. Great will be the devastation if not timely quenched or allayed by some more lenient Measures." Her mind, Abigail told Mercy, was shocked at the thought of shedding human blood, "and a civil War is of all Wars, the most dreadful." Still, she knew that many would willingly give their lives for the cause. "Such is the present Situation of affairs that I tremble when I think what may be the direful consequences. . . . My Heart beats at every Whistle I hear."[9]

John Singleton Copley was another Bostonian singularly affected by the situation. He was an unlikely man to try—single-handedly—to stop a revolution, yet in an amazing moment of courage, that is exactly what he did.

A shy, good-natured thirty-five-year-old, Copley had created "the first major American works of art in any medium," and was already recognized as an artist of the first rank. Paul Revere often made frames for the miniature portraits his friend painted.

Copley had been brought up by his widowed mother in rooms over the tobacco shop she operated on Long Wharf and had spent many hours in the shop helping her earn a living. From this vantage point, he saw the extremes of Boston life.

On the one side, as a little boy, he stared in grave-eyed wonder at the magnificence of the prosperous merchants dressed in imported clothes who frequented her shop, as his mother curtsied to them from behind the counter. On the other, he watched the sailors who crowded into the shop for a last hunk of tobacco before they set sail. He saw rebellious sailors hanging from the yardarms; he heard the cut of cat-o'-nine-tails on naked backs; and he watched as terrified black children were herded off slave ships and driven down Long Wharf to the markets to be sold.

When some of the tough waterfront boys dared him to come out of the shop and fight, nine-year-old John would run to an empty room in the back and draw pictures on the walls. His art was already providing him an escape from the sordid life around him. He would grow up to paint portraits of the wealthy merchants and their families whom he admired. And he would model his own manners on them.

By the age of thirteen, John had set himself up as a painter and engraver, working with passionate intensity. By nineteen he was becoming known as a fine portrait painter. His ability to depict character in faces was extraordinary. [10]

Hardworking and eager for self-improvement, Copley began to receive commissions for portraits from the wealthy of Boston. Invited to the homes of many of his sitters, he met numerous attractive and accomplished young women. Among them was the lovely Susannah Clarke, daughter of the rich Tory merchant Richard Clarke. They fell in love, and on November 16, 1769, when he was thirty-one, John Singleton

Mercy Otis Warren, sister to James Otis and wife of James Warren, brother to Dr. Joseph Warren. She possessed one of the sharpest minds in New England and was, perhaps, the most intellectually accomplished woman in revolutionary America. She was a good friend of Abigail Adams. *By John Singleton Copley, circa 1763.*

John Singleton Copley created "the first major American works of art in any medium" and, at the age of thirty-five, was already recognized as an artist of the first rank. Married into a Tory family, it was he who attempted in vain to effect a compromise between the merchants and the Patriots at the time of the Boston Tea Party. *Self portrait, 1769.*

Copley married into one of the leading Tory families in Boston. His father-in-law was an agent for the East India Company and one of the consignees of tea. It was Clarke's ship, the *William*, that had been wrecked off Cape Cod while en route from England carrying tea to Boston.

Now Copley found himself in an extraordinary position. His memories of the scenes from his childhood on Long Wharf caused him to look with horror at the British soldiers drilling in Boston and the ships with cannons poised ominously in the harbor. He recoiled from violence of any kind. And he had no interest in politics. He had managed to retain his friendships with Sam Adams, Joseph Warren, and John Hancock, now his neighbor on Beacon Hill, although he was now a son-in-law of Tory Richard Clarke.[11]

It was just this situation that made him the ideal person to attempt to negotiate a settlement between the merchants and the Patriots. A Whig married to a Tory, Copley saw both sides of the dispute. Compromise was essential. He was the man, he told himself, who could effect it.

In spite of his extreme shyness and his fear of any kind of confrontation, he forced himself to call on Adams, Warren, and Hancock in an effort to convince them that violence would only breed more violence. When this failed, Copley appeared before a town meeting in the Old South Church on the day after the tea arrived, pleading eloquently for moderation. All he gained here was time to consult with the consignees.

But the consignees were no more interested in compromise than the Patriots. They understood that if the tea was returned to England without any duty being paid, the ships carrying the tea would, by English law, be subject to confiscation, and the merchants thereby ruined. They sent Copley back from Castle William, where they were encamped, with a flat refusal.

With a heavy heart, Copley carried their letter of refusal back across the channel. There he paced back and forth along the wharf, at a loss to know what to do. If he delivered the merchants' letter to the Patriots, there was no telling how they would react.

Finally, determined to avoid violence and to reach a settlement, he turned back to the slip where the little boat that had taken him across the channel was docked, and struggling to overcome a fear of the sea that had plagued him since childhood, he took the boat back to Castle William. This time he convinced the merchants to agree to store the tea until they received further instructions from London.

The Patriots weren't interested.

Copley tried once more. If he could convince his in-laws, the Clarkes, to appear at their meeting, would the Patriots guarantee their safety? The Patriots voted and the Clarkes' safety was assured. They granted Copley two hours in which to bring them back from Castle William. The meeting adjourned.

Although he knew that the strong wind that had come up would make the passage out to the island a difficult one, this time Copley boarded the boat with a lighter heart. He was certain that if the Patriots and the merchants were to meet face to face, a compromise could be effected.

He was wrong. The Clarkes refused to leave the fortress, and Copley returned alone. He had done everything possible. The merchants' opposition, he told the assembled crowd of almost a thousand men, was due not to "obstinacy and unfriendliness to the community, but rather to the necessity to discharge a trust." They were fearful of ruining their reputations as merchants and wanted, also, to protect their friends who had invested large sums of money in the enterprise.

The merchants had promised not to bring the tea into town, Copley went on to assure the Patriots, but they "must be excused from being the active instruments in sending it back." If the tea remained unloaded, he reminded them, the captains of the boats would eventually have to take it back on their own initiative. The Patriots voted unanimously that this was not satisfactory, but they adjourned without doing anything.[12]

Fifteen days later a showdown occurred.

On Thursday, December 16, the last day before the deadline, seven thousand angry citizens packed the Old South Church and overflowed into the streets outside. Men had come from all over the colony. They would make one last attempt to persuade Governor Hutchinson to release the ships. The governor was at his country home in Milton, removed from the mobs, and consequently somewhat out of touch with the tension that had been steadily building in Boston over the last two weeks.

Frances Rotch, the son and representative of the *Dartmouth*'s owner, Benjamin Rotch, had already agreed to send his ship back to England if he could obtain clearance. Now he was persuaded to travel the six miles to Milton with the request. The meeting was adjourned until three o'clock.

By the time Rotch returned at a quarter to six, darkness had fallen on the short winter day. The crowd, restless and weary from the many long speeches, was waiting in the gloom of the church, dimly lit with candles. Rotch reported that the Governor remained inflexible. "You will not defy English law" was Hutchinson's message to the Patriots.

Pandemonium broke loose. Now Samuel Adams rose to speak. He had been certain what the governor's reply would be, and he had plotted his own response with Hancock, Warren, and many other Patriots. Now he banged his gavel three times and announced: "Gentlemen, this meeting can do nothing more to save the country!"

The Old South Meeting House outside and inside. This simple brick church was the scene of many meetings of Boston's citizens to demand their rights from British officials. It was the largest building in Boston, so when gatherings overflowed Faneuil Hall, they moved here. On December 16, 1773, thousands of citizens came to Old South, spilling out into the streets. It was then that Samuel Adams announced, "Gentlemen, this meeting can do nothing more to save the country," a signal for the start of the Boston Tea Party. *Photographs by L. H. Bober.*

As if at a signal, a war whoop sounded, then shouts of "Boston harbor a teapot tonight!" and "Hurrah for Griffin's Wharf!" The people streamed out into the night, headed for Griffin's Wharf. Above the tumult, John Hancock's voice rang out, "Let every man do what is right in his own eyes!"

Preparations had been carefully made in advance for what was to come. While Sam Adams, Joseph Warren, and Josiah Quincy Jr. were making speeches at the Old South, Paul Revere and his mechanics were getting ready to stage a brilliant piece of theater. Described by his contemporaries as "cool in thought and ardent in action," Revere had organized several groups of men. For the most part they were very young, with some in their early twenties and some just teenagers, not much known in town and therefore not likely to be easily recognized.[13] One thirteen-year-old apprentice, who had been locked in his room by his Tory master, the rope-maker John Gray, knotted his bedding together, hung it out the window, and slid down to join in.[14]

The men were roughly disguised as Indians, a symbol of freedom in the eighteenth century, their faces covered with lampblack, red ocher, or simply soot. Many were wrapped in blankets and carried a hatchet or an ax along with their pistols. Quietly, they proceeded to the waterfront and climbed aboard the tea vessels, about fifty men to a ship. There had been a steady drizzle all day, but the night had turned clear and a bright moon shone in the sky.

On each ship, the men politely requested some candles or lanterns and the keys to the hold so there would be as little damage to the ship as possible. The sailors complied. Some even helped the "Mohawks" attach block and tackle to the chests of tea and hoist them from the hold. The silence along the wharf

At the Boston Tea Party, which occurred on December 16, 1773, 342 chests of tea, worth about 10,000 pounds, were broken open and their contents dumped into Boston Harbor. It has been called the catalyst that precipitated the American War for Independence.

was so complete that the first blows of the hatchets on the chests were heard far into Boston.

Three hours later, 342 chests of tea, worth about ten thousand pounds, had been broken open and their contents dumped into Boston Harbor. One young "Mohawk" was heard to say, "What a cup of tea we're making for the fishes!"

Before they left the ships, each man took off his boots and shook them out over the railing. When one man was caught stuffing tea into his pockets, he was stripped of his loot *and* his clothes and sent home naked, in disgrace. Then the decks were swept clean, and the first mate of each ship was asked to testify that nothing besides the tea chests had been damaged. One broken padlock was replaced with a new one the next day. The Patriots' quarrel was *not* against property or order. Their only quarrel was with the right of Parliament to tax them. They had not wanted to destroy the tea. They had simply wanted to send it back to London in the ships in which it had arrived.[15]

Workers, craftsmen, and merchants had labored side by side to defend what they considered their sacred liberty. Hundreds more stood silently on the dock, witnessing the scene. It was their presence there that prevented the admiral of the royal fleet, at anchor in the harbor, from raking Griffin's Wharf with his cannon.

As they came ashore, the "Mohawks" formed into ranks and marched into town, their axes and tomahawks on their shoulders, a fifer playing at their side.[16]

Within a few days, a Boston street ballad called "The Rallying of the Tea Party" identified two leaders by name:

> Rally Mohawks! Bring out your axes,
> And tell King George we'll pay no taxes
> On his foreign tea.
>
> . . . .
>
> Our Warren's there, and bold Revere
> With hands to do and words to cheer
> For Liberty and laws.[17]

Now couriers galloped to the other colonies to spread the news. Paul Revere reached Philadelphia shortly before Christmas, carrying a hastily prepared note. For the most part, *t*'s were uncrossed and punctuation was omitted, evidence of the breathless haste in which it was written:

> Boston, December 17, 1773
>
> GENTLEMEN, — We inform you in great Haste that every chest of Tea on board the three Ships in this town was destroyed the last evening without the least Injury to the Vessels or any other property. Our Enemies must acknowledge that these people have acted upon pure and upright Principle.[18]

John Adams announced to Abigail that he considered the Boston Tea Party "the most magnificent Movement of all. There is a Dignity, a Majesty . . . in this last Effort of the Patriots, that I greatly admire." The destruction of the tea, he told her, is a "bold and daring act" that must have important and lasting consequences. It was an "Epocha in History." [19]

Chapter XXI

"The Dye is now cast"

London: 1772–1774

In London, Benjamin Franklin remained close to people on both sides of the controversy: those who understood and sympathized with the American point of view; and conservative officials, who somehow held Franklin responsible for the "American problem." These ministers were searching for a way to get rid of him.

At the same time, Franklin, who had always loved England, was coming to the conclusion that he would have to do something drastic if the British Empire were to be preserved. Through his many friends, he was kept informed of any attempts by the British to tamper with American interests, and he immediately took what steps he could to thwart those actions. He was always able to present a logical argument. Now he determined to find a way to calm the passions of men on both sides of the Atlantic Ocean. Perhaps, he reasoned, as a respected American in Britain, he might be able to effect a reconciliation between the two countries.[1]

Benjamin Franklin, when he was the chief spokesman for the American colonies in London. In England, Franklin had developed a deep love for the mother country, but his loyalty to America was never in question. He worked diligently to bring Britain and her American colonies together in friendly understanding. *By David Rent Etter, after Martin.*

Unwittingly, he played into the hands of those who were seeking to force him to leave England.

Near the end of 1772, a packet of thirteen letters had come into his possession, several of which had been written by Thomas Hutchinson during the time he was chief justice and lieutenant governor of Massachusetts. Others were written by Hutchinson's brother-in-law, Andrew Oliver, then secretary of the province. The letters, written between 1767 and 1769, were addressed to Thomas Whately, who had been secretary to George Grenville in 1765 and had played a key role in drafting the Stamp Act. Whately had died in 1772.

The letters were given to Franklin by a "gentleman of character and distinction," thought to be a member of Parliament who was sympathetic to the colonies. His name was never revealed. It was hoped that the letters would convince Franklin that Parliament had been misguided by Loyalists in America. The letters implied that it was the Loyalists, and not the British ministry, who were urging Parliament to enact oppressive measures on the colonists.

Six of the letters, written by Thomas Hutchinson, expressed the belief that constitutional changes would have to be made in the Massachusetts Charter, and that "there must be an abridgment of what are called English liberties" in

America if the empire were to be preserved. "I wish for the good of the colony when I wish to see some further restraint of liberty rather than the connection with the parent should be broken, for I am sure such a breach must prove the ruin of the colony," Hutchinson continued.[2]

Andrew Oliver suggested that officers of the crown should be made "in some measure independent" of the Assembly. Both men agreed that a firm hand was needed, perhaps even armed forces, to keep the colony in order.[3]

But some of Hutchinson's letters—letters in which he had expressed his opposition to abrupt action, his extreme reluctance to recommend the use of military force, and his uncertainty as to what course of action would be best to follow—had been removed from the packet.[4]

Franklin, knowing nothing of these missing letters, decided that the real enemies of colonial liberty were Loyalists like Thomas Hutchinson and Andrew Oliver, and not the ministry in London. Therefore Franklin resolved to send the letters he had been given to Boston in an attempt to prove this. He planned to send the entire packet to his friend and correspondent Thomas Cushing, Speaker of the Massachusetts Assembly and one of the leading Patriots in the colony. Perhaps the letters, by placing the blame on Hutchinson and Oliver, would serve to lessen Boston's resentment against England.

Since Whately had been out of office when the letters were written, they could have been considered confidential letters to a friend. But Franklin reasoned differently. Whately was still a member of Parliament at the time, and a close friend of Grenville. Thus, the letters had been written "by public officers to persons in public stations, on public affairs, and intended to procure public measures."[5] They could, therefore, be considered public.

On December 2, 1772, Franklin sent the letters off on their long journey. But he sent them with the stipulation that they were to be shown only to a few leading Patriots. They were not to be printed or copied. Franklin's name must not be revealed, and the letters must eventually be returned to him.[6]

For months he knew nothing of the disastrous effect they would have.

Franklin continued to hope for a cooling-off period in which the English government would work out some sort of accommodation. He urged patience: "I must hope that great care will be taken to keep our people quiet; since nothing is more wished for by our enemies than by insurrections we should give a good pretense for increasing the military among us and putting us under more severe restraints."[7]

Cling fast, he urged the colonists, to every right, privilege, and just claim, but avoid violence. Remember "that this Protestant country (our mother, though lately an unkind one) is worth preserving, and that her weight in the scale of Europe, and her safety in a great degree, may depend on our union with her."[8]

Franklin still hoped for peaceful, legal resistance on the part of America. He was certain that, in time, Great Britain would come to recognize the economic importance of the colonies. Then it would become possible for the colonists to achieve everything they wanted.

Franklin realized how wrong he was when he learned the fate of the letters.

"Nothing could have been more Seasonable than the arrival of these letters," one of the Patriots wrote to him. "They have had great effect. . . . [T]hey strip the mask from the writers who, under the professions of friendship to their country, now plainly appear to have been endeavoring to build up themselves and their families upon its ruins."[9]

Thomas Cushing had shown the letters to Sam Adams and several other Patriots, and for a short while Franklin's request for secrecy was honored. But Sam Adams, unwilling to heed Franklin's plea for patience, had begun a propaganda campaign in the press, hinting at the existence of the letters. He had then read the letters to a secret session of the assembly on June 2, 1773. The House voted that they tended to "subvert the Constitution and to introduce arbitrary power."[10]

Within a few days the letters appeared in the public press with several changes to make them sound even more incriminating. They were serialized in four colonial newspapers, with editorial comments that compared them to "footsteps stained with blood."[11] What was deliberately not mentioned was the fact that Thomas Hutchinson favored these restrictions ("abridgments of English liberty") because he wished to prevent revocation of the Massachusetts Charter—a step he believed inevitable if the turmoil in the colony continued. Liberty, Hutchinson felt, could be saved from complete overthrow only by restoring order. "I tremble for my Country [Massachusetts]," Hutchinson had written to a boyhood friend in 1769. "I wished to leave its Constitution at my death in the same state it was in at my birth." [12]

The Whately letters became a topic of conversation throughout Boston. John Adams took them with him when he made his legal rounds of the superior court in Massachusetts, allowing them to be read in towns outside Boston. Soon they were printed in pamphlet form and sent to the other American colonies. The colonists were outraged. Hutchinson was burned in effigy in Philadelphia and Princeton. Writing in the *Boston Gazette* under the pseudonym Novanglus, John Adams denounced Hutchinson as "this vile serpent." The letters bore the "evident marks of madness," he continued. [13]

For his part, Hutchinson swore that he had been misinterpreted. When he said, "There *must* be an abridgment of what are called English liberties," he had meant it in the predictive sense, a warning, not a desire. The Patriots wouldn't listen. [14] Thomas Hutchinson and Andrew Oliver were declared traitors, and a formal petition was sent to London to have them removed from office immediately.

Six weeks later it fell to Benjamin Franklin, as agent for Massachusetts, to submit the petition to Lord Dartmouth with a covering letter assuring him that the colony had "a sincere disposition . . . to be on good terms with the mother country . . . having lately discovered . . . the authors of their grievances to be some of their own people, their resentment against Britain is thence much abated." [15] Franklin had already admitted that it was he who had leaked the letters to the Boston Patriots.

Early in January of 1774, Benjamin Franklin received a summons to appear before the Privy Council to testify on behalf of the petition. The king had read it and had sent it on to the Privy Council for a hearing.

Privy Council meetings took place in a committee room in Westminster known as the Cockpit. During the reign of King Henry VIII, when

Westminster was used as his palace, the king had had a tennis court and a pit for cockfighting built on this spot. Eventually, this "playground" was rebuilt, and the cockpit became a committee room of Parliament.

On January 29, when Benjamin Franklin arrived at the Cockpit at the appointed time, he was surprised at what he found. Word had been circulated in London that this would be a trial worth hearing. Accordingly, the room was packed not only with thirty-six members of the Privy Council, but with members of London society, resplendent in all their finery, as well. Among those present were the Archbishop of Canterbury, Lieutenant General Thomas Gage, the earls of Dartmouth, Hillsborough, and Sandwich, Dr. Joseph Priestley, and Edmund Burke. Lord North, who arrived late, was forced to stand. No chair could be found for him.

"All the courtiers were invited, as to an entertainment," Franklin would describe it later. Never had there been such an immense gathering of spectators

The Privy Council hearing at which thirty-six English lords and a room filled with spectators heard Benjamin Franklin denounced as a liar and a thief by Alexander Wedderburn.

at a Privy Council meeting, nor so many of the councillors themselves. Council members were seated at a long table in the center of a spacious room. Alexander Wedderburn, solicitor general for the government, would hear the case.

Wedderburn, known for his acid tongue, was a politician with an unrelenting ambition to advance. He had already switched parties three times in two years, and was searching for a way to ingratiate himself with Lord North and King George. He was described by some as "a lawyer on the make." "His character as a man is by no means high," said another. Even King George had referred to him as "duplicitous."

Franklin, who had just turned sixty-eight, was dressed for the occasion in an elegant suit of dark brown Manchester velvet* and an old-fashioned full wig. He stood alone near the fireplace at one end of the room. Facing the lords at the table, his elbow resting on the mantel, he read aloud the text of the petition from the Massachusetts Assembly.

The petition appealed to the king's "wisdom and goodness" and asked, as a favor, that Governor Thomas Hutchinson and Lieutenant Governor Andrew Oliver be removed from office in order "to quiet the unrest" in Massachusetts and "restore the ancient peace and unity."

Franklin knew that the king and many of his ministers—Lord North somewhat less than the others—thought the British government had been too lenient for too long. There was little doubt, therefore, that the petition for the removal of Hutchinson and Oliver would be denied. But Franklin was not prepared for what came next.

Most of the Privy Council members were the king's friends. Many bore some grudge against Benjamin Franklin. They considered him the ringleader of all the tumult in America. And just a few days before, word of the Boston Tea Party had arrived in London. Here at last was a chance to punish America's most distinguished statesman and to get rid of him.

---

* It is said that Benjamin Franklin never wore this suit again until he signed the Treaty of Paris in 1783, ending the Revolutionary War.

Now Alexander Wedderburn turned the tables on Franklin. Leaping to his feet and standing between the chairs of two of the privy councillors, so close to the table that he could pound on it, Wedderburn let loose an attack on "Dr. Franklin" as the "prime conductor of the whole contrivance against His Majesty's two governors." It was sudden and unexpected.

It was not Thomas Hutchinson who should be removed from office, Wedderburn roared, but Benjamin Franklin himself. "This wily American, this man without honour," had obtained the Hutchinson-Oliver letters "by fraudulent or corrupt means, for the most malignant of purposes." He had stolen private letters and sent them to Boston, he continued.

"He has forfeited all the respect of societies and of men. . . . Men will watch him with a jealous eye; they will hide their papers from him and lock up their escritoires. Having hitherto aspired after fame by his writings, he will henceforth esteem it a libel to be called a man of letters," he thundered sarcastically.[16]

As Wedderburn unleashed on Franklin the full fury of Britain's frustration with her colonies, the assembled spectators began to laugh and nudge one another, visibly enjoying the show that the solicitor general was staging for them. Only Lord North displayed any sign of annoyance at the performance. Later, Edmund Burke, who in 1771 had been named agent for New York, called the attack "beyond all bounds and measure."

Through it all, Benjamin Franklin stood erect, barely moving, his anger held in check. Always patient under stress, now he endured Wedderburn's harangue for more than an hour, expressionless, scarcely moving a muscle, "as if his face were made of wood." Another eyewitness described him as "the whole time like a rock, in the same posture, his head resting on his left hand, and in that attitude abiding the pelting of the pitiless storm." [17]

The petition of the Massachusetts Assembly was denied.

As the session ended and the crowd moved slowly into an anteroom for a triumphant reception for Wedderburn, Franklin found himself walking alongside him. "I'll make your King a little man for this," Franklin is said to have whispered. Then he went home alone.

The next day a letter was delivered to Franklin informing him that he had been stripped of his royal appointment as deputy postmaster general of North America. In spite of this, Franklin told a friend, he considered his sending the packet of Whately letters to Boston one of the best actions of his life and would do it again in the same circumstances. "I have done nothing but what is consistent with a man of honour and with my duty to my king and my country," he wrote. "What I feel on my own account is half lost in what I feel for the public." His hopes for a reconciliation between Great Britain and her American colonies had turned to despair.[18]

Alexander Wedderburn, solicitor general for the British government, was known for his acid tongue. He verbally attacked and humiliated Benjamin Franklin, calling him a "man without honour" in front of an immense gathering of London society at a meeting of the Privy Council.

When the news of the Boston Tea Party reached London, Lord North had been dumbfounded. He could not understand how the colonists could rebel against a tax that made tea cheaper than it had ever been. Only "New England Fanatics" would do so. Even William Pitt, earl of Chatham, condemned it as "criminal." Boston must make restitution, he insisted. In fact, most Englishmen felt that Britain must not retreat in the face of such outrage. Here was a defiance of authority that could not be ignored.

Lord North claimed that the dispute was no longer over taxation. It revolved around whether Great Britain possessed any authority whatever over the "haughty American Republicans." King George agreed. "We must master them or totally leave them to themselves and treat them as Aliens," he said.[19]

The anger in England was intensified by the fact that the dispute was chiefly with Bostonians—the most hateful to Britons of all the colonists. All colonial troubles, said the English, could be traced to Boston. Even Americans living in London disapproved of Boston's misbehavior and sent a letter of protest to Parliament. Englishmen clamored for the use of force against the colonists.

Lord North would handle it his way. Instead of a bloody reprisal, he would close the port of Boston, lifeline to Massachusetts, the very element that made her great. He would cut her off from the sea, and thus from her neighbors and the world. The industry of a city that lived by building, sailing, freighting, and unloading ships would be annihilated in a single moment. He would starve the colonists into submission. Early in March of 1774, he submitted his Boston Port Act to Parliament.

Edmund Burke, a brilliant young Irish lawyer, became private secretary to the marquess of Rockingham. Burke used his literary talents to further the cause of the American colonies. *By an artist in the studio of Sir Joshua Reynolds.*

In the debates that followed, Edmund Burke ridiculed the idea of punishing Boston to preserve British dignity. Surprisingly, though, Isaac Barré, that staunch defender of the colonists, rose and with an unusal confusion of ideas, exclaimed—to the snickering of his colleagues—"Boston ought to be punished. *She* is your eldest *son!*" [20]

George III understood the stakes. "The Dye is now cast. The colonies must either submit or triumph," he wrote to Lord North. "I do not wish to come to severer measures but we must not retreat." [21]

Lord North was confident. Certainly, he thought, the

other colonies would not protest. They would welcome the opportunity to enjoy the trade denied to Boston. He was sure that New York and New Hampshire merchants would jump at the chance to grow rich on Boston's ruin.

The Port Act passed unanimously. It became law on March 25. It would remain in effect until Boston compensated the East India Company for the loss of the tea *and* gave evidence to the king of their good behavior.

The ease with which the first bill had passed encouraged North's ministers to propose three additional acts, which collectively became known as the Coercive Acts. The first, the Massachusetts Government Act, completely overturned the sacred Massachusetts Charter of 1691. It changed the constitution of Massachusetts to decrease the power of the legislature and increase that of the royal governor. The town meeting, that symbol of freedom as New Englanders understood it, was abolished. This would effectively end its role as a focal point of resistance and agitation. Town meetings could be held *only* with the governor's permission. Further, the king, not the Massachusetts Assembly, would now have the power of appointing the governor's council.

The Administration of Justice Act provided that government officials who might be brought to trial for enforcing the law (killing colonials in the line of duty) would *not* be tried in Boston. They would be sent to another colony, or to England, where they would likely escape punishment. And the Quartering Act provided, once again, for the quartering of British troops in the private homes of citizens of Boston.

Both Edmund Burke and William Pitt spoke out forcefully for the Americans. In what has been called one of the outstanding speeches of his career, Burke pleaded with Parliament:

> Again and again, revert to your old principles—seek peace and ensure it— leave America, if she has taxable matter in her, to tax herself. . . . Be content to bind America by laws of trade; you have always done it. . . . Let this be

your reason for binding their trade. Do not burthen them by taxes. . . . [Otherwise] you will teach them . . . to call . . . sovereignty . . . in question. When you drive him hard, the boar will surely turn upon the hunters. If that sovereignty and their freedom cannot be reconciled, which will they take? They will cast your sovereignty in your face. Nobody will be argued into slavery.

A noble lord has said, that the Americans are our children, and how can they revolt against their parent? . . . They are 'our children'; but when children ask for bread, we are not to give a stone. . . . Reflect how you are to govern a people, who think they ought to be free, and think they are not. Your scheme yields . . . nothing but discontent, disorder, disobedience. [22]

A month later, Pitt repeated his belief in the unconstitutionality of *all* parliamentary taxation of the colonies, and pleaded:

I am an old man, and would advise the noble Lords in office to adopt a more gentle mode of governing America; for the day is not far distant when America may vie with these kingdoms, not only in arms, but in arts also. . . . This has always been my received and unalterable opinion, and I will carry it to my grave, *that this country has no right under heaven to tax America*. It is contrary to all principles of justice and civil policy. . . . Instead of adding to their miseries, as the bill before you most undoubtedly does, adopt some lenient measures which may lure them to their duty; proceed like a kind and affectionate parent over a child whom he tenderly loves; and, instead of those harsh and severe proceedings, pass an amnesty on all their youthful errors.

He concluded with the prayer for America, "Length of days be in her right hand, and in her left riches and honour; may her ways be ways of pleasantness, and all her paths be peace!" [23]

King George refused to budge. Lord North echoed his king. He told Parliament: "The Americans have tarred and feathered your subjects, burnt your ships, denied obedience to your laws and authority; yet so clement and so forbearing has our conduct been that it is incumbent on us now to take a different course. . . .We must control them or submit to them." [24]

Now Lieutenant General Thomas Gage, who had traveled to England to apprise Lord North of the situation in the colonies, reinforced this view. He told the king, in language King George described as "very consonant to his character of an honest determined man," that the colonists "will be lyons, whilst we are lambs; but, if we take the resolute part, they will undoubtedly prove very weak." [25] Gage, therefore, was instructed by Lord Dartmouth to return to Massachusetts to replace Thomas Hutchinson. In 1773, Hutchinson had written to Lord Dartmouth requesting a temporary leave of absence from his position as governor, and he had been waiting for an appropriate time to depart for England.

General Thomas Gage was the British commander in chief in America. In 1754 he had served in the British army with George Washington. *By John Singleton Copley, 1768–1769.*

Lieutenant General Thomas Gage would become military governor *and* commander in chief of the British forces in North America. Thus, Parliament gave to the governor of Massachusetts the full resources of the military. Gage now had the power to deploy any force needed to suppress riots without the agreement of the council.

He was advised to move the capital of the colony from Boston to Salem, and the customshouse to Plymouth, which would effectively close the port of Boston, and to take all necessary steps to enforce the Port Act.

Three regiments of troops would accompany him. [26]

Chapter XXII

"a blot on the page of history"

The American Colonies: 1774

As church bells tolled in mourning, signaling that the Port Act was scheduled to go into effect in Boston that day, Thomas Hutchinson, his son Elisha, and his daughter Peggy quietly boarded the man-of-war *Minerva*, bound for England. He left behind a province seething with discontent. He had requested a short leave of absence and had anxiously awaited the arrival of Lieutenant General Thomas Gage, who would become acting governor in his absence. Hutchinson couldn't know then that he would never return to his homeland, a land he truly loved.

Two weeks earlier, on May 17, 1774, a raw and rainy day, General Gage had entered Boston amid much fanfare. He was met at the dock by an elegant John Hancock and the governor's cadets. Militia lined the way as Gage marched up King Street to the State House. That evening a banquet was held in his honor. The Patriots would show General Gage that Bostonians could be as elegant and polite as the general. This, despite the fact that they guessed, correctly, that General Gage had in his pocket orders to arrest John Hancock, Samuel Adams, and Dr. Joseph Warren.

Gage had first sailed into the harbor four days before, on Friday, the thirteenth, and had disembarked at Castle William. There, he conferred with Thomas Hutchinson before proceeding to Boston.

It was at precisely that time that many of Boston's citizens were at a town meeting in Faneuil Hall, listening to Sam Adams and the Patriots attack the Port Act as "intolerable." Word of its passage had arrived the day before. Terrified conservatives could think only of making restitution for the tea and

The Bostonians in Distress satirizes the blockade of Boston after the Boston Tea Party. The caged, starving Bostonians, surrounded by British soldiers, are receiving food and clothing from other colonists. *By Johann Martin Will, mezzotint, November 19, 1774.*

begging Great Britain for mercy. But Sam Adams and his followers wanted none of it. Rather than pay for the tea, they would "abandon their city to flames."

Committees of correspondence were quickly put into action. Once again, Paul Revere was called upon as the "patriot express" to appeal for aid to New York and Philadelphia. Soon all the colonists learned of the so-called Intolerable Acts, their nickname for the Coercive Acts, and patriot newspapers were printing their texts surrounded by thick black borders, symbolizing the death of American liberty.

The colonists feared that Boston's punishment would establish a precedent that might be used against every other seaport in America. If Boston were destroyed, British tyranny might sweep down the coast. The British government, the colonists felt, was waging "war on liberty wherever it existed in the empire, and there could be no refuge in neutrality." The blow had been aimed at Boston because it was foremost in the struggle for American rights. In Boston "lie the VITALS of *American freedom*." "The blow struck at . . . Boston is a Blow at all the colonies," said one Salem patriot.[1]

Donations poured in from towns near and far sympathetic to Boston's plight. Charleston, South Carolina, sent rice; Maryland sent flour; Baltimore, rye and bread. Fishermen in Marblehead, Massachusetts, who frequently sent barrels of dried codfish by ship to the poor of Boston, transported it by land in wagons. Philadelphia, and even London, sent cash. A farmer arrived from one little community in Connecticut driving a flock of 125 sheep, "hoping thereby you may be enabled to stand firm . . . in the glorious cause." To each, Boston wrote a grateful letter of thanks.[2]

On June 1, the day the Port Act was scheduled to go into effect, shops were closed in Philadelphia and flags were hung at half-mast. Churches were filled and the muffled bells of Christ Church "rung a solemn peal at intervals, from morning till night." In New York, effigies of Hutchinson, Wedderburn, Lord North, and the devil were carried through the streets and burned. In Connecticut, the Port Act was burned publicly.[3]

In Virginia, a day of fasting, humiliation, and prayer to signal the closing of the port was held. Thomas Jefferson, together with Patrick Henry and Richard Henry Lee, had proposed the plan. "It will inspire us with firmness in support of our rights, and . . . turn the hearts of the king and parliament to moderation and justice," Jefferson had said. "We must boldly take an unequivocal stand in the line with Massachusetts."

"An attack on any one colony should be considered an attack on the whole," the others agreed. Who could object to their praying for the people of Boston? they reasoned.[4]

Jefferson was coming to the realization that leadership could no longer be left in the hands of those older and more cautious members of the Virginia Assembly who were still clinging to the futile hope that they could gain colonial rights by more petitions to the king. They moved too slowly, he thought, and they were fearful of change. But gentlemen who knelt together side by side in prayer might suddenly find themselves on the same side of the controversy. Jefferson recognized the power of the church over the people and knew how strong its influence could be. A day of fasting and prayer would give a religious appearance to a political maneuver.[5]

"The effect of that day through the whole colony," Jefferson wrote later, "was like a shock of electricity, arousing every man and placing him erect and solidly on his center."[6]

Thomas Jefferson traveled more quickly down the road to revolution than most of his fellow Virginians. Although usually silent in general sessions of the Congress, he was extremely effective in committee, and had what John Adams called "a masterly pen."

Obviously, Lord North had made a mistake. He had misread the colonists. The Port Act, instead of isolating Boston, seemed to be "the very means to perfect *that union* in America, which it was intended to destroy."[7]

All up and down the seaboard men were coming to the conclusion that they must band together. "The whole continent seems inspired by one soul, and that soul a vigorous and determined one," reported the *Boston Gazette*.

Sam Adams had for some time been considering the possibility of a general congress of all the colonies, similar, perhaps, to the congress that Benjamin Franklin had initiated in Albany in 1754, and to the Stamp Act Congress that convened eleven years later.

So when he learned that New York's Committee of Correspondence was proposing such a meeting, Adams intensified his own efforts. He met secretly with members of the Massachusetts House of Representatives. They chose five delegates to represent them at a general congress: James Bowdoin, Thomas Cushing, Robert Treat Paine, John Adams, and Samuel Adams.

Virginia, too, agreed that there should be a meeting of all the colonies. Some of the burgesses met quietly in the Apollo Room of the Raleigh Tavern and decided that deputies of the various counties of Virginia should meet in Williamsburg on August 1 to appoint delegates. They instructed the Committee of Correspondence to "propose to the corresponding committees of the other colonies to appoint representatives to meet on September 5, 1774, in Philadelphia,"[8] the largest city and geographic midpoint of the colonies. This association would be known as the Continental Congress.

Thomas Jefferson realized that the delegates to this congress would need formal and exact instructions. As he pondered the problem, Jefferson looked for a *historical* precedent for the freedom he was so certain was right. He remembered reading that, more than a thousand years before, the Anglo-Saxons in England had lived under customs and unwritten laws based on the natural rights of man. These customs and laws had permitted individuals to develop freely, normally, and happily. This would become the basis for the resolutions he would draft. He hoped they would be moved as instructions to Virginia's delegates to the Congress. He hoped, too, that they would be incorporated into an address to the king. But, he cautioned, the Congress should address the king so that he understood that the colonists were asking not for favors but for rights: "Our ancestors, before their emmigration [*sic*] to America, were the free inhabitants of the British dominions in Europe, and possessed a right, which nature has given to all men, of departing from the country in which chance, not choice, has placed them."

He went on to say that the wilds of the American continent were settled at great sacrifice by the colonists. "Their own blood was spilt. . . . For themselves they fought, for themselves they conquered, and for themselves alone they have right to hold."

Kings, he boldly informed George III, are the servants, not the proprietors of the people. "Open your breast, Sire, to liberal and expanded thought," he lectured him. "Let not the name of George the Third be a blot on the page of history." Jefferson was directly, publicly, and fearlessly criticizing George III. No one had ever done that before.

Men were born to freedom, not to slavery, Jefferson continued. He had said this publicly four years before, when, as a new lawyer, he had tried to win freedom for a young slave. Now he was saying that the colonists were independent of the British constitution. They were subject to no laws except those they had freely adopted when they had consented to a new compact and formed a new society. Parliament had no right *whatsoever* to exercise authority over the colonies. Self-government, Jefferson knew, was right: "The God who gave us life, gave us liberty at the same time."[9]

He had studied, he had thought carefully, and he had come to the conclusion that the only solution was rebellion. His words would set aflame the imagination of the people and become their battle cry.

Unfortunately, Jefferson fell ill with a severe case of dysentery on his way to Williamsburg and was forced to return home. He sent the two copies he had prepared to his friend Patrick Henry and to his cousin Peyton Randolph, who, he was sure, would be elected chairman of the Virginia Convention. Henry didn't read it. Peyton Randolph did read his copy—aloud—to a large group of delegates who had assembled at his house. The younger men present were wildly enthusiastic, but the older, more conservative members shifted uncomfortably in their chairs as they pondered Jefferson's bold statements. They were hearing for the first time a categorical denial of Parliament's authority over the colonial legislatures. The resolutions were not adopted.

"The leap I proposed was too long, as yet, for the mass of our citizens," Jefferson explained later. But some of Jefferson's friends, inspired by his daring ideas, had the resolutions, titled *A Summary View of the Rights of British America*, printed by Clementina Rind, Williamsburg's only woman printer, without asking his permission. Among the first to purchase a copy was George Washington, who noted in his diary that it cost him three shillings nine pence.

The pamphlet was reprinted in newspapers throughout the colonies. Eventually it found its way to England. Jefferson learned that when it was read in Parliament by Edmund Burke, as he pleaded the case of the colonies, the name Thomas Jefferson was placed on the rapidly growing list of "outlaws" to be brought to England for trial.[10]

Chapter XXIII

spare the rod and spoil the child

London: 1774

Wind, weather, and three thousand miles of rolling sea stood between the British government and news of the response in the colonies to its unyielding policy. When Thomas Hutchinson was summoned to meet with King George immediately after his arrival in London, he was unable to answer directly the king's questions about the effect of the Massachusetts Government Act. All Hutchinson could speak of was the Port Act. News of the other "Coercive Acts" had not reached Boston by June 1, the day he had sailed for England. Therefore, with great deference to an overpowering monarch who knew what he wanted to hear, Hutchinson gave an ambiguous answer. After the meeting, the king told Lord North that he was certain the colonies would "soon submit."[1]

Other ministers seemed to feel that attempts were being made by their correspondents in the colonies to pressure them into concessions by painting the situation blacker than it actually was. The ministers remained set on their course.

Further, the people of England were beginning to resent the apparent tendency of the Americans to seek independence. Many Englishmen were convinced that American colonists were inferior to true-born Britons. They were not fellow subjects; they were merely "runaways" who lacked the courage to remain in England. The very word *colony*, they said, implied *dependency*. The colonists must be taught humility and obedience. Englishmen must not spare the rod and spoil the child.[2]

Thomas Hutchinson confirmed this. In a letter to a friend in Massachusetts, he wrote: "I am fully persuaded that there never has been a time when the nation in general has been so united against the colonies. . . . Even Lord Chatham, Burke, and Barré . . . condemn . . . the principles of the people there, and the actions consequent upon them." [3]

Neither the king nor his ministers had any grasp of the intensity of the colonists' feelings about their constitutional liberties. That the colonists might take up arms against them was inconceivable.[4] And a visit by a monarch to his colonies to assess the situation was unthinkable.

On September 21, Lord North told Thomas Hutchinson that if the colonists refused to trade with Britain, then "Great Britain would take care they should trade no where else." [5] The British were still certain that New York and Philadelphia were plotting to take over the Boston trade.

Less than two weeks later the king and his ministers learned how wrong they had been. Letters arrived from General Gage reporting that "popular fury was never greater" in Massachusetts "than at present." Gage went on to describe the virtual collapse of royal government, and his inability to remedy the situation without large troop reinforcements.[6]

This was devastating news. As Lord Dartmouth expressed it: "It is not the mere claim of exemption from the authority of Parliament in a particular case that has brought on the present crisis: it is actual disobedience and open resistance that have compelled coercive measures."

Dartmouth had already indicated in a letter to General Gage just how critical the situation had become. Not only the dignity and reputation of the British Empire, but its very existence depended on his success, Dartmouth warned him. Britain dared not lose her American colonies. If the Americans were to break free of the British Empire, the strength they provided Great Britain in the life-and-death struggle with France for international power would be lost. "Destruction must follow disunion," he wrote.[7]

Many Whigs in Parliament, particularly the earl of Chatham, William Pitt, agreed. France was the eternal enemy. Instead of quarreling with her colonies, Britain should be preparing for the next war with France. The colonists must have their rights restored, he counseled. Only then would they unite in defense of the British. Both Chatham and Lord Shelburne predicted that the loss of the American colonies would leave England easy prey to a vengeful France.

"The sun of Great Britain is set," exclaimed Shelburne, "and we shall no longer be a powerful or respectable people, the moment that the independency of America is agreed to by our government. . . . The commerce of America is the vital stream of this great empire."

And Isaac Barré declared, "You have not a loom nor an anvil but what is stamped with America: it is the main prop of your trade." It must not be destroyed in order that the mother country might be spared the humiliation of conciliating her oppressed subject. By meddling with America, another Whig warned, there was nothing to gain and everything to lose.

Why, some asked, should Great Britain seek from Americans "a pitiful Pittance in the Form of a Tax, while we may, with a Good Will, obtain Millions on Millions by fair Commerce?"[8]

But Lord Dartmouth was certain that "the thinking part" of the people of Massachusetts would soon rally to the support of Parliament. He was about to learn that to the American colonists, the Coercive Acts were "intolerable."[9]

Chapter XXIV

"a Nursery of American Statesmen"

The American Colonies: 1774

I have taken a long walk. . . . I wander alone, and ponder. I muse, I mope, I ruminate. The Objects before me are too grand . . . for my Comprehension. We have not Men, fit for the Times. We are deficient in Genius, in Education, in Travel, in Fortune, in every Thing. I feel unutterable Anxiety. God grant us Wisdom, and Fortitude!

Should . . . this Country submit, what Infamy and Ruin! God forbid. Death in any Form is less terrible.[1]

These were the thoughts recorded by John Adams at the end of June, as he contemplated the forthcoming Continental Congress and his role in it.

"I am at a loss, totally at a loss, what to do when we get there; but I hope to be there taught. It is to be a School of Political Prophets, I suppose, a Nursery of American Statesman," he wrote to his friend James Warren.[2]

John recognized the potential importance of the letters he was writing to his wife from the Congress, and had asked her "to put them up safe and preserve them. They may exhibit to our posterity a kind of picture of the manners, opinions, and principles of these times of perplexity, danger, and distress."[3]

The next month, when John was on the court circuit in Maine, he spent an afternoon, after court had adjourned, with his oldest, closest friend, Jonathan Sewall. Sewall was a Tory, and he had been attempting to lure John to his side for many months. Neither man had allowed their political differences to come between them.

Now the two went for a walk together on the hills above Casco Bay. When they reached a summit, they sat down on the warm rocks, and Sewall hesitantly broached the subject again. He begged his friend, for the sake of their old, deep friendship, to listen to him one more time.

He pleaded with John to try to understand that John would ruin his career, that men of property and standing were not on his side. But even more important, he must try to see that Britain's power was secure, irresistible. Britain will never change, Jonathan Sewall told his friend. She won't give in. The Sons of Liberty will drive this country to a civil war. "You will tear your country apart, rend it in two, set brother against brother." He reminded John of his own safety, and the safety of his wife and children. Then he begged him to withdraw from the delegation to the Continental Congress.

As John Adams listened to the pounding surf below, and to the pounding of his own heart, he felt a tremendous loss. While he recognized that much of what his friend said was true, he could not alter his course. "Sink or swim, live or die, survive or perish, I am with my country from this day on," he told him.

Both men knew that this was the end. They parted, each going his separate way down the hill to town. This was, as John later described it, "the sharpest thorn on which I ever set my foot."[4]

Now Wednesday, August 10, arrived, the morning on which the Massachusetts delegates were to set out from Boston for the Congress in Philadelphia. It was

A view of the city of Philadelphia from New Jersey, engraved in 1768.

a hot, dry, and dusty day. As the delegates—John Adams, Sam Adams, and Robert Treat Paine—gathered at the home of Thomas Cushing, the fourth delegate (James Bowdoin, the fifth delegate, remained at home because of illness in his family), they looked impressive in their new clothes and freshly powdered wigs. Even Samuel Adams was elegantly attired.

A few days before, a trunk had arrived at Sam Adams's door. It contained a suit of clothes, two pairs of fine shoes, a set of silver shoe buckles, sets of gold knee buckles and gold sleeve buttons, silk hose and cotton hose, a gold-headed cane, a cocked hat, a wig, and a new red cloak to replace his tattered old one. His friends had seen to it that he would represent Massachusetts properly in Philadelphia. He would hold his head high among the delegates from the other colonies. The name of the mysterious donor was never revealed.

Boston was sending its delegates off in style. They rode out of town in a coach with four horses. Two armed servants on horseback preceded them, and four in livery followed—two on horseback and two footmen. Five regiments of British troops watched silently from their encampment on the common. Their

THE CITY AND PORT OF PHILADELPHIA.

commanding officer predicted that the delegates would never agree to anything among themselves.

Cheering crowds had gathered to see them off. The three-hundred-mile trip would take nineteen days. They made "official" stops along the way in Hartford and New Haven in Connecticut; in the cities of Rye and New York in New York State; and in Princeton, New Jersey. They were feted all along the way.[5]

As they made their way on the long journey, they used the time to plan strategy for the meetings that would take place at the Congress. They must feel their way cautiously, they counseled one another. They must strive to avoid quarrels and factions that would split the delegates and set back their cause. They knew that many of the delegates feared the New England radicals.

In fact, shortly before they reached Philadelphia, several of the most active Sons of Liberty of that city rode out to meet them. These men were concerned, they told the four New Englanders, that they "had independence in view." The New Englanders must not even use the word, or give the least hint of it, they were warned. "Independence is as unpopular in Pennsylvania and in all the Middle States as the Stamp Act itself." They must be very cautious; they must not take the lead. The Virginians think they have the right to take the lead, and all must yield to them.[6]

On August 28, the day before their arrival in Philadelphia, John Adams put some of his fears—and the fears of all the delegates—into words in a letter to his wife, Abigail: "Tomorrow We reach the Theatre of Action. God Almighty grant us Wisdom and Virtue sufficient for the high Trust that is devolved upon us."[7]

As the fifty-six delegates from twelve colonies* began filtering into Philadelphia, "dirty, dusty, and fatigued," they met at the famous City Tavern, "the most genteel one in America," where they would take their meals. Here they tried to take one another's measure. On Tuesday, August 30, the Massachusetts delegates met Charles Thomson, who, they were told, was the Sam Adams of Philadelphia—the life of the cause of liberty. The next day they met John Dickinson, the Pennsylvania "farmer," whom John Adams described as "a Shadow—tall, but slender as a Reed—pale as ashes."[8]

On Friday, the Massachusetts delegation hurried to the City Tavern with great trepidation to meet the newly arrived members of the Virginia delegation. The New Englanders knew only too well that Massachusetts and Virginia, the two oldest colonies, epitomized the most striking features of their respective sections of the country. Their lifestyles could not have been more different. Would the northern merchants and the southern plantation owners find their differences irreconcilable? they worried. They found, instead, that they had one thing in common—their devotion to the cause of American freedom.

Among the Virginians were the portly and affable Peyton Randolph, a scholar and a masterful diplomat, and Richard Henry Lee, "a tall spare man," one of the Virginia firebrands. George Washington and Patrick Henry would arrive a few days later.

The delegates were a diverse group of men who had never before cooper-

* Georgia had been unable to send representatives.

ated among themselves. There were sober Quakers from Pennsylvania; elegant gentry from South Carolina and Virginia; frugal, pious New Englanders; worldly New Yorkers; and men from tiny Delaware and Rhode Island. In fact, the Congress included "a diversity of religions, educations, manners, interests, such as it would seem almost impossible to unite in one plan of action," as John Adams summed it up.[9]

But the Congress owed its very existence to consensus. Both radicals and conservatives had already agreed that this assembly was the only way to attempt to solve their problem. Not all were optimistic about its outcome. But all shared a sense of a virtuous American identity as opposed to what they saw as a corrupt British society. They came to this Congress with instructions to find a way to reestablish the harmony that, before 1763, had characterized colonial relations with their mother country. They came with hope for reconciliation.

It was with this hope in their hearts that all the delegates assembled at City Tavern at ten o' clock on Monday morning, September 5. From there they walked together to nearby Carpenter's Hall, a newly built, modest structure barely as large as City Tavern. The first session of the First Continental Congress in North America was about to convene. The "brace of Adamses," as Sam and John were referred to, sat quietly together in the back. They knew that many of the delegates from other colonies feared and condemned their radical stand.

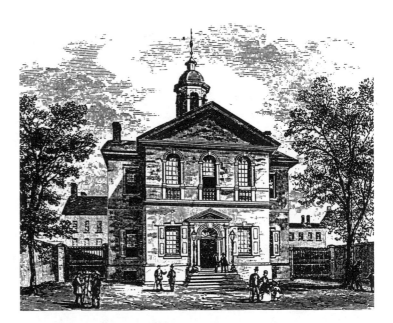

The first Continental Congress in North America convened at Carpenter's Hall, a newly built, modest structure in the city of Philadelphia.

This Congress was far too important for them to risk alienating its members.

In the end, though, Caesar Rodney of Delaware would write that "the Bostonians, who had been condemned by many for their violence, are moderate men when compared to Virginia, South Carolina, and Rhode Island."

One of the first orders of business was the choice of a presiding officer. Peyton Randolph, known to have "presided with great dignity over a very respectable society, greatly to the advantage of America," was quickly and unanimously approved. He gracefully accepted the title "President of the Continental Congress." He satisfied the conservative delegates and helped to create harmony within the Congress.

Randolph had been Speaker of the Virginia House of Burgesses, and in 1773 became chairman of Virginia's Committee of Correspondence. The following year he presided over the Virginia Convention, the unofficial surrogate for the dissolved House of Burgesses. Discreet, intelligent, and polite, he could be trusted by conservatives *and* radicals. A member of the colonial gentry, he was a staunch defender of colonial interests, skillful at balancing the rights of the colony against the demands of Great Britain. His was a voice of caution and moderation.

Charles Thomson, who had not been elected a Pennsylvania delegate because he was considered too radical, was nonetheless appointed secretary.

The next order of business for the delegates was to decide how they would vote. Should they vote by colonies, by poll, or by interests? Patrick Henry pointed out that since this was the first general congress that had ever been held, there was no precedent. A precedent must be established. But when he suggested that votes should be in proportion to each colony's population, the smaller colonies were immediately fearful that Virginia and Massachusetts might dominate the Congress. Too much power must not be given to anyone.

After much debate, it was decided that Congress did not have and could not at present "procure proper materials for ascertaining the importance of each Colony." Therefore, "each Colony or Province shall have one Vote."

By the second day, it had already become apparent that Congress was divided into two distinct groups in their attitude toward the mother country. One group hoped to form a more solid and constitutional union between Britain and America. The other wanted to throw off all subordination and connection to Great Britain. Patrick Henry seemed to want to establish a new national constitution: "Government is dissolved," he thundered. "The Distinctions between Virginians, Pennsylvanians, New Yorkers and New Englanders, are no more. I am not a Virginian, but an American."

To this, John Jay, an argumentative young lawyer from New York who represented the feeling of the opposing group in Congress, replied: "I can't yet think that all Government is at an End. The Measure of arbitrary Power is not full, and I think it must run over, before we undertake to frame a new Constitution."

Peyton Randolph was a moderate burgess from Virginia who was elected president of the First Continental Congress. He was well liked by all. It was said that had he not died suddenly in October, 1775, he might have become the first president of the United States.

Jay's argument prevailed. But Patrick Henry had set the tone. He had encouraged unity and avoided the possibility of sectional differences dividing the delegates along regional lines.

Now Thomas Cushing of Massachusetts proposed that sessions be opened with a prayer. But John Jay pointed out that the variety of sects in Congress made it impossible to find a form of prayer agreeable to all the delegates.

Sam Adams was ready. In a brilliant piece of strategy, he suggested that the Reverend Mr. Duché, a Church of England clergyman from Philadelphia, lead the prayers. Assuring his colleagues that he was no bigot, Sam Adams maintained that he "could hear a Prayer from a Gentleman of Piety and Virtue, who was at the same Time, a Friend to his Country." He had heard, Adams told his colleagues, that Mr. Duché was such a man.

The delegates were startled. Many were intolerant of any religious beliefs different from their own, and Sam Adams, particularly, was well known as an ardent critic of the Church of England. Sam was a stern Puritan, and he knew that many members of the Church of England held his religion in contempt. Now his proposal inspired a new spirit of harmony.[10]

While the Congress was in session in Philadelphia, in Massachusetts Josiah Quincy secretly boarded a ship at Salem and set sail for England. His mission was to try to explain the American point of view to Lord North, Benjamin Franklin, and others. When it was discovered that he had left, the Tories were fearful that he might convince the British ministers of the rightness of the American cause. His friends were afraid that he might be hanged on sight as a rebel.

At about the time that Josiah Quincy embarked for England, an express rider from Boston pounded into Philadelphia with news, later proved false, that the British had bombarded Boston. The reaction was startling. Every member of the Congress regarded the attack on Boston as an assault on his own capital. The delegates were drawn together even more solidly than they had been.

"WAR! WAR! WAR! Was the cry," John Adams wrote to Abigail. "If it had proved true, you would have heard the thunder of an American Congress." The alarm, occasioned by a report that British soldiers had fired on the people of Boston, sprang from the bloodless seizure by Gage's troops, in the early hours of September 1, of gunpowder kept in a public magazine (storehouse) in Charlestown.

As the delegates continued, over the next few days, to spell out their grievances with Great Britain and debate their suggestions for resolving them, John Adams was beginning to feel reassured about the quality of the delegates. In spite of their differences, he recognized that he was in the company of some of the most distinguished, thoughtful, intelligent Americans of the time. "There is in the Congress a Collection of the greatest Men upon this Continent, in Point of Abilities, Virtues and Fortunes," he wrote to Abigail. "The magnanimity and public spirit which I see here makes me blush for the sordid, venal herd which I have seen in my own province."[11]

The delegates spent a considerable part of each day outside of Carpenter's Hall. The extensive eating and drinking they engaged in, which seemed excessive to the frugal New Englanders, had a useful political as well as social purpose. As the good food and wine and talk bound them together, they came to understand and like and trust one another, and their feeling of being engaged in a common cause was strengthened.

On September 17, John Adams wrote in his diary, "This was one of the happiest Days of my Life. In Congress We had generous, noble Sentiments, and manly Eloquence. This Day convinced me that America will support the Massachusetts or perish with her." On that day they learned of Dr. Joseph Warren's "Suffolk Resolves."[12]

In early August, when General Gage had banned town meetings in Boston in accordance with one of the Coercive Acts that Parliament had passed in March, 1774, the Patriots had simply convened county meetings. Nothing had been said about *them*. In fact, they had never even been heard of in England.

Then, while the Continental Congress was meeting in Philadelphia, between sixty and seventy delegates appointed from towns in Suffolk County, which included Boston, were meeting in Milton for the third time since August. There, they unanimously approved a fiery set of resolves drawn up by Dr. Joseph Warren that protested the severe and unrelenting actions of a cruel monarch toward his "guiltless Children" of Massachusetts.[13]

Warren then entrusted the resolves to his faithful friend Paul Revere, who mounted his large gray saddle horse and rushed them to Sam Adams in Philadelphia in just six days.

The resolves urged Americans to "resist that unparalleled usurpation of unconstitutional power, whereby our capital is robbed of the means of life; whereby the streets of Boston are thronged with military executioners." They went on to say that no obedience was due to any of the Coercive Acts, "the attempts of a wicked administration to enslave Americans." Massachusetts must collect its own taxes and withhold them from the Royal authorities until the acts were repealed. They must form and arm their own militia, and "acquaint themselves with the art of war." Finally, the resolves urged the formation of a new provincial congress and a strict policy of nonimportation and nonexportation with "Great Britain, Ireland, and the West Indies." [14]

When Peyton Randolph read the resolves aloud to the Congress, the hall exploded in wild applause, cheering, and shouting. Men swarmed to the Massachusetts delegation to congratulate them.

The Congress adopted the resolves without a single change. But Joseph Galloway, a conservative delegate from Pennsylvania and a close friend of Benjamin Franklin, warned that it was tantamount to a declaration of war.

Galloway was an experienced politician in close touch with provincial agents in London. He understood the points of view on both sides of the Atlantic Ocean. Now he put forth his own "Plan of Union," which called for a complete reorganization of the British Empire. It recommended a union of the colonies under a Grand Council which, with the British Parliament, would care for America. Thus, political power would be distributed within the empire. Many of the delegates were impressed.

But John Adams, listening carefully as Galloway outlined his plan, saw it for what it truly was. Galloway made it sound like a fair proposal, while in reality, John knew, it was a dangerous illusion. It provided for American home rule, *but* under British direction. The assent of the parliament of Great Britain would be necessary to approve any acts or statutes passed by the colonists. [15]

After a lengthy debate, the plan came within one vote of being accepted and was eventually "laid on the table," where it remained buried. Ultimately, all mention of it was removed from the journals of Congress. [16]

John Adams had arrived at the Continental Congress with a sense that reconciliation with Britain was highly unlikely, and that war was probably inevitable. His wife reinforced this view. With her keen interest in political events and her skill at observation, Abigail Adams became her husband's best informant. Her letters to him included up-to-date, detailed, and accurate information about events in New England. Thus, while many in Congress continued to advocate a cautious and conciliatory policy toward Great Britain, John was reminded regularly by his wife that New England was ready to explode into war.[17]

"I am as fond of Reconciliation . . . as any Man . . . [but] the cancer is too deeply rooted, and too far spread to be cured by any thing short of cutting it out entirely," he wrote to a friend. He had little faith in compromise. There was no middle way, he insisted. He already had a clear vision of where they were headed.[18]

As he eloquently attempted to sway his colleagues in Congress toward a revolutionary course, he began to emerge as a leader. Now he was chosen to draft a "Declaration of Rights and Grievances." A sweeping rejection of Parliament's right to legislate for the colonies in any respect whatsoever, his declaration included a detailed list of bills enacted by Parliament since 1763 that infringed on colonial rights and "demonstrate a system formed to enslave *America*." "Repeal of them is essentially necessary in order to restore harmony between Great Britain and the American colonies," he wrote. He insisted that the colonists were entitled to "all the rights, liberties, and immunities of free and natural born subjects, within the *Realm of England*."

If Britain accepted the document, and Parliament repealed *all* the legislation that controlled American affairs, there would be peace and harmony between the two countries. Until that occurred, all the colonies agreed to "enter into a Non-importation, Non-Consumption, and Non-Exportation Agreement or Association," to begin on December 1. An exemption was granted to Virginia. She might wait until the following summer, after her next crop of tobacco had been harvested, dried, and shipped. South Carolina, also, would be permitted to delay the export ban until September 1775. A nonconsumption ban on all English goods would take effect immediately. Watchdog committees, to be elected in each town, would oversee its strict enforcement.

An embargo on trade with Great Britain, the delegates decided, would prove "the most speedy, effectual, and peaceable measure" for effecting redress.

The Association further prohibited the importing and purchasing of slaves and the use of imported tea from *any* country. In an effort to encourage American self-sufficiency, it urged the colonists to promote their own agriculture and manufactures. It also limited expensive diversions and entertainment, and encouraged frugality and industry.[19]

This document, known as the Continental Association, became the closest approach to a written constitution that the colonies as a unit had as yet devised.

As its final act, Congress decided it would prepare "a loyal address to his Majesty" for a redress of grievances. Richard Henry Lee, Patrick Henry, and John Adams headed the committee to draft the petition. Their version was deemed too radical. John Dickinson then prepared a more temperate draft, which appealed to the king's goodness, wisdom, and love of liberty. Its moderate language testified to the fact that the colonists were still loyal to their King. Their anger was directed at Parliament.

As the documents issued by the Congress were published and distributed throughout the colonies, and as committees were chosen to enforce the provisions of the Continental Association, a storm of protest arose from moderates and conservatives. They recognized that the Congress had evolved from a mediating body into a revolutionary government. The original purpose of the Congress had been to attempt a reconciliation of colonial differences with Britain. Passage of the Association had made such a reconciliation difficult. Many moderate Americans believed that Congress had gone far beyond its mission. They condemned its proceedings in pamphlets and newspapers.

One of the most articulate protests came from Dr. Samuel Seabury, rector of St. Peter's Church in Westchester County, New York, and considered "a Man of great good Sense, of a cheerful Disposition." Writing under the pseudonym A. W. Farmer (A Westchester Farmer), Seabury asserted that America's farmers were being asked to make sacrifices for a quarrel that city dwellers had started. It was the farmers, not the British, he contended, who would be hurt by the association. Nonimportation and nonconsumption would rob farmers of their best market and deprive them of reasonably priced supplies. Bostonians, he declared, believed that "God had made Boston for himself and all the rest of the world for Boston."[20]

In a mood of reluctant defiance, the Congress broke up on October 26, 1774. If colonial grievances were redressed, well and good, but if they were not, the Congress would meet again in May 1775. Many realized that their greatest achievement may well have been the demonstration of colonial unity and the coming together of many of the ablest men in the various colonies.

Before the delegates departed "the happy, the peaceful, the elegant, the hospitable, and polite city of Philadelphia," the Pennsylvania Assembly gave a dinner for them at the City Tavern. When a toast was proposed—"May the sword of the Parent never be Stain'd with the Blood of her Children"—John Adams overheard a Quaker sitting near him say to his companion, "This is not a Toast but a Prayer; come let us join in it."

Although at no time during the Congress had there been any mention of a declaration of war or of independence, the Tories branded the Congress a "blast from the trumpet of sedition." The drift toward war was gathering momentum.

Both Sam and John Adams believed that war was inevitable.

"I expect no redress, but, on the contrary, increased resentment and double vengeance," John Adams confided to Patrick Henry. "We must fight!"

"By God," exclaimed Henry, "I am of your opinion."[21]

Chapter XXV

"Blows must decide"

London: 1774–1775

In England, Benjamin Franklin was making one last effort to avoid war.

King George had already refused Lord North's recommendations to send a special commission to America to help resolve the crisis. "I do not want to drive [the colonies] to despair," the king explained to North, "but to submission, which nothing but feeling the inconvenience of their situation can bring their pride to submit to."[1]

Now Lord North and Lord Dartmouth, through an intermediary, turned to Franklin to help "bring about a reconciliation." Would Franklin draw up a plan that would offer a reasonable solution to both sides? Reluctantly, Franklin agreed. He suggested, though, that it would be better not to mention his name to other members of Parliament, since many were prejudiced against him.

He drew up a list of seventeen points, which he called "Hints for Conversation upon the Subject of Terms that might probably produce a durable Union between Britain and the Colonies." Franklin's "hints" recognized a continuing link between Great Britain and her American colonies, but his firm statement of what Britain must give up differed little from the demands of the Continental Congress.

When the Declaration of Rights and Grievances and the petition to the king arrived in London from the Continental Congress, Lord Dartmouth proclaimed them "decent and respectful," but other ministers were furious. The king reacted by instructing Lord North to prepare more punitive legislation. The king was certain that by helping those colonies that did *not* adhere to the Continental Association and punishing those that did, he would make the colonies quarrel among themselves.

Measures must be adopted, he insisted, that will "bring [the colonies] to a due obedience to the Mother Country." Then, on November 18, 1774, he declared, "The New England governments are in a State of Rebellion. Blows must decide whether they are to be subject to this country or independent." [2] King George could see no middle way for the colonies between unconditional submission and independence.

Just as the king was deciding that war was inevitable, Josiah Quincy Jr. arrived from Boston. He immediately went to tea with Benjamin Franklin. Within a week Franklin dispelled any fears Quincy might have had about Franklin's sentiments regarding the colonists. Quincy wrote to his wife that Franklin was "explicit and bold" on the subject of American rights and that "his hopes are as sanguine [hopeful] as my own of the triumph of liberty in America." A close bond of friendship developed quickly between the two men, one only thirty years old, the other about to turn seventy. They spent a part of almost every day together.

In London, Quincy met and talked with many great men—Lord North, Thomas Pownall, and Lords Dartmouth and Shelburne, among them. All told Quincy the same thing: They believed that the colonies would not unite and

Josiah Quincy was a zealous young patriot lawyer who, with John Adams, defended the British soldiers after the Boston Massacre. He became a devoted follower of Samuel Adams. "I speak it with grief—I speak it with anguish— Britons are our oppressors . . . we are slaves," he said in 1774. *Portrait by Gilbert Stuart, painted fifty years after Quincy had died.*

would soon submit. Lord North insisted that the authority of Parliament must be upheld in America. If he [North] were to yield on the question of parliamentary supremacy, North explained to Quincy, "he should expect to have his head brought to the block by the general clamor of the people, and he should deserve it."

But Shelburne indicated that if the Americans persisted, they would get all they asked. It was Shelburne's belief that the ministry could not carry on a civil war against them. He alone in Parliament admired and believed in Franklin. He fought the battle of sense and humanity single-handed within the cabinet.[3]

Among conservative Englishmen, there were many who feared that Josiah Quincy's visit to England boded ill for them. This most "pestilent Fellow," they said, had "come over from Boston with the lighted Torch of Rebellion in his Hand, and went Brandishing it up and down the Country, in hopes of kindling the flame of Civil Discord and Fury."

The English gentry feared, more than anything else, the doctrine of no taxation without representation. Since twenty-nine out of thirty Englishmen did not enjoy the right of suffrage—only gentlemen of property and breeding could vote—these men dreaded the possibility that the common people might push to gain an equal voice in government. To them, Boston was "full of a leveling, republican spirit." They felt Josiah Quincy had come with a mission to overthrow the established order in Great Britain with "American principles" of liberty and political equality.[4]

It was toward the end of the summer of 1774 that Benjamin Franklin had first met William Pitt, earl of Chatham. Franklin had been much impressed by "That truly great man." Chatham had talked to Franklin of "restoring the ancient harmony" between England and America.

Near the end of December, Franklin visited Chatham once again to discuss the colonists' Declaration of Rights and Grievances and the petition to the king, copies of which Franklin had sent to him. Franklin was encouraged when Chatham told him that the Congress had acted "with much moderation and wisdom." He hoped his government would "soon come to see its mistakes."

Then, on January 19, 1775, just two months after Josiah Quincy had arrived in London, Franklin accepted an invitation from Lord Chatham to attend the House of Lords the next day. When Franklin arrived, Chatham was waiting for him. The members of the House were stunned to see the two men together. Franklin listened as Chatham presented a motion to the Lords that troops be withdrawn from Boston. British troops, he said, were "an army of impotence and contempt, penned up in the town and unable to act." The Americans could never be defeated, he insisted. "It was our own violent proceedings that have roused their resistance," he continued. Nonetheless, his motion to withdraw the troops was defeated sixty-eight to eighteen. Quincy took careful notes of the speeches delivered that day.

To Parliament, the meeting of the Continental Congress appeared as a challenge, and congressional measures, however hesitant, as outright treason. Parliament, therefore, would not back down. In fact, they took even stronger measures. In mid-January, Parliament passed a bill restraining the entire trade of New England and excluding her from the rich fishing waters off Newfoundland "until they return to their duty." The Restraining Act would apply to Massachusetts, Rhode Island, and Connecticut. More troops were ordered to America, and discussions began with the German principalities about the hiring of mercenaries to supplement British troops.* General Gage was instructed to arrest "the principal actors and abettors," but the letter containing the instructions did not reach him until the following April.

By the end of January, the tuberculosis that had long plagued Josiah Quincy flared up anew. His friends feared he was dying. "His zeal for the public," Franklin wrote to a friend, "like that of David for God's house, will I fear eat him up." Ultimately, nothing the doctor attending him could do would save him. Quincy sailed for Boston on March 4, carrying in his head important information that Franklin felt was not safe to write. Josiah Quincy died at sea on April 26, within sight of Gloucester, Massachusetts, his messages never delivered. He was thirty-one years old.[5]

Quincy was mourned by many in Boston, but by none more so than Sam Adams. One of Quincy's last letters to his wife had expressed the devotion that Adams kindled in his young followers. "The character of your Mr. Samuel Adams runs very high here," Quincy had written from London. "I find many who consider him the first politician in the world."[6]

At the end of January, Lord Chatham visited Franklin at his flat on Craven Street. He remained there for two hours while his coach and footmen waited at the door, a signal to passersby that the two men were on friendly terms and attempting to effect a reconciliation between the two countries. Franklin wrote that Pitt's visit "flattered not a little my vanity," since it occurred exactly one year to the day after Franklin's disgrace at the hands of Alexander Wedderburn in front of the Privy Council.

Now Franklin and Lord Chatham discussed Chatham's "peace plan," which he had brought with him and which he would present to Parliament on February 1. Although Chatham reiterated his belief in "the supremacy of Parliament," and the king's right to station forces in the colonies, he did call for the Continental Congress "to be declared legal" in order that it might act for

* A mercenary is a professional soldier who is hired from a foreign country.

all the colonies, and he called for the suspension of "all grievous Acts whereof America had made complaints."[7]

Again, his motion was defeated. The next day, in the House of Commons, Lord North moved that the colony of Massachusetts be declared in a state of rebellion against the king. At the same time Franklin learned that his "hints" had been rejected by Lord Dartmouth.

Near the end of February, Lord North surprised Parliament by introducing a plan which would "offer grounds on which negotiation could take place." In one last effort to unite the country behind the ministry and avert a civil war in the empire, he put forth his Conciliatory Propositions by which he hoped to pacify the Americans, avoid a showdown, and satisfy his own peace-loving temperament. Instead of directly taxing the colonists, he proposed a system by which the colonists would tax themselves to the satisfaction of Parliament.

Lord North was shifting course. He believed that his plan would prove whether or not the colonists were sincere in their stated desire to settle their dispute with Great Britain. If they refused to accept his terms, then Parliament's moderation and the colonists' obstinacy would be apparent. North hoped, also, to spread dissension among the colonies. New York was already considered the weakest link in the chain of colonies. If New York agreed to his proposal, the union of the colonies would be broken and the Continental Congress would collapse.

But his motion infuriated the Tories. The majority in Parliament preferred to coerce the colonies into submission rather than hold out the olive branch. It was observed that when Lord North broached his plan, even his staunchest followers "turned pale with shame and disappointment."[8]

Two weeks later, news arrived from America that there would be a total embargo on the import and sale of English goods. Parliament retaliated by voting to extend the Restraining Act against American trade to include New Jersey, Pennsylvania, Maryland, Virginia, and South Carolina.

In the fiery debate that preceded the vote, Edmund Burke attacked the measure, saying that it was "new and unheard of in any civilized nation, to preserve your authority by destroying your dominions." Charles Fox, a leader of the Whigs in the Commons, said the measure was intended solely to exasperate the colonies into open and direct rebellion, and "to give an opportunity for drawing the sword and throwing away the scabbard."

Lord Sandwich, lord of the admiralty, countered by belittling the Americans: "Suppose the colonies do abound in men," he sneered, "what does that signify? They are raw, undisciplined, cowardly men. . . . Believe me, my lords, the very sound of a cannon would carry them off . . . as fast as their feet would carry them."

And in the House of Commons, Colonel Isaac Barré, remembering the battle outside Quebec in 1759, replied, "As to cowards—the very corps that broke the whole French column and threw them into such disorder at the siege of Quebec, were three parts composed of these cowards."[9]

So Parliament haggled.

As all this was happening, Benjamin Franklin was becoming more and more frustrated. Determined to leave nothing untried, he even offered to pay the East India Company for the tea the colonists had dumped into Boston Harbor from his own private fortune *if* the Massachusetts acts were repealed. Parliament refused. Then, on several occasions, and through intermediaries, Franklin was offered bribes if he could come up with more acceptable terms. He was disgusted by the offers.

He wrote to a friend in Massachusetts that if the Americans continued to stand firm and united in their boycott, the ministry could not possibly last another year. "The eyes of all Christendom are now upon us, and our honor as a people is become a matter of the utmost consequence. . . . If we tamely give up our rights in this contest, a century to come will not restore us in the opinion of the world," he counseled.[10]

In late February Franklin learned that his wife had died of a stroke on December 19. He decided the time had come to return home to Philadelphia. He had done all he could in England.

Friends began streaming to his rooms at Craven Street to say good-bye. Edmund Burke came for several hours. Joseph Priestley—a philosopher and supporter of the radical John Wilkes and the American colonists, and the scientist who had recently discovered oxygen—remained an entire day. Priestley later recalled that as Franklin was reading newspapers from America aloud to him, telling his friend what to extract from them for the English newspapers, "tears filled his eyes and ran down his cheeks." He was deeply saddened by the prospect of a civil war, Franklin told Priestley, but he thought he had done all he could to prevent it. If there should be a war, he was sure America would win, but it might take ten years and he would not live to see the end.

On March 21, Franklin took a carriage to Plymouth, where he boarded a ship bound for Philadelphia.

On the next day, Edmund Burke made one more passionate appeal for peace to the members of the House of Commons. Tall and imposing, with a commanding presence that matched his lofty phrases, Burke offered his proposals for conciliation:

> The people of the colonies are descendants of Englishmen. England, Sir, is a nation, which still I hope respects, and formerly adored, her freedom. The colonists emigrated from you, when this part of your character was most predominant; and they took this bias and direction the moment they parted from your hands. They are therefore not only devoted to liberty, but to liberty according to English ideas, and on English principles.
>
> The temper and character which prevail in our colonies, are, I am afraid, unalterable by any human art. We cannot, I fear, falsify the pedigree of this fierce people, and persuade them that they are not sprung from a nation in whose veins the blood of freedom circulates. . . . An Englishman is the unfittest person on earth to argue another Englishman into slavery.

He concluded his three-hour speech with the ringing words "Magnanimity in politics is not seldom the truest wisdom; and a great Empire and little minds go ill together."[11]

"Mr. Burke may fail to convince, but he never fails to charm," reported the *Gentlemen's Magazine*. "The attention of the House was rivitted [*sic*] to him."

While the members of Commons may have been moved to "the loudest, the most unanimous, and highest strains of applause," they did not change their minds about America. Burke's resolutions were defeated by a vote of two hundred and seventy to seventy-eight.[12]

Benjamin Franklin's voyage home was a long one. He used the time to write a ninety-seven-page journal of his last try for peace and to keep records of the changing water temperature and water color. The Gulf Stream might be studied like a river, he thought.

Franklin's ship dropped anchor in the Delaware River, opposite Philadelphia, on May 5. There he learned that General Gage had marched on Lexington and Concord on April 19. On the following day, he was elected a delegate to the Second Continental Congress, which would convene in four days.[13]

Chapter XXVI

"give me liberty or give me death!"

Virginia: 1775

By early 1775, Thomas Jefferson had become the most prominent citizen in Albemarle County in Virginia. When Committees of Safety were formed in Virginia to enforce the nonimportation and nonexportation of British goods, Mr. Jefferson was elected to head Albemarle's committee. Now he was about to represent his county at the Second Virginia Convention, to be held in Richmond on March 20.

The delegates met at St. John's Church, a simple white wooden building with about fifty or sixty pews. It was the only building in Richmond large enough to hold them.

On a fine spring day, Jefferson sat with George Washington and Richard Henry Lee, quietly, thoughtfully listening to the conciliatory resolutions being read. Soon these became too much for his friend Patrick Henry.

Inside St. John's Church in Richmond, Virginia, on March 23, 1775, Patrick Henry electrified the members of the Second Virginia Convention, including George Washington and Thomas Jefferson, when he cried out: ". . . give me liberty or give me death!" At that moment, Virginia was on the road to independence. *Photograph by L. H. Bober.*

Jumping to his feet, Mr. Henry called for a militia for the defense of the country.

Pandemonium broke loose. The members were still not prepared for such a radical step. Revolution had an ominous sound. The conservative members opposed Henry's resolution. They cautioned against armed resistance. Certainly, given time, the king would respond to their pleas for a redress of grievances. Military threats might hinder their progress.

Now Patrick Henry, with his perfect sense of timing, rose solemnly and majestically from his seat. He was recognized by Speaker Peyton Randolph.

He began slowly, praising the honor of those men who held a different opinion from his. Then he continued, "But this is no time for ceremony. The question before the House is of awful moment to this country." He went on:

Do not be lulled by an occasional smile from London. . . . Do not let yourself be betrayed with a kiss. Ask instead why British armies have come to your shores.

Has Great Britain any enemy in this quarter of the world to call for all this accumulation of navies and armies? No, Sir, she has none. They are meant for us. . . . They are sent over to find and rivet upon us those chains which the British Ministry has been so long forging. And what have we to oppose them? Shall we try argument? Sir, we have been trying that for the last ten years.

We have done everything that could be done to avert the storm which is now coming on. We have petitioned; we have remonstrated; we have supplicated; we have prostrated ourselves before the throne and have implored its interposition to arrest the tyrannical hands of the Ministry and Parliament. Our petitions have been slighted; our remonstrances have produced additional violence and insult; our supplications have been disregarded; and we have been spurned, with contempt, from the foot of the throne.

Henry had begun calmly, but as he spoke, his passion increased. Now he cried out, "There is no longer room for hope. If we wish to be free . . . we must fight! I repeat, Sir, we must fight! . . . Gentlemen may cry peace—but there is no peace. The war is actually begun."

His voice fell to a whisper as he continued. Then, eyes blazing, it rose to a thundering challenge and rang like an anvil through the timbers in the little church: "Is life so dear, or peace so sweet, as to be purchased at the price of chains and slavery? Forbid it, Almighty God! I know not what course others may take, but as for me . . . give me liberty or give me death!"

Not a sound was heard as Henry finished and sank into his seat. The men sat stunned and silent. Then, with his "usual elegance," Richard Henry Lee rose and supported Mr. Henry.

Suddenly, Thomas Jefferson asked to be heard. The delegates were amazed. Never before had Jefferson participated in a public debate. Overcoming his shyness and swept away by Henry's brilliant oratory and "the exact conformity of our political opinions," he argued "closely, profoundly, and warmly" in support of Henry and Lee. The radical delegates vehemently supported Henry. But George Washington remained silent, deep in thought.

The resolutions passed with a vote of sixty-five to sixty, an example of "the inequality of pace with which we moved, and the prudence required to keep front and rear together," Jefferson said. "We often wished to have gone faster, but we slackened our pace, that our less ardent colleagues might keep up with us; and they, on their part, differing nothing from us in principle, quickened their gait somewhat."

Mr. Jefferson was among the committee of twelve men appointed to prepare a plan for arming and training soldiers. He continued, as was his practice, to work behind the scenes, talking and planning in small groups. Good-natured, mild-mannered, never aggressive, he managed to instill his ideas into others so subtly that they came to believe it was they who had originated the ideas. He had a genius for friendship and a shy warmth that always attracted people to him. It proved extremely helpful now.

But he continued to hope that war could be avoided.[1]

At the same time, a short distance away in Williamsburg, John Murray, fourth earl of Dunmore and royal governor of the colony of Virginia, was writing to his superiors in London that a firm hand was all that was needed, and the present disturbances would soon be over. It was his "considered opinion," he wrote, that a few young men, no doubt well intentioned, "but spoil'd by a strange, imperfect, desultory kind of Education which has crept into fashion all over America," had been the cause.[2]

In April the impetuous and self-important Lord Dunmore secretly removed fifteen barrels of gunpowder from storage at Williamsburg and had them taken to a man-of-war anchored in the York River. The colonists were furious. Patrick Henry led an armed force of several thousand men to compel him to return them. It was only when Dunmore agreed to pay for the powder that Henry was convinced to retreat.[3]

Then, in the wake of angry demonstrations at the beginning of June, the frightened governor and his family fled the palace in the middle of the night, seeking refuge on a British frigate. From there, he scraped together a small force of British soldiers and marines and occupied Norfolk, the seaport of Virginia and a refuge for Loyalists. He was able to rally a large group of these Loyalists into companies of irregulars who then carried out a series of attacks on settlements and plantations along the river-banks.[4]

Finally, on November 7, Dunmore brought on the most dreaded event of all for white Virginians, an uprising of slaves against their masters. He issued a proclamation to the people of his "rebellious colony" in which he declared martial law and demanded that all able-bodied citizens of Virginia capable of bearing arms report "to his Majesty's STANDARD, or be looked upon as Traitors."

He then shocked most white Virginians by offering freedom to slaves "appertaining to Rebels" who would be willing and able to bear arms for the king "for the more speedily reducing this Colony to a proper Sense of their Duty." Thousands of slaves responded. They immediately fled to British lines, where hundreds joined the newly created Royal Ethiopian Regiment, under the command of British officers. Many wore shirts with the motto "Liberty to Slaves" stitched across the front, mocking the rebels' badges imprinted with "Liberty or Death."[5]

John Murray, fourth earl of Dunmore, was Virginia's last royal governor. In 1775 he promised freedom to slaves who would abandon their masters and fight for the king.

In December, the representatives of the Fourth Virginia Convention responded to Dunmore's proclamation with "A Declaration." In it "all slaves who have been, or shall be seduced, by his lordship's proclamation . . . to desert their masters' service and take up arms against the inhabitants of this colony . . . may return in safety to their duty, and escape the punishment due their crimes." They would be pardoned.[6]

Lord Dunmore had miscalculated. Moderate burgesses who had been unwilling to fight the British and who had been acting as a brake on their more radical compatriots, suddenly realized that the time had come to act. They viewed Dunmore's offer of freedom to their slaves as one more attack on private property, and worried about the inability of their plantations to function without slave labor, not to mention the actual fear for their own safety. White Virginians had long been haunted by the terror of a slave uprising. No issue could have solidified them more.

"If [Dunmore] is not crushed before spring," George Washington predicted, "he will become the most formidable enemy America has. His strength will increase as a snowball." [7]

The time had come to join the radicals.

Chapter XXVII

"O! What a glorious morning is this!"

Massachusetts Bay Colony: 1775

The die is cast. . . . Heaven only knows what is next to take place, but it seems to me the Sword is our only, yet dreadful alternative, and the fate of Rome will be renued [*sic*] in Britain.

—Abigail Adams to Mercy Otis Warren, February 3, 1775

Something was brewing. The redcoats and the royal marines were drilling more often, their horses were being exercised, there was a flurry of activity in Boston Harbor, and British officers had been seen examining the roads to Concord. Rebel leaders were being carefully watched. Sam Adams and John Hancock had already left Boston for the safety of the parsonage of the Reverend Jonas Clarke in Lexington, a quiet, rustic town about fifteen miles northwest of Boston. Reverend Clarke was married to Hancock's sister.

"Sam Adams writes the letters, and John Hancock pays the postage," it was said at the time. The Patriots knew that General Gage had been ordered, in the name of the king, to arrest them.

On April 14, a secret letter had arrived from Lord Dartmouth to General Gage. The colonists were in open rebellion, the document said. Gage must counter force with force. A cautious and conservative man, Gage had a scrupulous concern for the rule of law, and had tried to act with firmness and restraint. Even his enemies thought him decent, able, and full of good intentions. Respected as a man of honor and integrity, he had tried for a year to keep a lid on the colonial powder keg. Now he was being ordered to ignite it.[1]

Gage knew that to accomplish his mission he must strike at the heart of the rebel movement quickly and decisively, and with as little bloodshed as possible. And he must accomplish this before the Patriots could muster their own militia. Above all, he must keep his plans secret. He was certain that this would not be a difficult task to accomplish, in spite of the fact that he, himself, had recently found among the Patriots a man willing to sell *his* province's secrets for a price: a traitor who would keep Gage well informed of developments within the rebel network in Boston.

Paul Revere was a member of a voluntary committee of about thirty mechanics that had been formed specifically to watch the movements of the British. Now he knew that something serious was about to happen. Revere was already the Patriots' most trusted express rider and messenger. William Dawes, a canny young smuggler, was another trusted courier. He was a born actor. It would come in handy.

On Sunday, April 16, in spite of the fact that it was the New England Sabbath, Dr. Joseph Warren sent Revere to Lexington to warn Adams and Hancock that the British were planning some move. Warren suspected that General Gage would try to arrest the two men. But he had also learned that they were interested in a large cache of ammunition and flour stored in the nearby town of Concord. Adams and Hancock should know this. Warren himself had willingly risked remaining in Boston as the head of the rebel intelligence service.

Gage apparently believed that his plans were still secret. Thus, Revere had a pleasant and uneventful ride through the spring countryside to Lexington that Sunday. None of the British patrols stopped him.

Immediately after Revere's arrival at the Reverend Clarke's in Lexington, Hancock sent a messenger to Concord with instructions to divide and move the stores. He also sent warnings to other towns that their minutemen should be ready for action.

There had always been militias* in the colonies, originally assembled in the event of Indian attacks. Now, the younger able men of each village were arranged into separate militia groups and given the name "minutemen." When a warning came of a possible attack, these minutemen had to be ready, guns in hand, in a matter of minutes. They were well organized and alert.

On his way back to Boston, Revere stopped in Charlestown to confer with William Conant, colonel of the local militia, and several other patriot leaders from the town. Fearing that the British Regulars might try to stop all communication between Boston and the countryside, they worked out a plan for warning the country in the event that no couriers were able to leave Boston.

The town of Boston was a virtual island, confined to a diamond-shaped peninsula barely a mile wide and two miles long. It was linked to the mainland at its southern point by a narrow strip of land known as Boston Neck. The Back Bay, an expanse of tidal marshes and mud flats, lay on the west. Boston Harbor opened to the Atlantic on the east. On the northern side, the Charles River separated Boston from Charlestown.

Revere described their plan: "If the British went out by Water, we would Shew two lanthorns in the North Church Steeple; & if by Land, one, as a Signal;

---

* There was no police force in Boston—or London. Soldiers were the only means of keeping order.

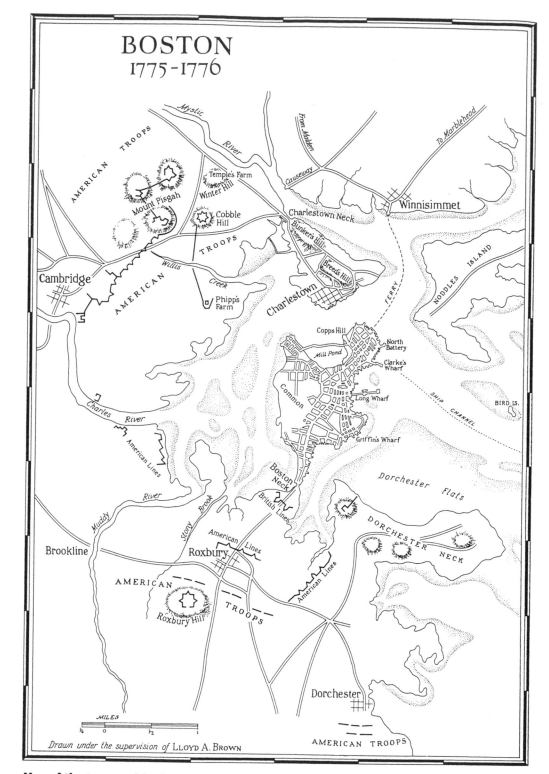

Map of the town and harbor of Boston and surrounding towns.

for we were apprehensive it would be difficult to Cross the Charles River, or git over Boston Neck."

In either case, Conant promised to meet Revere with a swift horse to carry him to Lexington and then on to Concord, six miles beyond.

They agreed that the best place to display the signal was in the steeple of Christ Church, commonly called Old North Church. It was Boston's tallest building and was clearly visible across the water in Charlestown.*

Although the rector of the church was a Loyalist, one of the vestrymen was a staunch Whig, and he agreed to help. The sexton of the church, Robert Newman, was also happy to help. That young man was known in town as "prompt and active, capable of doing whatever Paul Revere wished to have done."

By Tuesday, April 18, General Gage fully realized that it was all but impossible for him to make a move in Boston without Paul Revere spreading the word throughout the countryside—far more quickly than his men could march. Unless the rebel express riders could be stopped, his mission could not succeed. So all during the day mounted patrols were sent out to intercept them on the roads between Boston and Concord.

Instructed to pretend that they were simply out riding on a mild spring day, the soldiers were to hide in the bushes after dark to waylay any rebel messengers. But the people who saw them were quick to notice the thick bulge of pistol holders and sword pommels visible beneath their long and heavy dark blue riding coats. As they attempted to find the alarm riders, these British soldiers alarmed the countryside instead.[2]

At the same time, a young stable boy ran through the busy streets of Boston to Paul Revere's house to tell him what he had just overheard. Some British officers, watching to make certain that their horses were properly groomed and in top condition, had whispered to each other about "hell to pay tomorrow."

Revere thanked him, then confided to him that he was the third person

*Charlestown, like Boston, was attached to the mainland by a slender neck of land.

who had brought him that information. He immediately brought the news to Dr. Warren. Warren knew of the troop movements, but he wasn't certain of exactly when and where they would strike. Now he decided to play his trump card. He, like General Gage, had an informer. He would make inquiry. He must be absolutely sure. Both Warren and Gage understood the need for accurate intelligence. Each had a network of spies.

Warren's confidential source was unknown to anyone else. The identity of the informant was a carefully guarded secret, someone he could approach only in a moment of dire necessity. The person was very near the heart of the British command and therefore at great risk.[3]

The message came back to Warren: The troops were about to seize Sam Adams and John Hancock in Lexington and then move on to Concord to burn the stores there. They would go "by sea," across the Charles River, then along country lanes to avoid detection. His worst suspicions were confirmed.

Warren hurriedly sent for William Dawes and asked him to carry a warning to Concord. Dawes had played no part, as yet, in the rebel cause, but he was a loyal patriot whose business often took him through the British checkpoint on Boston Neck. The British sentries had no reason to suspect him, and "mounted on a slow-jogging horse, with saddle-bags behind him, and a large flapped hat upon his head to resemble a countryman on a journey," he was able to talk his way through the narrow gates by pretending complete innocence.

Warren then dispatched Paul Revere on a different route with the same message: "A large body of the king's troops were embarked in boats from Boston, and gone to land at Lechmere's point."[4] Revere, whose name, but not his face, was well known to the British, would go by boat to Charlestown. He would risk getting past the British man-of-war *Somerset*, which had been moved to the mouth of the Charles River, the place at which any boat headed for Charlestown must cross.[5]

At Province House, the palatial home where General Gage was living with his American-born wife, and which was serving as his headquarters as well,

Lord Percy, one of Gage's brigade commanders, had just completed a visit during which Gage had confided to him the movements planned for that night. Gage impressed upon Percy the tremendous importance of secrecy. The mission must remain a "profound secret."

Now, at dusk, Percy headed for the Boston Common, where troops were already lining up, waiting to embark. Townspeople were gathered about in groups, watching and talking. Percy was not recognized. Then, as Percy moved closer to one group, he overheard someone say, "The British troops have marched, but will miss their aim."

Margaret Gage, Thomas Gage's beautiful but headstrong American wife, was torn between her loyalties to her country and to her husband. John Singleton Copley called this painting of her his greatest portrait.

"What aim?" asked Percy.

"Why, the cannon at Concord," came the reply.

Percy was stunned. Hurrying back to Province House, he related to Gage what had happened. The mission was common knowledge.

Gage cried out in anguish. His confidence had been betrayed, he explained, for he had communicated his design to one person only, besides Percy.

Percy thought that Gage was referring to his wife.

We will never know for sure—Dr. Warren never revealed his source—but circumstantial evidence strongly suggests that Dr. Warren's informer was Thomas Gage's American wife, Margaret.

Torn between her loyalties to her country and to her husband, Margaret had told a gentleman that "she hoped her husband would never be the instrument of sacrificing the lives of her countrymen." Later, she confided her dilemma in a letter to a friend, quoting Blanch of Spain in William Shake-speare's *King John*:

> The sun's o'ercast with blood: fair day, adieu!
> Which is the side that I must go withal?
> I am with both: each army hath a hand;
> And in their rage, I having hold of both,
> They whirl asunder and dismember me.
>
> . . . .
>
> Whoever wins, on that side shall I lose;
> Assured loss before the match be play'd.

In an earlier speech, Blanch says to her husband, "Upon my knee, I beg, go not to arms."[6]

Gage loved Margaret dearly. Daughter of a prominent Brunswick, New Jersey, family, she was tall and proud, described as an "exquisite rare bird," "a daughter of liberty unequally yoked in the point of politics."[7]

As soon as it was dark, a large number of soldiers were marched to the foot of Boston Common, on the Charles River. Flatboats were made ready to ferry them across the river. They moved silently through the dark, cobbled streets, attempting not to arouse suspicion, in order to reach the beach where the boats with muffled oars were waiting to ferry them across. A dog that just then happened to bark was killed instantly by a bayonet.[8]

Now that they knew that the British would go "by sea," Paul Revere must inform Robert Newman, the sexton of the Old North Church, that it was time to hang the lanterns. But British soldiers were quartered in Newman's mother's house, which was just one block away from North Church. As the soldiers sat in the parlor playing cards, the young man, in order to avoid suspicion, announced that he was going to bed early. Then he climbed out of his upstairs bedroom window and dropped silently to the garden below, where he met Revere.

At the church, while his friend stood guard, Newman quietly mounted the wooden stairs to the belfry, lit two lanterns, and hung them for a few moments only, wanting to signal the men who he knew were waiting in Charlestown, but at the same time not wanting to alert anyone on the *Somerset*. His task completed, Newman, fearful of being seen if he left by the front door, climbed out a church window, then ran home, clambered over a roof and back inside through his own bedroom window.

Revere, for his part, hastened home, donned his overcoat and heavy riding boots, bade a hurried good-bye to his wife, and, followed by his faithful dog, set out for the north part of town where he had hidden a rowboat. It was about 10:15. He somehow managed to get through the troops that were rapidly gathering in North Square and heading for the common. On the way he met the two companions who would row him across the river.

Suddenly, he realized that he had forgotten his riding spurs. He wrote a note to his wife, tied it to his dog's collar, and sent him home. Soon the dog returned with the spurs in place of the note.

Then the men realized that in their haste they had also forgotten some cloth to muffle the sound of the oars. One of the men had a girlfriend who lived nearby. He whistled softly, and she came to the window. They told her they needed some cloth, and in a minute she wiggled a little, then tossed down her flannel underwear, "still warm from her body," as Revere would later tell the story to his children.[9]

Then, "two friends rowed me across the Charles River, a little eastward where the man-of-war *Somerset* lay. It was then young flood [the start of the incoming tide], the ship was winding [turning on its anchor], and the moon was rising. They landed me on Charlestown side."

Paul Revere was in luck that night. The moon hung low in the sky, making it possible for his little boat to pass safely in the dark shadows, unseen by lookouts on the *Somerset*. Revere was met on the opposite shore by Colonel

Conant, who had seen the lanterns and had brought him a "very good horse," named Brown Beauty. She was big, strong, and very fast.[10]

Now Revere rode swiftly, but carefully, toward Lexington. He had almost reached Cambridge when he ran into a British patrol. He turned about sharply and galloped for a road to Medford, outrunning his pursuer. After that, he "alarmed almost every house—shouting 'The Regulars [British soldiers] are out!'—till [he] got to Lexington."

It was midnight when Revere reached the Clarke parsonage in Lexington. Everyone had retired for the night. The house was dark and silent. A group of militiamen stood guard in the moonlight. When Revere called out to the sergeant, he ordered Revere not to make so much noise—people were sleeping.

"Noise!" Revere countered. "You'll have noise enough before long. The Regulars are coming out!" Revere knocked loudly on the door. Windows flew open. Reverend Clarke, not recognizing Revere, refused to allow him to enter. Then Hancock's head appeared at a window.

"Come in Revere. We are not afraid of *you*!" he called.

When Hancock learned of the British plan to seize the ammunition stored at Concord, he dramatically demanded his sword and his gun. He would march with the minutemen! The prudent Adams tried to stop him: "[Fighting] is not our business," he lectured him. "We belong to the Cabinet."

"If I had my musket I would never turn my back on the troops," Hancock insisted. But he relented, and the two men left swiftly for Woburn.

Dawes arrived soon after. He and Revere decided to continue on to Concord and alarm the countryside on the way. They mounted their weary horses just as Lexington's town bell began to ring in the night.

As the two headed west toward Concord, they met Samuel Prescott, a young doctor and enthusiastic Son of Liberty. He was just returning to Concord from Lexington, where he had been courting his girlfriend. Dr. Prescott offered to help, and rode along with them. About halfway there, they ran into a mounted patrol of Regulars. Prescott saw an opportunity and quickly jumped his horse over a low stone wall and escaped. He reached Concord with the alarm. Dawes also made a dash for freedom, yelling "Haloo, boys, I've got two of 'em," hoping to confuse the enemy. But this merry actor was thrown from his horse. Eventually, having lost his horse and being badly frightened, he limped back to Lexington in the moonlight, keeping a wary eye out for more British Regulars.

Paul Revere was caught. He was ordered to dismount. Some of the Regulars began to abuse him, but an officer intervened.

"Sir," he said politely, "may I crave your name?"

"My name is Revere."

"What? Paul Revere?" the officer exclaimed in surprise.

"Yes."

The questioning continued. Revere answered truthfully. With

"I know what you are after, and have alarmed the country all the way up," Paul Revere boldly warned the British officers who captured him during his midnight ride the night of April 18, 1775.

six pistols aimed at him, he told them they had "missed of [their] aim." He had "alarmed the country all the way up," he continued.

His defiance infuriated the soldiers.

Now he was searched for weapons. Fortunately, he had none.

As the men continued to question him, warning him that if he did not tell the truth they would "blow his brains out," Revere responded angrily that "he did not need a threat to make him speak the truth."

"I call myself a man of truth, and you have stopped me on the highway, and made me a prisoner I knew not by what right. I will tell the truth, for I am not afraid."

But he knew he must turn the soldiers away from Lexington—away from Hancock and Adams. Now he did lie, glibly telling them that the British boats had run aground. By the time the delayed troops reached Lexington, he warned, five hundred men would fall upon them. If they remained near Lexington they would be in grave danger.

The sound of gunfire coming from the direction of Lexington seemed to substantiate what Revere had said. The country was rising up against them. The Regulars were becoming increasingly nervous. Finally, they freed Revere, but they took his horse, turned around, and galloped back to warn their commanders. Paul Revere headed for Lexington Green.

By now, many others had taken up the role of express riders, and the message was carried swiftly across the countryside. Paul Revere had organized a plan to warn town leaders and military commanders all the way to the New Hampshire border, a distance of about thirty miles—normally a full day's journey. As each leader was warned, he in turn warned others. Soon, church bells began to ring, and the heavy beat of drums could be heard for miles in the night air.

In some towns, such as Carlisle, just north of Concord, a prearranged system of beacon fires and signal guns was used. Warning guns were used in Wayland, also. In the nearby town of Sudbury, the town's alarm bell was rung.

The alarm was passed from one to another, and word spread from town to town in time for militias to muster aid for Lexington and Concord. It was a crucial gain for the Patriots. They were not caught unprepared.[11]

In the meantime, things had not gone smoothly for the British soldiers. When they landed at Cambridge Marsh, after being ferried across the river, they had to wade ashore, then, shivering in the cold night air, wait until 2 A.M. for their provisions to arrive. Again, they waded through marshes, then, wet to the waist, their feet squishing in their wet boots, they began their slow march to Lexington. Alarmed by an occasional distant musket shot and the ringing of bells, they sent back to Boston for reserves.

As the eastern sky paled and dawn began to break over Lexington, a scout came pounding over the hill from the direction of Cambridge. The Regulars were out—in force! More than a thousand men were less than half an hour from Lexington.

John Parker, chosen by the Lexington militia to be their captain, had waited on the green in the cold, clear moonlight for the Regulars to approach. Parker and his men had decided not to "meddle or make with said regular troops unless they should insult or molest us." Hancock and Adams, they knew, were fleeing Lexington, and the supplies that had been stored in Concord had been moved to other hiding places. They would let the soldiers pass through on their way to their already compromised expedition to Concord.[12]

Now Parker ordered his drummer boy, sixteen-year-old William Diamond, to beat the call to arms. William had just moved to Lexington from Boston, where a kindly British soldier had taught him the art of military drumming. The Lexington militia came running onto the green. Most of them were family men over thirty. Twelve were teenagers, eight fathers had sons by their sides, and one man was sixty-three. They came in their workaday clothes, carrying their own muskets.[13]

"Stand your ground. Don't fire unless

The Lexington militia marched to the tune of this drum and fife on the morning of April 19, 1775. Sixteen-year-old William Diamond beat the call to arms. The player of the fife is unknown. *Photograph by David Bohl.*

fired upon, but if they want a war, let it begin here!" Captain Parker instructed his men. The captain knew that it was not in character for an Englishman to massacre his compatriots. He was certain the redcoats would march past his men on their way to Concord and ignore them.[14]

The first British regiment was just reaching the green. They rode up and reined their horses to a halt before Parker and his men.

"Lay down your arms, you damned rebels, and disperse!" their leader, Major John Pitcairn, called out.[15]

The minutemen stood firm.

Suddenly, Parker realized that they *were* going to fight. His men were a ready target on the green. Instantly, he ordered them to disperse.

Slowly, still holding their guns, the minutemen began to move away. This seemed to excite the Regulars, who now began to run toward the green, their muskets at the ready, their bayonets gleaming, their red uniforms splendid in the first rays of sun. British officers were shouting conflicting commands as Parker's men, weapons in hand, continued to look for cover behind a stone fence, a tree, or a barn.

Then, without warning, a shot rang out. No one knows who fired it, but it really didn't matter.

Within a few seconds a full volley of shots was fired at the Lexington men. Eighteen men fell, eight of them dead or dying. Teenager Isaac Muzzy died at his father's feet. Jonathan Harrington, hit in the chest, crawled to the doorstep of his house and died there before the horrified eyes of his wife and son. Then the British came on with their bayonets.

Paul Revere, who had returned to Lexington in order to save a trunk of John Hancock's papers from falling into British hands, had just passed through the militia on the green. He "heard a gun fired, which appeared to be a pistol . . . then a continual roar of musketry when we made off with the trunk." Musket balls were "flying thick around him." Nonetheless, he and his companion, John Lowell, carried their precious cargo through the gunfire and into the woods beyond the green, remaining there for about fifteen minutes.[16]

As the sun rose over the town of Lexington, British Regulars, led by the mounted Major John Pitcairn, fired at the retreating colonists. *Engraving by Amos Doolittle.*

At that moment, Sam Adams and John Hancock were hurrying away from Lexington in their carriage. Sam Adams had said that it was essential that if shots were fired, the British must be the first to fire. Only then would America stand united, he warned. Now, hearing the firing, he exclaimed, "O! What a glorious morning is this!" Hancock thought he was referring to the lovely spring day. Adams corrected him: "I mean," he explained, "what a glorious day for America!"

It was over quickly. As the Americans scattered, the British fired a victory volley, then jubilantly marched on to Concord. At the same time, thousands of American men of all ages were pouring into Concord from all the surrounding farms and villages. They didn't know yet what had happened at Lexington, so, as the British columns approached, some of the Americans fell into line in front of them and marched to the sound of their own fifes and drums. The British responded by also beginning to play, "as if banded together in one great festive parade."

The Americans even "set out chairs on green lawns, under blossoming

Even as the redcoats attempted to retreat to Boston from Concord, they looted and burned some of the houses as they passed by, running through with their bayonets any men they found along the way.

cherry trees for the officers to rest in" while soldiers began searching for stored military supplies. Angered at not finding any, they set fire to the courthouse and cut down the Liberty Pole.[17]

Soon, the sound of shots came from the direction of Concord's North Bridge. Some of the British officers had continued on, deciding to take their men across the bridge to higher ground on the other side of the Concord River. There the battle began. The British were not prepared for what happened next.

The colonial method of fighting was very different from the British line-by-line attack in close formation over an open plain. From the earliest days of settlement, the Americans had had to fight over mountainsides and other rough ground. They had learned to hide behind trees, boulders, barns, or stone walls, constantly changing their positions. And, unlike the British, Americans had been trained to aim. They caught the British by surprise.[18]

Now the Americans relentlessly pursued the British troops with deadly accuracy of fire until the redcoats themselves had to be rescued by two regiments of troops sent out from Boston. Yet even as the redcoats attempted to retreat to Lexington, they looted and burned some of the houses as they passed by, and any men they found they ran through with their bayonets. But the six-mile walk was marked by constant assault by hidden colonials. Eventually, the redcoats limped back to Boston.

By the close of the day a change had taken place in the colonists. From Englishmen rebelling against the unjust laws of their king, they had become Americans fighting for their freedom. The dreaded message was carried throughout the colonies in shock waves. "The . . . bloodshed at Lexington . . . ,"

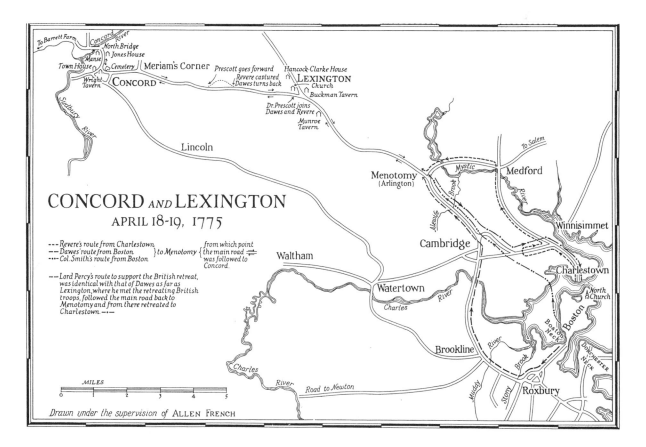

A map showing the routes to Concord and Lexington.

Edmund Randolph said, "had in Virginia changed the figure of Great Britain from an unrelenting parent into that of a merciless enemy."[19]

George Washington wrote to a friend in England: "A brother's sword has been sheathed in a brother's breast, and . . . the once happy and peaceful plains of America are either to be drenched with blood or we are to live as slaves—sad alternative! But can a virtuous man hesitate in his choice?"[20]

A war of words was turning into a war of bullets.

Lord North's Conciliatory Propositions reached New York the day after the news of Lexington and Concord.

Chapter XXVIII

English power, English honor

London: 1775

While Lord North was offering conciliatory proposals on the one hand and punitive programs on the other, he was also busily defending the policies of his government. For such a public defense, in early spring he turned to his friend and ally, the great Tory writer Dr. Samuel Johnson. As the author of the pioneering *Dictionary of the English Language*, as well as *The Rambler, Rasselas*, and numerous pamphlets, Johnson was already acclaimed as the literary giant of the age and a celebrity in his own right. He had come to North's aid before with defensive political pamphlets.

Now, in response to North's plea, he wrote *Taxation No Tyranny*, which was published in early March. The pamphlet was a forceful critique of the First Continental Congress's address to the king. Although a friend, Dr. Johnson had little respect for Lord North's ministry—he called it "feeble and timid."

Samuel Johnson was one of the most remarkable men of all time. King George III had great respect for his writings, and the two men came to admire one another greatly. They first met when Johnson was reading in the king's library, which was readily opened by the librarian to readers such as Johnson. "He is the finest gentleman I have ever seen," Johnson said of the king after this meeting. *Plaster cast by Joseph Nollekens, after the 1776 original by Herman W. Liebert.*

"[It] cannot act with that authority and resolution which is necessary," he explained.

Yet he had no love for the Americans, either. He considered them hypocrites who cried out for liberty while they would enslave "Negroes, Indians, French Canadians, and Loyalists." Johnson felt that all the colonists were being required to do was to pay the cost of their own safety. Their argument, he contended, was simply "We do not like taxes, therefore we will not be taxed." Surely, they could afford to pay taxes, he protested, pointing to reports of their "greatness and their opulence, . . . the fertility of their land, and the splendor of their towns." Those who "thus flourished under the protection of our government should contribute something towards its expense," he wrote.

An Englishman who voluntarily goes to America "cannot complain of losing what he leaves in Europe." Further, he stated, many Englishmen were "virtually represented" in Parliament; why not the Americans? Self-interest was at the heart of their outcry. How was it, he thundered, "that we hear the loudest yelps for liberty among the drivers of slaves?"

Dr. Johnson aimed his anger also at American defenders in England. They were the "Zealots of anarchy," the "libertines of policy." They had no patriotism, no virtue, if they did not love England more than they seemed to love justice in America. The obstinate, hard-hearted Americans were "rascals, robbers, and pirates."

He defined a Tory as "one who adheres to the ancient constitution of the State and the . . . hierarchy of the Church of England," even though he had many friends among Nonconformists and among those whom he loved to call "Whig Dogs."[1]

Dr. Johnson's bitter criticism mirrored the view of the country gentlemen who comprised Lord North's majority in Parliament. Uninterested in ideas, narrow in their concerns, and prejudiced against Americans, these men were ready to accept Johnson's accusations against the colonists.

Among those who were not was Edmund Burke, the most steadfast of the friends of America in Parliament. In September 1775 he wrote to Rockingham that the people of England were misled by the ministry and the court, "so that the violent measures towards America are fairly adopted and countenanced by a majority of individuals of all ranks, professions, or occupations."[2]

William Pitt persuaded his oldest son to withdraw from the army, rather than be sent to fight against the Americans.

Another who strongly disagreed with Dr. Johnson was Catharine Macaulay, a

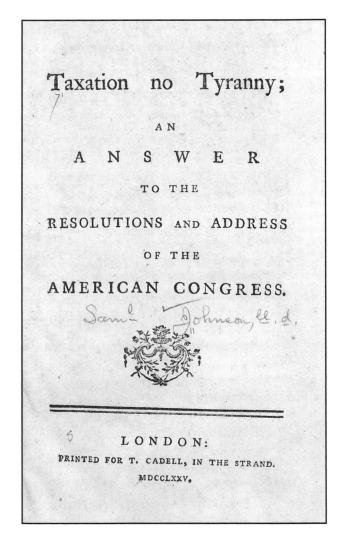

In *Taxation no Tyranny,* written at the request of Lord North and published early in March 1775, Samuel Johnson defended taxation without representation. How was it, he thundered, "that we hear the loudest yelps for liberty among the drivers of slaves?"

brilliant historian who had achieved recognition as an advocate of the American cause. Widow of a Scottish physician, Catharine Macaulay was the author of an eight-volume history of England. She corresponded with John Adams and Mercy Otis Warren.

In a radical pamphlet in support of the American cause, Mrs. Macaulay attacked George III's government. Her purpose, she wrote, was to rouse her countrymen to resist policies that might sink England "into the lowest abyss of national misery." The Americans, she continued, have been "stripped of their most valuable rights . . . to the eternal shame" of England. Her countrymen must act, she warned, for if they did not, "a civil war" would break out and "either the mother country . . . may ruin both herself and America, or the Americans . . . will gain an independency." In the latter case, Britain would lose the advantages of colonial trade, as well as the liberties and privileges that their ancestors had gained for them.

Dr. Johnson found Mrs. Macaulay's Whiggish principles and her sharp tongue distasteful. When she returned from a trip to Paris, much taken with current fashions there, Johnson remarked that she should "redden her own cheeks," rather than "blacken other people's characters."[3]

Despite the vigor of her attack, Mrs. Macaulay's pamphlet had little effect. The audience for whom she wrote in her pamphlet—primarily the masses, the laboring classes of Great Britain—had no voting power. Moreover, the reality of the situation in America was not fully understood in London. Whatever else made its way across the Atlantic Ocean, fresh and accurate knowledge of what was happening on the opposite shore most assuredly did not.

When an account of the action at Lexington and Concord reached London from the patriot leaders, the government chose to ignore it. From Salem, Massachusetts, Dr. Joseph Warren had rushed off eyewitness accounts of the action, an estimate of casualties, and a published account from the *Salem Gazette*. He had sent them, secretly, on a light, fast schooner that carried nothing but his report. The packet had arrived in England in just four weeks. The documents were delivered to the new Lord Mayor of London, John Wilkes, supporter of liberty. Within three days, the story was in all the leading British newspapers. General Gage's account, although sent off four days earlier than Warren's, but on a heavy cargo vessel, did not arrive until two weeks later.

One of the accounts sent by Joseph Warren described the redcoats as "seeming to thirst for blood." It accused them of having committed horrible atrocities on innocent people—including old men and pregnant women—and of wantonly burning houses. The Americans, the report contended, had been fired upon without provocation.[4]

General Gage, at the other extreme, wrote a letter to Lord Dartmouth without even mentioning the expedition to Concord. And in a letter to his superior, Lord Barrington, written three days later, Gage told him, "I have nothing new to trouble your lordship with, but an affair that happened here on the 19th instant." Gage followed this with a brief, factual account of the expedition, with the only mention of British casualties in a postscript reference to "a return of the killed and wounded."*

When King George read the Patriots' report, he was not disturbed. He sent his reaction to Lord Dartmouth: "By the newspaper report . . . which undoubtedly was drawn up with the intention of painting a skirmish at Concord in as favorable a light as possible for the insurgents, I am far from thinking the General [Gage] has reason to be displeased." Gage had accomplished his mission, the king continued, with the loss of an equal number of men on both sides. "The die is cast. I therefore hope you will not see this in a stronger light than it deserves."[5]

It took a while for the king and his government to comprehend the enormity of the news. In fact, many in England continued to believe that only a small minority of Americans were rebels. They were certain that the majority were loyal Britons at heart. Loyalists in the colonies encouraged this belief.

*Altogether, the British suffered 273 casualties, including 73 dead, out of a total force of about 1,800. Of the nearly 4,000 colonial militia who fought (not more than half at any one time), 49 were killed and 46 were wounded.

When a group of merchants in England began to draw up petitions to Parliament requesting repeal of the Coercive Acts, many other merchants rebuked them, accusing them of putting their own profits ahead of the good of the empire. Thus they were forced to stand by helplessly as their businesses were destroyed.

As King George continued to vacillate between policies of concession and coercion, the number of critics of his government began to grow. Soon, political debate could be heard not only in Parliament, but in the coffeehouses in London and in the countryside. Two themes were repeated: The policies of the administration were tyrannical and unjust; and they would not succeed in their object of subduing the colonies. Indeed, as Benjamin Franklin had said ten years earlier, these policies might very well ruin England in the process. But Franklin's wit had too much wisdom in it for the king to appreciate. For George III, English power and English honor were at stake.

Chapter XXIX

"we have taken up arms"

The American Colonies: Summer 1775

We live in Continual Expectation of Hostilities. Scarcely a day that does not produce some. . . .

Does every Member feel for us? Can they realize what we suffer? And can they believe with what patience and fortitude we endure the conflict?

"Courage I know we have in abundance, conduct I hope we shall not want, but powder—where shall we get a sufficient supply?"
—*Abigail Adams to John Adams*
June 25, 22, and July 16, 1775

When the members of the Second Continental Congress reassembled in May of 1775, it was John Adams who, patiently and relentlessly, led them down the path to independence. Long before most of the other delegates were ready to take the step, John had made up his mind. He had a clear picture from his wife of the devastating situation in Massachusetts. Her letters brought the reality of war home to him. He understood full well that Congress could no longer afford to offer an olive branch in one hand without pointing a musket with the other. While some members continued to press for conciliation with Great Britain, Abigail's letters echoed in John's mind, and he pressed for powder.

But no man in Congress had a clearer idea of what independence would entail: the risks, the obligations, the burdens that it would impose on Americans. To this end he persuaded Congress to enlist a Continental Army under the command of George Washington. Strong leadership, he knew, would be critical to success in further battles. Washington was a Virginian, experienced in the military, financially able, and of impeccable character and firm, quiet judgment. Adams was certain that the choice of Washington as commander in chief would have "a great effect in cementing and securing the union of these colonies."[1]

John Adams recognized, also, that America's ability to protect her own commerce on the high seas would be vital to her survival as a nation, and he became a leader in establishing the American navy.

But he was often annoyed at the length of time it took some of the delegates to make up their minds, and frustrated at their tedious debates and their "nibbling and quibbling," as he called it. He wrote to Abigail: "The Business I have had upon my Mind has been as great and important as can be intrusted to Man. . . . When 50 or 60 Men have a Constitution to form for a great Empire, at the same Time that they have a Country of fifteen hundred Miles extent to fortify, Millions to arm and train, A Naval Power to begin, an extensive Commerce to regulate, numerous Tribes of Indians to negotiate with, a standing Army of Twenty-seven Thousand Men to raise, pay, victual and officer, I really shall pity those 50 or 60 Men."[2]

He suggested to his wife that since he had so many great duties and responsibilities, and therefore not much time to write to her, she should rely on Paul Revere for detailed news of the activities of the Congress. But he continued to rely on her for news from Massachusetts. Living just half an hour's ride (nine miles) from the lines of American volunteers under Dr. Joseph Warren who had encircled the British army in Boston, she constantly had minutemen marching past her front door, as well as riders on the Coast Road who often stopped for a drink of water. They all brought news. Now she learned details of a great battle underway at Bunker Hill* in Charlestown, and of the death there of their dear friend Dr. Joseph Warren.

Before dawn on Saturday, June 17, Abigail had been awakened by the sound of far-off gunfire. All through the sweltering morning, as she went about her chores, the dull boom of cannons intruded on her consciousness.

Finally, she took her seven-year-old son, John Quincy, by the hand and together they walked to the top of nearby Penn's Hill. There, they climbed up on the rocks for a better view. In horror they stared across the bay into the black, smoking mass that was all that was left of Charlestown. It had been burned to the ground.

George Washington, in the uniform of a colonel in the Virginia militia, was nominated by John Adams to be commander in chief of the Continental Army at about the time this portrait was painted. *Oil by Charles Wilson Peale, 1772.*

"The Day; perhaps the decisive Day is come on which the fate of America depends," she wrote to John the next day. "My bursting heart must find vent at my pen." She went on to tell him of the death of Dr. Joseph Warren, who "fell gloriously fighting for his Country. . . . Great is our Loss."

*It was actually fought at Breed's Hill.

"The Day; perhaps the decisive Day is come on which the fate of America depends," Abigail Adams wrote to her husband, John, after she had watched the burning of Charlestown by the British.

Her letter continued: "Charlestown is laid in ashes. The Battle began upon our intrenchments upon Bunker Hill, a Saturday morning about 3 o'clock and has not ceased yet and tis now 3 o'clock Sabbath afternoon." She ended by telling her husband, "I cannot compose myself to write any further at present."[3] Two days later Abigail concluded her letter, alluding once again to the death of Dr. Warren: "The tears of multitudes pay tribute to his memory."[4]

Describing the situation in Boston, she compared the life of the inhabitants to that of "the most abject slaves, under the most cruel and despotic of tyrants." As for herself, she told her husband, "I have felt for my country and her sons, and have bled with them and for them. Not all the havoc and devastation they have made, has wounded me like the death of Warren. We want him in the Senate; we want him in his profession; we want him in the field."[5]

Warren had recently been named a general of the Massachusetts Provincial Army but had not yet been officially commissioned. He was chairman of the Committee of Safety, empowered to call out the militia, and after the Battles of Lexington and Concord he had been named president of the Massachusetts Provincial Congress. He was an inspiration to the amateur citizen-soldiers who were pouring into the camp in Cambridge, near Boston, where he had established army headquarters on April 20.

Warren had gone voluntarily to fight alongside his men, not as a general but as a common soldier, musket in hand. Hit on the right side of his head with a musket ball, he died instantly, his fine clothes soaked with blood. Whispered accounts said he was beheaded. "Everybody remembered his fine, silk fringed waistcoat," a British officer later recalled. Warren was only thirty-four.

After the Battles of Lexington and Concord, King George III had sent additional troops to Boston, increasing their number to ten thousand. Generals

A painting of the death of Dr. Joseph Warren, killed during the Battle of Bunker Hill. Abigail Adams wrote of his loss to her husband, John: "Not all the havoc and devastation [the British] have made has wounded me like the death of Warren. We want him in the Senate; we want him in his profession; we want him in the field. . . . When he fell, liberty wept." *Painted by John Trumbull in London about 1785.*

William Howe, Henry Clinton, and John Burgoyne had come as well, to aid General Gage. They knew what they would do.

Boston was dominated by high ground on two sides. To the north, on Charlestown Neck, were two mounds, Bunker Hill and Breed's Hill, half a mile across the estuary of the Charles River to the tip of the Boston peninsula. To the southeast, Dorchester Heights stood at the harbor opposite Boston Neck.[6]

The British plan had been to occupy and fortify Dorchester Heights and then, if possible, attack Boston from the heights. Once again, the rebels had gotten wind of their plan. Quickly, and secretly, on the night of June 16, under cover of darkness, they began to build fortifications on Breed's Hill, somewhat lower than Bunker Hill, but closer to Boston. There they staked out a V-shaped fortification, pointing, like an arrow, toward the slumbering city across the Charles. About midnight, in the starlight, the troops began to dig as noiselessly as possible. As they worked, the only sounds were the church bells and the cry of "All's well" from the watch on board the men-of-war anchored in the harbor.

But by the first gray light of morning, the watch on the warship *Lively* could see what was happening and sounded the alarm. The captain ordered a bombardment, and cannons were fired from the warships.

While Americans were feverishly working to fortify the path of retreat back over narrow Charlestown neck to the mainland, Gage sent in forty barges filled with troops for a frontal attack. He then ordered the ships in the harbor to set fire to Charlestown. "A large and noble town in one great blaze," General John Burgoyne described the scene. "The church steeples being of timber were great pyramids of fire above the rest."

Burgoyne told of the British troops ascending the hill, and the enemy pouring in fresh troops by the thousands, while British ships were cannonading them. "The hills round the country covered with spectators," he continued. "The enemy all in anxious suspense. The roar of cannon, mortars, and musketry, the crash of churches, ships upon the stocks, and whole streets falling together in ruins to fill the ear . . . and the reflection that perhaps a defeat was a final loss to the British Empire in America to fill the mind, made the whole a picture and a complication of horror and importance beyond anything that ever came to my lot to be witness to."[7]

The fire that consumed Charlestown continued to burn for two days.

The Americans, although exhausted from their all-night labors, and having had "little victuals and no drink," continued to resist as the British marched up Breed's Hill. They held their fire until the redcoats were within fifty feet, then "aimed at their bellies" and pulled their triggers. Line after line of British soldiers were mowed down. About twelve hundred Americans were confronting three thousand British troops.

Yet one soldier fighting for the rebel cause, who suddenly recognized a British officer as an old friend, shouted, "For God's sake, spare that man! I love him like

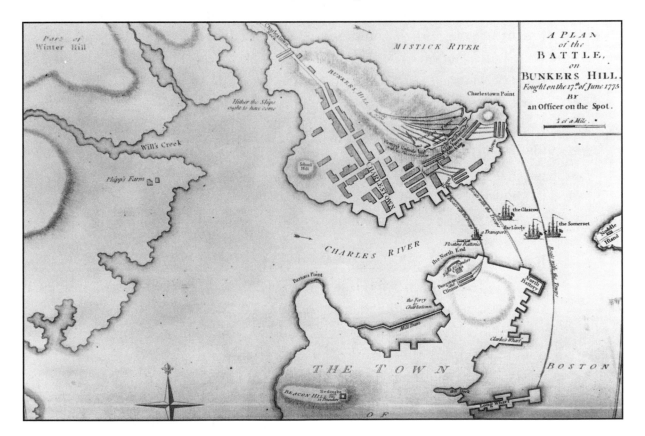

Map of the Bunker Hill area.

a brother." The officer, recognizing the voice, bowed to his friend for saving his life, then turned and walked out of range. Friendship was stronger than war.[8]

The American men continued to fight valiantly until they simply ran out of ammunition. As they retreated, they were raked by British cannons. When it was over, two hundred and seventy-one Americans had been wounded, one hundred and forty killed. But more than a thousand British Regulars had fallen, one quarter of them killed, including Major Pitcairn of Lexington. The British were left in possession of the field, but with a staggering number of casualties as the price of victory. With two more such "victories," it was said, the British would have no more army left in America.

The Battle of Bunker Hill, as it came to be called, changed the nature of the war for many Americans. The Battles of Lexington and Concord had been fought to defend their communities against an invading army. But at Bunker Hill, hundreds of soldiers from Connecticut, New Hampshire, and distant parts of Massachusetts risked their lives to establish and then defend an advance outpost against British-held Boston. Although they lost on the field of battle, they gained the respect of their opponents. General Gage described it in a letter to Lord Dartmouth: "The rebels are not the despicable rabble too many have supposed them to be. . . . They are now Spirited Up by a Rage and Enthousiasm, as great as ever People were possessed of.

"The conquest of this country is not easy," he ruefully concluded. [9]

Bostonians were still reeling from the destruction of Charlestown when Thomas Jefferson, newly elected delegate from Virginia to the Continental Congress, arrived in Philadelphia on June 20. News of the battle had not yet reached the city. It was a hot and humid day. The journey of more than two hundred and fifty miles from Williamsburg, over roads that were little more than trails through the wilderness, had taken Jefferson ten days.

For this meeting, Congress sat in the imposing red brick colonial State House, later known as Independence Hall, on Chestnut Street, instead of the smaller Carpenter's Hall, where the first Congress had met. The Pennsylvania

The red brick State House in Philadelphia, which later came to be known as Independence Hall. It was here that the delegates to the Second Continental Congress met to decide to fight for "independency."

Assembly had lent Congress its room on the ground floor, a large, beautiful, white-paneled chamber with windows lining two sides.

On the morning of June 22, when Jefferson arrived at the State House for his first meeting, crowds had already gathered outside to watch the Philadelphia Associators drilling their newly formed battalions of soldiers. A feeling of war was in the air.

Inside the building, to ensure secrecy, the delegates, wiping damp brows, locked the doors and opened the high windows just a crack from the top in spite of the sweltering heat. Insects buzzed and banged against the panes.

The tall, thin, sandy-haired new member from Virginia presented his credentials to Congress and was seated as a duly certified member. He was greeted warmly, and his concern about participating in this august group of men was soon eased. The other Virginia delegates had boasted about him, and many were anxious to meet this young man who, they had heard, wrote such eloquent prose about liberty and freedom.

Mr. Jefferson was introduced immediately to many of the members, but he was particularly drawn to two men. He had eagerly looked forward to meeting Benjamin Franklin, who had just returned from England, where, Jefferson knew, he had met many government leaders and had come to understand the workings of the British Parliament. Jefferson thought how wonderful it was to see him, his chair at the end of the row pulled out a little, his legs crossed as he sat, calm and composed, in his brown Quaker suit, his long gray hair falling on his shoulders.

And Jefferson was particularly happy to meet John Adams of Massachusetts. He had heard that Adams was a brilliant lawyer and a leader of the radicals, whose political opinions were exactly the same as his. Mr. Adams was talked of as the ablest debater for the revolutionary cause.

John Adams, in turn, was instantly drawn to Jefferson. "He soon seized upon my heart," John wrote to Abigail. Jefferson had not been in Congress for more than a few weeks when his quick, decisive way in committee became evident to all who worked with him. "He was prompt, frank, explicit . . ." Adams described his new young friend. "He will be given work at once."[10]

And he was. He and "the Pennsylvania Farmer," John Dickinson, were appointed to draw up a "Declaration of the Causes and Necessity for Taking Up Arms." It would be presented by General Washington to his troops.

Washington was preparing to leave for Cambridge, Massachusetts, where he would join the army just beginning to assemble there. Sitting quietly in his new uniform, a blue-and-buff coat with gold epaulets, a small, elegant sword at his side, and a black cockade in his hat, he was a silent reminder of where they might be heading. It was important, the delegates felt, that the soldiers understand recent political happenings in order to justify the steps that were being taken toward war.

John Dickinson, the conservative delegate who still hoped for reconciliation with Britain, wrote the first part of the paper. Of Jefferson's paper, only the final four and a half paragraphs were included. Dickinson considered Jefferson's draft "too harsh" and in need of "softening."

Though Dickinson's final draft did not incite the colonists to violence, it did speak firmly of the colonists' readiness to resist the British with force:

> Our cause is just. Our union is perfect. Our internal resources are great, and, if necessary, foreign assistance is undoubtedly attainable. . . . The arms we have been compelled by our enemies to assume, we will, in defiance of every hazard, with unabating firmness and perseverance, employ for the preservation of our liberties; being, with one mind, resolved to die freemen rather than live slaves.

Jefferson's stirring conclusion, read aloud by Washington to his men, echoed through the colonies and brought the people closer to the side of the radicals:

> We fight not for glory or for conquest. We exhibit to mankind the remarkable spectacle of a people attacked by unprovoked enemies, without any imputation, or even suspicion of offence. . . . In our native land, in defence of the freedom that is our birthright, and which we ever enjoyed until the late violation of it; for the protection of our property, acquired solely by the honest industry of our forefathers and ourselves, against violence actually offered, we have taken up arms.

Jefferson recognized that the moderates still shied away from independence, so he understood that he must move slowly and quietly. The colonies must be united in taking the final step. He did not want to instigate a civil war.

Dickinson, whose wife and mother were both Loyalists, immediately followed the declaration with a petition to the king. He saw no inconsistency in stating the colonists' readiness to take up arms at the same time that he pleaded with the king for a reconciliation. Affirming the affection of the colonists for Great Britain, Dickinson implored the king, in his "royal magnanimity and benevolence," to repeal the statutes that distressed the colonies so that harmony could be reestablished. Choose the olive branch of peace, he begged, over the sword of war. Perhaps the king would yet come to his senses.

The Olive Branch Petition, written by John Dickinson of Pennsylvania, was a final plea to George III to choose the olive branch of peace over the sword of war. The king rejected it.

Many members of Congress felt that the petition was humiliating. But Dickinson had another motive, as well. If the king rejected this petition, the colonists would have to realize that war was the only alternative.

Benjamin Franklin was enraged by the Olive Branch Petition. On the day that the Congress adopted it, he went home and wrote a letter to his old friend William Strahan, a publisher in England. Strahan published the works of Dr. Samuel Johnson, Edward Gibbon, and Oliver Goldsmith, among others. Over the years, he had printed many of Franklin's letters in the *London Chronicle*, one of London's most widely read and influential newspapers. Franklin's Philadelphia publishing firm had been Strahan's principle American outlet. But Strahan, in spite of his warm feelings for Franklin, had seen the Americans as rebels and had voted with the ministry. Now Franklin expressed his anger:

> Mr. Strahan:
> You are a member of Parliament and one of that Majority
> which has doomed my Country to Destruction. You have
> begun to burn our Towns and murder our People. Look
> upon your Hands! They are stained with the Blood of your
> Relations! You and I were long Friends. You are now my
> Enemy and I am
>
> > Yours,
> > B. Franklin

Franklin reconsidered his outburst and never mailed the letter. But he made certain that it was reprinted throughout America and England.

Congress adjourned for a short recess on August 2. It would reassemble on "Tuesday, the fifth of September next."[11]

One of the Patriots who had not attended the Second Continental Congress in Philadelphia was Benjamin Church, a prominent doctor in Boston. He ran the Continental Hospital, was a member of the Massachusetts Provincial Congress, and was one of the select members of the Committee of Safety who decided on the rebel policy, both political and military. He often delivered fiery orations, satirized the British in the newspapers, and wrote exaggerated reports of rebel achievements. He was considered a staunch patriot and was entrusted with their most important secrets. It was he who had written the elaborate justification of the militia's actions at Lexington and Concord that Joseph Warren had sent to London.

In September, the rebels learned the startling truth: Benjamin Church was a British spy. Church had expensive tastes, and he needed money, so he was selling the Patriots' secret strategy to General Gage. He was discovered when a coded letter he had written and given to his mistress to deliver for him fell into rebel hands. The letter was opened and quickly turned over to General Washington, who was now at his headquarters in Cambridge.

Washington immediately had the young lady brought to him. Under questioning, she broke down and confessed that its author was Benjamin Church, the man she loved.

When the code was broken, the letter revealed that Church was providing the British with details of the strength, supplies, and positions of the Continental forces surrounding Boston. The letter concluded, "Make use of every precaution or I perish."

When John Adams heard the news, he wrote, "Good God! What shall we say of human nature?"

Since there was no punishment for espionage in the disciplinary code of the new army, Church was sentenced to prison "without pen and ink." When his health broke in the spring of 1776, Congress decided to show mercy, and he was put on a "smalle schooner" bound for the West Indies. The ship was probably lost in a storm, for Church was never seen again.

Chapter XXX

"seduced into war"

London: 1775

When Richard Penn, grandson of William Penn, the peace-loving founder of Pennsylvania, rode into London in the middle of August 1775 bearing John Dickinson's Olive Branch Petition from the Continental Congress in Philadelphia, he found the city deserted. The king and his ministers had gone to the country for the summer. Penn delivered the petition to Lord Dartmouth's office on August 21.

Two days later, a proclamation was issued declaring the British government's determination to crush the "open and avowed rebellion" in America. On the following day, the Olive Branch Petition from his "Majesty's faithful subjects," with its plea for harmony and reconciliation, was handed to Dartmouth himself.[1] But it was too late. King George was determined to preserve his empire at any cost: "America must be a colony of England or treated as an enemy. Distant possessions standing upon an equality with the superior state is more ruinous than being deprived of such connections."[2]

The Proclamation of Rebellion put England and the colonies into an official state of war.

When the duke of Grafton, a longtime friend and supporter of the colonies, realized that "no notice would be taken" of the Olive Branch Petition, he, too, became alarmed. He was certain "that the connection of the two countries hung on that decision."

He would appeal to Lord North. Were there not "sufficient matters in the contents" of the petition to warrant opening "some intercourse between the two parties?" Grafton asked him.

Stubbornly, Lord North responded that "till the provinces have made some submission . . . it will be in vain to hope that they will come to any reasonable terms."

Grafton immediately requested an audience with the king to warn him that his ministers "were deluding his Majesty." Unconcerned, the king replied that a large number of German soldiers would soon join forces with Great Britain to subdue the colonies.

"Twice that number would only increase the disgrace, and never effect his purpose," Grafton angrily shot back at the astonished king.

But King George was certain he had justice on his side: "I know the uprightness of my intentions, and therefore am ready to stand every attack of ever so dangerous a kind with the firmness that honesty and an attachment to the constitution will support," he told Lord North.[3]

"As I now look upon ourselves as in an avowed state of war every means must be adopted to quicken that business." The king was determined. "We must persist and not be dismayed by any difficulties that may arise on either side of the Atlantic. I know I am doing my duty and therefore can never wish to retract."[4]

Two months later, in his address to the House of Lords at the opening of Parliament on October 26, King George III dismissed the Olive Branch Petition:

The authors and promoters of this desperate conspiracy have . . . meant only to amuse . . . whilst they were preparing for a general revolt. . . .

The object is too important, the spirit of the British nation too high, the resources with which God hath blessed her too numerous, to give up so many Colonies which she has planted with great industry, nursed with great tenderness, encouraged with many commercial advantages, and protected and defended at much expense of blood and treasure.

The Americans, he said, did not realize that "to be a subject of Great Britain . . . is to be the freest member of any civil society in the known world." "When the unhappy and deluded multitude . . . shall become sensible of their error," he concluded, he would be "ready to receive the misled with tenderness and mercy."

Lord Rockingham rose and suggested the king consider the "ruinous consequences" the decision to declare war on the colonies would have. With no attempt to hide his contempt, he warned that Parliament didn't understand "the true state and conditions of the Colonies." It would be a "dreadful calamity" to shed "*British* blood by *British* hands." The situation required reexamination.[5]

The earl of Sandwich angrily defended the king's policy: The American rebels were a "pusillanimous" lot, a people with "the most traitorous and hostile intentions." Force must be brought against the colonies. Only then would their "cowardice and want of spirit" be revealed.[6]

Now Grafton added his voice in support of Rockingham. Overcoming his usual reserve, Grafton condemned the king's address and the conduct of the administration. A bill must be passed, he said, that will repeal *all* the acts passed in Parliament relative to America.

Though his health was not good, Grafton told Parliament, he would "come down to this House in a litter" if necessary, "in order to express my full and hearty disapprobation of the matters now pursuing."[7]

King George was aghast. Such a public expression of opposition to his policies was unheard of.

The angry debate continued. Even Dartmouth believed that a petition from the American Congress could not be recognized "without at the same instant relinquishing the sovereignty of the British Parliament." The issue at stake, said Dartmouth, was no longer taxation but the allegiance of the colonies. Further, he was certain that the "softness of their language was purposely adopted to conceal the most traitorous designs." [8]

When a vote was taken, the king's address was supported by a majority of seventy-six to thirty-three. There were some who claimed that the victory was aided by Lord North, who slipped "bribes so elegantly under [the members'] ruffles."

One week later, the duke of Grafton was asked to resign.

Now the opposition united to sign a protest declaring that Parliament had "disgraced the nation, lost the Colonies, and involved us in a civil war, against our clearest interests, and upon the most unjustifiable grounds, wantonly spilling the blood of thousands of our fellow subjects."

A similar protest was made in the House of Commons. Charles Fox, a fearless spokesman for colonial rights and one of the strongest independent leaders of the Whig opposition in Commons, justified American resistance to the "tyrannical acts of a *British* Parliament." The administration, he said, should "place America where she stood in 1763 and . . . repeal every act passed since that period." He condemned Lord North as a "blundering pilot" who had "lost a whole Continent."

But the majority in Commons prevailed. Arguing that they must "put a speedy end to these disorders, by the most decisive exertions," they approved the king's measures to crush the rebellion in America.[9]

"We have been seduced into war," Edmund Burke wrote sadly to Lord Rockingham.[10]

Chapter XXXI

"steering opposite courses"

Virginia: 1775

Thomas Jefferson had long coveted his cousin John Randolph's violin. It was a Cremona, made in Italy in 1660 by the master, Nicolò Amati, and was considered the finest violin in the colonies. Both men loved music and were sufficiently accomplished to perform in musicales together. In fact, they had played in a very small group that met for dinner, conversation, and music at the governor's palace in Williamsburg once a week.

In the spring of 1771, the two cousins had struck a lighthearted bargain: Should Jefferson survive Randolph, he would inherit the fiddle and all its music; if Randolph were the survivor, he would receive books worth one hundred pounds sterling from Jefferson's library. The agreement was witnessed by George Wythe and Patrick Henry. It was unlikely that the pact was intended seriously, for at the time both were young men: Jefferson was only twenty-eight and Randolph was in his early forties.

But now, just four years later, Randolph was selling his violin to Jefferson, and on August 17, 1775, Jefferson received a letter from his cousin acknowledging receipt of the "purchase money" for it. The violin would remain a precious possession of Jefferson's for fifty-one years.

Randolph's letter to Jefferson was his sad farewell to his cousin. John Randolph, attorney general of the colony of Virginia, was going home to England. To Thomas Jefferson, this was incomprehensible. "We *are* home," he thought. But in just three weeks, John Randolph, his wife, and their two daughters would leave their elegant home in Williamsburg, ride to Norfolk, and there board a ship bound for England. In addition to dear friends and relatives, Randolph would leave behind his older brother, Peyton, now Speaker of the House of Burgesses, and his son Edmund, both of whom he deeply loved. Edmund, a strong patriot, had joined George Washington and the Continental Army in Boston. He would become Washington's aide-de-camp.[1]

Randolph's letter to Jefferson continued: "Tho we may *politically* differ in sentiments, yet I see no reason why *privately* we may not cherish the same esteem for each other which formerly I believe subsisted between us. . . .We both of us seem to be steering opposite courses; the success of either lies in the womb of time. But whether it falls on my share or not, be assured that I wish you all health and happiness."[2]

In his reply, Jefferson took advantage of the opportunity to implore his cousin to intercede for the colonists in England. He still looked "with fondness" toward a reconciliation with the mother country, if only Great Britain could give evidence of a return to "wisdom." Would Randolph contribute toward expediting this good cause?

He implored Randolph to advise the king's ministers that their officers in America had misrepresented the colonies' uniform opposition, describing ("for what purpose I cannot tell") a "small faction" of "cowards" ready to surrender at the appearance of an armed force. If Randolph could "undeceive" the British, he would be doing a "service to the whole empire."

His passionate conclusion was, perhaps, an accurate expression of the feelings of many of the Patriots: "I am sincerely one of those who would rather be in dependence on Great Britain, properly limited, than on any other nation on earth, or than on no nation. But I am one of those, too, who, rather than submit to the right of legislating for us, assumed by the British Parliament, and which late experience has shown they will so cruelly exercise, would lend my hand to sink the whole island in the ocean."[3]

John Randolph was taking a path followed by many Loyalists throughout the colonies. It was a decision he had not reached easily. His choice had not been clear-cut.

Loyalists had always been animated by a double patriotism. Now, they were tortured by it. They were as indignant as other Americans at what seemed an unjust and arbitrary exercise of British authority. They considered themselves moderate men, and they were alarmed at the possibility of a war between Great Britain and her colonies.[4]

They believed, as did John Randolph, that government must be composed of men who were competent to govern, and such men were found only in the upper class. They believed, also, that their position was based firmly on calm reason and dispassionate judgment, the result of their social position and their education. They loved America, but they could not go against what they most deeply believed. Many acknowledged that evils existed. But reform through law was, to them, the only justifiable procedure. Laws were meant to be obeyed.

Some Loyalists believed King George to be "as despotic as any prince in Europe." "I love the Cause of Liberty," one Loyalist wrote, "but cannot heartily join in the prosecution of measures totally foreign to the original plan of Resistance. The madness of the multitude is but one degree better than submission to the Tea-Act."[5]

The best of the Tories loved their country as much as the rebels did, but they were considered traitors nonetheless. To the Patriots, they were becoming more of an immediate threat than Parliament and the king, three thousand miles across a stormy sea. Increasingly, Tories in the colonies were becoming the primary enemy, more bitterly hated than the British themselves.[6]

The Patriots had adapted the word *Tory* to describe any supporter of British rule. Most of the "Tories" preferred to be called "friends of the government," or even "the Loyal Party." Eventually, they called themselves simply, Loyalists.

Now, in the aftermath of the Second Continental Congress, a war of pamphlets between the Tories and Patriots was flaring up with fresh vigor throughout the colonies. In one pamphlet, the actions of the Continental Congress were accused of meaning "total destruction of all LIBERTY." Another warned that meddling colonists would soon proceed from inspecting warehouses for British goods to examining "your tea-cannisters and molasses jugs and your wives' and daughters' petty-coats."

"They swear and drink . . . and pull down houses, and tar and feather, and play the devil in every shape, just as the devil and their own inclination lead them," the Tory Jonathan Sewall, John Adams's old friend, wrote, "and yet they cry out for liberty."

Others, furious, accused Congress of producing at home the tyranny it denounced in England. In place of the king, loyal Americans had to contend with "their *High Mightinesses* the MOB."

Lieutenant General Thomas Gage wrote to Lord Dartmouth, "The proceedings of the Continental Congress astonish and terrify all considerate men." [7]

Loyalists were gaining strength, particularly in Pennsylvania, New York, and New Jersey. Patriots spoke of those colonies as "the enemy's country." In New York, where an exceptionally strong Tory party was emerging, more Tory newspapers were published than in all the other colonies combined. The New York Assembly refused to adopt the Continental Association. They would stay clear of "treason" and "rebellion." In fact, the Loyalists' power was so strong that it seemed unlikely that New York would send a delegation to another congress in Philadelphia. [8]

Still, New Yorkers would *not* accept the principles of the Declaratory Act, which reserved England's right to tax the colonies. In the province in which England had the most friends—"the white hope of the British Ministry"—

there were very few supporters of parliamentary taxation. Parliament, by insisting on the right to tax, was making it difficult even for conservative Americans to uphold British sovereignty.[9]

John Adams estimated that one third of all the colonists were Patriots, one third clung to their allegiance to the king (usually at great personal sacrifice), and one third took no sides, wishing simply to be left alone.

Country, local policy, age, temperament, and private beliefs all operated to cause different views among the colonists. Religion also divided them. Quakers, for the most part, opposed independence. Their religious principles made them averse to war, and revolution, they feared, could only be accomplished by war.

While most of the wealthy, particularly in the northeastern and middle colonies, did not want a change, the reverse was true in the South. "There were in no part of America more determined Whigs than the opulent slaveholders in Virginia, the Carolinas, and Georgia." [10]

But there were Loyalists in every colony. Their story was, on the whole, a tragic one. Some left for Canada or Great Britain, where they lived the unhappy life of political refugees, incapable of truly finding a new home or returning to their old one. Many kept their opinions to themselves. Many were individuals respected and liked in their own communities, who showed great courage in opposing the majority of their friends and neighbors, and sometimes even members of their own families, breaking ties to the most precious associations of their lives.

One of the most poignant illustrations occurred in Benjamin Franklin's family. His son, William, whom he adored, refused to resign as royal governor of New Jersey, breaking his father's heart and causing many Americans who only knew his name to suspect that Benjamin Franklin was a British spy.[11]

When Boston painter John Singleton Copley, traveling in Italy, learned of the skirmish at Lexington and Concord, he immediately wrote home to his Loyalist half brother, Henry Pelham, hoping to persuade him to leave the country and the war to others: "The flame of civil war is now broke out in

America, and I have not the least doubt it will rage with a violence equal to what it has ever done in any other country at any other time." He predicted that "oceans of blood will be shed to humble a people which [England] will never subdue." "Americans will be a free independent people," he concluded.[12]

But many Tories never doubted that the mother country would be victorious. Then, they were certain, they would be vindicated, their fortunes restored, and their tormentors punished. They were confident that if war broke out, the mere sight of battle-seasoned British Regulars would be enough to overcome the rebels. British power would prevail. John Randolph was among these.

Ten years earlier he, along with other members of the House of Burgesses, had opposed Patrick Henry's resolves against the Stamp Act. At that time, John's brother, Peyton Randolph, had led the opposition. But by 1774, Peyton, despite the fact that he disliked controversy, had become convinced that recent acts of Parliament posed a genuine threat to the rights and liberties of Virginia landowners. He had become a staunch patriot.

From the beginning of the crisis that had developed between Great Britain and her American colonies, John Randolph, nicknamed "Tory-John" by the Patriots, had consistently supported the mother country, making no effort to disguise his position. In fact, in 1774 he published a treatise (anonymously) entitled, *Considerations on the Present State of Virginia*, in which he urged his countrymen to acknowledge their dependence on the mother country. "The Americans," he wrote, "are descended from the Loins of Britons, and therefore may, with Propriety, be called the Children, and England the Mother of them." Family ties were supported by common custom, law, language, religion, trade, and commerce.

The colonies, he believed, were subordinate to Britain. Randolph recognized that there were some defects in Britain's policy toward America. Still, he counseled, "our Interest is so interwoven with hers, that we ought to look with Horrour on any Attempt to cause a Separation." Independence was coming, but this was not the time. The British could easily crush a rebellion now. America must wait until she was stronger.

One of the most remarkable aspects of his pamphlet is that it reveals that in some ways John Randolph was actually whiggish. The sanctity of the Constitution was fundamental to his thought. The king's powers, he pointed out, were limited. The king must not infringe on the rights of the people, but the people must not exceed the boundary of their privilege. His aim, he said, was moderation and peace. It is the birthright of every Englishman to oppose injustice, he felt, but it must be done in "a Manner most likely to obtain Success."

Randolph had always taken for granted his place in politics and in society, and was contemptuous of his inferiors. Refusing to court public favor, he held to his principles despite public criticism. His hostility toward Patrick Henry and Richard Henry Lee, as well as his friendship with the hated Governor, Lord Dunmore (although he was sometimes critical of him), further tarnished his reputation among the Virginia Patriots.

Born in Williamsburg about 1727, he was the youngest child of Sir John Randolph, a leading lawyer and Speaker of the House of Burgesses. Sir John was the only colonial Virginian to be knighted. When he died, John was only ten years old, and he looked to—and received from—his older brother, Peyton, guidance and love.

He attended the College of William and Mary in Williamsburg, then sailed to England to "read" law for four years. He was called to the English bar at Middle Temple in London on February 9, 1749. It is likely that his experiences during his years abroad heightened his perception of the privileges as well as the responsibilities of a Virginia aristocrat. When he returned to Virginia, sometime in 1750, he quickly became one of the colony's leading lawyers, known for his "great erudition, just reasoning," and elegant speech.

While building his law practice, Randolph entered public service, which was the stronghold of the Virginia gentry, taking an active part in town and county government. His first post was Clerk of the House of Burgesses, a position second only to the Speaker. The clerkship had been handed down in the Randolph family for many years, and John was well aware that it could lead to more powerful positions in both law and government. He held the position for fifteen years.

Over the years he worked diligently to gain support in England. His efforts were rewarded when, in 1767, he was appointed by the king to the coveted post of attorney general. He succeeded his brother Peyton, who had just become Speaker. But he could not follow his brother down the road to rebellion.

John Randolph always had the best that money could buy. He dressed in the fashion of the time. Most of the family's clothes came from England. He indulged his wife and children and pursued his own interests in books, music, ornithology, and literature. His library contained more than eleven hundred books. Their large, expensively furnished home was renowned for gracious hospitality and was a popular literary and social center, frequented by the elite of the community. George Washington was a regular dinner guest whenever he was in Williamsburg, and the Randolphs often visited the Washingtons at Mount Vernon. In everything he did, John Randolph maintained a standard of living that was elegant, even for Virginia gentry.

Highly qualified by training and experience to serve as an interpreter and advocate of the law in Virginia, he performed his duties with authority tempered by sound judgment. George Washington, who was one of his law clients, continued to seek his legal advice despite the growing differences in their political opinions.

At the time that Randolph made the painful decision to leave Virginia for England, he was at the peak of his career. But he had become a very unpopular man. Whatever anguish he felt at leaving Virginia he kept mostly to himself. His worries centered on his son, Edmund, in Massachusetts with George Washington and the Continental army.

Before he left, he wrote a letter to Edmund pleading with him to return to Virginia:

Your military undertaking will not suit your Situation. Is not the Glory of the cabinet equal to that of the Field? Is not this better than broken Limbs, Fatigue, Shattered Health & an eternal want of money? For God's sake return to your family & indeed to yourself. Abandon not your Sisters, who are wretched about you. Come back & Heaven will prosper all your Undertakings.

I am your affected & afflicted Father,
J. Randolph

Before Randolph sailed for England, Lord Dunmore appealed to him to speak to Lord Dartmouth in London, and apprise him of the true state of affairs in America. That both Dunmore *and* Thomas Jefferson could agree that John Randolph was capable of honestly conveying this is a testament to Randolph's moderation.

John Randolph was confident that his loyalty to the king would be rewarded, and that the American rebellion would be crushed. He couldn't know then that he would never return to America.[13]

Chapter XXXII

The magic of the monarchy

London: 1776

By the beginning of 1776, after fifteen years on the throne of Great Britain, George III was still determined to be a patriot king who ruled his people in their best interests, above the interference of party. He was convinced that his way was the right way.

But the American problem was troubling him. There was nothing he more earnestly desired, he had told Lord Dartmouth just a few short months ago, than to remove the jealousies and quiet the apprehensions of his American subjects and to see them reconciled to the British government "upon principles that may secure the permanent peace and tranquillity of the British Empire."[1] He couldn't understand why they refused to look to their parent for assistance and security.

Six years ago he had counseled Lord Hillsborough that revoking the charter of Massachusetts, as Hillsborough proposed, was "of so strong a nature that it rather seems calculated to increase the unhappy feuds that subsist than to assuage them." King George prided himself on his good memory. He remembered all the many instances over the last few years when he had urged on his ministers that policy should be motivated by "a desire with temper to let them return to their reason, not with violence to drive them." [2]

But the colonists' recklessness was showing them to be unwilling to listen to reason. Their continued protests, their acts of rebellion, were exasperating. America was a "spoilt child" in need of punishment. Britain must take a stern line with her. King George would preserve the majesty of the British name and the British constitution.

He believed that the British constitution was "the most excellent form of government" that had ever existed, and considered it his first duty as monarch to preserve and protect it. He could not change it. Change, he knew, must come from Parliament, and he did not control Parliament. By refusing to find a solution for the American problem independent of the House of Commons, he was, in fact, preserving the constitution—and therefore, he felt, the freedom of his subjects. [3]

But this meant bringing the colonies firmly under the control of the mother country. In 1763, at the conclusion of the Seven Years' War, he had called the settlement of America "that greatest and most necessary of all schemes." The newly acquired territories must be absorbed into the old empire, and the whole must be organized for defense and profit, he had said. The empire was one unit.

He had advised that troops be stationed permanently in the colonies to guard against a recurrence of French aggression—and also to ensure that the colonists remained amenable to British authority. [4] But now America was defying the authority of Parliament. The colonists were in open rebellion. Britain must not retreat from its position that sovereignty is indivisible, and that taxation is its most vital element.

King George was not the brightest of monarchs, and he was certainly

King George III was involved in all matters of state. His intellectual curiosity encompassed music, literature, art, agriculture, astronomy, architecture, and mechanics. At Buckingham Palace he built four separate libraries, all of which contained remarkably fine collections of books that later became the nucleus of the British Library. *Print from a painting by Benjamin West, from circa 1778.*

not the most sparkling. Over the years he had matured in office and had become a practiced politician, but as he learned to rule, his opinions became more rigid. Always conscientious, he believed that it was morally essential for him to play a critical political role. A powerful and intense man who lived by a strict code of honor, he had an almost exaggerated respect for his duties.[5]

The word *compromise* was not in his lexicon. Indeed, after the skirmish at Lexington and Concord, and the battle at Bunker Hill, there was no room for compromise. The colonists had to be subdued. He would defend the British constitution. He would uphold the supremacy of Parliament. If this provoked a war between Great Britain and her colonies, so be it. He would exercise the powers that were clearly *his* by constitutional right and usage.

He was not overstepping the bounds of his powers as a monarch, nor was he being the tyrant many colonists considered him to be. It was the supremacy of Parliament, not the rights of the king, that was at stake.[6]

He knew that Lords Dartmouth and North still clung to the hope that the Americans would ultimately back down rather than risk war, and that a negotiated settlement could be arranged. But he didn't agree. He was now convinced that parliamentary sovereignty could be restored in America only by force.

Sure in his belief that he was hampered by irresponsible, self-seeking men, he was also certain that he alone was unswervingly following the path of duty. His failure to subdue the colonists, and the consequences of that were doubly bitter to him.

The king had been taught to believe that Great Britain should be governed by the will of the people. But no one had ever told him that America should be governed by the will of the American people.

In England, King George was held in great affection by his subjects—not because he was their king, but because "he was such a worthy gentleman, and that the like of him was never known in this nation before." Without in any way stooping to their level, he appealed to even the lowest of his subjects. In character and convictions he was the average Briton of his day—or what the average Briton aspired to be. The nation's affection for him never waned. He was truly thought of as the father of his people. [7]

Even the colonists had called him "the best of kings."

In some ways it is difficult to account for George III's popularity. He lived in a narrow world and saw very little of his kingdom. He saw very little of the world, either. He is the only monarch of the Hanoverian dynasty who never saw Hanover, nor did he ever visit the Continent, or Scotland, Ireland, Wales, or even northern England.

Nor had he and Queen Charlotte—or any member of the royal family—visited America. Perhaps, had the king met the ordinary American as he met the ordinary Englishman, the concept of monarchy in America might have become a reality. He would have appeared among them as their king, instead of remaining a distant symbol of the authority of Great Britain. The Americans never felt the magic of the monarchy.[8]

Chapter XXXIII

"an asylum for mankind"

Philadelphia: January 1776

Aitken's Bookshop was a congenial hangout in Philadelphia for writers and young professionals who believed strongly in the cause of liberty. It was here that an impoverished Englishman from London, with a letter of introduction in his pocket from Benjamin Franklin, caught the attention of Dr. Benjamin Rush, Philadelphia's most progressive physician and a staunch radical. His name was Thomas Paine.

Paine's long face was remarkable for its large, pockmarked nose, the amused curve to his mouth, and his startling blue eyes. He had grown up in poverty and had had little education, but he had always been an avid reader of history and political theory, and he was a talented writer.

His early experiences and suffering had sensitized him to social issues, and he tried to find out what could be done to change things for the better. He had learned as a poor child that the fine gentlemen in his town of Thetford had no scruples about sending hungry children to the gallows for stealing.

When Benjamin Franklin met Paine in London, he liked his politics and recognized his talents. He suggested that Paine make a fresh start in the New World. Paine took his advice and embarked for the colonies in October 1774, arriving in Philadelphia on November 30.

Now, with Franklin's letter recommending him as "an ingenious, worthy young man," [1] Paine had been able to obtain a position as editor of a magazine that the bookstore owner had just launched. By the second issue, Paine had doubled its circulation.

At the time that Rush met Paine, the doctor was preparing an essay

With his pamphlet *Common Sense,* published January 9, 1776, Thomas Paine paved the way for the decision to declare independence taken by Congress in July.

on the necessity of independence. But he was not sure that the time was ripe for such a revolutionary statement. He was also concerned that it might seriously hurt his practice as many of his patients were conservative, and he had a wife and young children to support. Rush suggested that Paine write the essay. Benjamin Franklin, now back in Philadelphia, had already suggested that Paine write a history of the Anglo-American controversy.

Delighted with the suggestions, Paine, who had been in the colonies only one year, set to work at once. What emerged was a passionate tract that was rooted in Paine's bitter years of poverty in England, his unfulfilled dreams, his anger and frustration at the English society that turned its back on misery and injustice. It was that passion flowing into his sentences that gave them their power and their eloquence.[2] Dr. Rush, thrilled by the force and vigor of the language and the boldness of its sentiments, suggested the plainspoken Scots title *Common Sense*. The pamphlet was published on January 10, 1776.

The effect of *Common Sense* was swift and universal. "It burst from the press with an effect which has rarely been produced by types and papers in any age or country," Rush declared. Benjamin Franklin called its effect "prodigious." It touched a sensitive nerve in American political awareness. Its sale was monumental. In less than three months one hundred and twenty thousand copies were sold. Paine refused to take a penny of the profits. He offered half to the printer, who took a risk in printing such a revolutionary work, and he earmarked the remaining half to purchase mittens for the American troops. At two shillings each, the pamphlet went through edition after edition, eventually selling half a million copies. But the publisher kept *all* the money and Paine, who had been penniless when he arrived from England, and ought to have made a fortune, actually lost money because he paid the printer's bill for a later enlarged edition, and the sum was never refunded.

Common Sense has been called the most brilliant pamphlet written during the American Revolution, and one of the most brilliant ever written in the English language.[3] It opens with an attack on the institution of kingship, one of the most radical statements Americans had ever read. It was the first vigorous attack upon the king, who was the strongest bond of union that remained in the British Empire, the umbilical cord that still bound the colonies to the mother country.

Paine attacked not one policy or another, but the entire structure of Britishness, subordination, and monarchy within which colonial Americans had lived: Monarchy and the "evil" of hereditary succession have "laid . . . the world in blood and ashes," he wrote. Hereditary right is ridiculed by nature herself, which frequently gives "mankind an *Ass for a Lion*."

No one doubted that the British system of monarchy, aristocracy, and the common people was the most successful in the world. Then why destroy it? Thomas Paine was certain he knew the answer: Independence was right and loyalty to Britain was wrong.[4]

What was different about *Common Sense* was not its rebellious spirit or its forceful language, but its association of the American cause with "the cause of all mankind." By extending the significance of the colonial cause from the local to the universal, Paine legitimized revolutionary action.

> This sun never shined on a cause of greater worth, [he wrote]. Tis not the affair of a city, a country, a province, or a kingdom, but of a continent — of at least one-eighth part of the habitable globe. Tis not the concern of a day, a year, or an age; posterity are virtually involved in the contest, and will be more or less affected even to the end of time by the proceedings now. Now is the seedtime of continental union, faith, and honor.

England was not "the parent country" of America, he continued. Europe, not England, gave birth to America, by sending to the New World "the persecuted lovers of civil and religious liberty. Hither have they fled, not from the tender embraces of the mother, but from the cruelty of the monster."

His resounding call to liberty must have echoed in every colonial mind that studied his pamphlet:

> O ye that love mankind! Ye that dare oppose not only tyranny but the tyrant, stand forth! Every spot of the Old World is overrun with oppression. Freedom has been hunted round the globe. Asia and Africa have long expelled her. Europe regards her like a stranger, and England has given her warning to depart. O! receive the fugitive, and prepare in time an asylum for mankind.[5]

Thomas Paine possessed a rare talent for reducing to simple language and memorable phrases the ideas that others were writing in a more diffuse and sophisticated fashion. "No writer has exceeded Paine in ease and familiarity of style . . . and in simple and unassuming language," was the way Thomas Jefferson described *Common Sense*.

Thomas Paine was not a learned man. His enemies said he was often dirty, he drank too much, and he was not scrupulous about financial matters. But all the passion of a flawed and damaged life cried out with a power beyond learning, and touched hundreds of thousands of hearts.

No scholar could have written *Common Sense*. Their background and their education made them too conventional in their language, too academic, too logical to speak with such power or touch such a common chord. John Adams was quick to recognize this: "I could not have written anything in so manly and striking a style," he wrote to his wife, Abigail. But, he told her, Paine was "a better hand at pulling down than building." He didn't like Paine's blueprint for the future.

When some speculated that *Common Sense* had been written by John Adams (Thomas Paine's name was not on the title page), Adams said he could not have equalled the strength and brevity of the author's style, "nor his elegant simplicity, nor his piercing pathos." [6]

As "two shillings worth of Common Sense" made its way into homes all up and down the seaboard, it gave focus and direction to a rising sentiment for independence. Although a few influential and articulate leaders were contemplating independence, independence was *not* the common opinion of the Continental Congress, nor was it the general view of the people at large. Not one colony had instructed its delegates to work for independence. The purpose of the Congress was to force Parliament to acknowledge the liberties it claimed and to redress its grievances. [7]

But to Thomas Paine, "the period of debate [was] closed." He put before the people the common sense of independence. He understood that without a declaration of independence, the colonists were merely rebels. No European power would jeopardize its own empire by encouraging rebellion.

After he had read the pamphlet, George Washington, who, like many others, still toasted the king at dinners and public gatherings, modified his toasts:

"May the crowns of tyrants be crowns of thorns." He wrote to his aide: "The sound doctrine and unanswerable reasoning contained in the pamphlet *Common Sense*," along with "a few more of such flaming arguments, as were exhibited at Falmouth and Norfolk,"* would soon convince most Americans of "the propriety of a separation." [8]

When Abigail Adams received a copy from John, she wondered how any friends of the colonies could hesitate one moment at adopting its appealing sentiments. She would try to spread it around wherever she could, she told her husband. She hoped it could be "carried speedily into Execution." [9]

Thomas Paine was forcing the people to think the unthinkable. He was forcing them to take the first step toward independence. The colonists were now fighting for an idea.

---

*Both towns had recently been burned by the British.

Chapter XXXIV

Independence!

Virginia and Philadelphia: May–July 1776

When Thomas Jefferson arrived in Philadelphia on May 14, 1776, to take his seat at the new session of the Continental Congress, he found waiting for him a month-old letter from his friend John Page. "For God's sake declare the colonies independent and save us from ruin," Page had written. But Jefferson knew that he was only a delegate, and he had to wait for instructions from the Virginia Convention, then meeting in Williamsburg.

In fact, Jefferson didn't want to be in Philadelphia. He would have preferred to be at the convention in Williamsburg, having a part in formulating "a plan of government" for Virginia. The Congress had approved a resolution calling on the colonies to adopt new governments, and he was anxious to draw up a plan of the kind of constitution he felt Virginia should have. The creation of a new government, he wrote to a friend, was "a work of the most interesting nature. . . . It is the whole object of the present controversy; for should bad government be instituted for us . . . it had been as well to have accepted at first the bad one offered to us from beyond the water without the risk and expense of contest."[1]

But Virginia had sent him to the Congress in Philadelphia.

Soon after he arrived there, still determined to have some voice in Virginia's constitution, he hastily drew up a plan. He then asked his old mentor and good friend George Wythe, who was returning to Williamsburg for a brief stay, to deliver it to the Virginia Convention, which had by now become the revolutionary government of Virginia.

The document stated that the "Legislative, Executive, and Judiciary Offices shall be kept forever separate," and it granted voting privileges to a far broader spectrum of the people beyond the wealthy landowners. It guaranteed religious freedom and freedom of the press, and abolished the inheritance laws that Virginians had brought from England, which gave everything to the firstborn son. All heirs, Jefferson felt, should have equal rights—male and female alike.

His plan arrived too late. A draft, called the Virginia Declaration of Rights, prepared chiefly by George Mason, had already been accepted. Williamsburg was hot, the delegates were tired, and they were not anxious to reopen the debate. Perhaps, too, Jefferson's "plan of government" was too radical a proposal for the conservative members of the Virginia Assembly. But they did adopt his preamble, a recital of all the wrongs the king had committed against Virginia.

John Adams, too, exulted in the idea of creating new state governments. It is independence itself, he thought. "How few of the human race have ever enjoyed an opportunity of making an election of government?" he wrote. Yet he understood that "to contrive some Method for the Colonies to glide insensibly from under the old Government, into a peaceable and contented submission to new ones" was "the most difficult and dangerous Part of the Business Americans have to do in this mighty Contest."[2]

His wife was also thinking about independence for the nation, and she was thinking about her own growing independence. She had already spoken out for separation from England: "They are unworthy to be our Brethren," she

The Second Continental Congress met in this simple, yet elegant and inspiring room in the State House in Philadelphia. It was here that the delegates decided to fight for "independency."

had written. Now she urged her husband to recognize the changing role of women in the new republic: "I long to hear that you have declared an independancy—and by the way in the new Code of Laws which I suppose it will be necessary for you to make I desire you would Remember the Ladies, and be more generous and favourable to them than your ancestors. Do not put such unlimited power into the hands of the Husbands. Remember all Men would be tyrants if they could."[3]

Before the end of May, the Virginia delegation in Philadelphia received instructions from Williamsburg to propose a declaration of independence and to call for the confederation of the colonies and for foreign alliances. Richard Henry Lee hastened to comply.

On June 7, he rose in the State House in Philadelphia and, in a three-part resolution, moved that "these United Colonies are, and of right ought to be, free and independent States, that they are absolved from all allegiance to the British crown, and that all political connection between them and the State of Great Britain is and ought to be, totally dissolved."

The fiery Lee, who had lost the fingers on one hand in a hunting accident, gestured for emphasis with the hand wrapped in a black silk handkerchief. He went on to propose that the colonies immediately "take the most effectual measures for forming foreign alliances."

Finally, he urged that "a plan of confederation be prepared and transmitted to the respective Colonies for their consideration and approbation." This would be known as the Articles of Confederation and Perpetual Union.

John Adams jumped to his feet to second the motion.

Congress was in an uproar. It sat until 7 P.M., then adjourned until "punctually at ten o'clock" the next day, Saturday. Heated debates continued all that day.

Pennsylvania, New York, New Jersey, Delaware, Maryland, and South Carolina were still under instructions to vote against a declaration of independence. Their delegates, led by John Dickinson, argued that the time was not right. The radicals, led by John Adams, Richard Henry Lee, and George Wythe, replied that the declaration of independence would simply "declare a fact which already exists."

As Dickinson continued his desperate plea for time, all of New England, Virginia, and Georgia argued that the debate had ended when American blood was shed at Lexington. Through it all, Thomas Jefferson said not a word, but sat quietly taking notes.

On June 7, 1776, the fiery Richard Henry Lee proposed to the Second Continental Congress "that these United Colonies are, and of right ought to be, free and independent States." *By Charles Wilson Peale.*

The Congress recessed on Sunday, then continued to struggle to come to an agreement on Monday. Finally, a compromise was reached. The resolution would be postponed for three weeks, until July 1. But a committee would be appointed at once to prepare the declaration. In this way, should Congress agree, no time would be lost in drafting it. It was clear, Jefferson would say years later, that the moderates were "not yet matured for falling from the parent stem."[4]

Drafting a resolution, they decided, was a necessary task because a mere assertion of independence by Congress was considered inadequate. It was essential, Congress felt, to clearly and simply define the reasons for the resolution in such a manner that all the colonists would understand the need for action and would be inspired to fight for independence.

The facts must also be explained to the rest of the world. Congress understood that it must promote the American cause and justify the severing of ties with Great Britain and the establishment of America's own government. The support of other nations might be critical to the new nation's success.

At this point, the tide was running strongly toward independence, but there was still much to be done. Canvassing, intriguing, caucusing, and persuading would be needed behind the scenes. Here was where Jefferson could shine. Never one to allow himself to be drawn into the battles waging among the delegates, he was always on good terms with the older, more conservative leaders, and he retained their confidence. He and Sam Adams, with that man's great skill in political organization and management, met regularly to devise plans and assign individual tasks to other members.

It is interesting to note that John Dickinson, while he led the opposition and refused to change his mind, never lost the respect of the radicals. It was he who, for the most part, worked out the plan for the governing document, the Articles of Confederation. The document proposed that the confederation be officially designated "The United States of America," reflecting a desire to organize the thirteen colonies under a united national government that would assume the authority previously held by Parliament.

Now Thomas Jefferson was chosen to head the committee to draft the declaration. He had already won for himself a reputation for his "masterly pen" and for his "peculiar felicity of expression." Benjamin Franklin, John Adams, Roger Sherman of Connecticut, and Robert R. Livingston of New York were also appointed to the committee. But the highest vote for any of the five went to the quiet young man from Virginia.

All the men elected were distinguished. But Jefferson was the one chosen to write the declaration. The members recognized that he could disagree politically, yet still remain on friendly terms socially. He was unyielding in his principles, they knew, but he "bore the olive branch." He was the one man who knew the history, the law, and the principles of government thoroughly, who had an unshakable faith in the ability of men to govern themselves, and who wrote graceful, elegant prose.

Accordingly, when the committee first met at the stone farmhouse several miles outside of the city where Dr. Franklin was recuperating from gout, they unanimously insisted that Jefferson should write the declaration. The committee members discussed the general content, or "articles" of the document, then nominated Jefferson "to draw them up in form and cloath [*sic*] them in proper dress."

He accepted the assignment, later saying of it simply, "The committee for drawing up the Declaration of Independence desired me to do it. It was accordingly done."

Forty-six years later, John Adams would give a somewhat different version. He *and* Jefferson had been asked to "make the draught," he said. Then "Jefferson proposed to [him] to make the draught."

> [He said,] "I will not."
> "You should do it!"
> "I will not."
> "Why?"
> "Reasons enough."
> "What can be your reasons?"
> "Reason first—You are a Virginian, and a Virginian ought to appear
> at the head of this business. Reason second—I am obnoxious, suspected,

and unpopular. You are very much otherwise. Reason third—You can write ten times better than I can."

"Well, if you are decided, I will do as well as I can."

"Very well. When you have drawn it up, we will have a meeting." [5]

Jefferson returned to his lodgings in a newly built brick house owned by Mr. Graff, situated on the southwest corner of Market and Seventh Streets. He rented the second floor, which consisted of a furnished parlor and bedroom. He had brought with him a revolving Windsor chair and a little travel lap desk that he had designed and had had made for him.

For the next seventeen days Jefferson followed a routine that varied only slightly. He arose each day at dawn, when there was just enough light in the sky by which to read, soaked his feet in a basin of cold water, which he believed helped to ward off colds, played his violin softly for a while, then sat in his chair in the sunny parlor, propped his new desk on his lap, took his quill pen in hand, and began to write.

He had no books in front of him as he composed, but his encyclopedic memory recalled much that he had read over the past years. As he pondered the task facing him, he knew that the time had come to express the conclusions he had reached slowly, gradually, as he had read the historians, the philosophers, and the old lawyers.

He would call now on

The desk, designed by Thomas Jefferson, on which he wrote the Declaration of Independence, is considered the most important object in American history.

all this earlier reading, on his own writing, and on his legal experience, and he would distill all the ideas already in his mind from these many sources into one short document. He would adapt some of the ideas he had put forth only last month in his preamble to the Virginia Constitution. He would try to write simply, clearly, logically.

He had read John Locke's *Second Treatise on Government*, as had many of his compatriots, again and again, and it was strongly impressed on his mind. Locke had written that no one ought to harm another in his life, health, liberty, or possessions. Jefferson would amend that. He would speak of life, liberty, and the pursuit of happiness, for he believed that happiness of the people was one of the objects for which governments existed. It was this concept, he felt, that could lay the foundation for a commonwealth of freedom and justice.

He would address this declaration to the American people, he decided, and he would express in it the principles that had directed his Saxon forefathers in their "settlement" of England. He would explain the rationale of their descendants, who had brought with them to America the right to settle in sparsely inhabited land and to live there freely and happily under their own chosen government. He would simply reclaim the colonists' Anglo-Saxon birthright.

He would include no new ideas, nor would he say things that had never been said before. To attempt to justify a revolution on principles that no one had heard before would be foolish, he knew. He would simply "place before mankind the common sense of the subject, in terms so plain and firm as to command their assent." He would say exactly what everyone was thinking. It would be "an expression of the American mind."

Now, bending his head over his little writing box, sipping tea that his servant had quietly placed in front of him, he began to put his thoughts on paper, adding, "interlining," and crossing out as he went along. As a page became too difficult to read because of all the changes, he copied it "fair," then repeated the process. He worked on it in sections, rather than as one continuous text, until he was almost finished. Only then did he put it all together.

Jefferson knew that should the colonies win their independence, the declaration would become an extremely important public document. He knew, also, that the fate of the colonies might rest on his document. He had been given the mandate of convincing the world that the colonists had a legal and a moral right to separate from Great Britain.

He had to convince the world that the colonists were *not* rebelling against established political authority, but were a free people maintaining long-established rights against a usurping king. Revolution, he knew, was not legal according to British law as stated by Sir William Blackstone. His task was to plead his country's cause in terms of the natural rights of men. His appeal would be to a higher law, "the Law of Nature and of Nature's God."

On Friday, June 28, after having shown the completed document to the other members of the committee, Jefferson presented it to Congress. As the delegates sat in their high-backed cushioned chairs, shuffling papers on the tables in front of them or whispering behind cupped hands, it was read aloud, then left on the table for perusal. There was no discussion. Numerous other matters of ordinary business were dealt with. Then Congress adjourned "until nine o'clock Monday next."

Such was the reception of the Declaration of Independence.

Monday morning, July 1, dawned bright and cloudless. By eight thirty, as Jefferson walked from his lodgings toward the State House, the bricks and cobbles were already giving off heat. As he walked up the three steps and through the wide double doors of the building, he was grateful for the cool of the hallway inside.

Tension mounted as the members began to assemble. Today they would vote on Lee's resolutions that the colonies were free and independent states.

John Dickinson, his face pale against his plum-colored coat, rose to defend for the last time the conservative point of view. He spoke for nearly an hour. John Adams answered him in what Jefferson would describe years later as "a power of thought and expression that moved us from our seats." As Adams spoke, pounding his hickory walking stick on the floor for emphasis, a storm broke outside and he had to raise his voice against the roll of thunder.

It grew dark. Candles were brought in. Still the debate raged on. It continued for nine hours, with no break for dinner. Even Sam Adams, who rarely spoke in Congress, spoke today, quietly and convincingly, rising on his toes in his characteristic manner as he ended a sentence.

Finally, the delegates from South Carolina requested that the decision be postponed until the next morning so they might have time to reconsider.

Everyone understood that voting for independence was voting for war, and a unanimous vote was essential. Colonies that voted against independence would not be included in the confederation and so would become, in effect, enemy states. No one wanted this to happen.

The delegates understood, too, that voting for independence meant jeopardizing their fortunes as well as their lives. They knew that English law provided that traitors could be partly strangled, their bowels torn out and burned before their eyes, their heads then cut off and their bodies quartered.

They recognized, also, that once Congress voted formally, its decision was final. A vote on independence taken too soon could destroy Congress. In order to prevent this, they had, the day before, turned themselves into a Committee of the Whole, in which both debate and vote were unofficial, a trial balloon, so to speak.

When Congress became a Committee of the Whole, John Hancock—who had been elected president when Peyton Randolph was summoned back to Virginia to preside at a meeting of the House of Burgesses—stepped down. Benjamin Harrison, a delegate from Virginia, took his place.

During the past weeks more and more of the delegates had come over to the side of the Patriots. Their faith was proving stronger than their fear. When they met this Tuesday morning, South Carolina announced that it had made the decision to join their ranks. John Dickinson, who could never bring himself to vote for independence, and Robert Morris, also of Pennsylvania, stayed away, thus allowing their state to vote "aye." Caesar Rodney, who had ridden eighty miles in darkness and heavy rain, arrived from Delaware drenched and covered with mud just in time to cast the deciding vote in favor of independence. Only the New York delegates, still waiting for instructions from home, did not vote. But their vote was promised, and within a few days they, too, sent approval. Independence was established.[6]

John Adams, writing to Abigail the next day, expressed the momentous significance of the decision:

> Yesterday, the greatest Question was decided, which ever was debated in America, and a greater, perhaps, never was nor will be decided among Men. . . . The Second Day of July, 1776, will be the most memorable Epocha in the History of America. I am apt to believe that it will be celebrated, by succeeding Generations as the great anniversary Festival. It ought to be commemorated, as the Day of Deliverance, by solemn acts of Devotion to God Almighty. It ought to be solemnized with Pomp and Parade, with Shews, Games, Sports, Guns, Bells, Bonfires, and Illuminations, from one End of this Continent to the other, from this Time forward, forever more.
>
> You will think me transported with Enthusiasm but I am not.—I am well aware of the Toil and Blood and Treasure, that it will cost Us to maintain the Declaration, and support and defend these States.—Yet through all the Gloom I can see the Rays of ravishing Light and Glory. I can see that the End is more than worth all the Means. And that Posterity will tryumph in that Days Transaction, even altho We should rue it, which I trust in God We shall not.[7]

The momentous "Epocha" that so excited John Adams would be reduced to a historical footnote by the event that was to follow two days hence.

Now the delegates turned their attention to the paper that Mr. Jefferson had placed before them the preceding Friday. Once again, the white-paneled chamber in the State House resounded with long and heated debate. It was not a happy time for Thomas Jefferson. Word by word, sentence by sentence, page by page, his document was criticized, ripped apart, changed—by men whose talents for writing certainly did not equal his.

As he listened to the often rude criticism, he sat silently squirming in his seat. He did not speak on behalf of his "instrument." But feisty John Adams, angered at the evident distress of his friend and at the mutilation of what he considered a brilliant document, kept jumping to his feet to defend it, fighting for every line as Jefferson had written it, as though he were fighting for his life. Jefferson would remember him always for this with gratitude and affection.

Now Jefferson was saddened as he heard a passage deleted that revealed his own feelings: "We must endeavor to forget our former love for [the English], and hold them as we hold the rest of mankind, enemies in war, in peace, friends. We might have been a free and a great people together."

He was particularly upset when Congress struck out the clause that condemned slavery and slave trade and denounced the king's determination "to keep open a market where men should be bought and sold": "[The king] has waged cruel war against human nature itself, violating its most sacred rights of life and liberty in the persons of a distant people who never offended him, captivating and carrying them into slavery in another hemisphere, or to incur miserable death in their transportation thither."

In deference to South Carolina and Georgia, which wished to continue slave traffic, this clause was struck out. "Our northern brethren also I believe felt a little tender over those censures; for though their people had very few slaves themselves, yet they had been pretty considerable carriers of them to others," Jefferson wrote of it later.

Congress continued to question, edit, harden the phrases, but much of Jefferson's simple, direct, precise prose was left intact. Congress speedily approved the preamble. Jefferson's final words—"we mutually pledge to each other our lives, our fortunes and our

John Adams, above, defended Thomas Jefferson's Declaration of Independence as though he were fighting for his life. Jefferson would remember him for this always with gratitude and affection. *By Charles Wilson Peale.*

sacred honour"—they agreed, could not be improved. In spite of what Jefferson may have thought, his colleagues were not ruthless, and the declaration emerged a stronger document.

A severe thunderstorm on the night of July 3, such as Philadelphia had not experienced in a long time, brought a cold and dreary morning with a bracing north wind on July 4. As the day progressed, the sun came out and the temperature rose. Later, it became oppressively hot and humid in the crowded State House chamber, even with the windows open.

The delegates continued their debate, but they were becoming increasingly uncomfortable and irritable. Next door to the State House was a livery stable from which swarms of flies emerged. They entered the delegates' room through the open windows, alighting on the legs of the delegates and biting hard through their silk stockings. The men lashed furiously at the flies with their handkerchiefs, but to no avail. Years later Jefferson would say that the debate that day came to an end and a vote was taken merely to get away from the flies. Treason was preferable to discomfort.

Late in the afternoon, Benjamin Harrison announced that the delegates had agreed to the document. The situation that afternoon was essentially the same as that which had existed on July 2. Twelve colonies voted in the affirmative, while New York remained silent.* [8]

Now Mr. Harrison read the title aloud: "A Declaration by the Representatives of the United States of America in General Congress Assembled." Then, overcome by the magnitude of the occasion, he paused, then continued:

> When in the course of human events, it becomes necessary for one
> people to dissolve the political bands which have connected them with
> another, and to assume among the powers of the earth the separate and

---

*New York adopted a resolution approving and supporting the declaration on July 9. It was laid before Congress on July 15. It then became "The Unanimous Declaration of the Thirteen United States of America."

equal station to which the Laws of Nature and of Nature's God entitle them, a decent respect to the opinions of mankind requires that they should declare the causes which impel them to separation.

The delegates sat in complete silence as the haunting cadence of the words of the preamble echoed through the hall.

Mr. Harrison continued with Jefferson's revolutionary philosophy of democracy:

> We hold these truths to be self-evident, that all men are created equal; that they are endowed by their Creator with certain unalienable Rights; that among these are Life, Liberty and the pursuit of Happiness.—That to secure these rights Governments are instituted among men, deriving their just powers from the consent of the governed.—That whenever any Form of Government becomes destructive of these ends, it is the Right of the People to alter or abolish it, and to institute new Government, laying its foundation on such principles and organizing its powers in such form, as to them shall seem most likely to effect their Safety and Happiness.

The body of the document is a stinging indictment of the king who caused the crisis. Relentlessly repeating "He has . . . " nineteen times, Jefferson listed all the specific grievances against George III. Read aloud, this steady piling up of offenses became a mournful bell tolling the death of American allegiance to the king.

The fourth and final section asserts that for men accustomed to freedom, there is only one choice:

> We, therefore, the Representatives of the United States of America, in General Congress Assembled, appealing to the Supreme Judge of the world for the rectitude of our intentions, do, in the Name, and by the Authority of the good People of these Colonies, solemnly publish and declare, That these United Colonies are, and of Right ought to be Free and Independent States; that they are Absolved from all Allegiance to the British crown, and that all political connection between them and the

State of Great Britain is and ought to be totally dissolved; and that as Free and Independent States they have full Power to levy War, conclude Peace, contract Alliances, establish Commerce, and to do all other Acts and Things, which Independent States may of right do.—And for the support of this Declaration, with a firm reliance on the protection of divine Providence, we mutually pledge to each other our Lives, our Fortunes, and our sacred Honor.[9]

As John Adams listened to Thomas Jefferson's words in the great, silent chamber, he was transported back in memory to that cold February day in 1761 when he had listened, rapt, as his old hero James Otis lashed out against writs of assistance. Then and there, he mused, on that day, in the old council chamber of the Boston Town House, was the first act of opposition to the arbitrary claims of Great Britain. Then and there, the child Independence was born.

Over the course of the last fifteen years, he thought, the revolution had been in the hearts and the minds of the people. It was effected "before a drop of blood was drawn at Lexington." Now, a newborn nation had emerged.

He reflected on the

A detail of the painting "Declaration of Independence," by John Trumbull, showing, from the left, John Adams, Roger Sherman, Robert Livingston, Thomas Jefferson, and Benjamin Franklin.

spirit and resolution of the people, and on the deep roots of American independence that existed in all the colonies. Their love of liberty and hatred of arbitrary government that blazed so fiercely within them had been present since their settlement. Time would "take away the Veil" and "lay open the secret Springs of this surprizing Revolution," John had written to Abigail. She would someday see, he promised her, that although the colonies "differed in Religion, Laws, Customs, Manners, yet in the great Essentials of Society and Government, they are all alike." [10]

The "accomplishment of [the Revolution] . . . was perhaps a singular example in the history of mankind," John Adams wrote. "Thirteen clocks were made to strike as one."

Reference Notes

Introduction

1. Miller, J., *Origins of the American Revolution*, 29–31.
2. Christie and Labaree, *Empire or Independence*, 20.
3. Trevelyan, G. M., *Illustrated History of England*, 510–11.
4. Ibid., 437–39.
5. Smith, *A New Age Now Begins*, 83–86.
6. Christie and Labaree, op. cit.; Smith, *A New Age Now Begins*, 1–8.
7. Miller, J., *Origins of the American Revolution*, 167.

Chapter I

1. Brooke, *King George III*, 73, 389, n. 4.
2. Ibid., 20–21.
3. Ibid., 390, n. 6.
4. Smith, *A New AgeNow Begins*, 1: 239.
5. Black, *Pitt the Elder*, 230.
6. Ibid., 253.
7. Brooke, *King George III*, 74.
8. Ibid., 75.
9. Ibid., 89.
10. Hibbert, *George III*, 79.
11. Brooke, op. cit., 79.
12. Ibid., 82.
13. Ibid., 84.
14. Bobrick, *Angel in the Whirlwind*, 29.

Chapter II

1. Draper, *A Struggle for Power*, 176.
2. Bowen, *John Adams and the American Revolution*, 208–17.
3. Adams, J., *Diary and Autobiography of John Adams*, 1: 306.
4. Miller, J., *Origins of the American Revolution*, 167–76.
5. Christie and Labaree, *Empire or Independence*, 41.
6. Bowen, *John Adams and the American Revolution*, 216.
7. Smith, *John Adams*, 1: 51–56.

Chapter III

1. Brooke, *King George III*, 88.
2. Ibid., 91.
3. White, *The Age of George III*, 63.
4. Plumb, *England in the Eighteenth Century*, 109–11.

5. Black, *Pitt the Elder*, 220.
6. Brooke, op. cit., 93.
7. Black, op. cit., 229–30.
8. Halliday, *England: A Concise History*, 147.
9. Cook, *The Long Fuse*, 45–6.
10. Brooke, op. cit., 102.
11. Ibid., 125.
12. Morgan and Morgan, *The Stamp Act Crisis*, 56–61, 68.

Chapter IV

1. Adams, S., *The Writings of Samuel Adams*, 1: 2.
2. Ibid., 1: 5, 219.
3. Draper, *A Struggle for Power*, 218, n. 7.
4. Adams, J., *Diary and Autobiography of John Adams*, 1: 239.
5. Canfield, *Sam Adams's Revolution*, 11.
6. Miller, J., *Sam Adams: Pioneer in Propaganda*, 18–19.
7. Cook, *The Long Fuse*, 61.
8. Miller, J., *Origins of the American Revolution*, 105.
9. Cook, op. cit., 57.
10. Morgan and Morgan, *The Stamp Act Crisis*, 15–20.
11. Otis, J., "The Rights of the British Colonies Asserted and Proved," in Beloff, *The Debate on the American Revolution*, 47–69.
12. Adams, op. cit., 39, 171, 161, 218.
13. Morris, ed., *The American Revolution*, 58–59.
14. Kennedy, ed., *Journals of the House of Burgesses of Virginia, 1761–1765*, 302–04.

Chapter V

1. Blackstone, *Commentaries on the Laws of England*, 142–61.
2. Morris, ed., *The American Revolution*, 64–71.
3. Morgan and Morgan, *The Stamp Act Crisis*, 72.

Chapter VI

1. Miller, J., *Origins of the American Revolution*, 114–115.
2. Tuchman, *March of Folly*, 129.
3. Harris, *America Rebels*, 11.
4. Wirt, *The Life of Patrick Henry*, 65.
5. Morison, *Sources and Documents Illustrating the American Revoluion*, 16–17.
6. Morgan and Morgan, *The Stamp Act Crisis*, 97; Bober, *Thomas Jefferson*, 42–46.
7. Morgan and Morgan, *The Stamp Act Crisis*, 102.

8. Miller, J., *Sam Adams: Pioneer in Propaganda*, 51.
9. Adams, S., *The Writings of Samuel Adams*, 1: 109.
10. Smith, *A New Age Now Begins*, 1: 201–202.
11. Miller, J., op. cit., 62; Hibbert, *Redcoats and Rebels*, 3–5.
12. Miller, J., *Sam Adams: Pioneer in Propaganda*, 26.
13. Bailyn, *Faces of Revolution*, 127.
14. Ibid., 127–28.
15. Hutchinson, *Diary and Letters*, 2: 359.
16. Maier, *The Old Revolutionaries*, 27.
17. Galvin, *Three Men of Boston*, 107.
18. Miller, *The Sam Adams: Pioneer in Propaganda*, 65–66.
19. Smith, op. cit., 1: 213.
20. Bailyn, op. cit., 125–36.
21. Zobel, *The Boston Massacre*, 26.
22. Harris, op. cit., 6.

Chapter VII

1. *Benjamin Franklin's Writings*, 4: 390.
2. Cook, *The Long Fuse*, 78.
3. Brooke, *King George III*, 106–108.
4. Christie and Labaree, *Empire or Independence*, 25–26.
5. Brooke, op. cit., 119.
6. Morgan and Morgan, *The Stamp Act Crisis*, 77.
7. Brooke, op. cit., 177.

Chapter VIII

1. Hosmer, *Samuel Adams*, 72.
2. Beloff, *The Debate of the American Revolution*, 73–76.
3. Hosmer, op. cit., 67.
4. Morgan, *Prologue to Revolution*, 118–22.
5. Miller, L., *In the Minds and Hearts of the People*, 102.
6. Draper, *A Struggle for Power*, 238–39.

Chapter IX

1. Morgan, *Prologue to Revolution*, 127–30; Morgan and Morgan, *The Stamp Act Crisis*, 273–75.
2. Franklin, *The Papers of Benjamin Franklin*, 12: 362–63.
3. Taylor, W. S. and J. H. Pringle, eds., *The Correspondence of William Pitt, Earl of Chatham*, 2: 362.
4. Beloff, *The Debate on the American Revolution*, 92–96.
5. Ibid., 97–99.

6. Ibid., 100.
7. Miller, J., *Origins of the American Revolution*, 202–203.
8. Beloff, op. cit., 100–105.
9. Draper, *Struggle for Power*, 277.
10. Van Doren, *Benjamin Franklin*, 335.
11. Bobrick, *Angel in the Whirlwind*, 30–31.
12. Cook, *The Long Fuse*, 91–94.
13. Van Doren, op. cit., 332–55.
14. Cook, op. cit., 104–105.
15. Trevelyan, *American Revolution*, 2.
16. Brooke, *King George III*, 171.
17. *Boston Gazette*, 19 May 1766.

Chapter X

1. Hosmer, *Samuel Adams*, 91–92; Smith, *A New Age Now Begins*, 1: 245–47.
2. Trevelyan, *The American Revolution*, 13.
3. *Boston Gazette*, Tuesday, 3 June 1766.
4. Trevelyan, op cit., 1–2.
5. Adams, J., *Diary and Autobiography of John Adams*, 1: 324.
6. Smith, *A New Age Now Begins*, 1: 251.
7. Morgan, ed., *Prologue to Revolution*, 158–59.
8. Adams, S., *Writings of Samuel Adams*, 1: 386, 387.
9. Forbes, *Paul Revere and the World He Lived In*, 83.
10. Fowler, *The Baron of Beacon Hill*, "Forward."
11. Hosmer, op. cit., 94.
12. Miller, J., *Sam Adams: Pioneer in Propaganda*, 94–102.
13. Ibid., 82–86.
14. Fischer, *Paul Revere's Ride*, 4–5, 14–22.
15. Smith, op. cit., 253.

Chapter XI

1. Brooke, *King George III*, 132; Plumb, *The First Four Georges*, 112–13.
2. Miller, L., *In the Minds and Hearts of the People*, 100–101.
3. Cook, *The Long Fuse*, 110–13; Brooke, op. cit., 135.
4. Miller, L., op. cit., 101.
5. Brooke, op. cit., 138–39.
6. Miller, L. op. cit., 101; Hibbert, *Redcoats and Rebels*, 11.
7. Christie and Labaree, *Empire or Independence*, 26.
8. Morison, *The Oxford History of the American People*, 190.

9. Miller, J., *Origins of the American Revolution*, 255.
10. Miller, J., op. cit., 101–102.
11. Christie, *Wars and Revolution*, 92–93.
12. Bobrick, *Angel in the Whirlwind*, 81.
13. Van Doren, *Benjamin Franklin*, 360–63.
14. Miller, J., *Origins of the American Revolution*, 255.
15. Brooke, op. cit., 154.
16. Namier, "A Much Maligned Ruler" in Reitan, ed., *George III, Tyrant or Constitutional Monarch*, 42–51; Brooke, op. cit., 154–58.
17. Langguth, *Patriots*, 116.
18. Draper, *A Struggle for Power*, 348–50.
19. Christie and Labaree, op. cit., 127.

Chapter XII

1. Bober, *Thomas Jefferson*, 59.
2. Miller, L., *In the Minds and Hearts of the People*, 102–105; Beloff, *Debate*, 125.
3. Smith, *A New Age Now Begins*, 1: 279.
4. Ibid., 1: 280.
5. Bobrick, *Angel in the Whirlwind*, 82.
6. Langguth, *Patriots*, 22.
7. Bober, op. cit., 60–61.
8. Bober, *Abigail Adams*, 36–37.
9. Miller, L., op. cit., 114; Langguth, op. cit., 95–97.
10. Hillsborough to Bernard, October 12, 1768 in Zobel, *The Boston Massacre*, 77.
11. *Boston Gazette*, 29 January, 1768.
12. Miller, L., op. cit., 115; Langguth, op. cit., 104.
13. Miller, L., op. cit., 115.
14. Langguth, op. cit., 111; Zobel, op. cit., 99–100.
15. Christie and Labaree, *Empire or Independence*, 130–131.
16. Bobrick, op. cit., 83.
17. Zobel, op. cit., 89–90.
18. Ibid., 101.
19. Miller, L., op. cit., 115.
20. Morgan and Morgan, *The Stamp Act Crisis*, 14.
21. Langguth, op. cit., 118; Galvin, *Three Men of Boston*, 181–82; *Boston Gazette*, 7 August 1769.
22. *Boston Gazette*, 4 September 1769.
23. Adams, J., *The Diary and Autobiography of John Adams*, 1: 343.
24. *Boston Gazette*, 11 September 1769; Zobel, op. cit., 146–49.
25. Adams, J., *The Diary and Autobiography of John Adams*, 1: 348–349.

Chapter XIII

1. Brooke, *King George III*, 158–59.
2. Cook, *The Long Fuse*, 148.
3. Hibbert, *Redcoats and Rebels*, 18.
4. Bobrick, *Angel in the Whirlwind*, 87–88.
5. Plumb, *The First Four Georges*, 114.
6. Brooke, op. cit., 155–56.
7. Johnson, *Eighteenth-Century London*; Plumb, *England in the Eighteenth Century* , 12–13, 15.

Chapter XIV

1. Benjamin Franklin to Joseph Galloway, 9 January 1769 in *The Writings of Benjamin Franklin*, 16: 10.
2. Langguth, *Patriots*, 127–28.
3. *Boston Gazette*, 5 March 1770; Zobel, *The Boston Massacre*, 172–75, 344 n. 26.
4. Adams, J., *The Diary and Autobiography of John Adams*, 1: 349–50; Zobel, op. cit., 178.
5. Adams, J., op. cit., 3: 289–90.
6. Hosmer, *Samuel Adams*, 160–61.
7. Langguth, op. cit., 114.
8. Christie and Labaree, *Empire or Independence*, 131.
9. Gage to Hillsborough, 10 April 1770, in Zobel, op. cit., 180–81.
10. Hibbert, *Redcoats and Rebels*, 15.
11. Zobel, op. cit., 194.
12. Ibid., 180–205, 301.
13. Smith, *A New Age Now Begins*, 1: 346; Zobel, op. cit., 211.

Chapter XV

1. Andrews, *The King Who Lost America*, 34; White, *The Age of George III*, 64.
2. Plumb, *The First Four Georges*, 102–105.
3. Christie, *Wars and Revolution*, 65.
4. Andrews, op. cit., 73.
5. Andrews, op. cit., 137–39.
6. Black, Interview with the author by Natalie S. Bober, April 1998.
7. Plumb, *England in the Eighteenth Century*, 118–23.
8. Cook, *The Long Fuse*, 136–37.
9. Ibid., 145–46.
10. Brooke, *King George III*, 149–52.
11. Miller, L., *In the Minds and Hearts of the People*, 132; Plumb, op. cit., 120–25.
12. Brewer, "The Number 45: A Wilkite Political Symbol" in Baxter, ed., *England's Rise to Greatness*, 356.

13. Cook, *The Long Fuse*, 137.

14. Christie, op. cit., 79, 94.

Chapter XVI

1. Adams, J., *The Diary and Autobiography of John Adams*, 1: 78.

2. Bober, *Abigail Adams*, 14–15.

3. Zobel, *The Boston Massacre*, 106.

4. Adams, J., *Works*, 3: 467.

5. Bowen, *John Adams and the American Revolution*, 316, 330; Miller, L., *In the Minds and Hearts of the People*, 124.

6. Adams, J., op. cit., 2: 210–12; Adams, J., *The Diary and Autobiography of John Adams*, 3: 286–89.

7. Ellis, *Passionate Sage*, 87.

8. Langguth, *Patriots*, 149.

9. Adams, J., *The Diary and Autobiography of John Adams*, 3: 292.

10. Zobel, op. cit., 210.

11. Adams, J., op. cit., 3: 291–93.

12. Miller, L., *In the Minds and Hearts of the People*, 122.

13. Hibbert, *Redcoats and Rebels*, 15.

14. Bowen, op. cit., 380.

15. Ibid., 399.

16. Adams, J., op. cit., 2: 79.

Chapter XVII

1. Miller, J., *Origins of the American Revolution*, 325.

2. Christie and Labaree, *Empire or Independence*, 146–51.

3. Brooke, *King George III*, 174–75.

4. Ibid., 90.

5. Ibid., 119, 260.

6. Cook, *The Long Fuse*, 14–17.

7. Brooke, op. cit., 84, 262–63.

8. Ibid., 288–97.

Chapter XVIII

1. *Records of the Colony of Rhode Island*, 3: 70, 71, 72, 82–86.

2. Miller, J. *Origins of the American Revolution*, 326–29; Smith, *A New Age Now Begins*, 1: 364–69.

3. Anonymous broadside, 1772 in Miller, L., *In the Minds and Hearts of the People*, 154.

4. Miller, J., op. cit., 235–330; Smith, op. cit., 1: 368; Miller, L., op. cit., 151–54.

5. Bober, *Thomas Jefferson*, 73–74.

6. Kennedy, *Journals of the House of Burgesses of Virginia, 1766–1769*, May 8, 1769, 187–89.

Chapter XIX

1. Miller, L., *The Dye Is Now Cast*, 167.

2. Harris, *America Rebels*, 35; Miller, J., *Origins of the American Revolution*, 339.

3. Hibbert, *Redcoats and Rebels*, 19.

4. Labaree, *Catalyst for Revolution*, 9.

5. Harris, op. cit., 37.

6. Ibid., 39.

Chapter XX

1. Labaree, *Catalyst for Revolution*, 11, 19.

2. Harris, *America Rebels*, 38.

3. *Boston Gazette*, 25 October 1773.

4. Christie and Labaree, *Empire or Independence*, 169–71.

5. Labaree, op. cit., 11.

6. Hibbert, *Redcoats and Rebels*, 20.

7. Labaree, op. cit., 13.

8. Bober, *Abigail Adams*, 45–46.

9. Butterfield, *Adams Family Correspondence*, 1: 88–89.

10. Flexner, *America's Old Masters*, 101–14; Weekley, *John Singleton, Copley*, 1–5.

11. Flexner, op. cit., 137.

12. Flexner, *America's Old Masters*, 127–141; *Boston Gazette*, 6 December 1773.

13. Fischer, *Paul Revere's Ride*, 25.

14. Forbes, *Paul Revere and the World He Lived In*, 189–90.

15. Labaree, op. cit., 9–19.

16. Hosmer, *Samuel Adams*, 251–54.

17. Miller, L., *In the Minds and Hearts of the People*, 175; Fischer, op. cit., 25–26.

18. Hosmer, op. cit., 256.

19. Adams, J., *The Diary and Autobiography of John Adams*, 2: 85–86.

Chapter XXI

1. Van Doren, *Benjamin Franklin*, 441.

2. Cook, *The Long Fuse*, 171–72.

3. Van Doren, op. cit., 444–45.

4. Bailyn, *Ordeal*, 350.

5. Franklin, *Writings*, 6: 284; Van Doren, op. cit., 446.

6. Franklin, op. cit., 6: 265–67; Van Doren, op. cit., 444.

7. Ibid., 22; Van Doren, op. cit., 447–48.

8. Bailyn, op. cit., 234.

9. Miller, J., op. cit., 331.

10. Ibid., 331–32; Miller, L., *In the Minds and Hearts of the People*, 148–49, 151.

11. Bailyn, op. cit., 242–43.

12. Bailyn, op. cit., 151; Miller, J., *Origins of the American Revolution*, 332.

13. Bailyn, op. cit., 243–44; Langguth, *Patriots*, 172.

14. Bailyn, op. cit., 238–51.

15. Ibid., 241–42.

16. Morris, *The American Revolution*, 110–13.

17. Fleming, *Liberty!*, 84.

18. Van Doren, op. cit., 462–75; Franklin, op. cit., 6: 185–89; Cook, op. cit., 181–86.

19. Brooke, op. cit., 175.

20. Hosmer, *Samuel Adams*, 265.

21. Brooke, op. cit., 175.

22. Edmund Burke, "Speech on American Taxation, House of Commons, 19 April 1774," in Beloff, *The Debate on the American Revolution*, 135–50.

23. Beloff, op. cit., 151–56.

24. Cook, op. cit., 190.

25. Trevelyan, *Illustrated History of England*, 117.

26. Christie and Labaree, *Empire or Independence*, 188–89.

Chapter XXII

1. Miller, J., *Origins on the American Revolution*, 360–62; *Essex Gazette*, May 24, 1774.

2. Forbes, *Paul Revere and the World He Lived In*, 215; Christie and Labaree, *Empire or Independence*, 201.

3. Miller, J., op. cit., 362.

4. Jefferson, *Autobiography* in *Basic Writings*, 413.

5. Bober, *Thomas Jefferson*, 79–80.

6. Jefferson, op. cit., 413–14.

7. Miller, J., op. cit., 362.

8. Wirt, *The Life of Patrick Henry*, 116.

9. Jefferson, *Summary View of the Rights of British America* in *Basic Writings*, 5–19.

10. Bober, op. cit., 80–85.

Chapter XXIII

1. Bailyn, *The Ordeal of Thomas Hutchinson*, 277–78; Christie and Labaree, *Empire or Independence*, 214.

2. Christie and Labaree, op. cit., 214–15; Miller, J., *Origins of the American Revolution*, 203–208.

3. Hutchinson, *Diary and Letters*, 1: 213, 230, 237; Christie and Labaree, op. cit., 215–16.

4. Christie and Labaree, op. cit., 225.

5. Hutchinson, op. cit., 1: 245.

6. Christie and Labaree, op. cit., 225.

7. Ibid., 192–93.

8. Miller, J., *Origins of the American Revolution*, 453–56.

9. Christie and Labaree, op. cit., 193.

Chapter XXIV

1. Adams, J., *The Diary and Autobiography of John Adams*, 2: 97.

2. Ellis, *Passionate Sage*, 38–39.

3. Adams, J., *The Familiar Letters of John Adams*, 8–9.

4. Bowen, *John Adams and the American Revolution*, 456–57.

5. Adams, J., *The Diary and Autobiography of John Adams*, 2: 97.

6. Adams, *Works*, 512–13; John Adams to Timothy Pickering, August 6, 1822; Butterfield, op. cit., 115.

7. Butterfield, *The Book of Abigail and John*, 68–70.

8. Adams, J., *The Diary and Autobiography of John Adams*, 2: 117.

9. Miller, L., *The Dye Is Now Cast*, 3.

10. Adams, J., op. cit., 2: 122–26.

11. Butterfield, op. cit., 70–71.

12. Adams, J., op. cit., 2: 134.

13. Miller, L., op. cit., 14–17.

14. Ibid.

15. Bowen, op. cit., 492.

16. Miller, J., *Origins of the American Revolution*, 382; Hosmer, *Samuel Adams*, 319.

17. Bober, *Abigail Adams*, 50.

18. Ellis, op. cit., 40–41.

19. "Declaration of Colonial Rights and Grievances," October 1, 1774, and "The Continental Association," October 18, 1774, in Morris, ed., *The American Revolution*, 130–40; Christie and Labaree, *Empire or Independence*, 211.

20. Miller, L., op. cit., 50–53.

21. Miller, J., op. cit., 392.

Chapter XXV

1. Cook, *The Long Fuse*, 202.

2. Brooke, *King George III*, 175.

3. Van Doren, *Benjamin Franklin*, 493–94.

4. Miller, J., *Origins of the American Revolution*, 211–12.

5. Van Doren, op. cit., 520.

6. Langguth, *Patriots*, 266–67.

7. Van Doren, op. cit., 510–11.

8. Miller, J., op. cit., 404–07.

9. Harris, *America Rebels*, 112.

10. *Writings of Benjamin Franklin*, 6: 310; Van Doren, op. cit., 516–17.

11. Beloff, *Debate*, 205–28.

12. Miller, L., *The Dye Is Now Cast*, 159.

13. Van Doren, op. cit., 487–523.

Chapter XXVI

1. Bober, *Thomas Jefferson*, 87–89.

2. Hibbert, *Redcoats and Rebels*, 101.

3. Bober, op. cit., 90.

4. Smith, *A New Age Now Begins*, 661.

5. Colonial Williamsburg, *Interpreter*, 16.

6. Ibid.

7. Bobrick, *Angel in the Whirlwind*, 162.

Chapter XXVII

1. Fischer, *Paul Revere's Ride*, 36–37.

2. Ibid., 88–90.

3. Ibid., 95.

4. Ibid., 97.

5. Forbes, *Paul Revere and the World He Lived In*, 242.

6. Shakespeare, *King John*, Act III, scene i, 326, 308; Fischer, op. cit., 96.

7. Time Life-Books, *The Revolutionaries*, 11–18.

8. Harris, *America Rebels*, 124.

9. Bobrick, *Angel in the Whirlwind*, 114.

10. Colby, *Lexington and Concord*, 50; Paul Revere Deposition, Massachusetts Historical Society, *Proceedings*, 16: 371, n. 119.

11. Fischer, op. cit., 129–37.

12. Time Life-Books, op. cit., 21.

13. Fischer, op. cit., 181.

14. Time Life-Books, op. cit., 21–22.

15. Bobrick, op. cit., 116.

16. Colby, op. cit., 55–56; Fischer, op. cit., 196.

17. Bobrick, op. cit., 117; Forbes, op. cit., 160.

18. Colby, op. cit., 42.

19. Randolph, J., "Essay," *Virginia Magazine of History and Biography*, 223.

20. Christie and Labaree, *Empire or Independence*, 259.

Chapter XXVIII

1. Miller, L. *The Dye Is Now Cast*, 162–63.

2. Smith, *A New Age Now Begins*, 867–68.

3. Ibid.; Miller, L., op. cit., 165–67.

4. Miller, L., op. cit., 88–90; Colby, *Lexington and Concord*, 91.

5. Christie and Labaree, *Empire or Independence*, 246.

Chapter XXIX

1. Butterfield, *The Book of Abigail and John*, 89.

2. Butterfield, op. cit., 112–14.

3. Adams, C., *Letters of Mrs. Adams, Wife of John Adams*, 1: 44, 49.

4. Butterfield, op. cit., 90–91.

5. Adams, C., op. cit., 1: 47–50.

6. Harris, *America Rebels*, 201.

7. Scheer, G. and Hugh F. Rankin, ed., *Rebels and Redcoats*, 59.

8. Marrin, *The War for Independence*, 70.

9. Christie and Labaree, *Empire or Independence*, 263.

10. Adams, *Works*, 357–58.

11. Van Doren, *Benjamin Franklin*, 539–40.

Chapter XXX

1. Miller, L., *The Dye Is Now Cast*, 147.

2. Christie and Labaree, *Empire or Independence*, 248.

3. Miller, L., op. cit., 169.

4. Christie and Labaree, op. cit., 249.

5. Miller, L., op. cit., 170–71.

6. Ibid., 174.

7. Ibid., 175–76.

8. Christie and Labaree, op. cit., 251.

9. Miller, L., op. cit., 178.

10. Ibid., 169.

Chapter XXXI

1. Bober, *Thomas Jefferson*, 96–97

2. Kimball, *Jefferson, Road to Glory*, 56.

3. Boyd, 1: 241–42.

4. Trevelyan, G. O., *The American Revolution*, 271.

5. Borden, *The American Tory*, 2.

6. Smith, *A New Age Now Begins*, 656–59.

7. Ibid., 447.

8. Miller, J., *Triumph of Freedom*, 55–57.

9. Miller, J., *Origins of the American Revolution*, 403–405.

10. Smith, op. cit., 658.

11. Fleming, *Liberty!*, 131.

12. Scheer, G. and Hugh F. Rankin, ed., *Rebels and Redcoats*, 45–46.

13. Cowden, "The Randolphs of Turkey Island," 668–753.

Chapter XXXII

1. Morgan, *The American Revolution*, 144.
2. Ibid., 142.
3. Brooke, *King George III*, 307–308.
4. Ibid., 144, 166–67.
5. Black, *An Illustrated History of Eighteenth Century Britain*, 218–20
6. Morgan, op. cit., 143.
7. Brooke, op. cit., 317.
8. Ibid., 297.

Chapter XXXIII

1. Franklin, *Writings*, 4: 248–49.
2. Smith, *A New Age Now Begins*, 1: 677–78
3. Bailyn, *Faces of Revolution*, 67.
4. Ibid., 69–73; Beloff, *Debate on the American Revolution*, 229–64.
5. Beloff, op. cit., 229–64.
6. Smith, op. cit., 681–83

7. Bailyn, op. cit., 68.
8. Miller, L., *The Dye Is Now Cast*, 240.
9. Butterfield, ed., *Adams Family Correspondence*, 1: 350.

Chapter XXXIV

1. Thomas Jefferson to Thomas Nelson, Philadelphia, May 6, 1776, in Boyd, 1: 292.
2. Smith, *John Adams*, I, 247.
3. Butterfield, *The Book of Abigail and John*, 120–121.
4. Randolph, J., "Essay," *Virginia Magazine of History and Biography*, 122.
5. Bober, *Thomas Jefferson*, 102–109.
6. Ibid., 109–115.
7. Butterfield, op. cit., 139–142.
8. Bober, op. cit., 115–120.
9. *Declaration of Independence*
10. Butterfield, op. cit., 143.

Bibliography

Adams, Charles Francis, ed. *The Familiar Letters of John Adams and his Wife Abigail Adams, During the Revolution.* Boston: Houghton Mifflin, 1875.

———, ed. *Letters of Mrs. Adams, Wife of John Adams.* 2nd ed. 2 vols. Boston: Charles C. Little and James Brown, 1840.

Adams, John. *Diary and Autobiography of John Adams.* Vols. 1–4. Edited by L. H. Butterfield and others. Cambridge, M.A.: Harvard University Press, Belknap Press, 1962.

Adams, Samuel. *The Writings of Samuel Adams, 1764–1773.* Vols. 1 and 2. Edited by Harry Alonzo Cushing. New York: Octagon Books, 1968.

Andrews, Allen. *The King Who Lost America: King George III and Independence.* London: Jupiter Books, 1976.

Andrews, Wayne, ed. *Concise Dictionary of American History.* New York: Scribner, 1962.

Bailyn, Bernard. "Butterfield's Adams: Notes for a Sketch." *William and Mary Quarterly* 19, no. 2 (April 1962): 238–256.

———. *Faces of Revolution: Personalities and Themes in the Struggle for American Independence.* New York: Knopf, 1990.

———. *The Ideological Origins of the American Revolution.* Cambridge, M.A.: Harvard University Press, Belknap Press, 1967.

———. *The Ordeal of Thomas Hutchinson.* Cambridge, M.A.: Harvard University Press, Belknap Press, 1974.

Beloff, Max, ed. *The Debate on the American Revolution, 1761–1783.* London: Nicholas Kaye, 1949.

Black, Jeremy. *An Illustrated History of Eighteenth-Century Britain 1688–1793.* New York: Manchester University Press, 1996; distributed in the U.S. by St. Martin's Press.

———. *War for America: The Fight for American Independence, 1775–1783.* Phoenix Mill, Far Thrupp, Stroud, Gloucestershire; Alan Sutton, 1991.

———. *Pitt the Elder.* New York: Cambridge University Press, 1992.

Blackstone, William. *Commentaries on the Laws of England.* Vol. 1. Chicago: University of Chicago Press, 1979.

Bober, Natalie S. *Abigail Adams: Witness to a Revolution.* New York: Atheneum, 1995.

———. *Thomas Jefferson: Man on a Mountain.* New York: Atheneum, 1988.

Bobrick, Benson. *Angel in the Whirlwind.* New York: Simon & Schuster, 1997.

Borden, Morton, and Penn Borden, eds. *The American Tory.* N.J.: Prentice Hall, 1972.

The Boston Gazette and *The County Journal*, 1760–1775.

Bowen, Catherine Drinker. *John Adams and the American Revolution.* Boston: Little, Brown, 1950.

———. *The Most Dangerous Man in America: Scenes From the Life of Benjamin Franklin.* Boston: Little, Brown, 1974.

Brewer, John. "The Number 45: A Wilkite Political Symbol." Pp. 349–80 in *England's Rise to Greatness, 1660–1763.* Edited by Stephen B. Baxter. Berkeley, C.A.: University of California Press, 1983.

Brooke, John. *King George III.* London: Constable, 1992.

Burton, Elizabeth. *The Pageant of Georgian England.* New York: Scribner, 1967.

Butterfield, L. H. and others, eds. *Adams Family Correspondence.* Vol. 1. Cambridge, M.A.: Harvard University Press, Belknap Press, 1963.

———. *The Book of Abigail and John: Selected letters of the Adams Family, 1762–1784.* Cambridge, M.A.: Harvard University Press, 1975.

Calhoon, Robert McCluer. *The Loyalists in Revolutionary America, 1760–1781.* New York: Harcourt Brace Jovanovich, 1973.

Canfield, Cass. *Sam Adams's Revolution, 1765–1776.* New York: Harper & Row, 1976.

Christie, Ian R. *Wars and Revolutions: Britain 1760–1815.* London: Edward Arnold, 1992.

Christie, Ian R., and Benjamin W. Labaree. *Empire or Independence, 1760–1776.* Oxford: Phaidon Phaidon, 1976.

Colby, Jean Poindexter. *Lexington and Concord, 1775.* New York: Hastings House, 1975.

Cook, Don. *The Long Fuse: How England Lost the American Colonies, 1760–1785.* New York: Atlantic Monthly Press, 1995.

Cootes, R. J. *Britain Since 1700.* London: Longman Group, 1975.

Countryman, Edward. *The American Revolution.* London: Penguin Books, 1991.

Cowden, Gerald Steffens. "The Randolphs of Turkey Island," (of "The Complete Story of John Randolph," Vol. 2. Ph.D. diss. College of William and Mary), 1977.

Currey, Cecil B. *Road to Revolution: Benjamin Franklin in England, 1765–1775.* Garden City, N.Y.: Anchor Books, 1968.

Davis, G. C. R. *Magna Carta.* London: British Museum, 1963.

Derry, John W. *English Politics and the American Revolution.* New York: St. Martin's Press, 1977.

Draper, Theodore. *A Struggle for Power.* New York: Times Books, 1996.

Ellis, Joseph J. *Passionate Sage: The Character and Legacy of John Adams.* New York: Norton, 1993.

Fischer, David Hackett. *Paul Revere's Ride.* New York: Oxford University Press, 1994.

Fleming, Thomas. *Liberty!: The American Revolution.* New York: Viking, 1997.

Flexner, James Thomas. *John Singleton Copley.* Boston: Houghton Mifflin, 1948.

Forbes, Esther. *Paul Revere and the World He Lived In.* Boston: Houghton Mifflin, 1942.

Fowler, William M. *The Baron of Beacon Hill.* Boston: Houghton Mifflin, 1979.

Franklin, Benjamin. *The Papers of Ben Franklin.* Vols. 1–10. Edited by Leonard W. Labaree and Whitfield J. Bell. New Haven, C.T.: Yale University Press, 1961.

Galvin, John R. *Three Men of Boston.* New York: Thomas Y. Crowell, 1976.

Gipson, Lawrence Henry. *The Coming of the Revolution, 1763–1775.* New York: Harper & Row, 1954.

Gravlee, G. Jack, and James R. Irvine, eds. *Pamphlets and the American Revolution: Rhetoric, Politics, Literature, and the Popular Press.* Delmar, N.Y.: Scholars' Facsimiles & Reprints, 1976.

Halliday, F. E. *England: A Concise History.* London: Thames & Hudson, 1994.

Hamilton, Ronald. *The Visitor's History of Britain.* Boston: Houghton Mifflin, 1964.

Harmsworth, Cecil. "Dr. Johnson: A Great Englishman." An address delivered to the Johnson Society, Lichfield, England 15 September 1923.

Harris, John. *America Rebels.* Boston: Boston Globe Newspaper Co., 1976.

Hibbert, Christopher. *George III: A Personal History.* New York: Basic Books, 1998.

——.*Redcoats and Rebels: The American Revolution Through British Eyes.* New York: Norton, 1990.

——. *The Story of England.* London: Phaidon, 1992.

Hosmer, James K. *Samuel Adams.* Boston: Houghton Mifflin, 1972.

Hutchinson, Thomas. *The Diary and Letters of His Excellency Thomas Hutchinson . . . Captain-General and Governor-in-Chief of . . . Massachusetts Bay.* 2 vols. London: S. Bay, Low, Marston, Searle, & Rivington, 1883–1886.

——. *The History of the Colony and Province of Massachusetts Bay, From the Year 1750 to June 1774.* Vols. 1–3. Edited by Lawrence Shaw Mayo. Cambridge: Harvard University Press, 1936.

James, Lawrence. *The Rise and Fall of the British Empire.* New York: St. Martin's Press, 1994.

Johnson, Nichola. *Eighteenth-Century London.* London: Museum of London, 1991.

Kennedy, John P., ed. *Journals of the House of Burgesses of Virginia, 1761–1765.* Virginia: The Colonial Press, E. Waddey Co., 1906.

Kimball, Marie G. *Jefferson: The Road to Glory, 1743–1776*. Westport, C.T.: Greenwood Press, 1977.

Labaree, Benjamin W. "Catalyst for Revolution: The Boston Tea Party, 1773." N.d.

Lancaster, Bruce. *The American Revolution*. Boston: Houghton Mifflin, 1987.

Langguth, A. J. *Patriots: The Men Who Started the American Revolution*. New York: Simon & Schuster, 1988.

LeMay, J. A. Leo, ed. *The Oldest Revolutionary: Essays on Benjamin Franklin*. P.A.: University of Pennsylvania Press, 1976.

Mackenzie, K. R. *The English Parliament*. Harmondsworth, England: Penguin Books, 1950.

Maier, Pauline. *American Scriptures: Making the Declaration of Independence*. New York: Knopf, 1997; distributed by Random House.

———. *From Resistance to Revolution*. New York: Knopf, 1972.

———. *The Old Revolutionaries: Political Lives in the Age of Samuel Adams*. New York: Knopf, 1980.

Marrin, Albert. *The War for Independence The Story of the American Revolution*. New York: Atheneum, 1988.

Maurois, André. *The Miracle of England: An Account of Her Rise to Pre-Eminence and Present Position*. New York and London: Harper & Brothers, 1937.

Miller, John Chester. *Origins of the American Revolution*. Boston: Little, Brown, 1943.

———. *Sam Adams: Pioneer in Propaganda*. Stanford, C.A.: Stanford University Press, 1936.

———. *Triumph of Freedom, 1775–1783*. Boston: Little, Brown, 1948.

Miller, Lillian B. "*The Dye Is Now Cast": The Road to American Independence*. Washington, D.C.: Smithsonian Institution Press in association with the National Portrait Gallery, 1975.

———. *In the Minds and Hearts of the People: Prologue to the American Revolution: 1760–1774*. Greenwich, C.T.: New York Graphic Society, 1974.

Morgan, Edmund S. *The American Revolution: Two Centuries of Interpretation*. Englewood Cliffs, N.J.: Prentice Hall, 1965.

———, ed. *The Birth of the Republic, 1763–1789*. Chicago: University of Chicago Press, 1969.

———. *The Meaning of Independence: John Adams, Thomas Jefferson, George Washington*. New York: Norton, 1978.

———, ed. *Prologue to Revolution: Sources and Documents on the Stamp Act Crisis, 1764–1766*. Chapel Hill, N.C.: University of North Carolina Press, 1959.

Morgan, Edmund S., and Helen M. Morgan. *The Stamp Act Crisis: Prologue to Revolution*. Chapel Hill, N.C.: University of North Carolina Press, 1953.

Morison, Samuel Eliot, ed. *The Oxford History of the American People*. New York: Oxford University Press, 1965.

———, ed. *Sources and Documents Illustrating the American Revolution, 1764–1788, and the Formation of the Federal Constitution*. 2nd ed. New York: Oxford University Press, 1977.

Morris, Richard B., ed. *The American Revolution, 1763–1783*. Columbia, S.C.: University of South Carolina Press, 1970.

Namier, Lewis B. *England in the Age of the American Revolution*. London: Macmillan, 1930.

Nelson, William H. *American Tory*. Oxford: Clarendon Press, 1961.

Norton, Mary Beth, ed. "John Randolph's Plan of Accommodations." Pp. 103–20. *William and Mary Quarterly* 28 January 1971.

Peterson, Merrill D. *Thomas Jefferson and the American Revolution*. Williamsburg, V.A.: Virginia Independence Bicentennial Commission, 1976.

Plumb, J. H. *England in the Eighteenth Century (1714–1815)*. Baltimore, M.D.: Penguin Books, 1961.

———. *The First Four Georges*. London: Batsford, 1957.

Reitan, E. A., ed. *George III, Tyrant or Constitutional Monarch?* Boston: D. C. Heath, 1964.

Roberts, S. C. *Samuel Johnson*. London: Longmans, Green, 1965.

Scheer, George F. and Hugh F. Rankin, ed. *Rebels and Redcoats*. Cleveland, O.H.: World Publishing, 1957.

Shaw, Peter. *The Character of John Adams*. Chapel Hill, N.C.: University of North Carolina Press, 1976.

Smith, Page. *A New Age Now Begins: A People's History of the American Revolution* 2 vols. New York: McGraw-Hill, 1976.

Stokesbury, James L. *A Short History of the American Revolution*. New York: William Morrow, 1991.

Sydnor, Charles S. *American Revolutionaries in the Making: Political Practices in Washington's Virginia*. New York: Free Press, 1965.

Time Life-Books, eds. *The Revolutionaries*. Alexandria, V.A.: Time Life-Books, 1996.

Trevelyan, George Otto. *The American Revolution*. Edited by Richard B. Morris. New York: David McKay, 1964.

Trevelyan, G. M. *Illustrated History of England*. London: Longmans, 1962.

Tuchman, Barbara W. *The First Salute*. New York: Knopf, 1988.

——. *March of Folly*. New York: Ballantine, 1984.

Uglow, Jenny. *Hogarth: A Life and a World*. New York: Farrar, Straus & Giroux, 1997.

Van Doren, Carl. *Benjamin Franklin*. New York: Penguin, 1991.

Viault, Birdsall S. *English History*. New York: McGraw-Hill, 1992.

Weekley, Carolyn J. *John Singleton Copley*. Williamsburg, V.A.: Colonial Williamsburg Foundation, 1994.

White, R. J. *The Age of George III*. New York: Walker, 1968.

Wirt, William. *The Life of Patrick Henry*. New York: McElrath & Bangs, 1831.

Wood, Gordon S. *The Radicalism of the American Revolution*. New York: Knopf, 1992.

Wright, Esmond, ed. *Benjamin Franklin: His Life As He Wrote It*. Cambridge, M.A.: Harvard University Press, 1990.

Zobel, Hiller B. *The Boston Massacre*. New York: Norton, 1996

Photo Credits

Colonial Williamsburg: frontis, 58, 87

Picture Library, National Portrait Gallery, London: 3, 5, 52, 55, 153, 202, 264

Museum of Art, Carnegie Institute: 7

Public Archives of Canada: 8, 112

New York Public Library Picture Collection: 12, 81, 119, 132, 157, 169

Historic Royal Palaces, Hampton Court: 13

Royal Collections Enterprises: 14, 170

New York Public Library: 16, 280

Library of Congress: 18, 85, 265

Massachusetts Historical Society: 19, 68, 183

New York Public Library Print Collection: 20

Petworth House, the Egremont Collection (The National Trust) Photographic Survey, Courtald Institute of Art: 33

William Loren Katz: 35

The American Revolution, A Picture Source Book by John Grafton. New York: Dover, 1975: 36, 39, 65, 107, 221

Museum of Fine Arts, Boston: 45, 109 **(Gift of Joseph W. Revere, William B. Revere, and Edward H. R. Revere),** 125, 185 **(Bequest of Winslow Warren)**

National Portrait Gallery (Art Resource): 67

National Archives: 71, 74, 99, 106, 122, 151, 190, 198, 205, 207, 218-219, 255, 259, 260, 271, 272, 273, 277, 298, 301, 309, 317, 320

Philadelphia Museum of Art (Gift of Mr. and Mrs. Wharton Sinkler): 77

American Antiquarian Society: 102, 133

Drumlanrig Castle, Scotland: 115

National Park Service: 130

Independence National Historic Park: 194, 209, 308

Winterthur Museum: 131, 186

National Galleries of Scotland: 201

Virginia Historical Society: 223, 243

Frick Art Reference Library: 232

Timken Museum of Art, San Diego: 251

Concord Museum: 257

Smithsonian Institution: 312

Maps: *Atlas of American History;* Kenneth T. Jackson, ed. New York: Charles Scribner's Sons, 1978.

Index